With her roots firmly planted in the South, #1 *New York Times* bestselling author **Sherryl Woods** has written many of her more than one hundred books in that distinctive setting, whether it's her home state of Virginia, her adopted state, Florida, or her much-adored South Carolina. Now she's added North Carolina's Outer Banks to her list of favorite spots. And she remains partial to small towns, wherever they may be.

Sherryl divides her time between her childhood summer home overlooking the Potomac River in Colonial Beach, Virginia, and her oceanfront home with its lighthouse view in Key Biscayne, Florida. "Wherever I am, if there's no water in sight, I get a little antsy," she says.

Sherryl loves to hear from readers. You can visit her on her website at www.sherrylwoods.com, link to her Facebook fan page from there or contact her directly at Sherryl703@gmail.com.

Jo McNally lives in coastal North Carolina with one hundred pounds of dog and two hundred pounds of husband—her slice of the bed is very small. When she's not writing or reading romance novels (or clinging to the edge of the bed), she can often be found on the back porch sipping wine with friends while listening to great music. If the weather is absolutely perfect, Jo might join her husband on the golf course, where she tends to feel far more competitive than her actual skill level would suggest.

She likes writing stories about strong women and the men who love them. She's a true believer that love can conquer all if given just half a chance.

#1 *New York Times* Bestselling Author

SHERRYL WOODS

FEVER PITCH

HARLEQUIN
BESTSELLING
AUTHOR
COLLECTION

**HARLEQUIN®
BESTSELLING
AUTHOR
COLLECTION**

Recycling programs
for this product may
not exist in your area.

ISBN-13: 978-1-335-20993-1

Fever Pitch
First published in 1991. This edition published in 2021.
Copyright © 1991 by Sherryl Woods

Her Homecoming Wish
First published in 2020. This edition published in 2021.
Copyright © 2020 by Jo McNally

This edition published by arrangement with Harlequin Books S.A.

For questions and comments about the quality of this book, please contact us at CustomerService@Harlequin.com.

Harlequin Enterprises ULC
22 Adelaide St. West, 40th Floor
Toronto, Ontario M5H 4E3, Canada
www.Harlequin.com

MIX
Paper from
responsible sources
FSC® C021394

Printed in Lithuania

CONTENTS

FEVER PITCH

Sherryl Woods

Chapter 1

"I am going to die!"

The dramatic declaration was accompanied by an exaggerated sigh. The teenager closed her eyes and clutched her still-flat chest with a swoon worthy of Scarlett O'Hara. She was propped upright by the two giggling girls on either side of her in the sun-drenched bleachers. Her eyes opened wide and she stared dreamily toward the dusty baseball field, where J.K. Starr was making his way toward the pitcher's mound.

"Did you see that, Heather? Did you? He winked at me. Midnight Starr actually winked at me. Did you ever see anyone that gorgeous in your entire life? Did you? I swear I am going to die."

J.K. listened to the breathless exchange and shook his head. He'd never gotten used to it, never understood why teenaged girls—or grown women, for that matter—carried on so just because he was wearing a baseball uniform. Not that he minded, but he was just an ordinary guy who'd grown up on a horse farm in Kentucky. He happened to throw a baseball with a fair amount of speed and accuracy. Women acted as if that made him some sort of sex god. His teammates never let him forget it, either.

As if on cue, Davey Ramon-Sanchez jogged up beside him and taunted, "Hey, amigo, you got another big fan over there. Why you not leave a few of the pretty ones for the rest of us?"

Davey, with his black curly hair and soulful brown eyes, had more than his share of adoring female followers. He also had a tiny spitfire of a wife who'd lynch him in center field if he even spoke to one of them. "You can have them all, my friend," J.K. offered generously. "Unless, of course, you're afraid of Maria."

Davey's grin faded and he quickly crossed himself while gazing devoutly heavenward. J.K. laughed at his comrade's instantaneous transformation into dutiful husband. "That's better, Sanchez. Now how about getting up to the plate and hitting the ball for a change, instead of letting me toss it past you?"

The third baseman rocked back on his heels and regarded him indignantly. "Tossing? What is this tossing? They clock you yesterday at ninety-seven miles an hour and that was after you slow down. No wonder the batters look like they sleep at the plate, Midnight Starr. They cannot even see your pitches."

J.K. was more pleased by Davey's compliment on his pitching than he was by the adoration of his trio of pubescent fans. Being named the league's most valuable player for the past three seasons had been like a dream. Back in Kentucky, he'd grown up listening to Cincinnati Reds games on the radio long after his parents had insisted on lights-out. He'd idolized players from the past like Johnny Bench and Pete Rose. He'd wanted nothing more than to grow up and play for the team they'd made great. Instead, he found himself playing against that team now and mourning Pete's downfall. Every time he struck out a Reds batter, he felt guilty. Well, a little guilty, anyway, especially if the score was already plenty lopsided.

"Hey, amigo," Davey shouted. "You going to throw the ball today or you taking the afternoon off?"

J.K. grinned. "You that anxious to make a fool of yourself, Sanchez? Let's see what you can do." Three straight fastballs over the inside corner left Davey standing flat-footed at the plate.

"Stop staring at the bleachers and keep your eyes on the ball," he advised the muttering batter. "Maybe I should throw it nice and slow, like I would for a girl. What do you think? I bet Maria could hit the ball better than you."

Davey muttered something—no doubt insulting—in Spanish, then resumed his stance with a look of fierce concentration. He slammed J.K.'s curveball into left field.

"I gave you one," J.K. asserted, laughing. "Nice and easy, just like I promised."

"You gave me nothing," Davey said, clearly affronted by the charge. "Again, amigo."

Before J.K. could complete his windup, though, manager Ken Hodges shouted at him from the dugout. "J.K., you got a phone call over here. The kid says it's important."

J.K. jogged across the field, once again winking at the girls who were still gazing raptly from the sidelines. They erupted into another fit of high-pitched giggles as he stepped into the fancy dugout and reached for the phone. Ken held it just out of reach.

"Make it snappy," he warned. "You know how I feel

about personal phone calls out here during practice. Besides, you ain't got no business giving this number to your fans."

"I don't give this number to my mother," J.K. swore, then snatched the phone from the still-grumbling manager. "Hello."

"Uncle Jake?"

J.K. recognized at once both the tentative little voice and the blending of his initials into one easy-to-say name. His heart seemed to go still. "Teddy? What's wrong?"

"You've got to come right away, Uncle Jake. It's an emergency. Mom…"

His heart revved up, pumping his blood harder and faster than any pitch he'd ever hurled. If anything had happened to Cassie… Blast Ryan Miles for not being there.

J.K.'s best friend and former teammate had had the morals of an alley cat. He didn't have a lick of sense either, as far as J.K. could see. Only a fool would have walked off and left a terrific woman like Cassie to rear his son alone. J.K. had admitted to himself long ago that there was a soft place in his heart for Ryan's fragile, blue-eyed wife. She was a real sweetheart, gentle, good-natured and so pretty it had made him go breathless the first time he'd laid eyes on her. It had killed him watching the awful pain in her eyes when Ryan had told her lie after lie. She'd been a master of the brave front, though, pretending that she didn't recognize the evasions for what they were. He'd never met a woman he'd admired more or felt more inclined to protect from life's hard knocks. Unfortunately, he hadn't been able to protect her from her ex-husband's infidelities.

All those old feelings came crashing back as he listened to seven-year-old Teddy, his surrogate nephew, declare that there was trouble at home. He didn't wait to hear what kind of trouble. He didn't stop to wonder why Cassie hadn't called herself. He only reacted, knowing in his gut that he'd walk through a blazing inferno for that woman if she needed him to.

"Ken, I'm out of here," he declared, already running. "I'll be back as soon as I can."

"You're going?" the manager sputtered incredulously as he tried to catch up, his arms pumping furiously. "What are you talking about, Starr? We're in the middle of practice, not some Sunday-school picnic. You don't just walk out in the middle of practice. I don't care if it is spring training. That's all the more reason to buckle down. We've got our first game next week. We've got a whole season ahead of us. These guys are playing like they ain't left the sandlot. You're supposed to be a leader, an MVP, for crying out loud. What kind of example are you setting?"

"A bad one," he admitted dutifully, not slowing down. He'd grovel later. "Fine me."

Leaving Ken still lecturing and waving his arms, J.K. accelerated across the practice field and went directly to the parking lot. He didn't even waste time getting out of his cleated shoes, despite the damage they were likely to do to his precious sports car.

Panicked thoughts sped through his brain as he made the familiar forty-minute drive in under twenty minutes. He wasn't sure what he expected to find, but it wasn't the serene picture that greeted him when he screeched to a halt in front of Cassie's house in the quiet neighborhood where Ryan had settled them before taking off. Teddy and a friend were sitting side by side on the front steps, elbows on filthy knees, chins in grubby hands. At the sight of the car, Teddy's face split with a crooked grin and they barreled across the yard, the friend lagging only a few paces behind an instantly animated Teddy.

"Uncle Jake! You came!"

He threw himself into J.K.'s waiting embrace. J.K. gathered the boy close, reveling in the sudden happiness that washed through him. He held Teddy in the crook of his arm as he anxiously scanned the porch and yard for some sign of Cassie. "Of course I came," he said. "I couldn't let down my favorite pal, could I? What's up?"

Instead of answering, Teddy turned to his friend. "See, Billy, I told you. I told you he'd come." His arm circled J.K.'s neck possessively. "He didn't believe me, Uncle Jake. He said I didn't know anybody as important as you."

The full import of Teddy's words took a minute to sink in. In the meantime, like a man coming home after a long absence, J.K. examined the tiny stucco house with its flamingo-pink trim, neat yard and splash of bright red geraniums beneath each window. A purple bougainvillea struggled to climb a lopsided trellis. Only when he'd reassured himself that nothing seemed to be dreadfully amiss did his pulse begin to slow. Hunkered down, he turned Teddy to face him. "Okay, pal, where's you mother?"

Teddy took a step back and shrugged, blue eyes downcast, his expression decidedly guilty. "Inside, I guess," he mumbled.

"You guess?" J.K. said, beginning to accept the fact that Cassie hadn't needed him after all. Just to be sure, he persisted. "What's the emergency, Teddy?"

The boy's freckled cheeks flamed red. He stared at the ground, scuffing his sneaker in the dirt. "Umm…"

"Teddy?"

"I told you," he said with a defiant lift of his chin that was all too reminiscent of his stubborn, bullheaded father.

"Billy didn't believe you were really my uncle. I had to show him, Uncle Jake. I had to."

Under J.K.'s stern look, Teddy's defiant mask began to slip. It was impossible, though, to miss the desperate yearning on his face. J.K. knew he should be furious. He knew Teddy needed a lecture, maybe even punishment, but first and most of all he obviously needed reassurance that somebody cared.

"Okay, sport," he said gently. "Here I am. If you guys have any baseball cards around, I'll sign 'em for you before I go back to practice, okay?"

Skinny arms circled his middle and he could feel Teddy's small, dirt-streaked body heave a sigh of relief. It brought a lump to his throat when Teddy whispered, "Thanks, Uncle Jake. I really, really missed you."

"And I really missed you, but don't thank me yet, slugger. We still have to talk about what's an emergency and what's not, okay?"

Teddy grimaced. "Yeah, I guess."

"There's no guessing about it. I'm going in to talk to your mom, while you say goodbye to your friend. Be inside in five minutes."

The walk to the front door was one of the longest J.K. had ever taken. It had been nearly a year since he'd seen Cassie. For a good bit of that time he'd been on the road, but he'd gotten back to town in the fall, right after the World Series and only weeks after her divorce from Ryan had been finalized. He'd wanted desperately to stop to see for himself that she was okay, but Cassie had made it plain that Ryan's friends were no longer welcome. Because J.K. recognized the hurt that ran deep inside her, he'd given her space and time to heal. He'd called once, just to let her know that he was around if she needed him, but Cassie would never admit to needing anyone, least of all her ex-husband's best friend. She'd thanked him politely and hung up before he'd had a chance to say anything more. There were no shared jokes, no friendly teasing about his overly active love life, no hint of the old closeness at all.

The front door was standing open now and he could hear Cassie's cheerful, off-key singing coming from the kitchen. He listened and smiled. She never had been able to carry a tune, but oh, how she loved to sing. He and Ryan used to kid her unmercifully, begging her to quit, threatening to drown her out with something more pleasant, like the sound of a lawn mower. She'd always told them to go right ahead. The grass needed cutting, anyway. Listening to her now filled J.K. with nostalgia and an odd stirring of tenderness toward sweet-natured Cassie Miles.

She looked anything but sweet, however, when she walked out of the kitchen just then and saw him framed in the doorway. The song died on her lips. She stopped where she was, her expression frozen. Her hands balled into angry fists at her sides. He ignored that and drank in the sight of her. She'd lost weight. In shorts that bagged and a shirt that hung loose, she looked to be maybe a hundred and five pounds of pure resentment. Her blond hair was caught up high on her head and shaggy bangs framed a face that seemed to be all gumdrop-blue eyes.

"Hi, Cassie," he said quietly, wishing it didn't hurt quite so much to see her look at him as if he were ten times more disgusting than pond scum.

"What are you doing here, J.K.?" The question was edged in ice and twice as hard. The Cassie he remembered had been all warmth and sunshine.

"It's nice to see you again, too, Cassie."

Only a man totally attuned to the quicksilver shifts in

her moods would have noticed the subtle stiffening, the fleeting guilt that darkened her eyes at his barb. Cassie had been reared by kind, salt-of-the-earth parents who didn't insult guests in their home, not even a man she equated with everything that had gone wrong in her marriage. Still, guilt-ridden or not, her unwelcoming expression didn't soften the tiniest bit.

"How've you been, Cassie?" he asked more gently, worried by the weight loss, the dark smudges under her eyes, her pale complexion.

As if the question were a challenge, she drew in a deep breath. Her spine straightened perceptibly. "Fine, J.K. Teddy and I are just fine, if that's what you came to find out." Her words were emphatic and clearly meant as a dismissal. When he didn't budge, she continued to regard him warily.

Like a hunter stalking an uneasy prey, he took a cautious step closer. She didn't withdraw, but cast a disapproving glance at his feet. Suddenly conscious of the damage his baseball shoes could do the the carpet, he grinned apologetically and took them off. Standing before her in his stocking feet made him feel oddly vulnerable. "I think we need to talk," he said, awkwardly clutching the filthy shoes.

A dozen different emotions seemed to war on her face. Denial. Anger. Confusion. Fear. And more he didn't even recognize. She visibly fought for control, then finally asked, "Has something happened to Ryan?"

He supposed it was the obvious conclusion for her to reach, but the question and the raw emotions behind it were like blows to his midsection. He hadn't prepared himself to deal with so many still-unresolved feelings. Steering clear of the mine field, he said, "No, babe. It's your son."

Momentary panic turned her deathly white. She swiveled instinctively toward the porch and J.K. cursed himself for his insensitivity.

"Teddy's right outside," she said as if reassuring herself. Her tough guard dropped away. "I mean he was just a minute ago. J.K....?"

He touched her arm, then drew back at once when she flinched. "It's okay, Cass. He's there. I'm sorry. I didn't think. He'll be in in a minute."

She walked to the front door and looked out, her shoulders finally relaxing once she caught sight of Teddy. "What about Teddy?" she inquired, cool and barely polite again. "If you're here for Ryan, tell him to fight his own battles, J.K."

"This has nothing to do with Ryan. Or maybe it does. I don't know. Teddy called me, Cass. Out of the blue."

She looked stunned. "He called you? When? Why?"

"A little while ago, at the ballpark. Who knows how he came up with the dugout number."

She closed her eyes and apparent embarrassment flooded her cheeks with color. "It's still on the wall by the phone in the kitchen. I guess I never did take it down. I'm sorry, J.K. Ken probably pitched a fit."

He shrugged, downplaying the manager's reaction. "Ken enjoys snarling. You know that. It's no big deal."

"I don't understand, though. Why would Teddy call you?"

"Nothing catastrophic, though he claimed it was an emergency," he told her with the first hint of a smile. "As it turns out, he just wanted to prove a point to his friend. I gather Billy's new to the neighborhood."

She nodded, then shook her head in apparent bemusement. J.K. knew exactly how she felt. "What point?" she asked finally. "I still don't get it."

"That I was his uncle. I think maybe it was more than that, though. I think he must be missing Ryan."

Her expression, which had seemed almost friendly for just a heartbeat, instantly turned bitter. "Good guess, Dr. Freud. The last time his daddy called was when he passed through town three weeks ago. Judging from the length of the conversation, it amounted to hello and goodbye. Teddy went to his room right afterward and wouldn't come out. He still won't tell me what Ryan said to upset him so."

J.K. had to swallow an oath. "Didn't Ryan stop by? When I saw him at the ballpark, I was sure…"

She cut him off with one succinct comment. "He had a date."

He did curse under the breath at that, then sighed. "I see."

"I'm sure you do," she said, building up a new head of steam. "Nobody knows Ryan better than you do, right, J.K.?"

"Cassie, rehashing Ryan's bad habits won't do anybody any good."

"Don't you try to placate me with that patronizing tone. You're every bit as bad as Ryan Miles." Once she'd started, she couldn't seem to stop. The anger boiled up and spewed over him in furious waves. "That's why you never told me he was fooling around on the road, isn't it? Do you all take a solemn oath of silence, is that it? Forget decency. Forget friendship. To hell with marriage vows. You all figure the women, those hot little bleacher bunnies, just go with the territory, right?" She ran out of steam finally and threw up her hands in a gesture of disgust. "You all make me sick. You're nothing but a bunch of overgrown adolescents."

For someone who hadn't wanted to talk, she'd managed to say a mouthful and every word of it filled with condemnation. J.K. accepted the hurled insults, but not the blame. "That's not the way it was, Cassie," he said with careful patience. "It killed me, what Ryan was doing to you and Teddy, but it was between the two of you. It wasn't up to me to tell you anything."

"Then maybe you should have reminded him once in a while that he had a family at home waiting for him. Would it have killed you to do that much, J.K.? Or isn't it macho to talk about wives and kids?"

J.K. winced. Locker-room talk all too often had more to do with the scoring off the field than on. He wouldn't admit that to her, though. Some truths were better left unspoken. There was one hard truth, though, that it was about time she faced up to. "Cassie, if you couldn't make him stay, then all the words in the world from me weren't going to make any difference," he said.

The blunt, untempered statement brought quick tears to her eyes. Her shoulders drooped in resignation and all the anger seemed to drain straight out of her. "You could have tried, J.K." she said miserably "You could have made the effort."

Regret pierced through him. She would never know how hard he had tried, how Ryan had laughed at him for his feeble attempts to get him to ignore the feminine bounty that was available and go home to his wife and son. He wasn't about to tell her that now. She'd already been hurt enough and from what he could see the healing process was a long way from over. If heaping some of the blame on his shoulders helped her to cope, then he'd deal with it. Maybe there was something more he could have done. Maybe he wasn't blameless, after all.

"Cassie, isn't there something I can do to make things easier for you? You and I always could talk. Maybe we could go out to dinner sometime, like old times. I'm a good listener."

"I don't want your pity, J.K., and I don't need anybody to listen to me. I want to forget the past, not relive it. I thought I was doing real well until you walked in here and reminded me of everything. I guess I was overdue for an outburst. I'm sorry, though, for taking my problems out on you. Thanks for coming by to check on Teddy."

"Sounds to me as if you have a lot of anger left inside. If yelling at me helps, feel free. I've withstood far worse."

"No. I've said my piece now," she said, squaring her shoulders. "I'll speak to Teddy, too. He won't be bothering you again."

J.K. only barely resisted the urge to grab those pride-stiffened shoulders and shake her until she grasped how important she and Teddy were to him. They were like family, to all intents and purposes the only family he had. Instead of telling her that, though, he kept a tight rein on his patience and said, "I don't mind him bothering me, Cassie. I've missed you both. In fact, why don't you let him come back to the ballpark with me? He can watch practice, then I'll pick us all up a couple of hamburgers and bring them back for dinner. Hanging out with the guys might be good for him."

Cassie looked as if he'd suggested a rendezvous with the devil himself. Furious eyes blazed at him. "No! Absolutely not! I won't have him around that place. Not ever!"

The irrational outburst stunned him. "Cassie, be reasonable. The ballpark's not the problem. I'm not the problem. Don't you think it would be good for Teddy to have a father figure in his life? That's really what this call of his was all about. If Ryan can't be around, let me fill in. You know I love him."

He could tell he'd struck a nerve. She twisted the dish towel she still held in her hands, wrestled with a whole ton of maternal guilt, then finally shook her head. "Not you," she told him, evading his gaze. "Teddy needs someone, J.K., but not you. You'll just up and leave him, too. He doesn't need to be abandoned twice."

Even though he understood that her attitude toward him was all mixed up with her feelings for Ryan, the outright rejection hurt. He wasn't about to accept her decision as final, though. Not this time. Not now that he'd seen how badly she and Teddy needed someone in their lives, how lost and alone they both seemed. Not with all this guilt she'd heaped on him. And not since he'd realized in that split second when she'd walked out of the kitchen that he was still more attracted to her than he'd ever been to another woman.

That reaction probably should have been a warning, but to J.K. it was more like a call to arms. He'd never walked away from an attractive woman in his life. Flirting came as naturally to him as breathing. Cassie always had been a great target for practicing his technique. As long as she'd been married to Ryan, she'd been safe and she'd kept him honest, taking him to task for his flaws in a way most women never dared.

The decision to stay in touch firm in his mind, he could afford to back away for the time being, let her settle down a bit and get used to the idea of his coming around more often. "Okay, Cass. I won't press this time, but I will be back."

She shook her head, that haphazard blond ponytail bouncing violently. "Nothing personal, J.K., but don't come." She faced him down. "Teddy and I don't need you."

"A less confident man would take that as an insult, babe."

"I meant it to be one," she admitted, meeting his gaze with an unflinching stare.

He took one step closer, admiring the fact that she didn't retreat, even though he could tell she wanted to. He reached out a finger and touched her cheek. It felt like silk and it was still damp with the tears she hadn't bothered to wipe away. The pad of his thumb swept across her lower lip and he wished desperately that he had the power to still the trembling. Wished even more that he had the right to kiss her the way he'd longed to for one jealous instant the very first time he'd ever seen her. He'd felt like a heel then and he felt like even more of one now. Lusting after his best friend's wife, for God's sake. Maybe Cassie was right about him. Maybe he was every bit as bad as Ryan. Maybe he ought to walk out the door and let her be.

Still, he owed her.

"I think you do need me, sweetheart," he said quietly. "And until you prove me wrong, I think I'll just stick around awhile."

Without waiting for a reaction he turned and walked outside, pausing on the front steps to tug his shoes back on. He spotted Teddy hiding out around the corner of the house.

"Okay, sport," he called, beckoning him over. "It's time to face the music."

Teddy approached cautiously, his blue eyes every bit as huge and round as Cassie's. "I didn't mean to do anything wrong, Uncle Jake. Really."

"I know you didn't, but an emergency is something that's really, really serious. Something like maybe you're sick or your mom's hurt herself…"

"Or the house is on fire. I know to call nine-one-one for that."

"Exactly like that. Those are real emergencies. Anytime

you need to see me, though, you can just call. It doesn't need to be an emergency. If you want to talk or maybe have a hamburger or toss a few balls around, you let me know."

He glanced up and saw Cassie in the doorway watching them, a frown on her face. "Your mom and I will work out the details, okay?"

Teddy flung his arms around his neck again. "Thanks, Uncle Jake."

"No problem, slugger," he said, raising his eyes to meet Cassie's disapproving gaze. "No problem at all. You might want to call my cell phone, though, instead of the ballpark. It takes messages and I promise I'll get back to you right away. Your mom will put that number by the phone in the kitchen, where the ballpark number was." He strongly emphasized the past tense, while staring pointedly at Cassie.

The beginning of a smile teased at her stubbornly set lips when he said that. They both knew that Ken Hodges would develop an ulcer—and J.K. would wind up paying half his much-publicized, exorbitant salary in fines—if Teddy repeated today's interruption of the team's practice session. Heaven forbid he should ever get it into his head to call during a game.

"Will you take me to a game one day, Uncle Jake? Dad used to let me sit with him in the dugout sometimes."

"I remember," he said as the last trace of Cassie's smile vanished. J.K. took the hint and kept his response cautious. "We'll have to see about that one, though. Maybe one of these days, if you're real good and ask her nicely, your mom will bring you by."

She glared at him. He smiled back innocently. "See you two later," he promised, getting to his feet. "Take care of yourself, Cassie."

She nodded curtly and turned away. "Teddy, I want to see you inside right now," she called over her shoulder.

"I guess I'm gonna get it now," Teddy said with a resigned sigh.

J.K. grinned at his attempted bravado. "I guess you are."

"I'm still glad I called you, Uncle Jake."

"Me, too. Let me give you a tip, sport. There's no point in trying to wriggle out of this one, but maybe if you just tell her the truth about why you called, she'll go easy on you."

"I guess," Teddy said doubtfully.

"Try it. Your mother's a reasonable woman."

He said the last loudly enough to stop Cassie in her tracks. When she whirled around to glower at him fiercely, he waved jauntily and climbed into his car. As he drove back to practice, he caught himself whistling. It was the same song Cassie had been murdering so cheerfully right up until that moment when she'd found him in her living room.

Chapter 2

There were millions of men in the United States, Cassie observed as she attacked the huge stack of dishes in the sink. There were thousands right here in town. Why, of all of them, had Teddy called her ex-husband's best friend? The more telling question, the one she didn't care to examine too closely, was why it bothered her so much. It had been a week since J.K.'s unexpected arrival on her doorstep and she was still as jumpy as a June bug. She was also no closer now to understanding her violent reaction than she had been at the time.

Okay, so J.K. was a link to the past, a past she very much needed to forget. So what? They'd been good friends once. It was nice of him to worry about her, wasn't it? What was so terrible about the fact that he'd hotfooted it over in response to a little boy's call? Nothing, she admitted. It was a generous gesture.

Probably.

She couldn't forget, though, that J.K. was cut from essentially the same opportunistic cloth as Ryan. If she lived to be a hundred and ten, she would never permit another selfish, skirt-chasing, macho jerk near her and Teddy, especially not one as drop-dead attractive as J.K. Starr. Women would be swooning over the man when he was eighty. She'd even felt a guilty pang or two of fascination herself, especially when her marriage was falling apart and J.K. was rock steady beside her. But she was no fool. Any man could muster up compassion and sensitivity when he wanted to, for the short term. She had learned from her mistake. Now all she wanted out of life was to settle down to a nice, peaceful, ordinary existence with her son. Maybe, someday, that life would even include a man again…preferably one who hated baseball as passionately as she did.

"You scrub that plate any harder, you're going to wash off those little bitty flowers."

Cassie jumped at the sound of J.K.'s lazy, amused, Kentucky-bred drawl. His arrival wasn't totally unexpected, but it was every bit as devastating as she'd anticipated. The plate crashed to the floor and shattered. She shot a furious look at the man who was standing just outside the screen door. She opened her mouth, but before she could say an accusing word, he held up his hands in a placating gesture.

"Don't blame me," he said. "I'm just an innocent bystander."

"You weren't innocent the day you were born," she muttered, picking up the pieces and tossing them into the trash. Now that J.K. was actually here, filling the doorway with his broad shoulders and that sexy, end-of-the-day shadowed jaw, Cassie discovered that there was some perfectly ridiculous part of her that was glad to see him, relieved just to have an adult for company no matter his motives.

She decided she'd better stomp on that part until it was well and truly dead. That meant resisting J.K.'s beguiling grin and his effortless charm. He was directing one of those magazine-cover smiles at her now. She steeled herself against the powerfully sexy effect, ignored the gentle and surprisingly familiar tug on her senses.

"Now that's a fine thing to be saying about the man who's going to take you away from all this," he said as he came through the door and settled himself on one of her kitchen chairs, his faded jeans molded tight, his baseball cap like worry beads in his strong, restless hands.

How many times had he done just that, she thought, regarding him warily. He'd always lingered in the kitchen while she cooked, chatting about inconsequential things, expressing interest in her observations, always making her laugh while they waited for Ryan to turn up. Now J.K.'s blue-green eyes were filled with that familiar humor and something more. A dare? Surprised, she realized the man was actually daring her to fight him. Welcoming the prospect on some instinctively feminine level, Cassie braced herself for the heady thrill of battle. J.K. knew exactly how to get her goat, knew her better, she'd thought sometimes, than her husband had.

"I don't want to be taken away," she said firmly, ignoring the contradictory fluttering of her pulse. Her chin tilted up a defiant notch, for her benefit as much as his. "And even if I did, you'd be the last man on earth I'd want taking me."

"Oh?"

There was an indulgent, arrogant tone to that single word that made her want to throw another plate straight at his cheating heart. "Go away, J.K." To her everlasting regret, the words came out more plea than demand. She was going to have to use more starch in her voice if she was going to win out against J.K.'s determined persuasiveness. "Go give one of those bleacher bunnies a break or have they all gone home to their mothers for the night?"

"I never did date jailbait, Cassie. I prefer my women with a little maturity and a lot of sass." His impudent gaze traveled over her insinuatingly. "Just like you."

"Your nerve never ceases to amaze me. Why'd you come back, J.K., when I told you not to?"

"Call me a masochist."

"More like a martyr. You've done your duty. You can leave now."

"And disappoint Teddy?" he said, pulling out the big guns, the ones guaranteed to shoot down every argument. With a skill most likely born of too much practice, J.K. had zeroed in on her vulnerability more effectively than one of those heat-seeking missiles honing in on a moving target.

Her gaze narrowed. She busied herself by slamming a pot into the drainer, then picking up another one and scrubbing like crazy. J.K. waited her out.

"What does Teddy have to do with this?" she asked finally.

"I promised him ice cream."

She whirled around and planted sudsy hands on hips. This time there was nothing feigned about her anger. His arrogant disregard of her wishes was just one more indication that for all his good intentions, J.K. would always do exactly as he wanted. It was good that he'd done that. She might have softened toward him otherwise.

"You had no right, J.K.," she said evenly, proud of the fact that she wasn't screaming like a banshee.

"Cassie, what's the big deal?" he asked in a voice that seemed laced with genuine bewilderment. She didn't trust that innocent pretense for one millisecond.

"The big deal is that you didn't ask my permission. I won't have you making plans with Teddy without checking with me first. I told you that the other day."

He nodded slowly, his expression serious. "Okay, you're right. I should have checked with you first, but I got his message this afternoon and when I called him back over at Billy's, he sounded lonely. The invitation for ice cream just happened. I apologize."

The apology was meek enough, but the look in his eyes was anything but. It was the look of a man who knew exactly how to charm a woman into submission. He'd probably started practicing while he was still in the cradle. Still, she forced herself to murmur a polite, grateful response.

"I will remember next time," he vowed, reaching for her hand. The touch of callused flesh against her soapy hand was distractingly erotic. She began to forget all about the importance of keeping her defenses in place.

"As long as I'm here now, though, what do you say?" he prodded. "You always did like ice cream. Couldn't you go for a hot fudge sundae?" His voice dropped seductively. "Or maybe a banana split?"

Cassie's insides melted. She assured herself it was purely a reaction to the prospect of all that gooey hot fudge sauce running over triple scoops of chocolate ice cream and sliced banana and topped with a mound of whipped cream. She hadn't indulged in anything that deliciously decadent in months.

J.K. chuckled at her silence and kept up that relentless stroking of rough thumb over slick knuckles. "Tempted, Cassie?"

"You're not playing fair," she grumbled, yanking her hand away. She was definitely weakening and she wasn't one bit happy about it. No wonder women fell all over themselves to meet J.K. His style was smooth as aged whiskey and twice as intoxicating.

"Shall I call in my backup? If I get Teddy to work on you, we'll be at the mall in ten minutes flat."

She knew she ought to be made of sterner stuff. She knew she ought to protest his using her son to manipulate her, but the prospect of a treat for Teddy was something she couldn't bring herself to pass up. The tight budget she adhered to didn't often allow for such splurges.

"Maybe the two of you…" she began in an attempt to salvage her pride.

J.K. was shaking his head before she could complete the thought. "It's a package deal. You, Teddy and me. Think of it this way—if you're not along, I'll probably cave right in and let him have a double order of whatever he wants and then he'll be keeping you awake all night with a stomach-ache. You need to come along to keep us from overindulging."

She laughed at the ridiculous ploy despite herself. The tension that had knotted her shoulders for the past few days abated. She felt herself relaxing, looking forward to a brief respite from the dreary routine she'd settled into. It was just this one night and it was ice cream, for goodness sake. What possible harm could come of that?

"Okay, okay." She relented. "You win."

"Yeah!" Teddy's gleeful shout could probably be heard down the block. He poked his head out from behind the bush beside the back steps. "I told you it would work, Uncle Jake."

She faced the two of them indignantly, trying not to respond to their matching grins of satisfaction. "So, you two were plotting this, huh? Just for that, I'm going to order the most expensive thing they have."

"Do your worst, woman," J.K. said expansively. "I can't think of a better way to squander my money. Now let's hustle. A man could starve to death waiting around for you, right, Teddy?"

"Right. Hurry up, Mom."

"Can I at least run a comb through my hair?"

"Mom!" Teddy wailed impatiently.

"Give her a minute, son. Women aren't happy unless they've kept a man waiting. They think it'll show us who's boss."

"Don't warp my son's mind with your opinions of women, J.K. Starr."

"Why not? You seem to think I'm some sort of expert."

"I also think it's not something to be especially proud of," she retorted, then made a hurried exit to the sound of his laughter.

J.K. loved it when Cassie went all prim and proper on him. He knew just exactly how long to tease her to put the sparks in those blue eyes of hers. He was glad to see them back again. Standing up to him might give her back some of the self-confidence that Ryan's lousy treatment had apparently sapped right out of her. This ice cream thing wasn't totally for Teddy's benefit, either. Cassie needed to put a few pounds back on. By the time he was through, she'd be bright eyed, healthy and sassy as the dickens again.

While he waited he opened the refrigerator to grab one of the beers she and Ryan had always stocked. There wasn't one in sight. He settled for a box of grape juice, grimacing at the first sip of the excessively sweet drink.

"I'm glad to see you've finally decided to drink something healthy," Cassie said as she came back wearing jeans every bit as faded as his own and a blouse that matched the bluebonnet color of her eyes. She hadn't bothered with makeup, but her hair had been swept up in that ponytail that made her look about fifteen years old. She looked innocent and vulnerable and that powerful need to protect her swept through him again.

"No beer," he explained in a voice that was suddenly husky.

"No need."

He acknowledged the curt admission with a nod, trying to ignore the quick flash of pain in her eyes. He couldn't. "Cassie…"

"Don't say anything, J.K. It's all right."

"It's not…"

"I'm ready for that ice cream now," she said firmly.

He swallowed hard, wanting to say the right thing but not knowing whether he'd make things better or worse. When she was in this porcupine-prickly mood, maybe there were things best left unsaid. He nodded again. "Let's go, then."

At the mall they found seats in front of the crowded ice cream booth. "You save the table, Cassie. Teddy and I will get the ice cream. What do you want?"

"A banana split," she said without hesitation as Teddy ran off to get in line.

"Chocolate ice cream, extra hot fudge, no pineapple, just strawberries," he said.

"You remembered," she said softly. There was a look of pleased surprise on her face that made his heart ache for her. How many times had Ryan forgotten the piddling little things that two people building a life together should have remembered? Black coffee, two sugars, for instance. Or the fact that she hated pink, loved stuffed animals and wished on stars. He wondered what she wished these days.

"It's not that easy to forget, sweetheart. You used to have

the cast-iron stomach and appetite of a truck driver. I lived in constant awe of you."

"Right," she scoffed. "Who was the one who considered four servings of the hottest chili in town to be a snack, then wondered what we were having for a main course?"

"Hot? That chili of yours was made for wimps."

"You ate four bowls, J.K.," she reminded him. "And it may have been mild when I fixed it, but you dumped an entire bottle of hot sauce in it. Even the bowl was pleading for mercy. Ryan took one bite and spent the rest of the evening chasing it down with beer."

The laughter in her eyes faded before she finished the sentence. J.K. reached out impulsively and squeezed her hand. "No sad thoughts tonight, okay? It's just us guys out on the town."

She nodded, but couldn't hide the shimmer of tears.

"Cassie…"

"Uncle Jake!"

J.K. glanced over and saw that Teddy was next in line. "I'll be right there," he told him, almost grateful for the interruption. For all he thought he knew about women, he was definitely at a loss when it came to giving comfort. Tears just about undid him. Cassie's tears made him want to throttle Ryan Miles. He brushed one errant teardrop from her cheek and felt something give way in his chest. "I'll be back in a minute with that banana split."

By the time he and Teddy returned, she was composed again. He set the ice cream in front of her. She toyed with it for the first few bites. J.K. enjoyed watching the slow transformation from disinterest to enthusiasm. Even Teddy stared in amazement as the last bit of hot fudge vanished, carefully scraped from the sides of the dish.

"Awesome, Mom! You ate the whole thing!"

"It was wonderful!" she admitted with a sigh of pure pleasure. "Thanks, J.K."

"Care to go for two?"

"And spend the rest of the evening listening to you torment me about my appetite? Not on your life. What's wrong with you, by the way? You've barely touched your sundae."

"I've been too busy watching you," he admitted.

"How's the caramel?"

"Want to try it?" He held out a spoonful. Cassie leaned forward without hesitation. Her lips parted. And a jolt of pure electricity shot through him, startling him so badly he almost dumped the ice cream on the table. He was familiar with the hot, aching sensation, but not in connection with Cassie. For one brief instant he felt as though he were cheating with his best friend's wife. Then he remembered the divorce. He looked again into Cassie's clear, guileless eyes. Not even he could be low enough to take advantage of that innocence. He swallowed hard and with fierce concentration managed to get the ice cream into her mouth.

"Umm," she murmured. "That's almost as good as the hot fudge."

He shoved the bowl toward her. "Here, it's yours."

"J.K., I do not need your sundae."

"There's only a little left. Go for it."

"Maybe just another bite," she said, looking at him expectantly. Her tongue slid tauntingly over her parted lips. And another odd tremor jolted through him. He handed her the spoon with a sense of desperation.

"Be my guest."

When Cassie had finished his ice cream, she smiled in contentment. "I won't eat another bite for a week."

Worry began to nag at J.K. He sensed that there was

more truth than exaggeration in the claim. Impulsively he said, "Oh, I'd bet I could talk you into a pepperoni pizza with mushrooms and green peppers tomorrow."

"Wow!" Teddy said, his eyes lighting up. "That'd be great! We haven't had pizza in ages. Mom tried to make one, but the crust was all soggy."

Cassie was shaking her head. "No, really. That's very nice of you, but I'm sure you have better things to do, J.K. Don't put your social life on hold for us."

He brushed aside the protest without missing the barbed tag line. "I can't imagine anything I'd rather do than spend an evening with the two of you. It's settled. You rent a video and I'll bring the pizza. I'll be by as soon as practice lets out."

J.K. was on Cassie's doorstep fully an hour before dark, much too early to eat dinner. He hadn't planned it that way, but practice had let out a little earlier than usual. He'd rushed home for a quick shower and a change of clothes, rather than hanging out with the guys. The next thing he knew he was pulling up in her driveway, pizza in hand. He refused to analyze the motive behind his rush or the unexpected way his pulse hammered every time an image of Cassie flashed in his mind.

Teddy came running down the block, his friend Billy hard on his heels. "Uncle Jake, you're early. Mom's not even home from work yet."

"Work?"

"Yeah, didn't you know? She has a job in some office. I think maybe she types or something. She promised to take me one day, so I could see where she works."

A hard knot of anger formed in J.K.'s stomach. "What do you do after school?"

"Go to Billy's. His mom's home all the time. Sometimes she bakes chocolate chip cookies for us. They're not as good as Mom's, though."

Despite Teddy's staunch declaration of loyalty, J.K. was certain he detected a forlorn note in his voice. He vowed on the spot that before long Cassie would be back home baking cookies, too. The means for accomplishing that eluded him for the moment, but he had no doubt he'd manage it. He'd be damned if Teddy was going to grow up as one of those lonely, latchkey kids who came home to an empty house or to some neighbor's cookies.

"You wanna eat the pizza now?" Teddy asked, regarding the huge box hopefully.

"Nope. We'll wait for your mom. Why don't you get a baseball and we'll play catch until she gets here."

The two boys were off like a shot to get the ball. J.K. sat the pizza on the hood of his car and propped one sneaker-clad foot on the bumper. He studied Cassie's house more closely. Once again he was struck by still more evidence that all was not going nearly as well with her as she'd wanted him to believe. He'd been fooled the past two visits by the cheerful flowers and the neatly tended lawn. He hadn't noticed that the paint on the house was beginning to peel in spots or that some of the tiles on the roof had broken loose. Thank goodness the rainy season hadn't started yet. Once it did, she'd have a living room full of water if she didn't begin the tile replacement soon. He'd call a roofer in the morning and have him begin work at once.

Pleased to have found something constructive that he could do to help, he put the repairs out of his mind while he played ball with the boys. Teddy had his father's natural ability. Though Billy was older and strong, he was still clumsy and within a half hour his frustration was showing. J.K. empathized with him.

"I didn't want to play catch, anyway," Billy said, blinking back big, fat tears. "I gotta go eat."

J.K. draped a consoling arm around the boy's shoulders. "Next time I come back, we'll try it again. All it takes is a little practice."

Billy sniffed. "Teddy's good and he's littler than me."

"Hey, it's a fact of life that sports are easier for some people than they are for others. That's not your fault, but giving up without trying, that would be your fault. You see what I mean?"

"I guess."

"You keep practicing with Teddy and I'll bet before long you'll be good enough to make first string in Little League."

He shrugged indifferently. "It doesn't matter."

"Do you like playing ball?"

"I suppose."

"Then don't give up. I'll coach you guys until you're the best in the neighborhood."

"Come on, Billy," Teddy urged. "Uncle Jake's the greatest. We'll be awesome."

"Okay," Billy agreed finally. "I really do gotta go now, though."

"Okay. Bye, sport."

Teddy waved. "See you tomorrow, Billy. Will you play catch with me some more, Uncle Jake?"

"You bet."

"What do you think you're doing?" Cassie asked, appearing seemingly out of nowhere, her voice strained. Surprised by her quiet arrival, he turned and realized that her car wasn't in the driveway. Since he wasn't prepared to deal with her abrupt tone, he focused on the absence of the car.

"Hi, sweetheart," he said, planting a kiss on her cheek and admiring the way she looked in the neat skirt and short-sleeved blouse that were a far cry from the shorts and T-shirts he'd usually seen her wear. "I like the duds, but you look beat. How'd you get here? Did you just snap your fingers and materialize?"

"I'm afraid extraordinary powers are a little beyond me. I owe my arrival to the city transit system."

"A bus?" he said incredulously.

"Don't look so stunned. That's why they have them," she said, still scowling at him.

"But you have a car."

"It's in the shop."

"It's been there a really long time," Teddy chimed in.

"How long?" J.K. said, his jaw set angrily.

"A few days. It's no big deal."

"When will it be ready?"

"Soon, I guess."

"Mom," Teddy protested. "The guy called yesterday, remember?"

"Is that true?" J.K. asked.

Cassie shrugged. "It's true. So what?"

"So why didn't you go get the car?"

"The bill was a little higher than I expected, all right? I'll pick the car up when I get paid," she snapped and stomped off toward the house. J.K. grabbed the pizza and followed.

"How much is it?"

"I told you it didn't matter, J.K."

"It matters to me," he said, dropping the pizza on the kitchen table and reaching for his wallet.

"Put your money away."

"How much?" he demanded, peeling bills off and throwing them on the table. "Is that enough?"

"I don't want your money."

"Well, that's too bad. You're wiped out. I don't want you riding the bus. If it takes a few bucks to get your car out of the shop, I can certainly cover it."

Cassie picked up the money and threw it back at him. "I do not want your money, J.K., and I don't want you over here encouraging Teddy to play ball. Am I making myself clear?"

"You and that stupid stiff-necked pride of yours," he said, swearing loudly.

"Teddy, leave the room," Cassie ordered the wide-eyed boy.

"But, Mom…"

"Leave."

He inched closer to J.K. and tucked his hand in J.K.'s bigger one. "I'm staying with Uncle Jake," he said stubbornly.

"Don't you defy me, young man, or you'll spend the rest of the evening in your room. Now, go."

Teddy's lower lip trembled, but his back was stiff as he faced her. "You're going to make him go away, just like you did Dad. I know you are. I hate you! I hate you!" He whirled and ran from the room, leaving Cassie obviously shaken. Judging from her strained expression, she was also near hysterics.

As soon as Teddy was out of sight, she lashed out at J.K. "Don't you ever try to humiliate me like that in front of Teddy again."

"Humiliate you?" he repeated in astonishment. "Is that what you think I was doing?"

"It may not have been your intention, but that was the effect, just the same. I don't want him thinking I can't take care of the two of us. He's insecure enough since Ryan walked out. I won't have him scared out of his wits we can't afford the simplest little things."

J.K. felt the scared, desperate words slamming into his gut. "God, Cassie, I wasn't even thinking about that." He pushed his hand through his hair, feeling more helpless and frustrated than he'd ever felt before in his life. "I feel so lousy about the way things have turned out for you. I just wanted to help."

"I know you did," she said, her tone relenting slightly. "But that's not the way, J.K. The money's not important. We're managing."

"Managing," he repeated, as if the word were alien. Just *managing* wasn't good enough, not for her, not for Teddy. It offended his sense of order, his sense of what was right.

But with his hands tied, exactly what was he supposed to do to make things better for them?

"I meant what I said about baseball, too, J.K. Don't encourage it. I won't have Teddy turning out like his father."

"Ryan's behavior had less to do with baseball than it did with his values. You're here to see that Teddy stays on the right track. Participating in a healthy, all-American game is not going to hurt him."

"Stop it, J.K. Just stop it. Teddy is my son, not yours. I know what's best for him. If you can't accept that, then stay away." Her voice was climbing and her lower lip quivered.

"Simmer down, Cassie," J.K. said gently.

"I will not simmer down," she said stubbornly, tears streaming down her cheeks. She swiped at them furiously. "You have no right coming over here and taking over. No right. We were doing just fine until you showed up. Now everything's such a mess."

Her too-thin shoulders shook with sobs. It was as if a dam had burst and for an instant J.K. stood by helplessly.

Then he gathered her in his arms. "Oh, babe, don't cry," he pleaded, his voice gruff. "There's nothing wrong that can't be fixed. I promise you."

"You're wrong," she said, trying to break free.

"Shh," he said, holding her right where she was. "Trust me."

Her response to that was muffled. J.K. had a feeling it was just as well. Cassie was in no mood to trust anyone these days, least of all him. That might have been the very worst thing that Ryan Miles had done to her. A year ago Cassie had been the most open, trusting person he'd ever met. Ryan's betrayal had robbed her of her innocence, along with everything else.

Chapter 3

She'd lost it! Cassie wasn't sure what had come over her, but she had definitely lost it. Carrying on as if J.K. and Teddy were committing a crime just because they were playing catch didn't make a bit of sense. To top it off by throwing J.K.'s money all over the place was crazy. She had her pride, but that didn't give her the right to be downright rude in the face of yet another generous gesture.

She must be more exhausted than she'd realized from coping with all the changes. The tension of the past year had finally gotten to her, spilling out in this totally out-of-character, irrational outburst. She'd kept herself under control all these months for Teddy's sake and suddenly to-night she'd felt it slipping away the minute she'd turned the corner and seen J.K. with her son. She supposed that the argument that had followed had been inevitable.

Still, she kept hearing Teddy's angry cry: "I hate you! I hate you!" It echoed again and again, every bit as awful as the day Ryan had said he was leaving, that he didn't love her anymore. No, she corrected, it was worse than that. Deep down in an unacknowledged part of her heart, she had anticipated Ryan's going. Teddy's intentionally cruel words had blindsided her.

"What have I done?" she murmured, her heart aching. "What have I done to my baby?"

J.K.'s arms, solid, warm and comforting, tightened around her. "It's going to be okay," he soothed.

If he'd promised something easy, maybe the moon, she might have believed him. This mess would never be okay. It only seemed to get worse. Even so, she welcomed the embrace, the awkward attempt to console. God help her, for just this one moment she needed his strength and, like Teddy, she wanted his easy reassurance. She sniffed as he rubbed her back.

"J.K., I'm making such a mess of things. I'm trying so hard, but everything I do is turning out all wrong."

"Shh. No, it's not. You're doing just fine. Teddy's a great kid. Kids and parents fight all the time. He'll calm down and then you can make him understand."

She swiped at a tear and grinned at him ruefully. "How am I going to do that when I don't understand it myself? I sounded like a lunatic for a minute there, and look at your money. It's all over the place." She kicked at a balled-up twenty-dollar bill. Others were scattered from one end of the room to the other. There must have been two or three hundred dollars in all, almost as much as she brought home in a week after taxes. Unskilled receptionists, she'd discovered, were in short demand and far from the top of the pay scale.

"Stop being so hard on yourself. The money can be picked up. As for the rest, even I can figure out what's going on here and I'm no expert. Just about the only thing I know about psychology is that you pay shrinks a lot of money to tell you awful stuff about yourself that you wouldn't take from your best friend."

"Then explain it to me, please, because right now I feel as though I've made an absolute fool of myself. Even more unpardonable, I've upset my son. He's just a little boy, J.K. He shouldn't have to try to guess why his mommy's behaving like an idiotic shrew."

He brushed the trail of tears from her cheeks. "Enough of that. Sit down and rest for a few minutes. Then we'll talk about it."

She peered at him suspiciously from the comforting circle of his arms. "Is this your sneaky way of sticking around after I've repeatedly banned you from the house?"

"Did you ban me?" he inquired innocently, pointing her toward a chair and giving her a gentle shove. "I don't seem to recall that."

"Selective hearing," she muttered. "Ryan had it, too."

He frowned. "Cassie, I wish you'd stop comparing me to Ryan."

"If the shoe fits..." she said, but her animosity was beginning to falter. She was beginning to remember J.K.'s good traits.

"It doesn't," he said adamantly. "Besides, in the long run, it's only going to confuse Teddy. You saw how he reacted tonight. He doesn't understand why you keep slamming doors on people he cares about."

She sighed. "I suppose you're right. Why do I feel the compulsion to do it then?"

He tapped her on the nose. "To remind yourself what a rake I am, so you won't be tempted to fall madly in love with me."

"What conceit!" she declared, but she couldn't help a wobbly smile. She must be the only woman in the country who wasn't half in love with J.K. Starr. How many of them would kill for this chance to have him lounging comfortably around the kitchen? Were they crazy or was she the blind one? She gave him a quick, surreptitious once-over, from tousled dark blond hair to cleanly shaven cheeks and on to flat stomach and solid thighs. His butt wasn't bad either, she noticed as he turned toward the refrigerator. The man was definitely sexy, she decided objectively. Maybe it wasn't conceit, after all.

"I prefer to think of it as self-confidence," he said modestly enough. The devilish twinkle in his blue-green eyes gave him away. "Do you want a soda or milk?"

"I'd take a stiff shot of Scotch if I kept any in the house."

"Scotch makes you weepy," he reminded her. "It's the last thing you need. Milk or soda?"

"Diet soda, if there's one in there," she said, chagrined by his all-too-accurate memory. She might have a cast-iron stomach when it came to food, but she had no head at all for alcohol. One night she had foolishly tried to match him and Ryan beer for beer only to wind up turning melancholy after the second one.

"Hmm, there's no diet soda in here. Not unless it's disguised itself in one of these little cartons. How about apple juice instead? You can feel healthy and I'll feel virtuous. Remind me to bring you a six-pack of something stronger the next time I come over."

Cassie wasn't sure she liked the sound of that. She wasn't very proud of her tantrum earlier, but that didn't mean she wanted J.K. getting the idea he could pop in and out around here at will. Having a pal like J.K. would be risky business for any woman, but for her it would be flat-out dangerous.

Even if she was willing to risk it for herself, she wasn't for Teddy. He was the one who'd be hurt again in the end. Once spring training ended, J.K. would head north for the long baseball season and Teddy would know the feeling of being left behind all over again.

J.K. popped straws into the juice, handed one to her, then pulled out a chair for himself. He turned the back toward her and straddled it, his muscular arms resting on the back. "Feel better?" he asked, watching her intently as she took a sip of the juice. The sympathetic tone made her want to start bawling all over again. She nodded.

"Then let's talk about it," he said.

"It?" Suddenly she wasn't at all sure she wanted J.K. playing shrink with her emotions. As well as he knew her, she feared his analysis might cut a little too close to the bone.

"Don't play dumb with me," he chastised gently. "We're going to discuss that snit you worked yourself into a few minutes ago."

"It was not a snit."

"What would you call it?"

"A justifiable release of pent-up tension," she suggested hopefully.

J.K. actually grinned. "Sounds about right to me. In the future, you might want to consider taking a long walk instead. I hear it does wonders for stress and it's not nearly as disturbing to the neighbors."

"Very funny. I don't get it, though. I had a perfectly decent day at work. There were no major crises. I've finally figured out all the phone lines. I got paid. The bus didn't get stuck in traffic. Why did the sight of you and Teddy playing a simple game of catch in the yard turn me into some out-of-control crazy lady?"

"I can answer that with one word—Ryan."

She waved dismissively, unwilling to admit that there might be even a shred of truth in that observation. "You're not Ryan."

"Thank you for finally noticing."

She stared glumly back at J.K. and ignored the gibe. "He's been gone nearly a year now. I'm over him. He's history. Kaput. Nothing." In her head it sounded like the truth. Her gut told her it was a lie. Ryan Miles had been her childhood sweetheart, her first and only lover. Some women never forgot their first love. She was determined to. She glanced at J.K. and realized with a start that he could probably make her forget. In his arms... Whoa! She could feel the color flooding her cheeks and was grateful that J.K. would probably attribute it to irritation.

"I suppose you don't want to hear the line about protesting too much?" J.K. said, emphasizing the fact that so far she hadn't succeeded in forgetting anything.

She glared at him. "When did you get to be so obnoxious?"

"According to you, I've always been that way. Don't try charming me by calling me names. Stick to the subject."

"It's true," she said huffily. "I've accepted what happened. I've picked up the pieces and moved on."

"But you're still angry. Face it, Cassie, until you let go of the anger, you'll never be truly free of Ryan. Do you want him to have that kind of hold over you?"

"Of course not, but how am I supposed to go about doing that? Every time I see Teddy staring at a picture of his father, it breaks my heart. As for me, I can't get out of the supermarket without seeing Ryan's face on the cover of some tabloid or some sports magazine. It would have been hard enough if he'd been a nobody. Instead, he's got to have his best season ever last year. Then he tops it off by getting involved with that game-show bimbo and he's reached superstar status. The magazines can't get enough of him. Do you know he was on fourteen covers last year? *Fourteen!* The president wasn't on that many."

"Use the pictures for darts."

"Interesting notion. Don't you think that might get me arrested if I try it in the check-out lane?"

"Maybe all it would take would be one giant outburst. A little ranting and raving and crying. Did you ever do that, Cassie? Did you ever allow yourself to get really mad at him?"

"You mean before the last couple of days?" she said meaningfully.

"That was nothing. I mean a real hell-raising, dish-breaking fury?"

She shook her head. She'd cried herself to sleep more nights than she could remember, but she'd never raised her voice, not even at Ryan. She'd kept silent to avoid upsetting Teddy. It hadn't worked. He was obviously more shaken even now than she'd realized. "I couldn't," she told J.K. "I'm lousy at confrontation."

J.K.'s eyes rose in obvious disbelief. "You couldn't prove that by me."

"Okay, so I'm finally getting the knack of it," she said dryly. "At the time it seemed like such a waste of energy. Ryan was determined to leave. It wasn't going to change anything."

"Except, maybe, the way you felt. When I play lousy, you know what I do? I go back to the ballpark and get into the batting cage and slam balls for an hour or two. It doesn't change the way I played that day, but I feel a lot better."

"How do you think Ken would feel if he caught me in his batting cage?"

"Don't ask. I'll tell you what, though. We'll make a deal. One night soon we'll get a baby-sitter for Teddy and you and I will stock up on all those sleazy tabloids, get drunk and burn the bunch of them. We'll even dance around the bonfire. How about it? Could be fun."

Despite herself, she giggled at the prospect. "Sounds like a pretty kinky date to me."

"Hey, that's the kind of guy I am."

She saw straight through the teasing, lighthearted tone and caught the serious caring behind it. It gave her an insight into J.K. she'd never had before. She'd always lumped him into the same devil-may-care league as Ryan, but perhaps she'd been wrong. There was an underlying decency that she'd been fighting to ignore. "I don't think so," she told him softly. "I think maybe I've misjudged you."

Her statement seemed to make him uncomfortable. He shook his head. "Don't go that far, Cassie. It's dangerous. My halo slipped off years ago."

She nodded thoughtfully. "Thanks for the warning. It only proves I'm right."

He shoved back the chair and stood up. "What it proves is that this conversation is getting way too heavy. Why don't you go have a talk with Teddy while I pick up another pizza?"

"You brought a pizza."

"It'll taste like cardboard by now."

"That's okay. Don't waste your money. I'll throw it into the oven and it'll be fine."

"I have an ulterior motive," he admitted with a guilty grin. "I cannot possibly eat pizza with apple juice. I'm bringing back a six-pack of beer for me and some sodas for you."

Cassie laughed. "Go, then."

He hesitated at the door. "You won't lock this behind me, will you?"

She shook her head. "No. I promise."

After he'd gone, she said softly, "Not tonight, anyway. But if I have a grain of sense, I will tomorrow."

Upstairs she found Teddy huddled on his bed, his favorite bear clutched in his arms. Ryan had given him that bear for this third birthday. For years it had been ignored on a shelf until Ryan left. Now Teddy was seldom without it at night. She sat down beside him. She could tell from the rigid way he was holding himself that he wasn't asleep. When she put a hand on his back, a sigh shuddered through him.

"I'm sorry, baby."

He sniffed and clung more tightly than ever to his bear, but said nothing.

"I shouldn't have raised such a fuss," she told him. "But sometimes I get scared."

"Scared?" The possibility seemed to intrigue him. "How come?"

"Oh, because your daddy left me and I want so badly to be a good mommy and make up for his having gone. But you know what scares me most of all? The thought that I might hurt you. I don't ever want to do that, Teddy. You're the most important thing in my life and I want so very much for you to be happy. Forgive me? Please."

He sat up and flung himself against her, his arms wrapping tightly round her middle, the bear caught between them. "I was scared, too. I don't like it when you yell at me. I don't ever want to make you mad so you'll go away like Daddy did."

Cassie's heart constricted painfully at the depth of his fear. "Listen to me, kiddo. There is nothing in this whole world that you could ever do to make me leave you or stop loving you. Nothing. Do you understand that?"

His head bobbed against her. "Did you make Uncle Jake go away?" he asked. Even though his words were muffled, she could hear the sadness and wariness behind them.

"He went to get another pizza, but he'll be back."

"You're not mad at him anymore?"

"No," she said softly, realizing it was true. Something had shifted tonight in her relationship with J.K. The fight had opened old wounds and left them raw, but for the first time she thought they might be healing. Maybe she and J.K. could be friends, after all.

"I'm glad," Teddy said. "Uncle Jake's the greatest, isn't he?"

"The greatest," she echoed. With the memory of his gentleness still lingering, she realized she actually meant it. She also knew that probably ought to scare the daylights out of her.

The pizza shop smelled of garlic and oregano. For J.K. it was one of the headiest scents in the world. He'd spent most of his teenage years hanging out in a place just like this one, the booths crowded with couples, the jukebox filling the air with country-western songs. Back home in his part of Kentucky, there hadn't been any place much fancier to go without driving all the way into Lexington. Giuseppe's, owned by a man whose real name was Billy Joe Callahan, had been like a second home to a kid whose own house was less than inviting. Billy Joe had encouraged him, cheering his victories and sympathizing with the defeats. He'd kept the high school team's baseball trophies along the back counter, and clippings about their games were tacked on a giant bulletin board. Once J.K. had turned pro, those clippings had joined the ones about the local team and the TV behind the bar was always tuned to J.K.'s games.

As he sat on a stool in the small pizza shop waiting for his replacement pizza and listening to his country-and-western favorites, J.K. found himself wondering what it would be like to take Cassie home to Kentucky. What would Billy Joe think of the pretty little blond with the big-as-saucers eyes? And what would Cassie think of his hometown, a place so small a man could practically spit from one end of Main Street to the other?

Now, why was he thinking a fool thing like that, J.K. wondered, taking another sip of the draft beer that was ice cold, just like the ones at Giuseppe's. What had made him so nostalgic all of a sudden? Except for Billy Joe, he rarely thought of home and he'd certainly never considered taking a woman back there with him. He was still pondering that unexpected train of thought when a woman wearing tight blue jeans, a red Western shirt and a heavy, provocative scent of a zillion flowers slid onto the stood beside him.

"Hey there, Midnight," she said in a lazy drawl that sounded like home and lured like late night seduction.

His gaze wandered over her appreciatively. Her black hair was long and shiny, her lips red and tempting, just like the shirt which was opened one button below daring.

"I was watching you at practice earlier," she said in that low, sultry tone. "You were hot."

He acknowledged the double-edged compliment with a modest nod. "I had a good day."

Her hand covered his, bloodred nails against tanned male

skin, turning up the heat a notch. "Honey, if all your days are half that good, the team will be in first and running away with it by the All-Star break."

He grinned at the enthusiasm. "You're a real fan."

"I'm a baseball junkie. RBIs and ERAs turn me on," she said provocatively, her bold gaze traveling slowly down his body.

There had been a time—probably not much more than twenty-four hours earlier—when J.K. would have given her a second glance. She was gorgeous and sexy and willing. Tonight, though, she just reminded him of too many others who trailed the teams in the hopes of scoring—forever or even for a night—with a ballplayer. She seemed a little pathetic. And the image of an impish blond with the spirt of a hellion wouldn't go away.

"Sorry, sweetheart," he said just as his order arrived. "I have someone waiting at home."

"Sure you couldn't stick around for just one more beer?"

He grabbed the pizza and six-pack and put a twenty on the counter. "Take the lady's drink out of that, too," he told the cashier.

She gave him a smile filled with regret. "I sure hope she's worth it, lover."

He grinned, surprised by the direction of his thoughts. "You know something, babe, I think she is."

Back at the house, he found Cassie and Teddy in the yard. She'd changed into paint-streaked shorts and a T-shirt that was faded from too many washings. She was definitely not trying to impress him, though he found the unassuming outfit ten times more appealing than the tight jeans and red shirt he'd just left behind. He watched for a minute as she and Teddy played catch. She was obviously trying to make amends, but she was lousy at the game. He chuckled as she chased down another ball that had been right at her fingertips.

Teddy came running over to him. "Mom's pretty bad at this, huh?" he said in a conspiratorial whisper.

"Pretty bad," J.K. concurred. "Maybe we should give her a break and go inside for pizza."

"What are you two conspiring about now?" she asked, sneaking up behind them.

"Conspiring?" J.K. repeated, looking offended. "Us?"

"That innocent act doesn't fool me. You two are up to something."

"We were just deciding whether to risk my car windows by leaving it within your throwing range. What do you think, Teddy?"

"I think you'd better put it in the garage," he said seriously, then broke into giggles.

Cassie was all offended dignity. She glowered at the two of them. "With a little coaching, I'd be just fine. Maybe even great," she boasted.

J.K. and Teddy exchanged looks. "Is that a dare?" J.K. said, stepping closer. "You're willing to submit to a little coaching?"

She backed away from him and the deliberate taunt. "No. I just meant…"

"Come one, Cass, let me teach you a few things," he said, his gaze locked with hers. An embarrassed blush tinted her cheeks pinks. "We could have a training session every night. By the time I finished with you, you'd have great hands."

She regarded him warily. "What did you have to drink while you were waiting for that pizza?"

"One beer and I guarantee it didn't go to my head."

"Maybe not, but I think I know where it did go."

"Why, Cassie Miles, are you flirting with me?" he asked, laughing.

Thoroughly flustered now, she scowled. "No. I mean I don't think so. Oh, for heaven's sake, J.K., let's eat this pizza before it gets cold, too."

As they walked into the house, J.K. wondered for the second time that night what was coming over him. He'd always liked Cassie, but this sudden desire to tease her with sexual innuendo was something new. He considered flirting second only to baseball as his favorite sport, but he'd never engaged in the most casual sexual banter with her.

Sure, but she'd been Ryan's wife then. Now she was free and he couldn't seem to resist. He enjoyed those sweet blushes and that hint of breathlessness in her protests.

Careful, though, he warned himself. Cassie wasn't in the same ballpark as the women he was used to. With her he could very well by playing with fire. As innocent as she was, they could both get burned.

"How come you're not eating your pizza?" Cassie asked when they'd been sitting around the kitchen table for a while.

He glanced down and realized that his first slice was still untouched, while she and Teddy had eaten nearly half the rest. Teddy had already excused himself and gone to his room. "I guess my mind wandered."

"I don't suppose I have to ask what you were thinking about. Who is she, J.K.?"

He regarded her blankly. "Who's who?"

"The new woman in your life. I've seen that look on your face often enough. It always involves a woman."

"Is that so?" He leaned back and stretched out his legs. He looped his thumbs through the waistband of his jeans. "What if I told you I was thinking about you?"

"I'd say you were being either gallant or evasive."

"Can't take the truth, huh?"

She tilted her head thoughtfully, still not convinced but apparently willing to consider the possibility. "What about me?"

"I was just wondering why I'd never noticed before how sexy you are."

She immediately blushed a fiery red. "J.K.!"

"It's true. You're a real heartbreaker, Cassie Miles."

"And you've definitely had a few too many drafts."

He shook his head soberly. "That's not the beer talking. If anything, I'm more alert than I've ever been."

She was slowly shaking her head. "Don't, J.K. Don't try to change things between us."

He reached across and touched a finger to her chin, enjoying the way her eyes flared wide with that first spontaneous hint of arousal. "I may have to, Cassie. I just may have to."

Chapter 4

Hanging out with Cassie was turning out to be a lot more fun than J.K. had anticipated when he'd first decided to start looking out for her. It was also playing surprising havoc with his hormones, which he definitely hadn't counted on. Restraint wasn't something he was all that familiar with, but if he'd discovered one thing over the past few days, it was that Cassie couldn't be rushed about anything. If he honestly, flat out told her he was developing this insatiable need to get her into his bed, she'd slam the door in his face so hard he wouldn't be able to pry it open again with a crowbar.

Smart woman!

Still, when she stared up at him with those wide, innocent blue eyes, yearning shot through him with a force that almost toppled him right over. He came to think of it as The Look. Guileless or not, it made him wary. It was every bit as dangerous as dynamite and a lot sexier. He began to stare at her lips the way a dieter stares at forbidden chocolate. It was getting harder and harder to resist temptation.

"J.K.?" Cassie said now, giving him The Look as they sat in the kitchen snapping beans for dinner.

"Mmm?" he said, fascinated by her. Why had he never noticed the way her nose turned up or that it had the cutest little sprinkling of freckles across it?

"Why are you staring at me like that?" she demanded.

"Like what?" he said, struggling for his own innocent expression. Her blush began at her chin and disappeared beneath her bangs. He loved it.

"You know," she muttered.

"As if I wanted to kiss you?"

She nodded, looking up finally. Her gaze clung to his and left him weak.

"Because I think I'm going to have to."

Her mouth formed a startled "oh." A handful of beans spilled to the floor. When she'd gathered them up she took a deep breath, then stiffened her spine, squared her shoulders and faced him head-on. "No," she said simply.

Perfect, he thought. There was nothing he liked better than a chase. At least she couldn't say he hadn't warned her.

"Yes," he contradicted, inching his chair closer. "I definitely think a kiss is in order."

"J.K." Her protest was definitely getting weaker and this time she didn't look away. She didn't scoot her chair away, either. "We talked about this."

"No, we didn't."

"We most certainly did," she said, waving a handful of green beans at him. "There's a chance, just a chance, that you and I could be friends, but no more. I'm not looking for a man in my life. Any man," she added emphatically, apparently to make sure he got her point.

"You need one," he contradicted.

"Says who?"

"Says me. You can't afford to have your car fixed. The house is falling apart. Teddy needs a father figure. I'm telling you you need a man in your life."

"And that's about the most sexist thing I've ever heard you say. What I need is a better job, not a man. Being a receptionist is no challenge. The people are okay, but the pay stinks."

"You shouldn't be working at all," J.K. insisted. "Teddy needs you at home. The right man would get your life back on track."

"Are you volunteering?"

"Yes, as a matter of fact."

"For what? Marriage?"

The word registered in his brain and exploded. "No," he said, too quickly. He didn't miss her smirk. She'd deliberately set him up. He equivocated. "I mean, not exactly. Cassie, be reasonable."

"I am being reasonable and practical. I can survive quite nicely without you or any other man. The bus gets me to work. If the roof leaks, I'll crawl up there myself and fix it."

"Right," he said skeptically.

"I can do it, if I have to," she said, matching stubbornness with pit-bull defiance.

"But you don't have to," he said, his patience slipping. "I told you I'd hire someone to fix the blasted roof and what does that have to do with kissing, anyway?"

"You brought it up."

"I brought up kissing. You changed the subject."

"It needed to be changed."

He groaned. "Cassie, I'm a dying man. Take pity on me."

An unwilling smile flitted across those luscious, tempting lips. "Men die from starvation, J.K., and you haven't lacked for kisses since you were twelve."

"Ten," he corrected.

"Ten!"

"I was precocious."

"Then it's definitely time for you to start tapering off."

He tilted her chin up with the tip of one finger. He could practically feel the shiver that ran through her. "Not yet. Not without one kiss from you. You're a free woman now, Cassie. And you're sexy and desirable. I don't think I can wait another minute to taste you, to see if your lips are as soft as they look."

There was an unmistakable flare of passion in her eyes. "No, J.K." There was a breathless desperation in her voice that was unmatched by the longing in her eyes. He went with the longing.

His fingers swept over the curve of her cheek to tangle in her hair. She swallowed hard, but again she didn't retreat. He had to admire her pluck. He could tell she was scared to death...of him, of the kiss, and most definitely of the implications. God help him, he ought to give her time. He ought to leave her alone. But...

"Just one, Cassie," he murmured, leaning forward until his mouth hovered over hers, their breath mingling. Then finally, slowly, inevitably, he closed the gap, not sure whether he was going to be smacked for his audacity, but willing to risk it for just one taste of those lips.

The first touch was feather light, a mere brush against silk.

The second savored, a gentle persuasion.

It was the third that set off unexpected skyrockets. Hungry, bold, demanding, the third kiss was a passionate declaration that left him breathless and shaken by its intoxicating message. Judging from the bewildered expression in Cassie's eyes, she was every bit as undone by the unexpected thrill of it as he was. Her small, slender hands, with their neat, blunt-cut nails, rested on his tensed forearms, lingering indecisively, not quite sure yet whether to cling or push him away.

He saw the precise moment she made her decision. There was no missing the slow rise of anger, the renewed quickening of her breath, this time stirred by fury. All that misdirected passion, he thought briefly, almost wistfully, as he braced himself for the inevitable explosion.

"Damn you, J.K. Starr!" she said, slamming down the bowl of beans so hard that half of them flew out. "You're exactly like Ryan. I was starting to believe you. I wanted to believe we could be friends, but you couldn't let it go at that. You had to try out your famous seduction routine and ruin it all, didn't you? What's the matter, were you getting out of practice? Or did you just think any woman—especially a lonely divorcée—would be grateful to be seduced by the great superstar jock? Not me, J.K." She was near tears as she shouted, "Not me!"

He waited quietly for the tirade to end. It was all steam and very little substance. He knew—and so did she—that no kiss that powerful was just a game anymore. It was a victory, a triumph. It was something a man didn't walk away from, no matter how it terrified him. She wasn't ready to hear that, though, and with a struggle he intentionally made light of it.

"That was a simple kiss, Cassie, not a seduction," he said, hoping he sounded clinically instructive and endlessly patient. Then he went and ruined it all by winking. He couldn't resist as he concluded, "When the seduction happens, babe, you'll recognize it and you'll want it every bit as much as I do."

He decided that was the perfect exit line, one to give her something to think about. Besides, it was time to pick up Teddy. He walked out without waiting for her reaction. She made sure he knew just how she felt, anyway. Before he reached his car, he heard the sound of glass crashing against the door, followed by the thump of something heavier and less breakable. The emotional clatter tempered by quick practicality made him smile.

"You're getting to her, J.K. You're definitely getting to her." One tiny little twinge of conscience told him that should make him feel guilty as hell, but it didn't. It made him want to shout at the top of his lungs.

Cassie stared after J.K., her emotions in a terrible tangle. He was wrong. This wasn't what she wanted from him at all. She didn't want to be kissed, not like he'd just kissed her. It made her want too many other things, things she couldn't possibly have—maybe never and certainly not with a man like J.K.

Stability, security, fidelity. Those were the qualities she yearned for. It sounded like the name of an insurance company and with J.K. the one thing she knew for sure was that there were no guarantees, no insurance for happily ever after. He'd kiss her today, woo her just the way he had all the other women in his life and then he'd abandon her the minute spring training ended. He wouldn't mean to. It was just the natural evolution of things with a ball player. An automatic, no-excuses way out of a sticky situation. She, better than anyone, knew the routine.

Experience had toughened her up, made her wary. Hadn't she tried to keep him away in the first place? She'd known he was trouble. But he'd kept coming around any-way, giving Teddy the masculine companionship he craved, ignoring her temper, chipping away at her defenses until she'd almost believed that she was safe with him. That kiss had snapped her back to reality. No woman's heart would ever be safe from J.K. Starr.

So, why had she responded when she knew the logical outcome? Why had that one long and dreamy kiss left her weak-kneed and hungry for more? Loneliness. That's all. Any kiss would have had the same breathtaking impact, she reassured herself. It had nothing to do with J.K.

Maybe she ought to experiment, kiss a few frogs as the saying went, just to prove that J.K. was no prince.

Maybe she ought to have her head examined.

Well, it wasn't something she had to figure out to-night. She'd been granted a reprieve. J.K. obviously had his tim-ing down pat. Kiss and run. Give 'em something to think about. Well, she wasn't going to think about it for one sec-ond more. She was sitting in her kitchen all alone, just the way she usually did. When it came right down to it, noth-ing cataclysmic had happened to change the ordinariness of her life. Teddy would be home for supper any minute. He'd take his bath. She'd take her shower. And they'd both be in bed by ten. She took comfort in the promise of a per-fectly normal routine.

"So, did you think about me while I was gone?"

Startled, she stared into J.K.'s twinkling eyes and groaned. "What are you doing here? I thought you'd gone home."

"And miss dinner, after I snapped all those beans? Not a chance."

"Then where did you go? Was that just another of your strategic maneuvers to throw me off guard?"

"Maneuvers?" he repeated with indignation. "I'll have you know that I do not *maneuver*. I went to pick up Teddy at the park."

Cassie moaned. What was happening to her? "Good grief," she murmured. "I forgot all about getting him."

"Fortunately, some of us are not so easily distracted," he taunted deliberately.

"Go to hell, J.K."

"Can I wait until after dinner? I'm starved. What are we having besides the beans?"

"We?"

"You did invite me over, Cassie. Did you forget that, too?" He placed a hand on her forehead. "Are you sure you're feeling okay? You seem a little warm."

Warm? She was burning up. She felt her pulse quicken. Tell him to go, she ordered her brain. It responded by saying, "Go. Stay. It makes no difference to me."

Liar! her brain shouted.

"Liar," J.K. accused, smiling confidently. He dropped a kiss on the top of her head in passing. "Don't ever try it on the big stuff, Cass. You're lousy at it."

"Not enough practice. Give me time."

"Cassie, there are not enough years in a lifetime for you to master that. Do I have time for a shower?"

She gulped. The very idea of J.K. naked did fascinating things to her heartbeat. Why had this blasted attraction smacked her between the eyes just when she was getting comfortable with J.K. again. "A what?" she said in a choked voice.

"A shower? I'm filthy. I came here straight from practice, remember?"

Her gaze traveled over the dirt-streaked, formfitting uniform. He was already unbuttoning the shirt, displaying a broad expanse of tanned, muscular chest. She'd seen J.K. bare chested before. It hadn't affected her like this. She swallowed hard, then cleared her throat. If it hadn't been so obvious she would have gulped down a glass of ice water as well. Better yet, she would have dumped it over her head and cooled off her hot thoughts. She cleared her throat again.

"Where are you planning to take this shower?" she asked. Despite the preparation, her voice squeaked anyway.

"In the bathroom. Care to join me?"

Her heart thumped unsteadily. "I have no intention of joining you in my or any other shower. Couldn't you go home and take one?"

"And be late for dinner and have you fussing at me?"

"I wouldn't fuss," she vowed breathlessly.

"I don't want to chance it. I figured practice might run late tonight. I've got a change of clothes in the car. I'll be right back."

The minute he walked through the door she began fanning herself with the magazine he'd brought in with the mail. The kitchen had gotten downright steamy in the past few minutes and she had yet to turn on the stove. What was he trying to do to her?

Don't be naive, she told herself. He was trying to rattle her.

And succeeding admirably, she had to admit, dropping the magazine and fighting for composure the second she heard him approaching the back door. She was not about to let him see how well he was doing. J.K. could flirt and tease all he wanted, but she was every bit as tough-minded as he was. She could withstand his assault. Sooner or later he'd tire of it and move on to someone who was easier prey.

The prospect depressed her. After he'd gone to the bath-room to shower she tried singing to cheer herself up, but the only songs that came to mind were country ballads about star-crossed lovers. She gave up, only to hear J.K. in the shower belting out the lyrics of a Kenny Rogers tune that always reminded her of Ryan. Terrific! Now she was going to get really depressed.

But she didn't. After a few minutes of waiting for the nostalgia to settle in, she realized that she wasn't think-ing about Ryan at all. She was thinking about J.K.'s kisses and how very much she'd like to experiment some more. She was envisioning his body, sudsy and slick and hard. Oh, my, she thought, fanning frantically and to no avail.

"Talk about jumping from the frying pan into the fire," she muttered under her breath.

"Hey, Mom, how come you're talking to yourself?" Teddy asked, standing in the doorway.

"Because I'm losing my mind," she retorted. "Come give me a hug and help me save my sanity."

Teddy reluctantly submitted to the hug, then squirmed free. "What's for dinner? I'm really, really hungry."

"You are always really, really hungry. We're having spa-ghetti and fresh green beans."

Teddy made a face. "We just had spaghetti last night."

"It was two nights ago," she said wearily. "I thought you loved it."

"I do, but not every night."

"What's this?" J.K. interrupted, still bare chested but dressed in clean running shorts and rubbing a towel over his still-damp chest. Cassie's gaze locked on the dark blond hair that arrowed down to the elastic waistband of his shorts. She had to force herself to listen to his conversation with Teddy.

"You're tired of spaghetti?" he said, his expression astonished. "How do you expect to grow up to be the best ballplayer ever to graduate if you don't eat all this healthy stuff?"

Teddy looked skeptical. "You like spaghetti?"

"I eat it every chance I get, especially if your mom makes the sauce."

"She doesn't make the sauce anymore. She says she doesn't have time and that the stuff that comes in the jar is just as good."

J.K. regarded Cassie intently, but he kept up the valiant pretense. "It is just as good. Go wash your hands."

Teddy retreated without a battle.

"Thanks, J.K."

"I gather he's getting a pretty steady diet of this."

"It's nutritious and easy and I don't want to discuss it."

He held up his hands in a placating gesture. "Fine. I won't bug you," he vowed, tugging an out-of-shape team T-shirt over his head. Cassie wasn't convinced by the promise. Sooner or later he was going to start pestering her about money again. She appreciated his concern, but it was none of his business and she was getting very tired of telling him so.

Teddy ate his dinner without complaint, mimicking everything J.K. did to doctor up the spaghetti that Cassie suddenly found tasteless. They sprinkled on a heavy coating of Parmesan, added some hot peppers and mixed in the green beans.

"Wow! This is radical," Teddy said when he took his first bite. His eyes were watering from the peppers.

Cassie caught J.K.'s eye and grinned. "Hot enough for you, too, J.K.?"

"Better," he said. "Next time I'll toss in a little more oregano and garlic while it's simmering."

"Maybe next time you should be the one making it from scratch," she said, unable to keep an edge from her voice.

J.K. didn't rise to the bait. "Why do that when all it takes is a little ingenuity to fix this right up? Now, why don't you go sit in the living room and put your feet up, while Teddy and I do dishes."

Cassie stared at him, startled by the thoughtful offer. When J.K. was like this, it was all too easy to forget the danger of letting him get too close to her or to Teddy. Just look what had happened earlier, when she'd let down her guard. The man had practically kissed her senseless. She was about to object when she glanced at Teddy. He was nodding enthusiastically. "I can dry real good, Uncle Jake."

"I'm sure you can," he said, getting up and gathering the dishes from the table. "Go on, Cass. Leave us men to our man talk."

"Just don't offer him a cigar," she warned.

"Got it," he said, chuckling. "Any other ground rules for this occasion?"

"None I can think of."

"Then go."

She appreciated the gesture. She really did. But the minute she was in the living room, all alone, she felt lonely. She could hear the happy sounds of J.K. and Teddy at work in the kitchen and she wanted to be a part of it. She convinced herself to stay where she was. It wouldn't do to get too used to having J.K. around the house, doing chores, teasing Teddy, helping her. It certainly wouldn't be wise to pretend they were a real family.

But, oh, how the idea was beginning to tempt! It was

getting harder and harder to keep J.K. at arm's length, even though she knew that in the long run it was for the best.

J.K. sent Teddy to take his bath, then went into the living room. He found Cassie curled up in a corner of the sofa, her feet tucked under her, her head on the armrest. She was sound asleep, her cheeks flushed, her hair fanned out in tempting disarray.

Unable to help himself, he went to hunker down beside her. An increasingly familiar tug made him ache to hold her in his arms. She was worn out and, again, he was struck by a helpless anger that she had to work so hard and for so little. Teddy's unwitting revelation about the spaghetti had infuriated him. Sure, they weren't about to starve to death, but the constant cost-cutting measures were demeaning and unnecessary. He'd seen the published reports of the deal Ryan had struck with the new team. It had been in the millions. That was more than enough to support Cassie and Teddy in this modest little house. He could have moved them into a mansion, complete with pool and housekeeper. There was no reason for them to be struggling so just to make ends meet.

Unless Ryan wasn't getting the alimony and child support payments to them on time. As soon as the notion entered his mind, he knew that had to be it. Ryan had always been a big spender. No matter how much he had, he always spent more. His much-publicized generosity with lavish gifts was one of the reasons he'd had so many women chasing after him, even when he'd been married. More than once, he'd spent money on his friends while leaving Cassie to cope with the household expenses on the bank account leftovers.

It took everything in J.K. to keep him from going to the

phone and placing a call to tell Ryan what a no-good, lousy son of a… Forget it. Cassie wouldn't thank him for the interference and her pride would never allow her to admit—especially to him—that Ryan was late with the payments. She'd been embarrassed enough when J.K. had overheard her arguing with Ryan for enough to pay the utilities one month. The night before that incident he'd seen Ryan lose a thousand dollars in a poker game without blinking, money that obviously should have gone toward the overdue electricity and phone bills.

Since Cassie seemed determined to cover for Ryan's bad habits, he would just have to find his own subtle ways of helping out, nothing as overt as trying to hand her cash again. She'd made it plain how she felt about that. But surely he could think of something else.

In the meantime, though, he wanted to get her into bed. Alone, he thought with a sigh of regret. Much as he wanted her, it was still too soon and she was far too exhausted. He scooped her into his arms, his breath catching as she snuggled against him, innocently tempting him. As he carried her through the house to her room, she burrowed her head into the crook of his neck, her breath a hot whisper against his flesh. Desire arrowed through him with an intensity that almost rocked him off balance.

"Oh, Cassie," he muttered, his voice husky as he tugged down the comforter on her bed, spilling her crazy collection of stuffed toys onto the floor. He gently placed her on the fresh sheets, then picked up a ragged, long-eared bunny and tucked it in beside her. He wavered on the issue of undressing her, then wisely decided against it. He had only so much willpower and it was already being tested to the limits.

"What are we getting ourselves into here?" he said, staring at her with longing.

She stirred sleepily. "J.K.?"

"Shh, sweetheart. Go back to sleep." There was an urgency underlying the request. Asleep, Cassie was provocative enough. Awake, she'd be dangerously irresistible. And he needed to get out of here tonight before they made a mistake from which neither of them would ever recover.

Chapter 5

The spaghetti incident, on top of a few other alarming signs, put J.K. on the alert. His protective instincts rallied, fueled by his overwhelming desire to bolster Cassie's spirits, to see her smiling again instead of worn out and blue.

Not that he was being totally altruistic, to be perfectly honest. He just recognized the fact that not even he could seduce a woman who didn't have the energy to resist him. When they finally wound up in each other's arms, he wanted Cassie every bit as spirited and passionate as he knew she was capable of being. He decided to turn detective to see just how bad things really were.

The next few times he went to get something to drink from Cassie's refrigerator, he took stock of the scanty contents. What he discovered was pitiful. There were a couple of containers of leftovers, a package of dried-out cheese, sandwich meat for Teddy's lunches, a few eggs, a carton of milk, some juice, lettuce and the usual assortment of condiments. One cupboard held peanut butter, bread, a few canned goods, a box of spaghetti and a bag of cookies. On Thursday night, increasingly worried, he stole a glance into the freezer. It was discouragingly empty as well, except for a couple of trays of ice cubes, two frozen dinners that looked about as appetizing as dog chow and some frozen orange juice. He slammed the door, wishing he could slam his fist into Ryan's face instead.

The time had definitely come to take action. He spent the whole day Friday thinking about it. Unfortunately, his pitching went to hell as a result. He blew more three-two counts than he had in all of his previous seasons of play combined. He actually walked in a run in the first inning. After taking about as much as he could of J.K.'s disastrous inning and a third, Ken delivered an ear-blistering lecture at the mound and yanked him. To add insult to injury, he replaced him with a kid who'd just been called up from the minors the day before.

"I don't know what kind of burr you've got stuck in your behind, but see to it that it's gone by this time tomorrow," Ken growled, stalking him back to the dugout. "The way you're playing, you might as well be back on the farm team. What kind of leadership is that? I've got green kids out here pitching better than you."

The charge hurt, mostly because it was valid. "I won't make excuses, Ken," he said. "It was my mistake. I've got a lot on my mind."

"Some woman, you mean. I've seen it time and again. Some guy makes MVP a couple of times, gets a little publicity and bingo, he can't concentrate because his mind ain't on the game. Believe me, Starr, there ain't a woman in the world worth blowing your career over."

"Maybe one," J.K. said to himself as Ken, satisfied with

having made his point, stomped off to sit at the other end of the bench. Cassie was worth every ounce of energy he had to spend on her. Why hadn't Ryan realized that before it was too late?

As he tried to figure out his friend's stupidity, recalling all the great times the three of them had had together, the solution to Cassie's food problem finally came to him. It was so simple he couldn't imagine why it hadn't occurred to him earlier. He'd casually waylay her in the store, add a few extras to what she picked up, then pay for it all, swearing they'd divvy up the bill later. It was perfect, absolutely foolproof.

After all, he theorized as he looked for flaws, it wouldn't be the first time they'd wound up grocery shopping together. He and Ryan used to go with her occasionally, dropping junk food into the cart while she overloaded it with fruit and vegetables. They always left with the cart piled high. If his suspicions about money being tight were valid, he'd be able to tell at once just by looking into her grocery cart.

Tonight was the perfect time to try out his plan, too. It was Friday and Cassie had always shopped on Fridays, stocking up for the barbecues and impromptu parties Ryan liked to throw on the weekends after the games.

As soon as he'd showered and dressed, J.K. headed for her neighborhood supermarket. It was five-twenty. Cassie ought to be on her way home from work just about now. He waited for her in the parking lot for a while, then went inside. He stationed himself in the produce section, lingering over the oranges and apples for so long he began to draw curious glances from the help.

With some sort of ESP that he seemed to be developing where Cassie was concerned, he knew the instant she walked into the store. By the time she turned down the produce aisle, sashaying along in a cute little dress that skimmed her knees and showed off her figure, he was fingering a head of lettuce as if it were a ball he was getting ready to pitch on a full count. He waited expectantly for her to discover him.

She stopped in front of the tomatoes, picked up and discarded several, glanced at the price posted on the counter, sighed and took two steps to her left and began examining the lettuce. When she reached for a head, J.K. reached for the same one. Their fingers collided. Cassie began a quick apology, then looked up. A spontaneous, heart-melting smile broke across her features.

"J.K., what are you doing here?"

He bounced the lettuce idly in the air. "I was in the mood for a salad. What about you?"

"I always pick up the groceries for the week on Friday."

"Of course," he said. "I should have remembered. Everything going okay? How was your day?"

"Fine."

"Teddy?"

She regarded him suspiciously. "He's great. You just saw him two nights ago."

Whoops! He'd been so busy being nonchalant, he'd forgotten to use his brain. He glanced toward her still-empty cart and shifted his plan into action. "You haven't gotten much yet."

"I just got here."

"Mind if I shop along with you? You can give me some advice."

One brow arched deliberately. "Advice?"

"You know, about brands and stuff."

"I don't think lettuce comes in brands."

"Sure it does," he improvised hurriedly. "What we have here is your basic iceberg lettuce." He bounced it gently, then put it back and reached for another package. "Now there's also your endive, a little bitter for my taste. Maybe some Boston bib lettuce. What do you think? Maybe I should just go for spinach, instead. Spinach makes a great salad, don't you think?"

She laughed. "I think you're crazy. Nice, but definitely wacko. Do you have a similar problem with the tomatoes?"

"Indeed. We have beefsteak. These aren't looking too hot after that freeze back in January. Notice how they've gassed them to make them ripe. Nothing but mush. The plum tomatoes. I'm not so sure about those. I've never much liked them. But these," he said, lowering his voice to a seductive purr. He met her gaze as he held out a container of perfect, ripe cherry tomatoes. "These look just right…"

He watched the pulse in her neck begin to beat more rapidly. "For a salad," he concluded.

This was turning out to be more fun than he'd anticipated. Cassie was clinging almost desperately to her cart. She blinked and took the cherry tomatoes and placed them into the cart. He doubted she was even aware of it. "I don't think you need me for this," she said, her voice oddly husky. "You're doing just fine."

"But we haven't gotten to the salad dressings."

"J.K., in all the time I've known you, I have never seen you use anything except Italian dressing."

"But even with Italian there are so many choices," he protested.

"I have great confidence that you'll be able to make a selection on your own. Read the labels. Check out the herbs in the bottom of the bottle. Shake it. You can do it," she said, giving him an encouraging pat.

"Are you so sure? Practically since the day we met, you've been accusing me of letting indecisiveness ruin my love life."

Her gaze turned skeptical again. "What does your love life have to with this?"

"Nothing, exactly," he admitted candidly. "It's just indicative of a definite character flaw, isn't that what you've said?"

She regarded him incredulously. "So, because I think you'll never settle down with one woman, I'm also supposed to believe you can't decide among the various brands of Italian salad dressing."

He smiled cheerfully. "That's logical, isn't it?"

"That's bull—" She caught herself and quickly amended, "That's baloney."

"So you won't help?"

"Oh, I'll help, all right. By the time I'm finished with this lesson, you'll know every ingredient in every salad dressing on the shelf. Never let it be said that I allowed you to flounder through life not knowing how to fix a proper salad. Let's go."

"Great," he said and quickly dropped a couple of heads of lettuce and two more little baskets of tomatoes into her cart.

"Where's your cart?" she asked.

"Oh, I'm not getting that much. I might as well share yours. Do you want some fruit before we move on?"

"Just a couple of bananas for Teddy's lunch box."

"No oranges? You always loved oranges."

"They're too expensive right now. The freeze hit the groves up in Orlando pretty hard."

"Just take a couple. See, these are from California. You need your vitamin C. How much can three oranges cost?"

"Ninety-nine cents."

"A bargain, really. Just think about it. These little suckers flew all the way across country for thirty-three cents apiece."

"J.K.," she protested, but he'd already turned the corner and planted himself in front of the meat counter.

"How about a couple of steaks? The sirloin looks good."

"It's not in my budget," she said, her amusement visibly beginning to fade.

J.K. wasn't daunted. "They're on sale."

"No steaks."

"Hamburger, then. You used to make the best hamburgers. Maybe we ought to organize a barbecue this weekend. You know, the way we used to. What do you think? I'll invite a few of the guys and their wives. It'll be fun. They ask about you all the time."

"The last thing I want to do is spend an evening with Ryan's old pals. Come on, J.K., what is this all about?"

"What?"

"You are no more in here to buy stuff for a salad than I am to buy prime rib. What's the story?"

He hadn't prepared himself for a direct confrontation. He knew darn good and well that Cassie's pride would be shattered if he said anything directly about her financial situation. She'd rub his nose in that package of hamburger, then stalk off and leave him to explain the mess to the manager. Maybe he could turn this around simply by inviting himself over for dinner again and offering to bring the food.

"Maybe I was just angling for another dinner invitation," he ventured.

"And maybe you wanted to fly to the moon. Get real. You've dropped in for dinner five times in the last two weeks. You didn't grovel for those meals in the middle of the supermarket."

"I forgot my manners. I figure it's payback time. Besides, I enjoy your company and you do make great hamburgers. I'll grab the fixings and you cook again tonight. Consider it repayment for the meals I've been bumming the last couple of weeks. How about it? Or I could cook, if you're too wiped out. I can manage hamburgers."

The last trace of amusement vanished. "You never give up, do you?" she said wearily.

"I don't know what you mean."

"In a pig's eye. Look, I appreciate what you're trying to do here, but you're wasting your energy. I won't take money from you."

"I'm not trying to give you money."

She waved the two-pound package of ground round at him. "Okay. I won't take meat from you." She glanced in the cart and realized just how busy he'd been. "Or lettuce. Or tomatoes. Or California oranges. Am I getting through that thick skull of yours yet? I'll see you around, J.K. Maybe you can stop by to see Teddy over the weekend. He says I throw like a sissy."

Head held high, she made a quick turn onto the cereal aisle. Something inside J.K. snapped at the sight of that proud, stubborn posture. He caught up with her in front of the corn flakes and dumped an armload of meat and chicken into her cart. She whirled on him with startled indignation. He didn't care. He was ready for the outburst she was bound to make, looking forward to it, in fact. She'd been suffering in silence long enough. It was about time she got mad. Blowing off steam at him was a start. They'd tackle Ryan together.

"What do you think you're doing?" she snapped.

"Seeing to it that you and Teddy get a proper meal for a change. You're through living on spaghetti."

"There's enough food there for half a dozen meals and I don't want any of it," she fumed.

He leaned across the cart and stared her down. "Think about Teddy, for once, instead of that damned obstinate pride of yours." He decided to go for broke and lay it all on the line. "When was the last time Ryan sent you child support money, Cassie? Have you talked to his lawyer about it? Or are you just struggling quietly along?"

"I don't want to hear this," she said, stalking off empty-handed. "Drop it, J.K. You have no right."

He grabbed her cart and caught up with her, trapping her next to the peanut butter. He grabbed the biggest jar on the shelf and defiantly tossed it into the basket. "I care, Cassie, that gives me the right," he said, adding a jar of grape jelly. "I will not sit by and watch you starve yourself to death and scrimp to put a meal on the table for Teddy, when Ryan could afford caviar on the Riviera for the two of you."

"You have nothing to say about it. This is my life, J.K. Starr," she shouted. "Stay out of it!"

"I will not," he said, suddenly aware that shoppers had stopped dead in the aisles to stare at the scene. He abandoned the cart, grabbed Cassie by the arm and propelled her out of the store.

"What do you think you're doing now?" she said, resisting him.

"Taking you someplace where we can sit down and discuss this situation rationally. Don't fight me, Cassie, or I'll carry you."

Her eyes widened. "You wouldn't dare."

"Test me."

They matched stares for several tense seconds before she finally said, "J.K., please, there's nothing to discuss. I have a job. I can support Teddy and me just fine. I don't want your money, your meat or your meddling. I certainly don't want your pity."

"Sorry, babe. Pity has nothing to do with it. I've walked away from a lot of responsibilities in my lifetime, but not this one."

She glared at him, sparks in her eyes, but her voice stayed soft. "You are not responsible, J.K. This is not your fault."

"That's not what you were saying a couple of weeks ago. You couldn't wait to heap the blame on me then."

"I was wrong, okay? I should have kept my big mouth shut. If I'd known this was going to happen, I would have. I wanted to blame someone for what had happened and you were handy. You told me yourself, though, that it was up to me to keep Ryan from walking out and you were right. It is also up to me to get him to face up to his responsibilities. I seem to be failing at that, too. I don't know what I could do differently, but it's my problem, not yours."

J.K. shook his head. "No, honey, I was wrong about that, too. It's Ryan's problem. He's the only one who could make the decision to stay or go and not a thing you or I could have said could have influenced him. As for the money, he's a man who'll always do exactly what he wants to, regardless of the pain it causes. Maybe it's going to take hauling him into court to get him to wake up."

She shuddered visibly. The color drained out of her cheeks. "And have the story on the front page of every sleazy magazine on the rack? No, thank you."

"Just the threat would probably do it. He doesn't want that kind of publicity any more than you do."

"For Teddy's sake, I'm not willing to risk it. Now, if you don't mind, I do have groceries to buy and a dinner to fix."

"Stop running away from this, Cassie. I'll take you out to dinner. We'll talk it out."

"I do not want to go out to dinner and I don't want to spend another minute talking about this."

"You're just being pigheaded."

"Talk about the pot calling the kettle black. You're not exactly being a paragon of compromise."

"You want compromise, we'll compromise. I'll buy your groceries this week and you can buy them next week. We'll take turns cooking. You'll be doing me a favor. I'm lousy in the kitchen."

"It's probably the only room in the house where you are," she grumbled under her breath.

"Thanks for the compliment."

"I meant it as an insult."

"Whatever. So, Cass, what's it going to be? Do I buy the groceries or do I talk to Ryan?"

"That's blackmail."

"Not a pretty word, but fairly accurate."

She regarded him helplessly. "J.K., what exactly will it take to get you to drop this savior role you've adopted? I will say this one last time. I do not want to be protected. I do not want to have my roof fixed. I do not need a father figure for my son. And I do not need to be fed like some sickly calf you're hoping to fatten up for market."

He flinched at her interpretation of what he was trying to do. "Terrific. You know what you want and you know exactly how to get it, right? There's no room in this scenario for friends. No, indeed. Just Cassie struggling to beat the odds, just Cassie so determined to prove a point that it doesn't matter that it could have been easier. What a martyr! You'll accomplish it all on your own and then you can sit around in lonely isolation and rejoice in it. Is that what you want?"

"No. What I wanted was a till-death-do-us-part marriage

with a man I loved. When I said those vows, I meant them. I wanted my son to grow up knowing his father, instead of reading about him in the sports pages or on the cover of some supermarket rag. I didn't have big dreams, J.K. I didn't think I was asking a lot," she said, her eyes bright with unshed tears. "But life's not always fair. I am alone. Teddy doesn't have a father ninety-nine percent of the time. This is the hand I've been dealt and I'm doing the best I can to cope with it. If that makes me a martyr, so be it."

Her shimmering gaze blazed up at him. "The one thing I really don't need is you coming round constantly and telling me what I've accomplished is not enough."

J.K. felt as if she'd landed a solid blow with a bat. There was so much pain in her voice, but he couldn't miss the determination as well. She was going to make it and without his help, if she had her way. He sighed heavily and searched his brain for a compromise, one she'd accept.

"I'm sorry, Cassie," he said softly, wiping at the tear that trickled down her cheek. "I swear I never meant to make things worse for you. I don't know how to do this. I know I'm blundering but you gotta believe me, I just want to help."

She blinked back fresh tears. "Don't you think I know that? But I don't need your money, J.K. It just makes me feel more like a failure. Everybody warned me I was making a mistake marrying Ryan when we were both just kids. I was too stubborn to listen and I was wrong. I wasn't ready for marriage."

"Stop kicking yourself. Ryan wasn't ready, not you. You didn't fail. He did. Don't you understand that?"

"And now? Who's failing now, J.K.? There's no one around to put the blame on except me."

"You're not a failure. You're just struggling to get on

your feet. You'll make it, Cassie. You're tough. You'll get through this rough patch."

"Not if you keep trying to pick me up. I need to do it on my own, J.K. Don't you see? It's important to me to prove I can do it all on my own. The job I have now may not be much, but it's a first step. I got it without anyone's help. I'm good at it and I'm going to get better. Who knows, I may even go back and finish college. One of these days I'll actually have an identity of my own, instead of just being Ryan Miles's ex-wife. No matter how long it takes or what kind of sacrifice I have to make, I'm going to make something of my life. I'm going to be somebody."

"You are somebody, Cassie. Cassie Miles is the most special woman I've ever met."

"Not yet," she denied, her expression fiercely determined. "But I'm getting there."

For the first time, he began to understand her point of view and to accept her determination. "Okay," he relented finally and with great reluctance. "I won't try to interfere anymore. Just remember that I'll always be around to back you up. Think of me as an insurance policy."

Something about his words made her smile. "Insurance, huh? Couldn't you just be my friend, J.K.? That's what I need the most," she said softly. "I could really use a friend."

Without conscious thought, J.K.'s arms opened and Cassie moved into them. He felt her whole body shudder as he closed the embrace. "You have one, babe. You have one."

It wasn't exactly the role he'd had in mind, but it would do for now. It would do.

Tomorrow, however, would be a different story.

Chapter 6

Now that the ground rules had been spelled out, Cassie felt as if she could finally relax and just enjoy J.K.'s company. There would be no more subtle attempts to underwrite her expenses, no more pestering her to get into a legal battle with Ryan over money. There would definitely be no more unexpected, bone-melting kisses. That's the way she wanted it—the only way it could be—and J.K. had agreed.

Well, he'd agreed about the money, anyway. In retrospect, she wasn't so sure about the kisses. She carefully reconstructed the conversation in the supermarket parking lot and realized she might not have mentioned that ground rule as clearly as she should have. She had insisted that all she was looking for was a friend. That should imply no kissing, shouldn't it?

Probably not to a man as blatantly sexual as J.K., she admitted reluctantly. He'd looked very much like a man intent on kissing, even when they'd been in the middle of that face-off over the shopping cart. And as mad as she'd been, the idea had definitely crossed her mind, too. The man's appeal was impossible to ignore. He had a body like... Oh, brother! she thought, catching herself in midlust. She hoped she'd gotten that no-kissing point across, because obviously her traitorous hormones had other ideas.

Still, overall she was feeling pretty good about making herself heard, standing up for herself, not letting him ride roughshod over her. It would be all too easy, especially in her present circumstances, to give in and let a take-charge man like J.K. handle things. She hadn't done that.

She was so busy congratulating herself on her victory that she was stunned when the florist's delivery boy came waltzing into her office with a bouquet less than one week later. Fortunately, he looked as if he lifted weights in his spare time, because the awesome arrangement of colorful spring flowers he was carrying was just about the size of Texas.

Her co-workers, three blatantly curious nurses and the only slightly more restrained office manager, surrounded her desk before she could gather her wits. She grabbed the card, which was tucked amid the tulips, daffodils and irises, and hastily stuck it into her desk drawer.

"Aren't you going to look to see who they're from?" Ellen, the office manager, said.

"I know who they're from," she said with a little sigh of resignation. Why hadn't she thought to include flowers in the ground rules? She struggled to pick them up and move them to a credenza where they'd be out of the way and almost out of her sight. She didn't want to be reminded of exactly how persuasive J.K. could be once he set his mind to it. The man had been practicing seduction since the age of ten. He was bound to be a master at it by now. Sending lavish flower arrangements after an argument was probably second nature to him. Considering his bossy temperament, he probably kept a standing order at the florist's.

"Come on, Cassie, tell us," Jennifer Martin pleaded. "Are they from your ex?"

"Hardly."

"Then you have a new beau. How romantic!" She sighed. She was barely twenty-one and still thought romance came directly from the florist. Cassie wasn't quite ready to disabuse her of that notion. She figured reality would set in soon enough.

"No new beau," Cassie asserted. "They're from a friend."

"Some friend," said Mary Beth, casting another envious look at the spectacular arrangement. "I'm doing good if John picks up a bunch of carnations from the vendor on the corner for our anniversary."

"The size of the gesture is not necessarily indicative of the sincerity." Even as the words were tripping off her tongue, Cassie realized how stuffy she sounded.

"Come on, Cassie. Any guy who'd spend all that money must really care," Ellen contradicted.

"He's just spending what I save him on hamburger."

"Huh?" All four women stared at her in confusion.

"Never mind."

"You're really not going to tell us, are you?" Jennifer said.

"Sorry."

They sighed in collective disappointment and slowly returned to their own work, leaving Cassie to mull over the implications of J.K.'s latest tactic. She was still mulling—and reaching no conclusions she liked—when the door to the office swung open ten minutes before closing time. Looking tanned, virile and breathtakingly gorgeous, J.K.

strolled in. His pleated gray slacks were straight from the pages of the latest men's fashion ads. His navy blazer was more traditional, but it hugged his shoulders in a way that would have made most men weep with envy. His shirt was pristine white and was offset by a daring pink-and-navy tie. Much as she wanted to, Cassie couldn't drag her eyes away from him. Her co-workers more than made up for her speechlessness.

"J.K. Starr!" Jennifer shrieked. "Oh, my God! Sandy, Ellen, Mary Beth get back out here. Midnight Starr is in the waiting room."

"Hey, sweetheart, how ya doing?" J.K. said, sweetening the drawled greeting with his famous grin. Jennifer sank back in her chair. The other nurses stood in the doorways of their respective treatment rooms, mouths gaping. Ellen dashed out of the rest room so fast only her top lip had lipstick on it. Cassie shook her head at the display of female hormones screeching into overdrive.

Why was he doing this to her? First the supermarket. Now her office. Was there to be no place where she was safe from his determined assault on her senses? Why tonight and why, dear God, here? These women would never, ever let her forget it. There was little hope that J.K. had turned up by accident, unaware that she worked in this particular office. Nor was it likely he wanted to see one of her employers. They were pediatricians. Even so, she was tempted to ask if he had an appointment. Maybe that, with a pointed glance at the waiting room filled with toys, would reduce him to size. Before she could gather her wits, though, J.K. was hovering over her, an all-too-familiar glint of mischief in his eyes. He dropped a friendly kiss on her forehead to a chorus of background sighs.

"Damn," she said.

"Make that *hot damn* and I'll feel better."

She regarded him malevolently. "Don't press your luck. What are you doing here? How did you even know where to find me?"

"Why are you cursing?" he evaded.

"The kissing," she moaned, whacking her forehead where only seconds before J.K.'s lips had been. "I knew I should have been more explicit about the kissing. No more, J.K." She shook her head, speaking firmly. He was laughing at her. Her gaze narrowed. "And don't laugh at me."

"Maybe you'd better write out all these rules. I remember the one about the money, but I'm getting confused about these new ones."

"You remember. You're just being stubborn and selective."

"Maybe so," he agreed cheerfully. He glanced at the flowers dominating the credenza. "I see you got the flowers."

"Yes, thank you," she said politely, refusing to meet the perfectly enthralled gazes of her co-workers. "They're lovely." She swallowed hard and tried not to notice that he was perched on the edge of her desk, his rock-solid thigh within inches of her fingertips. She would have told him to move, but the only other chairs nearby were built for five-year-olds. "Why are you here?"

"I thought maybe we could go to dinner. Take in a movie. How about it?"

She shook her head. "I can't. Teddy's waiting for me."

"Nope. Billy's mom said he could stay there tonight."

"He has school tomorrow. He can't spend the night with a friend."

"No school. A teacher planning day, I think."

"What do you know about teacher planning days?"

"I made it my business to know about this one. Even as we speak, the boys are working their way through a stack of the latest videos."

"Supplied by you, no doubt."

"I didn't want to leave anything to chance."

"You forgot one thing."

"What?"

"You're supposed to ask me before you go making all these arrangements for my life. That was definitely part of the deal we made. I remember specifically discussing that the very first time you came by."

"Could be, but I decided I prefer a sure bet. If I'd asked you first, you'd have made some excuse or other, just like you're doing now. This way I've already covered all the contingencies."

"Except one," she insisted. "I'm saying no."

Four women moaned in the background. J.K. winked at them.

"Don't be stubborn, Cass. I had a lousy day at the ball-park. I need someone to talk to."

If he meant to appeal to her kindness and understanding, he was off base. She was feeling about as understanding as Attila the Hun. "Go down to the Blue Dragon. I'm sure some of your teammates will be able to cheer you up."

He apparently didn't intend to give up that easily. "I don't want to talk about baseball. I need a woman's comfort."

She gestured grandly at the still-staring women behind her. "Take your pick. Except for Mary Beth. She's married."

"That's okay," Mary Beth said, wide-eyed. "I could make an exception."

"Sorry, ladies," J.K. said. "I've already made my choice."

He said it with such confidence, such sincerity. Cassie began to waver. She stared at the pile of medical records on her desk. She'd planned to have them all filed before she left for the night. Ellen caught the direction of her gaze and apparently guessed where her thoughts were headed. "Don't worry about the filing," she said. "Jennifer and I will finish up. You deserve a night on the town."

"Traitors," she muttered.

"See," J.K. said, ignoring her comment and grinning in satisfaction. "No more excuses."

He was right, she thought in resignation. She couldn't think of a single one. And there was this one movie she'd been dying to see, a romantic comedy. It was the sort of movie J.K. and Ryan had always hated. It would serve him right.

"I'll only go if I get to pick the movie," she said finally.

"You're on."

She managed a weak smile for her still-gaping friends. For some reason she didn't feel all that victorious. In fact, she felt as if she were walking into a deadly trap.

The restaurant only accented her fears. It was expensive and romantic. The maître d' greeted J.K. with deference and led them to a secluded table, lit by candlelight. The low, mellow music was provided by a pianist who could have performed for elevator recordings. Her menu had no prices and no entrées that she recognized. She glanced across at J.K. and felt her pulse begin to hammer to an unexpectedly sensual rhythm.

"You're not playing fair," she accused, deciding the best defense was a good offense. Would a baseball player understand that tactic or was it football? Or politics? Whatever, it didn't seem to be fazing J.K. He met her gaze evenly.

"Who's playing?" he asked.

"You are. First the flowers. Now this."

"I'm just treating you the way you deserve to be treated."

"No, you're treating me the way you would a lov—" She stammered to a halt, her face turning fiery.

"A lover," he said softly, leaning toward her. The candlelight made the blue in his eyes dance with invitation. "Is that what you were going to say?"

She nodded, captivated by that barely contained hint of aggression, the definite sizzle of passion. Even out of practice she recognized desire when it was sitting across from her. It made her very, very nervous, especially since it seemed to be striking some responsive chord deep inside her.

"That's how I see you, Cass."

"You promised, J.K.," she said, her voice weak with sudden longing. If only… She snapped herself back to reality. Old apprehensions made her cautious. Men like J.K. left women like her. She wasn't flashy enough or provocative enough to compete with all those women who waited willingly on the sidelines in every ballpark in the country. She wasn't Susan Sarandon in *Bull Durham,* witty and self-confident and looking for nothing more consequential than a short-term fling with a summertime hero.

"I'm just here as your friend, if that's all you want," J.K. reassured her. "I'm just hoping that sooner or later I can change your mind."

"Why? For the challenge of it? Those four women in my office, Mary Beth included, would have died to be sitting here with you tonight. Why me? It can only be because I'm the one saying no."

"You're not giving yourself enough credit. Now let's not debate this anymore. We're here because we both want to be here, whether you're ready to recognize the fact or not. Why don't I order for us both? Is that okay?"

"Please."

They'd finished the escargot, sampled the pâté and were well into the veal before Cassie finally relaxed and realized she was actually having a good time. It was like the old days, only Ryan wasn't there. This was just J.K., her pal. What harm could she come to with an old and dear friend?

Her guard was down by the time they arrived for the late show at the big multicinema mall. J.K. looked at the poster advertising her movie choice and faltered. To his credit, though, he didn't argue, didn't try to persuade her to switch to an action movie starting at the same time. He bought the tickets and, over her protests, the biggest container of buttered popcorn, two large sodas and a giant box of candy.

"J.K., we just ate a huge meal," Cassie said as he tried to juggle his purchases. She made a grab for the popcorn just as it tilted precariously.

"Force of habit. Movies require very specific sustenance. Can you get the door?"

She rolled her eyes and opened the door to the already-darkened theater. As soon as their eyes were accustomed to the shimmering light from the huge screen, J.K. led the way down the aisle and found two seats in the middle. Cassie was sure they were the same two seats in the same row he sat in every time he went into the theater. "Another habit," she murmured.

"Hmm?"

"Nothing."

A nearby chorus of hisses silenced them as the credits began to roll. The director's name hadn't even completely rolled up the screen before Cassie realized she might have made just the tiniest miscalculation. The emphasis in this particular comedy was clearly going to be on the romance. And the star looked a lot like J.K., whose knee was bumping hers and whose fingers kept grazing hers over the popcorn.

She tugged at the collar of her dress. Where the heck was the air conditioning in this place? By the time J.K. draped his arm across the back of her seat, his hand resting lightly on her shoulder, Cassie felt as if she'd been sequestered in a steam room.

Midway through the first of what seemed destined to be a great many love scenes, J.K.'s fingertips brushed lightly along her nape. Sparks shot through her. Then he began a slow, sensual massage that made every bone in her body melt.

Science fiction, she thought desperately. She should have insisted on science fiction. Or maybe a techno-thriller. Then she wouldn't have understood what was happening, wouldn't have cared and would have drifted happily off to sleep. Asleep, she would not have noticed the effect of J.K.'s touch.

Wanna bet? She scrunched down in her seat in what turned out to be a futile attempt to escape J.K.'s provocative touch. Four love scenes later and after at least fifteen views of an incredibly tantalizing male posterior that resembled the shape of J.K.'s—or at least looked like J.K.'s in a bathing suit, she amended with all due modesty—Cassie was on fire. Her whole body hummed with awareness. J.K. leaned over to whisper in her ear and the sensation of his warm breath on her neck make her cling desperately to the armrest. She had no idea what he said. Fortunately, he didn't seem to expect a response. Or else he was content just to listen to her heavy breathing.

It doesn't mean anything, she told herself. It's habit, just like the popcorn and fruit-flavored candy.

It didn't feel like habit. It felt incredibly special.

Who was she kidding? It felt like danger. Wonderful and alluring, but dangerous nonetheless. She shivered as he whispered something more, then brushed an innocent kiss across her cheek.

Innocent, my Aunt Tilly! Nothing J.K. ever did was innocent, she lectured, trying to ignore the way her blood was pounding just as hard as if he'd meant it. He was still determined to seduce her and he was doing a fine job of it. One more love scene on screen and one more fleeting kiss by J.K.'s velvet-soft lips and she'd be ready to throw him down in the aisle and have her way with him, audience or not. The man ought to be declared a lethal weapon.

Cassie was on her feet, shaken but steady, the second the final credits began to roll. J.K. grabbed her hand and pulled her down. "I want to check out the cinematographer. He did a great job, don't you think? Especially on that shower scene. Pretty steamy stuff, huh?"

Steamy? They could have cooked broccoli in that shower. "I didn't notice," she said.

"Liar," he accused, grinning and still clinging to her hand. "I can feel your pulse racing just at the mention of it."

"Caffeine," she improvised. "We drank all that coffee at dinner and then the soda. It always makes my pulse race."

"Nice try, but we had decaf at dinner and the sodas were caffeine free."

"Oh." Even in the dim, flickering light, Cassie could see his smirk. She had to get away from that knowing look. It might be cowardly, but she'd never claimed to be anything more. "I think I'll go to the ladies' room. Meet you in the lobby," she said and hurriedly slid out of her seat before he could react.

In the rest room she dawdled. She splashed cool water on her face and then let it cascade over her wrists. It was meant to chill the white-hot sensations running riot through her, but it failed dismally.

"You are heading for disaster," she warned her wide-eyed reflection in the mirror.

"Cass?"

Her eyes flared even wider at the sound of J.K.'s hushed, anxious voice just outside the door.

"Cassie, are you still in there?"

She groaned.

"You can't hide forever, you know. They want to lock this place up before morning. They'll throw you out eventually."

She dried her hands and face and marched out, head held high. "What makes you think I was hiding out?"

He grinned. "Experience."

"Maybe I was just trying to make myself more beautiful for you before we went home. Isn't that what your dates usually do this time in the evening?"

Bad move, she thought as J.K.'s whole body visibly tensed at the unintentionally flirtatious remark. He stared at her with an intensity that was unnerving.

"Cass?" There was a sudden questioning look in his eyes. His voice hovered between vulnerable and hopeful. That tone almost did her in. She drew in a deep breath and steeled herself against it.

"I mean you go to your home and I go to mine," she said desperately. "Not the two of us together."

She watched the flare of passion being rekindled in his eyes and shook her head emphatically. "Oh, no! Forget it. You get that notion out of your head right this minute, J.K. Starr."

He nodded seriously, but there was the faintest suggestion of a smile playing about his lips. "Whatever you say, Cass. Whatever you say."

Chapter 7

"Whatever you say."

That's exactly what J.K. had said to her. Cassie distinctly remembered not only the words but the precise context in which they'd been spoken. Apparently, however, she hadn't said nearly enough or maybe she'd said all the wrong things. At any rate, J.K. drove straight past her office and car and on toward her house at a breakneck pace. She knew there was something in politics called damage control, a quick fix when a misstatement caused seemingly irreparable harm to a campaign. She really, really needed a little damage control right now. Unfortunately, she had no idea how to bring it into play in this situation. She'd set something into motion back there at the movies and for the life of her she couldn't imagine how to stop it.

No, a persistent, self-confident little voice nagged. That voice obviously belonged to someone with a complete grip on her senses. Cassie hadn't been that controlled since the day J.K. had turned up in response to Teddy's call. Any two-year-old knew that decisively negative word. Why couldn't she get that one, firm syllable past her frozen lips?

Cassie wasn't sure she liked the answer that popped into her mind. She did, too, want to object. She wanted to stop this before it went any further. She knew she had to. Having a casual fling with J.K. might help her temporary hormone imbalance—which she'd only just recently noticed—but it would play havoc with her life. Sex, even the very best sex, didn't last forever and she would not be the one being left behind next time. So, she would say no.

At the door.

J.K. had her out of the car and inside the house before she could say spit. She'd forgotten he had keys, forgotten that Ryan had given them to him so he could look out for things that time they'd taken a camping vacation in the mountains up in Georgia. She'd also forgotten he could move that fast. It was the one thing she should have remembered about any ballplayer. They were trained to have moves so quick that only a dead-on fastball could catch them between bases. Obviously they practiced those moves off the field and J.K. was at the head of the class.

As his mouth swooped down to cover hers with velvet demand, she realized the one thing she hadn't forgotten was the devastating power of his kisses. She remembered that in spine-tingling detail. And she melted into his embrace with a tiny sigh of resignation and a whole ton of reservations.

Any minute now, she would say no, she promised herself. Any second she would pull away, regain control of her senses and slug J.K. in his arrogant, presumptuous jaw.

Just not this second, she thought as his tongue slid over hers, setting off yet another riot of bone-melting sensations. Maybe not even this hour, she thought as his fingers found the curve of her breast. A hand swept down the curve of her spine, then over her buttocks, tipping her firmly into his heat and hardness.

Maybe not tonight, she conceded breathlessly. Maybe just this once she would indulge in feeling sensual and feminine and loved. Even if it was make-believe. Even if it didn't last.

"Let me love you, Cassie. Please."

It was the plea for permission that flipped her heart over. Not the kisses. Not the blatantly sensual, impossible-to-resist touches. Not even the impressive evidence of his desire. Just "please," and she was undone.

She couldn't make herself say a word—not yes and definitely not no. Whatever was happening between her and J.K., she couldn't walk away from it. Not yet. She simply nodded and slid her arms around his neck. Her lips brushed over the sandpapery texture of his jaw, leaving them tingling and aware. Her tongue tasted, discovering the lingering lemon and cherry of candy.

J.K. pulled back, his fingers trembling hesitantly against her cheek as he searched her eyes. "No regrets, Cass. I don't want there to be any regrets."

"No regrets, my friend," she said, trusting him that there would be no need for any. The man who was her friend would see to that. The man who was about to become her lover might be incapable of long-term commitment, but he would never abandon her as a friend. Despite the obstacles she'd placed in his way, he'd proved that many times over in the past few weeks. He'd stuck it out. He would be beside her through thick and thin and there was a lot to be said for that. It was more than she'd had from the man who'd vowed before God to stay.

At the door to her room she hesitated. Ryan was the

only man who'd ever crossed that threshold. She'd never expected to want another man as much. The implications left her weak. As if he sensed her mounting reservations, J.K.'s hand cupped her chin, his thumb stroking the bottom lip she'd been biting in that instant of gut-wrenching confusion and indecision.

"Any time, Cassie. You can stop this anytime you want to."

"No," she said now, when it had a different meaning entirely. "No. This is what I want. Promise me, though, that we won't try to pretend that it's anything more than what it is."

"Meaning?"

"Don't say you love me, J.K., and don't let me say it, either. The lie would cheapen it. This can be something special, just for what it is."

He opened his mouth, but she stood on tiptoe and sealed her lips over his, stopping the protest, changing the direction of his thoughts back to wicked, back to devil-may-care, back to loving. She didn't stop the kissing and the tasting until she was sure that only the heat flaring between them mattered anymore.

J.K. wondered how Cassie would react if he took her right where they were standing. His whole body trembled with the effort it took to keep from losing control. Her deep, wet kisses first startled, then delighted him. Now they were turning him into a quivering mass of needy male protoplasm. Make that a hardened mass. He was aching with his hunger for her. Her king-size bed, littered with her silly, charming collection of stuffed animals, seemed much too far away. If they didn't slow down, they'd never get there.

"Cass," he murmured, placing feathery little kisses along

the column of her neck. He nibbled on her ear. "Slow down, babe. We have all the time in the world."

She murmured a protest as her fingers began working the buttons on his shirt. He clasped her hands and stilled them against his chest. A puzzled look crossed her face as she stared up at him. "Why?"

"Because I am about to toss you down on this floor and I don't want it to be that way. I've been hungry for you for too long now. I hurt all over."

Her hands slid down, tentatively grazing the front of his slacks. He groaned as a shudder swept through him. "You're playing with fire, Cassie."

She gazed up at him with a pert smile. "Oh, is that what you call it?"

He shook his head. "Why is it that I never suspected this cruel streak in you?"

"Cruel? I'm just giving you a dose of your own medicine."

Satisfaction surged through him. "So, it did get to you when I touched you in the movies."

"Don't feign innocence with me. You knew exactly what you were doing."

"Oh, I knew what I was doing. I just wasn't sure if it was working. You're a pretty tough customer."

"Just because I didn't swoon at your feet the first time you made a pass at me doesn't mean I wasn't aware of you. I just have a little more class than some women you've met."

"Honey, when it comes to class, you're the leader of the pack. Now that we've established that, why don't we try to find our place in this scene."

"You're calmer now?"

He nodded.

"Well, we can't have that," she said, reaching for him

again. His shirt vanished and her lips found the masculine nipples buried in the thatch of dark blond hair on his chest. Every muscle in his body went taut. So much for slowing down.

"I think we'd better get into that bed, Cassie," he said, scooping her up and carrying her across the room. He shoved plush toys in every direction, then placed her squarely in the middle of the bed, her dress riding high on her thighs. He knelt at the foot of the bed and slipped off her shoes, then slid his hands slowly up one silky leg until he found the snaps of her garters. With a flick, he undid them and slowly rolled her stocking down, leaving a trail of searing kisses in the wake of cool, shimmery silk. By the time he'd repeated the process on her other leg, she was beginning to twist beneath him and her bare flesh was on fire.

"Help me with the dress, sweetheart," he whispered, kneeling now behind her and working on the zipper. Slow, lazy kisses burned down the column of her spine. When he was finished, she lifted the whisper of fabric over her head, turned slowly around and sat before him in lacy bra and bikini pants. He'd seen her before in no more. But quick, responsive heat swelled inside him as it never had before.

"Cassie," he began in a choked voice. He reached toward her, then hesitated.

She was the one who completed the touch, taking his hand and placing it on her breast, then sighing with pleasure. "Love me, J.K.," she pleaded. "Hold me close."

As badly as he wanted to be sheathed inside her, he settled for simply taking her into his arms, savoring the sweet scent of her, delighting in her sensuous warmth and the promise of passion. How heavily would all this weigh on his conscience once tomorrow came, he wondered, then dismissed the thought. They were consenting adults. They were friends. They could handle being lovers without it changing anything essential between them.

It always changes things, his conscience warned. Always. But the temptation and the need were too great. Cassie was liquid fire in his embrace, drawing him as the eternal flame attracts the moth.

"This will be special, Cassie. I promise you that," he vowed as he slowly stroked and caressed until she cried out, coming apart beneath his touch, leaving herself vulnerable and unafraid. He stared into eyes shiny with tears and whispered, "There's more, sweetheart. Don't quit on me yet."

Her hips rose eagerly to meet his first slow thrust and her eyes widened with wonder. "That's it, sweetheart. Come to me." His whole body was alive with anticipation as each sure stroke took her higher and brought him closer and closer to a shattering climax in her arms. This waiting, this edge-of-the-precipice excitement was new to him. "That's it, babe. Let go for me."

"J.K.?" she murmured, part disbelief, part fear.

"It's okay. Go for it, Cass. All the way."

As shuddering contractions swept her along, he felt his own intense release wash endlessly through him until at last, filled with unmatchable joy and weak with exhaustion, he slept, Cassie in his arms.

He woke to find Cassie curled tight against his side, wide awake and intent on running her fingers through the hair on his chest.

"Did you sleep?" he asked groggily.

"Nope. I was too busy."

He opened one eye and encountered a glassy stare. He blinked and realized it belonged to an oversize panda. He heaved it aside and regarded Cassie intently. "Busy?"

"I had exploring to do," she said, her hand increasingly

adventurous. J.K. moaned as desire rocketed through him again.

"What did you discover on this exploration of yours?"

"Oh, all sorts of interesting things," she said, pointing them out with magical fingers. J.K. had a feeling he'd unleashed a tiger. The thought was delightful and a little terrifying.

"Maybe we should talk," he suggested, drawing a sheet up and settling it over them. The suggestion met with blatant disobedience. "Cassie, that's not talking."

"Tell that to the phone company."

"Cassie!"

She grinned. "Do you really want me to behave, J.K.?"

"I really do," he said soberly.

"Oh."

Her disappointment was gratifying. His body agreed with her. After a fleeting wrestling match with his conscience, he gave in to the two of them.

Some time later, still damp with sweat and sleepily contented, Cassie murmured, "I do like the way you talk, Mr. Starr."

"You have quite a way with words yourself."

"J.K.," she began, then went silent.

"Hmm?"

"Why don't you ever talk about home?"

"Home? You've seen my house. What's to talk about?"

"Don't be deliberately obtuse. I'm talking about Kentucky and you know it. Why don't you ever say anything?"

The question whispered through the hairs on his chest and stirred a responding sigh deep inside him. He supposed she had the right to ask. Lying here in his arms gave her that right. But the question prodded like one of those pitchforks he'd used on never-ending bales of hay back on the farm.

"J.K.?" she repeated, then waited, endlessly patient.

"I suppose I just don't think about it much anymore. I haven't been back in a couple of years now."

"Don't you miss it? As much as I love being here where it's warm year-round, I've never quite gotten over longing for the change of seasons in Wisconsin."

"You'd trade blue skies and palm trees for bitter winds and icy streets?"

"Not forever, but yes, I think I'd like to go back sometime. Since my parents moved here, too, I haven't been back at all. I want Teddy to experience the way I grew up, the hot chocolate in front of the fire on Christmas Eve, making snow angels, skating on the pond down the road in winter and swimming there in summer. Didn't you ever do stuff like that?"

"Sure, but that's not what I remember when I think of home."

"What do you remember?"

"The loneliness," he said at once, startled to discover that the bitterness and anger of that time was still very much with him. He'd been so sure he'd slammed the door tight enough so that he'd never have to look back.

"But I thought you had a sister," she said, confusion in her eyes. "And I know you played ball. Surely you had friends."

"I had friends."

"Then what? Tell me what was so rough."

"Who said it was rough?"

"You said it was lonely. Do you want to fight over definitions?"

He sat up and the sheet fell to his waist. His movement dragged it off Cassie, leaving her bare chested and vulnerable, but she didn't waste a second trying to hide herself from him. She was too intent on her cross-examination. The question made him uneasy. All the probing, the hunt for intimacy nagged at him like a burr. J.K. had never let anybody get close. He'd let them into his bed often enough, but never into his heart. Cassie was doing her best to sneak onto forbidden turf. She was trying to break her own fool ground rule about not pretending this was anything special between them.

"I have to go," he said, edging out of bed as his defenses slid into place.

"If you leave now, don't ever come back." Her voice was whisper soft, but deadly serious. He stared at her. "I mean it, J.K. If we can't talk, then all this…" She waved a hand over the bed in an all-encompassing gesture. "It was a terrible mistake."

He stood there naked and feeling hideously vulnerable. The chill in her voice scared him as nothing else had scared him in all his rough-and-tumble years. "You've got quite a way of getting to the heart of things, don't you, Cass?"

She smiled demurely. "I do try."

Only a man who'd watched her wrestle with demons in the past would have caught the flash of relief, would have noticed the tiny sigh. J.K. saw both and knew he couldn't walk away, no matter how badly he wanted to. She'd laid herself on the line getting into this bed with him. She'd compromised a lot of things she believed in, given herself to him wholeheartedly. The least he could do in return was tell her what she wanted to know. Talking about the past wouldn't kill him. Living it had made him tough enough to withstand almost anything—except the prospect of losing Cassie when he was just beginning to discover her.

"What do you want to know?"

"Everything."

"I don't suppose we could have this talk over breakfast."

She shook her head. "Nope. You'll talk faster if you have a goal of pancakes and eggs in mind."

"Lordy, but you're tough."

"It's something to remember," she said, her expression thoroughly satisfied.

He sat back down then, stretching out on the bed with his hands linked behind his head. The posture was relaxed enough, but his head was spinning with a kaleidoscope of painful memories. He sorted through until he found one simple, uncomplicated place to start: the farm.

He'd loved that farm. He'd even loved waking up at dawn to let the thoroughbred horses out into the fields. "Ah, Cass, you should see it sometime, especially at dawn when a gray mist hangs over everything. The bluegrass just goes on and on, rolling hill after rolling hill. There's nothing, *nothing* that smells quite like that earthy scent of fresh-cut grass, horseflesh and morning mist."

She sighed and curled herself against him. "It sounds lovely. How can you not miss it? Are your parents still there?"

The tension, easing for a time, slammed back into him. "They're there," he said curtly.

"Didn't you get along?" she said, obviously sensing his turmoil.

"About as well as any kid gets along with his parents, I suppose."

She lifted herself up and studied him closely. "There's something you're not saying, isn't there? I can hear it in your voice."

He shook his head.

"J.K.?"

"It doesn't matter."

"Obviously it does. What was your father like?"

"He was a great guy. A little too absorbed with working the farm, but by all accounts a success and an all-round nice guy."

He sensed that Cassie was sifting through what he said, listening for nuances, searching for clues. Finding none, she said, "And your mother? Did she like living on a farm?"

His whole body froze with the ache of remembering. "Yeah, she liked it." He tried to keep his tone even, but Cassie clearly caught the bitterness.

"And?"

"And what?"

"There's more, J.K. Spit it out."

He thought back to that horrible, gut-wrenching day when he'd walked into the barn. His stomach turned over even now. "She was especially fond of the stable hands," he said finally.

Cassie sucked in her breath and then her arms went around him. "Oh, J.K., no," she whispered as she held him tight. Her compassion surrounded him, made the remembering a little easier.

"I'm afraid so, as I discovered rather vividly one sultry night. Near as I could tell, the whole town knew about her little habit, but they kept it under wraps out of respect for my dad. Funny, isn't it? Just when I realized how much he was respected by everyone, I lost all respect for him myself. He should have thrown her out."

"Obviously, he loved her very much."

"He was a fool."

He didn't realize he was crying until Cassie wiped away the dampness on his cheeks. He was so caught up in those awful emotions that he was hardly aware of her touch.

"Quite a story, huh? Mr. and Mrs. Middle America. They deserved each other."

"Stop it," she said, her voice tender but impatient. "Apparently they'd made their peace with each other and it's not for you or me to judge them."

"Come off it, Cassie. Don't tell me you're not shocked."

"It doesn't matter what I feel. They had to live with it, not me."

"I had to live with it."

"No," she insisted. "You had to live with the way they treated you, and for all your bitterness I've never heard you say one thing to suggest that they didn't both love you, that they didn't do right by you. You grew up wanting for nothing. You got a good education. Some kids never have chances like that."

He'd never looked at his life from that perspective before. He supposed she had a point. That didn't make it any easier, though, to accept that his mother had been little better than a common whore.

"It does explain a lot, though," she said thoughtfully.

"What?"

"It's no wonder you've never settled down. You've convinced yourself that all women are untrustworthy, haven't you?"

"I've never given the matter any thought."

She tweaked the hairs on his chest, breaking the somber mood. "Maybe you should, big guy. You can do that while I fix the pancakes."

He didn't, though. He took a shower instead, dismissing Cassie's dime-store analysis. He was the way he was. What did it matter why?

When he walked into the kitchen, dressed in his slacks and the shirt he'd worn the night before with its sleeves rolled up, she gave him a questioning glance, but Teddy's presence saved him from the need to respond.

"Hi, Uncle Jake," Teddy said, accepting J.K.'s appearance readily. Fortunately he'd spent many a night in the guest room after those barbecues that had run on into the wee hours of the morning. It saved them all from an awkward moment.

"Are you here to take Mom to work? Is the car busted again?" Teddy wanted to know.

"Yes," Cassie said, clearly grabbing the easy explanation, "I had to leave it at work last night. J.K. said he'd drop by and take me in."

"I don't have school today," Teddy told him. "Maybe you could stay and play with me while Mom works."

"Sorry, pal. I have a game."

"Oh, wow! What time? Can I come?"

J.K. lifted his gaze to meet Cassie's. She was concentrating intently on her eggs. J.K. sighed. "I guess you'll have to work that out with your mother, slugger."

"Mom, can I go, please? You don't have to buy hot dogs or anything. I could probably even sit with Uncle Jake in the dugout, just like I used to with Dad. Please?"

J.K. watched the struggle on Cassie's face. "I'll think about it," she said finally.

"But, Mom…"

"I said I'd think about it, Teddy," she said sharply. "Now drop it."

Teddy's bottom lip went out. "May I be 'scused?" he mumbled.

"Yes," Cassie said. "Go."

Teddy gave J.K. a quick hug, then vanished. As soon as he was gone Cassie lifted a defiant gaze to J.K. "Go on and say it."

"Say what?"

"I blew it again, right?"

"I didn't say that. I do think you're making too big a deal about not letting him come to the ballpark. The guys adore him. He'd be out in the fresh air. There are a lot worse things he could be doing."

"Okay, okay. I will think about it. Did you consider what we talked about?"

"I was too busy thinking about last night. You were sensational, Cassie."

She battled against a smile and lost. "Thanks for the flattery, but it doesn't get you off the hook, J.K. You think I have all these unresolved feelings about Ryan that are standing in the way of my getting on with my life and that may be true. But you have just as many unresolved feelings about your mother. Promise me you'll give some thought to making peace with your parents. It might make a difference to your whole future."

He sighed heavily. "I'll think about it." He stood up and touched a brief kiss to her forehead, then realized he needed much more to get him through the day. His lips moved to her mouth for a slow, leisurely kiss.

"For good luck," he said, winking as he walked out the door.

"Yours or mine?"

"Maybe both."

Chapter 8

Cassie's goodbye kiss had been potent. J.K.'s luck held through eight and two-thirds near-perfect innings. He had pitched a shutout so far, but now there were three men on base in the ninth and he was getting nervous. Still, he had two outs and he was two strikes up on Yankee first base-man Red Grady, a powerhouse hitter who couldn't seem to get a handle on his fastball today. One more strike and his team would have a shot at breaking the scoreless dead-lock. After the way he'd pitched the other day, he needed this victory for his self-confidence.

It was the first time since the start of spring training that J.K. had gone the entire nine innings. He'd had to beg Ken to leave him in the game after the fifth, but he was tiring now and wondering if he hadn't made a serious mistake. His shoulder ached. He wanted the inning and the game to be over with in the worst way, but he wasn't about to ask Ken to pull him with only one batter between him and that shutout.

He watched for the sign from catcher Kyle Rogers, acknowledging it with the faintest suggestion of a nod. Never was he more aware of the tension in his muscles, the soft leather of his glove, the weight of the ball and the roughness of the stitching than at a turning point like this. He could feel the blazing afternoon sun beating down on his shoulders, the trickle of perspiration running down his back. Every sensation was gloriously magnified.

Grady shifted nervously at the plate, going through a familiar ritual. He took a few practice swings, tapped his bat on home plate, resettled his batting cap on his head and muttered something under his breath. He glared ferociously toward the pitcher's mound in an attempt to intimidate, but J.K. was long since onto him. Unlike other players who psyched themselves with threats and obscenities, Red Grady recited still-remembered chunks of his high school poetry assignments. The first catcher who'd mocked him for it had been eating dust five seconds later. That had taught J.K. an important lesson about body language and tone being every bit as important as content.

That's why he figured it was so much easier for him to see through Cassie's defensiveness. There was an underlying message every time they communicated and he doubted if she was even aware of it herself. Last night had been all the proof he'd ever need that he'd been reading her right all along. This, however, was no time to be thinking about Cassie, he reminded himself as he began his windup.

One more, Starr. One more strike and you're out of here. Let some other sucker pitch the extra innings if the guys can't pull it out in the bottom of the ninth.

The tension in the stadium was almost palpable. Even

though it was only spring training, the fans took each exhibition game seriously. J.K. tried to make himself relax into the throw, but his fingers gripped the ball too hard. Sweat beaded on his brow and ran into his eyes, but he never once looked away from Grady. For him there was an intensity, an undercurrent of electric anticipation in that instant before a pitch that was unmatched by anything he'd ever experienced, except maybe great sex.

Grady stepped out of the batter's box in an attempt to break his concentration. J.K. turned his back on the plate, picked up his resin bag, dusted off his hands and wiped them on his uniform. When he turned back, Grady was in place and he was ready. J.K. brought the ball in to his chest, then out again. As he reached the peak of his pitching motion, an excited voice split the air.

"Uncle Jake! Hi, Uncle Jake!"

"Balk!" the umpire shouted as J.K.'s motion jerked to a stop in midwindup.

J.K. groaned. He couldn't even bring himself to look toward the dugout as the third-base runner sauntered home, putting the Yankees into the lead. He could hear Ken's furious stream of objections and could imagine the expression on his face. His own feelings were mixed. He almost never balked. He had a smooth pitching motion that rarely faltered. The fact that he had at such a critical point in the game was humiliating.

But knowing that Teddy was in the stands almost made it worth it. If he was there, then Cassie had brought him after work, which had to mean she was coming around. Maybe, at long last, she was putting things back into perspective. Maybe the fantastic lovemaking they'd shared last night had been a critical turning point in her recovery. The memory of the way she'd come apart for him was every bit as hot and disturbing as the afternoon sun.

Thoroughly distracted by Teddy's one innocent yell and all it implied, J.K. finished the inning in a daze. The Yankees scored twice more before he got the side out. Disgusted, he walked to the dugout and took a seat as far away from the furious manager and his teammates as he could. Ken would have plenty to say once they hit the locker room, but for now he was going to try to get them out of the last half inning with some pride.

"Sorry, guys," J.K. apologized after the game ended as their first loss of the still-young training season.

"Hey, J.K., it happens to the best," Kyle told him with a pat on the back.

"Sure, amigo," Davey said. "We take them next time. Come, have dinner with Maria and me. We'll drink a few beers. You'll forget all about it."

He thought of Cassie someplace nearby, waiting for him, he hoped, as she used to linger at the locker-room entrance waiting for Ryan. "I don't know, Davey. I might have a date tonight."

"Bring her. She can help Maria in the kitchen."

"Don't let her hear that sexist talk. She'll have you scrubbing pots and pans before the night is out. I'll talk to her and see what she wants to do. I'll give you a call if we're coming." His expression turned sober. "Thanks, pal."

Davey waved off his gratitude. "*Por nada.* We are friends, right? Besides, Maria has been complaining about missing you. I think she has a crush on you like all the others. You will watch your step with her, *si*?" There was a mock threat in his voice.

J.K. laughed at the thought of tangling with the feisty

Maria. "Definitely *si*, my friend. Your wife is safe. She's too much woman for me."

The exchange with Davey improved J.K.'s mood, but Ken was less forgiving than his teammate. "In here," he hollered, when he spotted J.K., a towel draped around his hips, on his way to the showers. Anxious to get cleaned up, J.K. hovered in the doorway of the manager's dingy office. The place was such a mess it was rumored that a couple of his teammates had gotten lost in there and were never seen again. The bodies were probably under that stinking pile of towels in the corner.

"What the hell happened to you out there?" Ken demanded. "That was the sorriest excuse for pitching I've ever seen."

"Hey, lay off," he said defensively. "I had eight great innings."

"It takes nine to win a game."

"So why didn't you yank me after eight?"

Ken didn't even deign to answer that one, since they both knew perfectly well that it was J.K.'s own stubbornness that had kept him in the game. "Maybe there's a lesson in here, Starr."

"Maybe so."

His ready acknowledgment seemed to startle Ken. "Just think about it," the manager mumbled before waving him off.

"I'll do that," he agreed, hurrying off to shower so he could get back outside to see if Cassie was still around. His hair was still damp when he emerged from the locker room ten minutes later. Teddy was waiting for him right outside.

"Uncle Jake, you were great!"

J.K. scooped him up for a hug. "Thanks, slugger, but I blew it."

Teddy patted his shoulder sympathetically. "That's okay, Uncle Jake. You did real good till the end." He frowned. "I guess maybe it was me yelling that messed things up for you."

Startled that Teddy was that astute, he said, "What makes you say that?"

"That's what the man next to me said. He told me to shut up."

"Don't worry about it, pal. I get paid to pay attention to what I'm doing. If I foul up, it's nobody's fault but my own." His gaze searched the area, but he saw no sign of Cassie. "Where's your mom?"

"In the parking lot. She said she'd wait by the car."

"Let's go find her, then."

"Can I have a drink first? I'm really, really thirsty."

"Let's check with your mom. Maybe we can stop for hamburgers or something. I'm pretty hungry myself."

"Wow! That'd be great. Hey, mom," Teddy yelled, taking off across the parking lot. "Uncle Jake's gonna take us for hamburgers."

J.K. winced, wondering how she was going to react to that news. He'd hoped to broach the subject a little more diplomatically, then casually mention the invitation from Davey and Maria. He should have known that a seven-year-old understood nothing about tact and strategy. He followed Teddy's progress across the nearly empty parking lot until his gaze finally fell on Cassie. She was leaning against the side of her car, wearing white shorts and a bright pink T-shirt that was knotted at the waist. With an old baseball cap perched on her head and no makeup on, she looked to be about fifteen. She was staring down at the scuffed toes of her sneakers, but glanced up at Teddy's untimely announcement.

"Hi," J.K. said, suddenly feeling awkward after last night's intimacy.

"Hi," she responded warily.

"How was your day?"

"Okay. Everyone at work was full of questions about you."

"I'm sorry."

She regarded him skeptically. "Are you?"

He decided to change directions. "I'm glad you decided to come."

She nodded curtly. "Did you win?"

"Afraid not. You didn't come in?"

"No." She shook her head as if to ward off the very idea. "I couldn't."

J.K. nodded. "Maybe next time. I'm still glad you brought Teddy."

She shrugged. "He gets his persistence from his father and I was running out of excuses," she admitted wryly. "What's all this about hamburgers?"

"Teddy's thirsty and I'm starved. I suggested maybe we could stop someplace. Davey and Maria wanted us to drop by there. How about it?"

He watched her whole body tense up and knew what was coming. "You told Davey about us seeing each other?" she said uneasily.

"Not exactly. I just said I had plans. He told me to bring along anyone I wanted. Come on. You and Maria used to be great pals. She'll be thrilled to see you. I think she's getting very tired of being pregnant. She'd probably enjoy a little female company. Davey's about as sensitive as a steel practice bat."

"Come on, Mom. Let's go someplace. I'm really, really hungry, too."

"I'm sure you are," she said with a shake of her head. "It's been at least two hours since lunch."

"Wait'll he gets to be a teenager," J.K. warned, laughing.

Cassie groaned. "I know. I remember what Ryan was like. He'd clean out the refrigerator at his place, then come over to work on ours. My father said he was going to have to take a second job just to support Ryan's milk habit."

"And bread," J.K. recalled. "I ate at least three sandwiches for lunch and another two for a midafternoon snack. Our housekeeper finally said if I was going to consume an entire loaf of bread by myself every day then I could bloody well go to the store and get it. That lasted about a week, until she realized how much extra money it cost once I got near the doughnuts."

"That's disgusting. You men act like pigs and wind up with muscles. If I ate like that, I'd be a hundred and eighty pounds of flab."

"I'd love you anyway," he said nobly.

"It would serve you right if I put you to the test on that."

Teddy was gazing back and forth between the two of them. Finally disgusted, he grumbled, "Are we going to eat or not?"

J.K. looked at Cassie, who gave a resigned shrug. "I guess we are."

"At Davey's?"

She hesitated. "Why not. Just don't give them the wrong idea about us, J.K. You know how talk like that travels."

"And you don't want it getting down to Ryan that you and I are seeing each other, right?"

"I don't want it getting out at all," she said, casting a meaningful look at Teddy, who was already heading for J.K.'s car.

"Let's ride in Uncle Jake's car. It's neater than ours."

"A World War Two jeep is in better shape than ours," Cassie commented dryly. "Maybe we ought to take both cars, though. It'll be simpler later."

The prompt defensive maneuver worried J.K. He studied her questioningly. "Are you sure you're okay?"

"Why wouldn't I be?"

"I mean about last night."

"It was no big deal, J.K. That's what we agreed."

"People agree to a lot of things and then find the rules tough to live with. That's why there are so many divorces." He touched her cheek gently. "Don't regret last night, Cass. It was special."

She closed her eyes and sighed. "I know, J.K. I guess that's why it scares me."

"We need to talk some more, I think. How about cutting the visit to Davey's short and then I'll swing by your place for a while."

She shook her head. "Let's play it by ear."

J.K. sensed that she was retreating and he wasn't sure what to do about it, especially with Teddy waiting anxiously in the back seat of the car. Alone, he would have known exactly how to reach her. In bed, they had instantaneously attained an almost perfect understanding. He settled now for squeezing her hand, trying to communicate without words that he knew exactly the qualms she must be having and that they would work them out.

Once they were on the road, J.K. used his cell to call Davey and let him know they were coming.

"Let me talk, Uncle Jake," Teddy pleaded. "Mom doesn't have a cell phone."

"Too late, kiddo. He's already hung up."

"Could I call Dad?"

J.K. glanced over at Cassie. Her mouth was set in a thin,

disapproving line. "Maybe you can try your father later on," J.K. said. "He's probably out at the ballpark now, anyway."

Teddy heaved a disappointed sigh. "Oh, yeah, right. I forgot." He sank back in the seat.

Glancing into the rearview mirror, J.K. saw that he was staring dejectedly out the window. "We'll try him after dinner, son. I promise."

"It doesn't matter," Teddy said stoically. "He never calls me."

J.K. bit back a stream of obscenities and vowed that he would call Ryan tonight himself. He'd track him down wherever he was and have a long heart-to-heart talk with him about parental responsibility.

Even with all the reminders of Ryan's faults and their impact on his son, J.K. realized he was feeling astonishingly contented being with Cassie and Teddy. If he didn't watch his step, he was going to find himself caught up in something he'd never expected when he'd first started spending time at Cassie's place. His goal had been to give her a little moral support. Then he'd developed a few immoral ideas and suddenly other wicked thoughts were creeping into his mind when he was with her.

Love. The word slipped into his head with all the sneakiness of a cat burglar. He could feel his stomach knotting at the very idea. *Whoa! Slow down, Starr. You don't even believe in love.*

But he did believe in Cassie and the warmth of their friendship. They were growing closer day by day. The sex was spectacular. And he adored Teddy. He guessed that was a form of love, just not the happily ever after kind, he reassured himself.

Whew!

"J.K., are you all right?" Cassie asked, her voice laced with concern.

He blinked and turned to her. He found that he had to fight the urge to slam on the brakes and kiss her right there in the middle of the street with Teddy looking on. "Fine," he said in a choked voice.

She regarded him skeptically. "Are you sure? For a minute there you looked a little pale."

"Just hungry, I guess. Here's Davey's just ahead. I'll be terrific as soon as I get some food." He sounded far more confident than he felt. He had a feeling he wasn't likely to be fine until he could get his rampaging hormones and crazy thoughts under control.

He watched as Cassie swung her slender, tanned legs out of the car. Immediately his muscles tightened and heat blazed through him. So much for control. He abandoned the effort and stared, imagining his hands against the silken flesh, cupping that sweet little derriere, bringing her hips tight against his.

Holy mother of all the saints! He was definitely in trouble here. He gulped fresh air and thought of air conditioning and icy showers. The effect was only moderately successful. At least it would get him into Davey's without embarrassing all of them. Inside, with Cassie's legs discreetly under the table—please God, let Maria have a tablecloth on the picnic table—he might have a reasonable shot at getting himself under control. If he didn't, Davey and Maria wouldn't have to guess about the details of his relationship with Cassie.

Cassie approached Davey and Maria's front door as if she were being walked to the guillotine. This was the last place she wanted to be tonight, but she owed it to J.K. to make an effort to normalize her life. She'd been hiding too long and he was right—she had always liked the diminutive, fiery Maria. For all his machismo and bravado, Davey doted on his wife. Seeing them again would be okay, she reassured herself.

Maria swung open the door, a radiant smile on her face directed at J.K. Then she spotted Cassie. *"Mi amiga,"* she said, hurrying down the walk to throw her arms around Cassie. "You look *muy bonita.* J.K., why you not tell us you were bringing Cassie and the *nino*? Davey, hurry. Look who's here."

"Maria, it's so good to see you again," Cassie said sincerely. "How are you feeling? When's the baby due?"

"Yesterday, I wish," she said, grimacing. "I am very tired of this waiting. Come in. Come in. The others are on the patio."

Cassie hesitated. "Others?"

"Johnny and his new lady," she said with a meaningful lift of her expressive dark eyebrows. "Roberto and Anna. Kyle and Lauren. You know them all, except this new one. They will be so glad to see you, *amiga.*"

Teddy bounded up to Maria when he heard Roberto's name mentioned. "Is Joey here?"

"By the pool, *nino.* Go. He has missed you very much, I think. He has had only girls to play with for a long time now."

As Teddy took off around the side of the house, Cassie cast a desperate look at J.K. He put a reassuring hand on her shoulder. "It'll be okay, sweetheart."

She supposed if she had to confront Ryan's old gang again, she was glad to be doing it with J.K. at her side for support. In her heart she knew that they would be diplomatic. Ryan's name most likely wouldn't be mentioned. In fact, everyone would probably tiptoe around it until she felt like screaming.

"Come," Maria urged, apparently sensing her reservations. "You can help me in the kitchen for a minute. I am not so good at lifting these days."

Cassie smiled gratefully. "Of course. I'd be happy to help. J.K., you go on out."

He appeared torn, but he finally nodded. "I'll grab a soda for you and bring it in."

"That would be great and keep an eye on Teddy, please. I don't want him jumping into the pool with his clothes on," she said just as they heard a gigantic splash, followed by childish shrieks of laughter.

J.K. peeked out the door and grinned ruefully. "Too late. Don't worry, though. I think he did manage to get his shoes and socks off before he jumped."

"Terrific."

"There's still plenty of daylight left. He'll dry out in no time."

"I suppose," she said, silencing her worries. She was not going to start babying Teddy the way some divorced mothers did. This would not be the first time he'd been swimming in Davey and Maria's pool. It would just be the first time that Ryan wasn't around to watch him.

"I'll keep an eye on him," J.K. promised. "He's a good swimmer, Cass."

"I know that."

When J.K. had gone, she turned to Maria. "Now tell me, what can I do to help?"

"You can get that platter of hamburgers out of the refrigerator and take it to Davey, then come right back here and talk to me."

Cassie nodded, grabbed the heavy ceramic platter with its burden of burgers and took it outside. At the door she plastered a smile on her face and kept it there. She was greeted with friendly surprise and hugs from the wives. When she handed Davey the food and turned to go back in the other women trailed after her.

"You've been such a stranger, Cass," Anna said. "We've missed you."

"I've been busy. I'm working now and it seems as if there's never enough time in the day."

"Well, I'm glad J.K. was finally able to get you out of the house."

"He's been a good friend to Teddy and me."

"That's all?" Lauren said with blatant curiosity. "I thought I caught a little spark when he saw you come outside just now."

"An automatic response," Cassie said, feeling the heat rise in her cheeks at the lie. "J.K.'s eyes spark at the sight of any woman under the age of seventy."

"If you say so," Lauren said doubtfully.

"I know so. Now tell me what you all have been up to."

The conversation thus diverted and the first awkward meeting past, Cassie relaxed and enjoyed herself. J.K. was attentive without being obvious about it. She vowed to thank him later for his discretion.

It was only as the evening was winding down that all the careful subterfuge went for nought. Teddy was perched on J.K.'s lap, barely able to keep his eyes open.

"I think we'd better get this young man home," J.K. said.

"You're probably right."

"Are you going to stay at our house again tonight, Uncle Jake?" Teddy asked innocently, bringing the conversation on the patio to a screeching halt. No one said a word.

"Out of the mouths of babes," Lauren muttered under her breath.

"I'm…we're…" Cassie began, then floundered, hot pink color flooding her cheeks.

J.K. shrugged. "Cassie thought she heard a prowler last night. I went over to check it out for her."

The others nodded. The story was perfectly plausible. Clearly, however, not a one of them believed it.

"What prowler?" Teddy demanded, no doubt confirming that their skepticism was justified. "You didn't tell me about a prowler. I miss all the neat stuff."

Cassie turned to Maria and hugged her. "Thank you for everything. It really was good to see you again. If I can help when the baby's born, you call me."

"I will, *amiga*." She lowered her voice. "And do not let what the others think bother you. I think that you and J.K. would make a very good couple. He is, how do you say, more melted…"

"Mellow," Cassie corrected, grinning.

"*Si*, more mellow around you. And you have the light in your eyes again. That is very good."

"Thank you."

Once they were in the car, Teddy fell asleep at once. Cassie stared out the window.

"Cass," J.K. ventured, his voice tentative.

"Hmm?"

"You aren't upset, are you?"

"What would be the point," she said with a little sigh of resignation.

"It's true, you know."

"What?"

"What Maria said. I am more mellow since I've been with you and you do have a light in your eyes again. Let's not throw that away."

She turned and saw that his expression was grave. "Are you so sure we're not just deluding ourselves?"

"I'm not so sure of anything anymore. You seem to be turning my life upside down."

"And you think that's good?"

He reached for her hand, caressing her knuckles with the callused pad of his thumb. "I think that's very good. Let me stay tonight and prove it."

Desire spread slowly through her, just as he'd meant it to. "No," she whispered, her voice husky. "Not with Teddy in the house."

"When?"

"I don't know, J.K. If it's meant to be, we'll find a way."

"You're relegating me to cold showers?" he grumbled, but there was an amused twinkle in his eyes.

"You have other options."

His gaze caught hers and held. "No, Cass. As long as we're together, you're the only woman in my life."

The only woman in my life. The words sang in her heart, only to shatter a moment later when she remembered how they'd been prefaced: *As long as we're together.*

How long, she wondered. How long before he would tire of her? How long before some other woman would arouse his curiosity and stir his desire?

"Cass?"

"What?"

"We'll be playing out of town tomorrow and Sunday, but I'll be back late Sunday night. I'll call, okay? Maybe we could spend the whole day together on Monday. Teddy'll be in school, right? Could you get the day off?"

A whole day to be with J.K., to be held in his arms, to feel his touch again. It would be magic. Who knew how long it might have to last her. She nodded. "I suppose I could call in."

"Would you like to spend the day with me?"

How long? The question echoed. *You have now. Take it, Cass. Grab it and hold on.*

She lifted her gaze to meet his. "Yes, J.K.," she said, bold longing overcoming hesitance. "Yes, I'd like that very much."

He nodded, looking pleased. "Then I'll be by early."

At the door, with Teddy safely upstairs in his room, J.K.'s lips met her in a tender, fleeting caress that inflamed every bit as cleverly as the deep, hungry kisses they'd shared the night before.

"Very early," he amended.

Chapter 9

J.K. made a point of calling Cassie on Saturday and again the minute he got back to town on Sunday night. It was the first away series the team had played since they'd been seeing each other and he suspected it would arouse all sorts of uncertainties for her. Besides, he admitted reluctantly, he missed the sound of her voice.

"Hi, sleepyhead," he murmured when she answered. "Sorry to call so late, but we just got back. I missed you."

"Did you win?" she asked groggily, stirring all sorts of memories. Waking up with Cassie could definitely turn out to be addictive, he thought as his body began to respond to her sleepy, sensual tone.

"We trounced 'em, nine to two."

"Did you have to pitch?" she asked.

"Nope. I sat around the bullpen wishing I were back here with you. What did you do today?"

"Cleaning, laundry, the usual chores. Teddy and I went to the mall for ice cream."

"A banana split?" he asked, remembering the last time and that instant when he'd first become shockingly aware of Cassie as a desirable woman.

"Nope, just a cone."

The thought of her tongue slowly licking a cone of soft, melting ice cream made J.K.'s entire body ache. "Cass, don't do this to me," he pleaded.

"Do what?" Her voice was filled with innocence.

"You're teasing me," he accused.

"Not me. I'm too sleepy to tease."

"Maybe I should let you go back to sleep again, then."

"I suppose so," she said without conviction.

"Do you still want me to come over in the morning?"

"Yes," she said with far more enthusiasm. The yearning in her voice set his blood on fire.

"I'll call first," he promised. "Good night, Cassie."

"Night."

The phone was almost back in the cradle when he heard her call out his name.

"What, babe?"

"I missed you, too."

That sweet, breathless declaration kept him up the rest of the night. At six in the morning he went out for coffee and picked up a bag of doughnuts. At seven he was pulling up in front of her house. He walked around to the kitchen door, hoping to find Cassie awake and alone.

She was awake, but to J.K.'s shock she definitely wasn't alone.

The sight of Ryan Miles standing in the doorway to the kitchen with his arm draped possessively around Cassie's pajama-clad shoulders was like a blow to J.K.'s midsection. Ryan was doing all the talking, his expression intense. Cassie seemed to be clinging to his every word.

Damn! J.K. thought furiously. His friend's arrival today wasn't totally unexpected. He'd known since the beginning of spring training that Ryan's team would be heading into town on this date for a night game. He'd even looked forward to getting together over a few beers, trading a few insults and telling a few tall stories the way they used to when they shared a room on the road before Ryan was traded.

That, however, was all before Cassie became so much a part of his life. Finding Ryan here at the crack of dawn was the last thing he'd anticipated when he'd walked around the corner of the house. What kind of game was the man trying to play with Cassie's head now? She'd come a long way over the past few weeks. Friday night at Davey's had been a major hurdle, but she'd gotten over it. Even Teddy seemed to be feeling more secure. J.K. didn't want to see them hurt again, if this was just another of Ryan's thoughtless games. He assured himself that the sick feeling in his gut was sheer protectiveness, nothing more.

"And I'm destined for sainthood," he muttered in self-disgust as he paced the driveway trying to decide whether to go or stay. "Admit it, man, you're hung up on the woman and you're scared witless that she's going to dump you and go running straight back to Ryan."

He wasn't sure which astonished him more, the sudden awareness of the depth of his feelings for Cassie or his lack of self-confidence. Both were firsts. He'd never been attached to any woman so deeply that it had mattered whether she stayed or went. He'd always known he could walk across a ball field and pick just about any replacement he liked from the women in the bleachers. Right this minute, though, he didn't care about a replacement. He didn't care about anything but this newly discovered caring for Cassie and the whisper of fear that he could lose her.

Taking a deep breath, he tapped on the screen door, then opened it and walked in. Cassie's startled gaze collided with his. She looked guilty, which only accelerated the racing of his pulse. What would she have to feel guilty about unless Ryan was getting to her?

"So, buddy, how're you doing?" he said with forced cheer, dragging his attention from Cassie to the blond giant at her side. A familiar easy smile broke across Ryan's face as J.K. came through the kitchen into the living-room, dining-room area just beyond.

"J.K., what the devil are you doing here at this hour? I didn't think you ever got up before noon."

"I, umm, I thought I'd drop these doughnuts by for Teddy's breakfast. He hasn't left for school yet, has he, Cass?"

She shook her head, looking thoroughly uncomfortable.

"So, J.K., I hear you had a tough game against the Yankees the other day. One of the online baseball bloggers did a piece on it. He said Ken had just pulled you in the second inning a few days before that. He wondered if you were losing your edge. You know how these jokers are. One or two bad days and they make a federal case out of it, you know what I mean?"

"Yeah," J.K. said. "That guy in Ohio wrote me off three weeks into the season last year. If he'd seen me in the ninth on Saturday, he'd be writing up my professional obituary."

"Don't worry about it, pal. You're bound to be a shoo-in for MVP again, maybe even the Cy Young Award. You've got a few more great years left in that arm of yours."

J.K. shook his head, puzzled by Ryan's too-jovial attitude. "Hey, the end of season's a long way off. I just worry about one pitch at a time," he said, snatching the cliché out of the repertoire he saved for interviews.

Ryan's arm slid down and settled around Cassie's waist. He squeezed and J.K.'s blood pressure rose. "Spoken with true humility, right, Cassie? Is this guy the greatest or what?"

J.K. watched as Cassie tried to extricate herself from Ryan's casual embrace. She refused to look at either of them.

"Would you like some coffee? I just made a fresh pot. I'll go get it." She took off for the kitchen before either of them had a chance to respond.

"What's bugging her?" Ryan said, staring after her. He shrugged. "Oh, well, you know women. Never will understand them. So, sit down here and tell me what's been happening with you."

J.K. bristled at Ryan's assumption that he was still the man of the house with the perfect right to issue invitations and play host. For one immature instant he wanted very badly to stake his own claim, but the image of Cassie's disapproval and possible embarrassment stopped him. It was obvious she found the whole situation awkward. The last thing she needed was two grown men having a territorial dispute in her living room. She'd probably toss them both out on their ears, just to prove exactly who was really in charge. Instead, he asked, "Have you seen Teddy yet?"

"No. He's still asleep. I told Cassie not to wake him, so she and I could have a little time alone."

"What for?" J.K. asked bluntly.

"Hey, man, what do you think? She's my wife."

"Your ex-wife," J.K. corrected, barely keeping his temper in check.

"Hey, what's bugging you?"

"Nothing. I just don't think you've got any right to come in here and play games with her head."

"Who's playing games? You know how I feel about Cass."

"No, I don't. How do you feel?"

"She's the greatest."

"Then why'd you divorce her?"

Ryan's gaze narrowed. "You're acting weird, you know that? If I didn't know better, I'd say you had the hots for my wife."

J.K. felt every muscle in his body go tense. "Don't be crude, Ryan. That's Cassie you're talking about."

"No. I was talking about you. Have you suddenly decided to do your playing around a little closer to home?"

J.K. rose to his feet with murder in his eyes. Fortunately, Cassie came back just then with the pot of coffee. The color in her cheeks told him she'd overheard every word. For her sake and her sake only, he backed off.

"Did Teddy know you'd be here this morning?" he said, shifting to more neutral turf.

"No. I thought I'd surprise him."

Which meant, J.K. thought uncharitably, that he hadn't been sure he'd be willing to leave his date in time to stop by. Before he could say anything to that effect, Cassie jumped in with an offer to go and wake Teddy.

"Why don't you let Ryan go?" J.K. suggested. "It'll be more of a surprise that way."

Ryan appeared startled by the suggestion. "Sure. That's a great idea. I'll be back in a few minutes."

Cassie sat down across from J.K. and began fiddling nervously with a napkin.

"What's wrong, Cassie?"

"What do you think is wrong?" she snapped. "Ryan

shows up here out of the blue, practically in the middle of the night. He's acting like everything's perfectly normal. How do you expect me to react?"

"Are you glad to see him?" he probed.

Her gaze shot up and bright pink spots appeared on her cheeks. "Why would you ask anything crazy like that? Of course I'm not glad to see him. If it weren't for Teddy, I wouldn't care if I never saw him again."

"Then why can't you look me in the eye?"

"Because…"

"Because why?"

"It just feels weird, that's all. The man had the nerve to walk in here and make a pass at me. Do you believe it?"

J.K. believed it so readily he felt like slamming his fist down Ryan's throat.

"It's been months since he's been around," Cassie went on. "He got the divorce he wanted and he thinks I'll still fall into bed with him whenever it's convenient."

Which explained the tension he'd noticed when he first walked in. Ryan's overtures had apparently clashed head-on with Cassie's newfound sense of independence. He might have gloated if he hadn't been more inclined to go after Ryan and wipe up the sidewalk with that famed posterior of his.

"You have every right to be mad, Cassie, but what does that have to do with me? You're acting as if I'm at fault here, too."

"I guess I am," she agreed. "You and Ryan, you were always such great pals. Listening to him this morning, watching him make his predictable moves just as if I were one of the bimbos he'd met on the road reminded me of everything I went through when we were married. He'll never change, not as long as he's wearing that uniform."

"And you think I won't, either?"

Her chin rose defiantly. "Well, will you? Can a leopard ever change his spots? Ryan certainly hasn't."

"I'm not Ryan. You've seen the change in me yourself, Cassie. You're responsible for it. The last few weeks I haven't looked at another woman."

The declaration drew a faint smile. "A few weeks, J.K. That's hardly a glowing testimonial. Am I supposed to risk my whole future because you've managed to be faithful for the first couple of weeks of spring training? What happens once the team goes north?"

"I don't know," he admitted honestly. "What I'm feeling for you is still pretty new to me. I don't know how I'm going to react over the long haul. Does anyone?"

"Maybe not, but the odds are better for some than others. I think you definitely fall into the high-risk category."

"What do you want to do about that?" he asked, filled with tension. Ryan's arrival couldn't have been more ill timed. The fragile faith she was beginning to have in him was too easily shattered. Ryan had done it in a heartbeat.

"I don't know," she said miserably. "The only thing I want right now is to get through the next twenty-four hours with a minimum of damage to Teddy. Seeing his father always upsets him. How is a seven-year-old supposed to understand a daddy who fits him into his schedule for one morning a year?"

J.K. shook his head. "If you and I can't understand it, we can't expect Teddy to. All we can do is to be here for him and make him realize that it has nothing to do with him, that Ryan just can't be any other way."

"So we excuse him?"

"Will it do any good not to? Is he likely to change just because we point out his flaws?"

"No, though God knows I've tried."

"Then let's just make the best of it and see that Teddy has a wonderful time with his father."

"You won't mind?"

"I can't say I'm crazy about it," he admitted, "but I'll live with it for Teddy's sake."

She lifted eyes shining with tears to meet his. "There are times, J.K. Starr, when I think you're very special."

"Hang on to those thoughts, sweetheart. I'm doing my best." He held out his arms and Cassie moved into them for a quick, nervous hug. She was close one instant and back across the room the next. At his questioning look, she shrugged apologetically. "I told you, it feels weird with Ryan around."

"Cassie, he's clear back in Teddy's room. Besides, he's going to hear about us soon enough. We were at Davey's together the other night. If he and Maria don't talk, one of the other guys will."

"I know."

"Are you worried about how he's going to react?"

"I suppose."

Something inside him froze at her evasiveness. "Or is it that you're worried he won't react at all?"

"What is that supposed to mean?"

"Maybe I'm the one in the way here. Would you go back to Ryan if I weren't in the picture?"

"Absolutely not."

He listened for a false note, but there didn't seem to be one. "Cass, have you talked to him about the money?"

She bit her lip and shook her head.

"Why not?"

"I couldn't face the thought of a fight right off the bat."

"Let me talk to him."

"No. We agreed you wouldn't fight my battles for me, remember?"

"I don't mind."

"I do."

They were still at a standoff when Ryan and Teddy came in. Teddy was chattering a mile a minute. "And then I yelled at Uncle Jake and he… What was it you did, Uncle Jake?"

"I balked."

"Yeah, and the runner came in and scored and everybody was really mad. That man, Mr. Hodges, he came running onto the field and he yelled at the umpire, but it didn't help. We lost the game anyway."

"I see," Ryan said, studying Cassie thoughtfully during his son's recitation. J.K. watched the speculative gleam form in his friend's eyes. "I'm glad you're still getting out to the ballpark. Have you been playing ball yourself?"

"Mom plays catch with me sometimes, but she's not very good. Sorry, Mom. Uncle Jake's helped a lot, though."

"I see," Ryan said again, turning his gaze on J.K. quietly, "Thanks for taking such good care of my family, old buddy."

J.K. opened his mouth to respond, but Cassie said quietly, "We're not your family anymore, Ryan. J.K.'s been a good friend, but I take care of Teddy. We do okay."

"No thanks to you," J.K. muttered without thinking.

Ryan shot a questioning look at him.

"Maybe we'd better have a talk," J.K. said, refusing to face Cassie. He knew she was going to be furious.

Her hand clamped down on his arm. He looked at the nails biting into his flesh, then up into her warning expression. "Sorry, babe. I can't leave things the way they are. It's about time…"

"Don't do it, J.K.," she pleaded.

Ryan took the matter out of his hands. "I think maybe you're right, buddy. You and I seem to be long overdue for a talk."

Teddy watched the two of them anxiously. "Daddy, you and Uncle Jake aren't going to fight, are you? I thought you were best friends."

Ryan looked as if he were suddenly itching for a good brawl, but J.K. squeezed Teddy's shoulder reassuringly. "Nope, we're not going to fight. We're just going to talk. I promise. Your dad will be back inside in no time."

Cassie looked as if she wanted to strangle both of them. Instead, she said in a voice tight with strain. "Teddy, if you want your father to take you to school today, you'd better hurry and get ready."

His eyes widened with excitement. "You mean it?"

She nodded.

"Yippee!" He took off at a run.

"Okay," she said, staring at J.K. "If you want to talk, do it in here."

"I think it would be best if we did this outside," J.K. said.

Ryan nodded his agreement. "It's between us, Cassie."

"Do either of you intend to bring my name into this private, all-male conversation?"

"Well..." J.K. squirmed uncomfortably.

"Hon..."

"I am not your *hon* anymore, Ryan Miles. I am your ex-wife," she said flatly before turning on J.K. "As for you, I've made it perfectly clear on more than one occasion that I don't want you interfering in my life."

"I think I have the right."

"No," she said emphatically. "You have no rights where I'm concerned. None!"

"Then what the hell was the other night all about?"

"What happened the other night?" Ryan demanded, his face flushing.

"Nothing," Cassie and J.K. said in unison, then stared at each other.

"Well, at least we agree about that," she said wryly. "J.K., I think you ought to go now."

"Not until Ryan and I have talked."

"Is this some sort of macho game with you? I told you to drop it."

"Okay. If that's the way you really want it, I'm out of here. Don't expect me to come running back, either."

"What are you two talking about?" Ryan asked. "I feel as if I walked into one of those foreign films and found out they left the subtitles off."

"I know exactly what you mean," J.K. said. "Cassie's a hard woman to understand."

"Cass?" Ryan said, looking bemused. "There's nothing complicated about her."

"Maybe it just takes more practice than I've had yet. See you two at the ballpark."

J.K. got in his car, drove straight to the ballpark and walked into the weight room. Maybe if he spent the next few hours lifting weights he'd be too exhausted to punch Ryan out when he saw him with Cassie again tonight. And he had no doubts at all that Cassie would be there with Ryan. He'd practically forced her straight back into the man's arms.

There was a hard knot in J.K.'s gut all during the game against the Orioles. The anger ate away at him as he sat idly in the bullpen just thinking about Cassie and Ryan together. He watched Ryan's moves on the field, as smooth as ever, and couldn't help thinking that the man was just as smooth off the field, too. If he decided he wanted Cassie back, he'd talk her into it. J.K. had heard Ryan's line often enough. He knew just how persuasive he was capable of being.

And he had Teddy on his side. Cassie would do just about anything to make her son happy.

Including going back to an ex-husband who'd cheated on her, a man who'd repeatedly humiliated her? Come off it, Starr! Don't be a fool!

No matter how often he told himself that's just what he was being—a jealous jerk—he couldn't help feeling that Cassie was slipping away from him and heading straight for trouble.

It didn't help that he exited the locker room just in time to see Cassie, Teddy and Ryan getting into Ryan's car. Davey saw them, as well.

"I think we should go get a beer, amigo," he suggested, his dark brown eyes filled with sympathy.

"Good idea," J.K. said, slinging his jacket over his shoulder. "I think that's a very good idea."

"Ryan is your friend?" Davey asked later, after they'd downed the first cold draft.

J.K. shrugged. "I thought so. I guess I never paid much attention to the way he was, you know what I mean?"

"He is not so reliable when it comes to women. Is that what worries you?"

"What worries me is that he's going to hurt Cassie again."

"Then tell her so. Warn her. Isn't that what a friend would do?"

"A friend, yes."

"But you want to be more than that," Davey said, astutely. "You think she will confuse your intentions?"

"I think she'll tell me to mind my own business."

"Is that so bad, if you think she needs to hear what you have to say?"

"No," he said thoughtfully. "You are right, my friend. You are very right. It doesn't matter if she gets mad at me, as long as she listens to what I have to say."

Unfortunately, the six beers it took for him to reach this momentous decision did nothing to enhance his equilibrium or his coherence. He stumbled up the front walk, leaned against the doorbell and waited for Cassie. She opened the door wearing a nightgown and a belted robe. She looked sleepy and flushed and infinitely desirable. She also seemed to be slightly irritated at being awakened. Not a good sign, he decided fuzzily. Definitely not a good sign.

"It is three o'clock in the morning," she observed. "What are you doing here?"

"I came to tell you…" he began, then lost his train of thought as he stared at the deep V of flesh where her robe was falling down. "I came to tell you that you are very beautiful." His voice was husky, but he thought fairly sincere.

She scowled, clearly exasperated, and tugged the gaping robe closed. "Thank you, but couldn't that message have waited until morning?"

"No. It's very important that I…" He swayed. "Whoops!"

She gave a heavy sigh of exasperation. "Get in here, J.K. I'll get you a blanket."

"I'm not here to sleep, Cassie. My sweet Cassie. Talk. We have to talk."

"Later, when you're making sense," she said curtly. J.K. stood in the doorway, still weaving unsteadily, while Cassie disappeared down the hall. She came back with a blanket and a pillow, tossed them onto the sofa and pointed. "Sleep it off, J.K."

"Could I have a little kiss?"

"Not in this lifetime," she said and vanished.

Too bad, he thought as he sat on the edge of the sofa and tried to master his shoelaces. They seemed to be beyond him, so he just tugged the shoes off and grabbed a corner of the blanket. It seemed to be stuck under him. He gave up and rolled over.

The last thought that flitted through his muddled brain was that Cassie was going to be furious with him in the morning. And that he might very well deserve her wrath.

Chapter 10

J.K. felt as if the entire percussion section of the local symphony orchestra was playing in his head.

Thrum! Loudly.

Thrum! Thrum! Thrum! Relentlessly.

Dragging himself to his feet, he staggered into Cassie's tiny guest bathroom and splashed cold water on his face. One glance in the mirror told him all he wanted to know about just how stupid he'd been last night. He'd been hoping it had been a bad dream.

Why had he allowed Ryan to get to him? Why had it mattered so much that Cassie had left the ballpark with Ryan? What right did he have to come charging in here, loaded with more beer than sense, and warn her that she was making the biggest mistake of her life? Which she was, of course, but it wasn't any of his business if she was fool enough to give Ryan Miles a second chance.

The only positive thing he could recall about his foolish

display of righteous anger was that Ryan apparently hadn't been around to witness it. Even in his drunken state, he'd taken heart from the fact that Cassie apparently hadn't let Ryan spend the night. Maybe this morning, after a gallon or so of coffee, he could calmly and rationally talk some sense into her.

If she was still speaking to him. The fact that she'd let him sleep on her living-room sofa wasn't exactly a promise of forgiveness. Quite the contrary in fact, considering where he'd slept the last time he'd spent the night in this house. All it proved was that even infuriated, Cassie was too tenderhearted and too sensible to put him back behind the wheel of a car in the condition he'd been in last night. Today might be an altogether different story. Today she'd probably have his hide and take pleasure in every punishing second of it.

With that prospect facing him and those blasted drummers drumming in his head, he headed into the kitchen for coffee. While he waited for it to perk, he slumped down at the kitchen table, head in hands. It was several minutes before he realized he wasn't alone. It was the press of Teddy's body into his side that finally registered. He turned his head to find the boy studying him sympathetically.

"You and Mom had a fight last night, huh?"

"What makes you say that?"

"I heard you. She made you sleep on the sofa."

J.K. nodded.

"She used to make Dad do that, too. You want some breakfast? I can fix cereal."

The very thought of all those little, healthy flakes floating in milk turned J.K.'s stomach. "No, thanks, sport. Maybe later."

"I think what your Uncle Jake really wants is some humble pie," a voice said from the doorway.

J.K. listened hard for any evidence of amusement, but Cassie's tone was absolutely even. No humor. No anger. No feeling at all. It was worse than he thought.

"Teddy, why don't you get your cereal and take it into the family room," she said. "Aren't your favorite cartoons on this morning? You can watch until it's time to get ready for school."

"I'd rather stay here with you and Uncle Jake."

"Not this morning."

Teddy must have heard the soft but indisputable thread of warning in her voice. He fixed his breakfast and left without another word. Cassie poured two big mugs of coffee, silently passed one to J.K. and went to work at the stove. In no time the kitchen was filled with the greasy scent of bacon frying.

"You're trying to get even with me, aren't you?" J.K. said suspiciously, gesturing toward the frying pan. The aroma made his stomach turn.

"Why would I do that?"

"Because I behaved like an idiot last night."

"You'll get no argument from me about that."

"Would it help it I told you I was sorry?"

"It would help more if you explained why you felt it necessary to get drunk as a skunk and come charging over here like Sir Lancelot. My honor was never endangered, J.K."

"I'm not so sure about that. I didn't like what I saw here yesterday."

"What exactly did you see?"

"Ryan putting the moves on you. You even admitted he'd made a pass."

She waved a spatula at him dismissively. "I am perfectly capable of handling Ryan."

"Not if you're still in love with him."

"Who said I was still in love with him?"

J.K. studied her closely. "You're not?" he said doubtfully.

"Definitely not," she said and went back to stirring pancake batter. A minute later she was humming cheerfully. Any second now she was going to burst into off-key song and J.K. wasn't at all sure his pounding heart could take it. He decided he'd better sober up fast.

"Cass, do you have an aspirin?"

"In the medicine cabinet."

"A compassionate woman would offer to get them."

"If you can find one, suggest it. I'm busy. Some of us have to get to work this morning."

"I'll get 'em myself."

"Wise man."

J.K. got the aspirin, took three and sat back down, praying that Cassie wouldn't get it into her head to start singing until they took effect. He sipped his coffee and pondered her attitude toward Ryan. She had sounded pretty sure of herself and he'd always credited her with knowing her own mind.

He looked up at her and announced casually, "He wants you back, you know."

"No, he doesn't," she replied just as casually.

"Cassie, I saw the way the man looked at you. I, of all people, can recognize lust when I see it."

"Then you also know that there's a rather wide gap between lust and love. Ryan just had a momentary twinge of jealousy. He picked up on the vibes between you and me and decided to get all territorial."

"He made a pass before I ever showed up," J.K. reminded her.

"Doesn't matter. Whatever the timing, he wasn't serious about it. It's instinct with him. I'm woman. He's man. Let's go for it. That's how he operates."

"Did you?"

"Did I what?"

"Go for it?"

"You seem to be missing the point here. I am not interested in my ex-husband, thank you very much. As for him, I guarantee he'll forget all about me the instant some sweet young thing winks at him from the bleachers." She put a plate of eggs, bacon and pancakes in front of him. "You know I'm right, so I'll ask you again, why'd you get so worked up over it?"

"I just didn't want to see you get hurt again," J.K. said, poking a fork tentatively into the center of the egg. The sight of all that yellow oozing out almost did him in. He covered it quickly with a pancake, then looked up just in time to see Cassie trying to wipe a smile off her too-expressive face. She seemed to know something he didn't or at least she thought she did. He couldn't imagine what.

"I don't think so," she responded, blithely digging into her own breakfast. She was apparently having no problems at all with her appetite.

J.K. was too busy trying to follow the conversation to eat. Still baffled by her attitude, he said, "You think I want to see you get hurt?"

"Of course not. I just don't think that's the whole story and until you can figure out the rest, maybe you'd better not come around so much."

He stared at her blankly. "Now why would you say a fool thing like that? I thought you and I were working on a real relationship."

"I thought so, too."

"Then what's the problem?"

"I don't have one. You're the one who's drinking and behaving like an adolescent."

"One little attack of jealousy," he grumbled. "You go and make a big deal out of it."

"Unjustified jealousy," she noted. "And all I'm suggesting is that you figure out why you found it so tough to think of me out with Ryan."

"Because…" He couldn't think of a reason that made a bit of sense.

"Because why?"

"I never thought I'd say this, but you're a hard woman, Cassie," he said, scowling at her. "I'm hurting here and you're playing word games with me."

She shrugged indifferently, changing forever his image of her as sweet and vulnerable. Cassie was tough as nails. Her words confirmed it. "Maybe so," she said as if she rather enjoyed the idea of giving him grief. "I just know what I see." That secretive look was back on her face.

"Which is?"

"I'm not going to be the one to say it, J.K."

"Cassie!"

"Eat your breakfast."

They ate in stubborn silence, J.K. trying to figure out what bee Cassie had in her bonnet now. He couldn't understand a woman who got such a kick out of talking in riddles.

"I guess I'll be going," he said eventually, expecting an argument or at least a mild protest.

"I hope you feel better," she said just as nonchalantly. "Though you don't deserve to."

He glared at her. "I'll just say goodbye to Teddy."

"Fine."

He walked into the family room still muttering under his breath. Cassie was singing happily before he reached the door, the off-key tune grating on his nerves worse than squeaking chalk on a blackboard. What did she have to be so blasted cheerful about? Since he wasn't likely to come up with an answer to that one, he turned his attention to Teddy, who was lying on the floor in front of the TV on his stomach, his chin propped in his hands. He barely spared a glance for J.K. Apparently the whole family was uninterested in his presence this morning.

"So, what're you watching?" J.K. asked after staring at the dizzying rush of colorful cartoon action for several minutes.

"It's about these giant bugs," Teddy explained enthusiastically. "They turn into people sometimes and nobody knows that they're really bad guys until it's too late and they zap 'em with these poison things."

J.K. nodded. The explanation made about as much sense as his conversation with Cassie.

"Wanna watch with me?" Teddy asked hopefully.

"Maybe for a minute," J.K. agreed, sitting down on the floor. Teddy promptly snuggled closer.

"See," he said, pointing. "That's one of the bad guys. Any minute now he's gonna kill the good guy, unless this guy Lionel can get there in time to save him."

"Lionel?" Whatever happened to the really tough guys like the Duke or Rambo, J.K. wondered, feeling increasingly out of sorts.

"Yeah, Lionel's really neat. He's in comic books and everything." Teddy paused. "Can I ask you something, Uncle Jake?"

"You can ask me anything."

"What's love?'"

Oh, brother. It was not a question to ask a man with a boot-stomping jamboree going on in his head. "Ask me an easy one, pal."

"Don't you know?" Teddy asked, obviously surprised by this gap in his knowledge.

"I'm not sure I do," he said frankly. "What does you mom say?"

"She says there are different kinds of love. She says my dad can still love me, even if he doesn't love her anymore. Do you think that's right?"

J.K. felt the weight of all sorts of childish terrors behind that question. Teddy's expression was serious as he waited for an answer. "Absolutely," J.K. told him. "I think your dad loves you very much."

"I wish he'd come to see me more," he said wistfully. "It's great having a dad who's on television sometimes and stuff, but I miss having him around to, you know, hang out with. It was really neat seeing him yesterday, don't you think? Why do you think he and my mom don't live together anymore?"

"Grown-ups can't always get along the way they should when they're married. When that happens, sometimes it's better if they don't stay married anymore."

"You don't have a wife. Is that why? 'Cause you didn't get along?"

"Nope. You know I've never been married."

Suddenly Teddy's eyes lit up with excitement and he sat up. He put his hands on J.K.'s knees and leaned in close. "I know what, Uncle Jake."

"What?" J.K. said cautiously.

"You and Mom could get married!" he announced, clearly thrilled with the cleverness of his idea. "Wouldn't that be great? Then you'd be my dad, too. I'd have two dads."

Maybe if he'd been anticipating it, J.K. wouldn't have been so stunned. Instead, he reacted as if Teddy had suggested that he fly to the moon. Married? To Cassie? He wasn't sure which idea startled him more. He supposed that in the back of his mind he'd envisioned getting married one of these days, maybe after he'd left baseball behind him. But now? To Cassie?

"I don't think so," he protested, too quickly. Disappointment registered immediately on Teddy's face. He immediately felt guilt welling up. "Sorry, sport."

Teddy's excited expression began to change. He looked more indignant, though, than hurt. "How come? You like her, don't you? You come over a lot. That must mean you like her some."

"Of course I like her."

"Well, then?" His voice faltered. "Is it me, Uncle Jake? I'd be really good. I wouldn't be any trouble at all."

Oh, hell. "Teddy, this has nothing to do with you. You're the greatest kid in the whole world and I'd love to have you for my son. It's just…" He felt himself floundering.

"It's that love stuff, isn't it?" Teddy said wisely. "You don't love her?"

"Yeah, it's that love stuff," he agreed softly, but as Teddy turned back to the TV, J.K. began to wonder.

What if… The images that swept through his mind were powerful and seductive. Cassie had everything he'd ever wanted in a woman, at least those qualities that he'd ticked off on the rare occasions when he'd taken a serious look at the future. She was bright and beautiful and stubborn as the dickens. She'd never be dull. And loving. God, how he'd envied Ryan the tenderness in Cassie's eyes when she'd looked up at him on the day that Teddy had been born. Someday, he'd said to himself then. Someday, he'd have a woman like that. A woman who wasn't a bit like his cheating mother.

Well, why not now? And why not Cassie?

Because she wouldn't have him on a bet. It was as simple as that. Cassie was looking for reliability, steadfastness of heart and sensitivity. She credited him with none of those qualities. Even though he'd been on his best behavior for weeks now, she still didn't trust him worth spit. She tended to regard him with a prejudiced eye.

And rightly so, he admitted guiltily. He'd seduced her the first chance he got and hadn't said the first thing about the future.

That didn't mean he wasn't capable of changing, though. He'd win her over. She was already attracted to him. That was definitely no problem. He'd just have to prove to her that he was also the most reliable, the most faithful, the most sensitive man she'd ever met. Now that a plan was beginning to crystallize in his mind, J.K. could hardly wait to get started.

There was only one tiny little problem. How did he go about proving all that to a woman who already knew him better than he knew himself?

Chapter 11

J.K. had pitched no-hit ball games that were less stressful than planning this campaign of his to get Cassie to take him seriously. It took him a full week to figure out his first tactic, an endless week during which he denied himself the pleasure of even calling her, a week during which he growled at everyone else. His teammates began to give him a wide berth. Maria, however, had no such instinct for self-preservation.

"You are a fool if you do not see what is before your very eyes, J.K. Starr," she told him, her own eyes flashing.

"What are you talking about?"

"Cassie. She is in love with you."

"No, she's not."

Maria acted as if he hadn't spoken. "And you, I think, are in love with her, *si*?"

His gaze narrowed. "What makes you think that?"

"You have all the, how do you say, evidence."

"Symptoms," he corrected automatically, then looked at her. "It's that obvious?"

"It is to me. I see the way your eyes follow her. It is definitely the look of love. My Davey look at me that way before I get so huge," she said, rubbing her pregnant belly.

J.K. detected a certain wistfulness in her voice, something he probably would never have noticed if he weren't so attuned to shifts of mood these days. He hugged her. "Davey will always look at you that way."

Maria beamed. "You think so?"

"I know so."

"You see, that is why Cassie is in love with you. You have the charm, the gift of words."

"I'm not sure she sees that as an attribute," he admitted candidly.

Maria's expression grew puzzled. "What is this—attribute?"

"It means she doesn't take my charm all that seriously. She thinks it's a flaw."

"Cassie may see you with wide-open eyes, but that is good, is it not? She will never expect what you cannot give."

"Oh, I think she expects quite a lot and she deserves it."

"But not more than you can give," Maria insisted. "Have you told her how you felt?"

"Not yet."

"Why not? It does no good to speak to me of your feelings. Cassie is the one who needs to hear."

"It's going to take more than words."

"Then show her."

He grinned. "You make it sound so easy, Maria."

"It should be easy to speak what is in your heart."

But it wasn't. For the first time in his life, J.K.'s glib charm and clever seductiveness let him down. He sent flowers. He called. He thought of a dozen different ways to surprise her. She responded exactly the way he'd hoped, with enthusiasm and delight. But there was always a sense of reserve. It was as if she was still waiting for something else. He was at a loss trying to figure out how many other ways there were to say he loved her. The longer the emotional limbo went on, the more frayed his nerves became. While one part of him wondered if they would ever work things out, another part, a part he didn't acknowledge except in the darkest hours of the night, was terrified that they would.

Cassie decided she had a surprisingly sadistic streak. She was really enjoying watching J.K. squirm. Now that she'd recognized exactly how deep his feelings for her were and accepted that her own feelings ran just as deep, she could sit back and watch the developments with a certain amount of equanimity.

It was interesting, she decided from a purely objective, psychological standpoint, that the number of bouquets arriving decreased in direct proportion to the increasing seriousness of J.K.'s intentions. And without the tulips and daffodils and irises to boost his cause, J.K. seemed to be floundering. She considered it a good omen that he'd apparently never reached this stage with another relationship. She also knew that he had to face this part of the struggle on his own. He had to believe in the power of their love or it would never work. He thought he had only to overcome her doubts. She realized he had to overcome his own.

It was after midnight when the phone beside her bed rang. Predictably. J.K. apparently saw these late-night calls as a way of offering proof that she was always on his mind. She wondered if he also saw that he was testing her, checking on her, still doubting after all this time that any woman would remain faithful for long. Either way, if he didn't realize soon that what they had was built on mutual trust, she was going to be walking around like a sleep-starved zombie.

"Hi, J.K.," she murmured into the receiver, a smile in her voice.

"How'd you know it was me?"

"Who else would be calling at this hour? Where are you?"

"Tampa. In my motel room," he added hurriedly. "Alone."

Clearly he wanted to cover all the bases, relieve all her doubts.

"J.K., it's not that I don't appreciate these reports. I do. It's just that you seem to have a slightly misguided reason for giving them."

"I just want you to know that you're the only woman I care about. I thought if I called you'd begin to understand how I feel."

"I do understand, but the calls aren't the reason it's so clear."

"They're not?"

"Sweetheart, for all I know you could engage in wild revelry the minute you hang up. You could have women locked in your bathroom, even as we speak. You could leave the room and head to the nearest bar and drink till dawn. I'd never know it unless Davey or Kyle tattled and we all know how likely that is to happen."

"Oh," he said, sounding deflated. "I never thought of that. Should I call back later? Check in more often? Do you want to call me?"

She laughed. "Oh, J.K., don't you see? It's all a matter of trust. If I didn't trust you, you could call me every hour on the hour and it wouldn't matter. The reverse is just as true. Do you worry about what I'm doing while you're out of town?"

"Of course not."

"Why?"

"Because I trust you implicitly. You'd never cheat on me."

"You thought I might with Ryan."

"Just a temporary aberration." There was a long silence. "Wasn't it?"

"It was," she assured him.

"So, you're telling me I'm wasting my time making these calls."

"Not if all you want is a chance to say good-night." She lowered her voice seductively. "I very much like hearing your voice just before I go to sleep."

There was a heavy sigh on the other end of the line. "I miss you, Cass."

"I miss you, too."

"Good night, my love."

"Night, J.K."

When J.K. hung up the phone, he took yet another cold shower, then climbed into the too-empty king-size bed. He plumped up the pillows just right. He fussed with the sheets until they were just so over his naked body. He turned out the light. And his brain promptly went into overdrive with thoughts of Cassie. Sweet, sensual, arousing thoughts. Thoughts that sent him straight back into an icy shower.

Maybe it was time to stop all these subtle approaches, which didn't seem to be working anyway, and just tell her straight out what was on his mind. Maybe that's what Maria had been suggesting days ago. He could handle rejection. Probably. He wasn't so sure he could deal with having her laugh in his face, but Cassie would never do anything quite that tacky. Probably.

Thank heavens they were going home after tomorrow's game. Maybe once he'd kissed her, maybe after he'd held her in his arms, he wouldn't feel this sense of urgency. Maybe he'd be able to hold off actually asking her to marry him until he was sure he'd convinced her how much he'd changed. With something this important, he wanted all the odds stacked in his favor.

So, he decided, back in bed again with the light out, he'd slow down, hold off until the timing was exactly right. It was the sensible way to go.

"Marry me, Cassie," he blurted out seconds after he'd walked into her living room. She wasn't even looking at him when he said it. She was down on her knees looking for dust or something. J.K. knew it was all wrong, but the words just popped out automatically. It probably had something to do with standing there while her cute little derrière was poked up at him. He waited, holding his breath, for her reaction.

She wasn't laughing. He could tell that. She also wasn't moving. Maybe she wasn't even breathing. She'd probably gone into shock.

"Cass?" He bent down beside her. "Did you hear me?"

She rocked back on her heels and stared into his eyes. "You're serious, aren't you?"

He didn't trust himself to repeat the words again. He just nodded, hoping she could tell exactly how much love there was in his heart.

"Why, J.K.? Why now?"

"Because… Why does anyone ask somebody to get married? You know…"

"I can think of any number of reasons to get married. People marry for money. They marry for position. They marry out of some sense of family obligation. They get married because they can't stay out of bed and figure they ought to legalize it. So, J.K., which is it in your case?"

He could think of only one way to shut her up, to halt all this ridiculous talk of arranged marriages and get-rich-quick marriages. He kissed her. Long and slow and hard, until they were both so breathless neither of them could speak.

Cassie swallowed hard, her eyes dazed. "That's definitely one reason," she said, her voice a husky whisper.

"A good one?"

"Not bad."

"Not bad? Obviously I didn't do my best. Let's try again," he said, claiming her lips with every bit of mastery at his command.

"Oh, my," she said weakly.

He regarded her indignantly. "Is *oh, my* better than *not bad?*"

There was just the tiniest bit of amusement in her eyes. "About the same," she said, being deliberately provoking. Maybe this marriage idea he'd had was lousy, after all. Did he want to spend the rest of his life with a woman who taunted him?

Damn right he did.

"Do you want to be swept off your feet, carried off to bed and loved for forty-eight hours straight?" he asked, searching for a more successful approach.

She grinned at that. "You're definitely getting warmer."

"Damn right I am," he growled. "I'm burning up and so are you. What are we talking about here? You need a grand seduction to convince you?"

She sighed and shook her head. "Nope. I like the concept, but it's not the answer."

J.K. got to his feet and began to pace. "I don't get it. I've done everything I can think of. Are you just not in love with me? Is that it? Maria thinks you are, but maybe she's got it all wrong, too. Does she?"

She halted him in midstep by grabbing his hand and kissing his knuckles. Her velvet lips caressing his scarred flesh sent bolts of lightning flashing through him. "Cass?"

"You're off base, J.K. I do love you. I do trust you. I began to trust you weeks ago, when you ignored every bitchy, obnoxious thing I said and did and just kept trying to help. I think I fell in love with you when you were dumping peanut butter and grape jelly into my grocery cart. I saw exactly how caring, how sweet you were capable of being."

"You love me?" he repeated, dazed. He lifted her up until she was standing, then studied her. "Really? No doubts?"

"Not a one."

He dropped her hands and shoved his own hands through his hair. "Then I really don't get it. Why haven't you said yes?"

"Because I want to hear you say the words, J.K. I want you to admit that you love me. I know what you feel in your heart. I can tell it by the way you treat me, the way you treat Teddy. But I think it's important for you to recognize that it's really true."

"Why else would I be asking you to marry me?"

She grinned, apparently taking great delight in his frustration. "Shall I run through the list again?"

"No. Forget it. Once was enough."

"Why can't you say the words, J.K.? Do you know the answer to that?"

He sank down on the sofa. He searched his brain and

then his heart. He probably should have started with the latter. "I suppose it's because of what you said a few weeks ago," he admitted finally.

"About your mother?"

"Yes. I guess so. Ever since I found out what she was really like, I've never believed a woman could make an honest commitment."

"Yet you seem to think that I can."

"You're different, Cass."

She shook her head. "Am I really so different, J.K., or are you finally realizing that you've been intentionally setting out to fulfill your own expectations?"

He twisted her explanation around, stood it on end and still didn't know what the hell she was talking about. "Cassie, I'm not here for some psychobabble stuff. Talk English or we can forget the whole thing."

"Just think for a minute, J.K. You've always chosen exactly the kind of woman you knew would let you down. Then you dumped them, before they could move on leaving you behind."

There was something undeniably familiar about the pattern she described. "That's sick."

"Not so sick," she said. "A fairly normal reaction to the hurt you felt when you found out about your mother. But if we're going to make this work, J.K., it's every bit as important for you to trust me as it is for me to trust you. If you've just decided to marry me because it's time to settle down, we'll never make it."

"That's not it, Cass. I swear it. I love you."

"Well, hallelujah! Finally."

He grinned at her exuberance. "Okay, so it took me a long time to wake up to that. There might even have been a time when I figured if you were attracted to me, but still in love with Ryan, it made you like all the others..." He stopped, suddenly realizing what he'd said.

Cassie nodded as if she'd guessed it all along.

"That's why I went so crazy thinking you were going back to Ryan, isn't it? I thought you were just another cheating wife and it was tearing me apart inside."

All at once he felt totally drained. Tapping into the depths of his emotions was harder than anything he'd ever done before. It was worth it, though, if it meant he and Cassie were going to get off to the right start.

"I love you, Cass," he said again, this time with full understanding of the words. "Marry me."

Cassie's eyes were shining and even before she spoke he could read the answer in her joyous expression. "Yes, J.K. Yes!" she said, her fingers tunneling into his hair as she drew his head down for a kiss.

When he could finally draw a steady breath again, J.K. asked, "Is Teddy home?"

"Nope."

"Is he likely to come home in the next half hour?"

"Half hour?" she repeated with exaggerated disappointment.

"Okay," he said, grinning. "Make it an hour. Are we going to be alone for at least an hour?"

"I think we can count on that. Why?"

"Because I have plans for you, Cassie Miles. I've been thinking about these plans every night for the last week. I've almost gone crazy thinking about them."

"Sounds intriguing."

"That's one word for them," J.K. said wryly. "Let me show you."

He lifted her into his arms and carried her down the hall.

"First the shower," he said. "Do you have any idea how much time I've spent in showers this past week?"

"Are you so sure talking me into this one with you will be the solution to this problem you seem to have?"

"It will definitely be a solution to my most immediate problem. If you're concerned about the memories it's likely to arouse, I'll take my chances."

He flipped on the water, then slowly removed Cassie's clothes. His followed in quick succession. He drew her into the shower stall and picked up a bar of soap as the water cascaded around them. His hands slippery and sudsy, he began to wash her, his gaze riveted on the changes in her body as his touches became bolder and bolder. His fingers skimmed and teased, sliding over slick flesh until he could bear it no more. He lifted her slightly, settling her on him, his blood roaring, his body demanding. Her legs wrapped tight around his waist and her breasts were crushed against his chest. Only the slowest, most tantalizing movement was possible.

"Cassie," he whispered, his voice a tender moan. "God, how I've dreamed of this. Night after night. I haven't been able to get the feel of you out of my head."

The water turned to steam as their body temperature soared. "It's like the movie," she said, wonder in her voice and dazed sensuality in her eyes.

"But we're real, sweetheart. This is real."

Her head fell back and he pressed his lips against the hollow at her throat. "Sweet, sweet Cassie. I've been so hungry for you." He tasted fiery shoulders and slickened breasts as the slow rocking motion began to send gentle waves washing through him. The tempo of the waves increased, more demanding, crashing endlessly until at last they both shouted out with the sheer ecstasy of it.

J.K. reached behind him and turned off the water. When his legs were steady again, he wrapped Cassie in a towel and carried her to bed. "I never want to sleep another night without you beside me," he said, wiping strands of damp, blond hair from her cheeks.

"Not very realistic, all things considered," she said with a sigh that seemed heavy with regret.

"Cass, that is something we have to talk about."

"I don't want to talk, J.K."

"But we have to. Are you going to be okay about my playing baseball and being on the road so much? You brought up the subject of trust and I know right now you're convinced I'm being honest and honorable, but how long is it likely to be before the doubts set in?"

She tried to roll away from him, but he held her tight. "Come on, babe. Be honest."

"I can't answer that. I guess it depends on you."

"How so?"

"J.K., when I married Ryan he was already playing baseball. I knew what the life would be like or at least I had a pretty good idea. I didn't go nuts just because we were separated a lot. It all changed when I found out he was cheating on me. That's what ruined the relationship. The discovery that I couldn't trust him anymore."

"So you'll trust me until I let you down?"

"I guess that's about the size of it."

He leaned back, bringing her with him. Her head was resting on his chest. "I wish I could believe that."

"It's true. You're not the same man Ryan is."

"You haven't always felt that way."

"You've won me over," she said lightly.

"At the risk of indulging in some of that psychobabble I accused you of earlier, I think your vision may be clouded by your hormones. The reality is that you've been hurt by a man very much like me, who used his road travel as an excuse to be unfaithful. I don't want you getting nervous every time I pack my bags. Be honest, Cassie. There's a part of you that's going to be threatened."

"Maybe so," she admitted finally, angrily. "But I'll deal with it."

"There has to be a better way."

"Name one."

"You and Teddy will just have to come with me," he said at once, liking the prospect. "I'm not a bit crazier about the idea of leaving you behind than you are about being left."

"Not very practical."

"I'm not looking for practical. I'm looking for a way we can guarantee that this marriage will work."

"There are no guarantees, J.K."

"Maybe not, but we can improve the odds. We'll just have to make the travel thing work."

"That's all well and good during the summer, but Teddy has school and I have work."

"You won't need to work."

"But I'm not so sure I want to become totally dependent on you or any man."

"Sweetheart, if you want a career I'm all for it, but couldn't it wait until I retire in a few years and we can settle down in one place? Maybe you could just take classes during the off-season and get that degree you were talking about. Then you'd be ready for a really good job."

"I suppose I could do that. But what about Teddy's school?"

As hard as he tried, J.K. couldn't come up with an answer to that one. "I guess that gives us about four months of the year—April and May, maybe a little of June, then

September and part of October—when we're going to be separated, at least some of the time."

"Unless," Cassie began slowly. "J.K., what if we moved up north? You'd only be down here for the few weeks of spring training. The rest of the time you'd be home, except for road trips and we could at least come along on weekends."

He let the suggestion settle in his mind. It definitely had some merit. "I suppose that's workable," he said. "You really want to leave here?"

"I told you how much I've been missing snow and the change of seasons. I wouldn't want to go back forever, I don't think, but for a few years I think it would be great. What do you think?"

"I think you're a pretty terrific lady."

"You're pretty wonderful yourself."

"So, Cassie Miles, do you think we can make this marriage thing work?"

She scattered little kisses all over his chest.

"Is that your answer?" he inquired, his pulse quickening.

"Yes," she whispered. "My final answer. I wonder what Teddy's going to think of all this?"

"He'll love it," J.K. said confidently.

"You sound so sure of that."

"I am. It was his idea."

"What?"

"It might have been a little unorthodox, but your son proposed to me weeks ago, on your behalf of course."

"You're kidding."

"Nope. Obviously that's one very bright child. He recognized what we hadn't figured out yet."

"Remind me to raise his allowance," she said. She was

still in his embrace for the longest time before she added, "Thank you, J.K."

"For what?" he said.

"For loving me."

"It seems as natural as breathing," he said, realizing it was true.

"Do you know how rare it is, though, to find what we've found?" she demanded, then grinned. "Besides, how many women can claim they have their very own Midnight Starr to light up the night?"

"Oh, Cassie," he said, laughing. "We are going to have one helluva good time together, aren't we?"

She snuggled closer. "The very best," she said softly. "The very best."

* * * * *

HER HOMECOMING WISH

Jo McNally

To first responders everywhere,
who balance family and personal lives
against their stressful jobs, and who carry
the weight of people's expectations every day.

Thank you.

Chapter 1

How could a liquor store owner not have any booze in his house?

Mackenzie Wallace kept opening and closing her dad's kitchen cabinets as if she hadn't searched each and every one already. Hell, she'd even checked the bedroom closets and the cabinet in the laundry room.

She did *not* want to go downstairs to her father's liquor store in the middle of the night.

But she *did* want a glass of scotch.

And Dad's apartment was dry as a bone.

There was no sense procrastinating. She grabbed the keys hanging by the back door. Dad's old gray hoodie also hung there, worn and faded. Mack looked down at her purple pajama shorts and green cotton camisole. No one would see her in the dark, wee hours of the morning, but she was still a little *too* naked for venturing outside. The hoodie barely fell past the hem of her shorts, but at least it covered her almost see-through top. And it would protect her from the cool night air. It might be the end of April, but in the Catskill Mountains of New York, that could mean snow flurries as easily as daffodils.

If nothing else, she'd have a great story to tell Dad when she visited him at the hospital tomorrow morning. No, later *this* morning. Ugh. She needed some serious sleep after too many hours packing, driving and unpacking in one day. Surely a glass of Dad's top-shelf scotch would do the trick. All she had to do was let herself into the liquor store and find it.

She'd watched her brother do it dozens of times when they were kids. As much as she'd tried to distance herself from Ryan's bad behavior, he'd pressed her into lookout duty more than once—a nervous ten-year-old standing outside the door, praying no one would come by. *Especially* Mom and Dad. Young Mackenzie could never bear the thought of disappointing her parents. And look at her now—slinking back to her childhood home as a bitter divorced woman in need of booze.

She side-eyed her reflection in the small mirror by the back door—put there by her mom, who'd never had a hair out of place when she left the apartment. Mom, who'd been gone so many years now, would definitely *not* approve of Mackenzie's appearance *or* her behavior. Mack raised her chin. As much as Mack had adored her late mother, she didn't want to *be* her. Not anymore. Her days of living up to someone else's standards were *over*.

She tucked her unruly hair behind her ears and slipped her feet back into her bright red leather flats. If the ladies of Glenfadden Country Club could only see her now. Mack snorted, talking to the large orange tabby cat watching her from the armchair, "As if we care what that group of two-faced Connecticut snobs think anymore, right?"

Her cat, Rory, meowed in response, casting a malevolent gaze around the apartment. He was clearly ticked off about being stuffed into a canvas cat carrier for the four-hour drive from Greenwich. Mack walked over and scratched the top of his head. The Maine coon cat was as big as a small dog. Her ex-husband hated him. But it was Rory's attitude of fierce independence that drew Mack to him in the shelter two years ago. Maybe she'd had a premonition that she'd need a tough friend, and Rory was it. He tried to ignore her touch in true Rory fashion, but he couldn't disguise the purr that rumbled in his chest. She grinned. "You stay here and guard the place. I'll be right back."

The closest full-time residents in the row of shops and apartments in downtown Gallant Lake lived three doors down and were surely sound asleep. Still, she tiptoed down the stairs outside the back door. The metal fire escape stretched the length of the block on the second level, connecting the buildings. Stairs to the parking lot were spaced along the walkway. She was going to a ridiculous length for a drink, but now that it was on her mind, she couldn't turn back. It would only take her a few minutes to grab a bottle of Macallan and get back upstairs.

She used the back door to the store, knowing she'd be able to find her way through the familiar space without needing to search for any light switches that might attract attention at 2:00 a.m. The door opened easily, letting out a low groan as it swung closed. She waited, then let out a long sigh of relief at the silence that followed. Didn't look like Dad ever installed that alarm system he kept threatening to buy.

She'd just let herself into her father's store without permission, barely dressed, sneaking around as if she was some kind of thief. She couldn't help feeling a little thrill at doing something so out of character. She had every right to be here, of course, but it still felt deliciously naughty.

She used the flashlight app on her phone to work her way around the boxes in the back hall and into the store itself. And that's where her plan took a turn. Her father may not have installed an alarm, but he'd completely rearranged the store in the year since she'd been home. There were three café tables and a bunch of stools pushed together in the back corner of the store, and the display shelves had been rearranged. More space was devoted to wine now, which was a change she definitely approved of, but where was the top-shelf liquor that used to be displayed back here?

Working her way down the aisle with her phone light, she found the gin and vodka. She wasn't looking to make cocktails, so she kept going, being careful not to bump into the displays on the endcaps. A car drove by slowly outside—probably some poor soul heading home from working the night shift somewhere. She found the good stuff behind the checkout counter.

"Sorry, Dad," she whispered. Hopefully, he'd forgive her for helping herself to store inventory. It was a small price to pay for bringing her back to Gallant Lake ahead of schedule. She'd really been hoping for a few weeks on a beach somewhere before she swallowed her pride and moved back home with Dad to figure out her next steps. It wasn't as if Dad planned on falling off that ladder, but it *had* succeeded in giving him what he'd wanted—one of his children running the family business. At least for now.

Well played, Dad.

She tore the wax seal from the bottle and tugged the top off. Reaching under the counter, she found the heavy crystal tumblers Dad always kept handy for after-hours tastings with friends. Her phone sat on the counter near the cash register, light shining upward, casting soft shadows, but the old-fashioned streetlights on Main Street spread enough light into the store that she didn't need it. Those lights were new, and she liked the quaint atmosphere they created in the village. The rim of the glass had just touched her lips when she heard the muted groan of the back door closing.

No. It couldn't be. She'd locked it. She was *sure* she'd locked the door. But that was definitely the same sound the door made when she'd come into the store. A hot flush of adrenaline washed under her skin, spiking her heart rate to the point where it threatened to jump straight out of her chest. Would the intruder be able to hear it? Because there was no doubt in her mind—there *was* an intruder. Someone had just let themselves into the store in darkness. Time seemed to slow as she listened to what were definitely soft footsteps coming down the hall.

Now what? Hide? Run? Scream? No. She'd vowed to herself on the drive over here from Greenwich that she was done acting meek and playing nice. This was Wallace Liquors. She was Mackenzie Wallace, and she wasn't going to let some low-life criminal mess with her family's business.

She swallowed the scream still threatening to break free. She needed a plan. A fast one, because there was another footstep. Damn it, she wasn't good at thinking on the fly. Good girls who never got in trouble didn't need escape plans. Her shoulders straightened. Good thing she wasn't a good girl anymore, wasn't it? She took a quick inventory.

Her phone was only a few feet away, but with the flashlight app still on, it would send a beam of light moving around and draw the intruder's attention to her location. Calling 911 would mean speaking aloud, again exposing her to the bastard who'd dared to enter her father's store while Dad was lying in a hospital bed. Fear began to morph into rage. She pulled the hood up over her long blond hair and toed off her shoes for silence. Logical or not, she couldn't help thinking the element of surprise was her greatest advantage.

What would Dad do in this situation? She reached under the counter and smiled. There it was. Dad's old baseball bat, suspended on brackets. He'd always called it his "burglar alarm." Mack slowly lifted and removed the bat. This would at least give her a chance. If she scared him away, or even incapacitated him a little, she'd have time to call for help. Or run.

She crept toward the back corner by the hallway. This was just the perfect end to a far-from-perfect day. *Focus, Mackenzie.* She heard one footstep. Another. He was at the end of the hall. The beam of a flashlight cut into the darkness. If she didn't move now, he'd see her with his next step. She raised the bat, breathed a quick prayer and stepped forward, swinging with every ounce of strength she had.

There was a sharp, shouted curse, and the next thing she knew, she was being slammed against the wall so hard she saw stars. The bat was wrenched out of her hand, her body spun to face the wall, her arm twisted so high behind her back she was sure it was going to break. Something hard and cold touched her neck, directly under her ear. Her bad day just got a whole lot worse. For the first time, it occurred to her that this could be her *last* day.

Was this really what her final moment on this earth would be like? Half-dressed, defending her dad's liquor store in freaking Gallant Lake, New York? It hardly seemed fair. Her vision blurred, but she refused to pass out and let this jerk have his way without a fight. *Focus!*

In between some of the harshest swear words she'd ever heard, she heard some others that refused to compute.

"Don't move, you son of a…"

Swear. Swear. Swear.

"Give me your other hand."

Swear. Swear. Swear.

"You're under arrest, pal."

Wait.

What?

She tried to make eye contact, but he had her face pressed so tightly to the wall she could hardly breathe, much less move.

"*Arrest?* Wait, no… Are you…a cop?"

There was no humor in his responding laughter. "Yeah, it's your lucky night. Breaking and entering *and* assaulting a police officer. You picked the wrong town…"

Mack gathered the deepest breath she could, blinking back tears at the pain in her arms.

"I'm not a *thief*! This is my *father's* store! I didn't break into anything. I used a *key*!"

A thick, tense blanket of silence fell on the hallway. Not a sound. No breathing. No movement. Finally, the pressure on her arms and against her chest eased. He stepped back half a step. The man's voice went from cold and command-ing to incredulous.

"Mac*kenzie?*"

Deputy Sheriff Dan Adams willed his heart to fall back into a steady rhythm again, but the damn thing wouldn't cooperate. He'd expected to confront some dumb-ass teens looking for trouble in Carl's store. The whole town knew about Carl's fall from a ladder. The popular local business-man had ended up with broken ribs and a badly broken ankle. Dan figured some punk was taking advantage of Carl's situation to get some free booze or easy drug money. The one thing he didn't expect? Seeing the distinctive dark shape of a baseball bat whipping toward his face.

At that point, his training took over. He went through the motions without a lot of thought. Other than thinking he was royally pissed off.

Disarm the perpetrator. Subdue him. Restrain him.

Express extreme displeasure with the perp's behavior.

Throw him in the car and haul him to jail.

And then the perpetrator spoke. A *woman* spoke. And claimed to be Carl's daughter.

Well, son of a…

Carl only had one girl.

Dan reached up and tugged at the hood, uncovering a tumble of thick blond hair.

Mackenzie freakin' Wallace.

He'd just held a nightstick to the head of Mackenzie Wallace. Little Mack. The sweet baby sister of his best friend in high school. She was still face-planted against the wall, probably afraid to move, even though he'd released her. That was when the old protective feeling kicked in, along with a flood of horror at how many ways this could have gone seriously wrong.

"Jeez, Mack, what the hell?" Dan turned her around. "I could have *killed* you. You know that, right? What the fu… what are you doing here?"

She stared at him, wide-eyed. "*Danny?* Danny Adams?"

He spread his hands. "I go by Deputy Sheriff Adams these days."

That didn't seem to compute.

"You're a cop? *You?*"

As Dan studied the look on her face, he couldn't blame

her for whatever mix of anger and shock she was feeling. If he'd seen teenage him do some of the things she had seen growing up, he wouldn't believe it, either. But that was a different time. A different Dan. He took another step back, but he had to ask.

"Mackenzie, seriously." He looked down at long, bare legs. "Are you *naked* under that hoodie? What are you doing in here at two o'clock in the morning?"

Her voice chilled. "What are *you* doing in here at two o'clock in the morning, Deputy Sheriff Adams? Besides assaulting innocent women on their own damn property?"

He understood why she was ticked off. He'd scared her. But he hadn't done anything wrong. "I drove by, saw some-one moving around in here with a flashlight and investi-gated. Your dad gave me a key years ago. I had no idea you were back in town."

"I didn't know I had to check in with the sheriff when I arrived." Sharp words, but some of the fire left her voice. Mackenzie rubbed her wrist, and Dan felt a stab of guilt.

"I'm sorry, Mack. You had the hood up, I had no way of knowing…"

"Was that a gun I felt against my neck?"

"Was that a baseball bat I saw swinging at my face?"

She gave a short laugh, and Dan felt something shift a little in his chest. It was the husky laughter of a grown woman, not the giggle of the cute little pigtailed girl from his memories. She nodded, running her fingers through her hair to push it off her face.

"Fair enough. I couldn't get to sleep, and Dad didn't have any good stuff upstairs. So I figured I'd pull a Ryan and help myself."

"That's definitely something your brother would do." Dan frowned into the darkness. Ryan and Mack had always been as different as night and day, with Mackie being the Goody Two-shoes to Ryan's wild ways.

"I don't suppose you can join me while you're on duty?"

"Join…?"

"There's an open bottle of very expensive scotch on the counter, just waiting for someone to enjoy it." She laughed again, softly this time. "And I'd *really* like to hear the story of how Danger Dan turned into a lawman."

Dan grimaced. He hated that stupid nickname Ryan made up, especially coming from Mack. Even if he *had* earned it back then.

"Is your husband waiting upstairs?" Dan wasn't sure where that question came from, but, to be fair, all Mack ever talked about was leaving Gallant Lake, having a big wedding and a bigger house. The girl had goals, and from what he'd heard, she'd reached every one of them.

"I don't have a husband anymore." She brushed past him and headed toward the counter. "So are you joining me or not?"

Dan glanced at his watch, not sure how to digest that information. "I'm off duty in fifteen minutes."

Her long hair swung back and forth as she walked ahead of him. So did her hips. *Damn.*

"And you're all about following the rules now? You really have changed. Pity. I guess I'm drinking my first glass alone. You'll just have to catch up."

He frowned. Mackenzie had been strong willed, but never sassy. Never the type to sneak into her father's store alone for an after-hours drink. Not the type to taunt him. Not the type to break the rules.

Looked like he wasn't the only one who'd changed since high school.

Chapter 2

Mack willed her hand not to shake as she poured two fingers of Macallan into a second glass and slid it across the counter in Dan's general direction. He hadn't moved from his spot at the end of the hall, where he stood—watching. *Damn*. Danny Adams.

Danny, of the dragon tats, hard-drinking and wrong-side-of-the-law escapades in high school. Danny, who'd spent most of his waking hours upstairs with her brother, Ryan. Smoking pot and playing stupid video games in Ryan's room. If they weren't hanging out upstairs, they were racing around the countryside in Ryan's souped-up Nissan, looking for trouble. And one night, they'd found it. At least, Ryan had.

She'd lost track of him after the accident. Ryan had been in the hospital for ages, and she didn't remember Dan coming around much. Then there was the trial. Then Mom got sick. And the life hits just kept on coming, until Mack finally made her escape from Gallant Lake, burning all her bridges on the way out.

Now she was back. And there was Dan. In a sheriff's uniform. Never saw *that* coming.

"Are your fifteen minutes up yet?" She gestured toward his glass. "I doubt your boss is wandering the streets to check up on you…"

Dan held his wide-brimmed hat in one hand and ran the other through his sandy brown hair. He stared at her like he'd just stumbled across a unicorn.

"It's not about getting caught, Mackie. It's about being responsible. If I get a call in the next few minutes, I need to be ready." Well, wasn't he a good little scout? He looked around the store. "How's your dad?"

"Tired and grumpy, but on the mend. You're really going to count down to your quitting time before you drink? The Danny Adams I knew would have crawled over broken glass to get to alcohol."

A weird shadow crossed over his face before he leveled a pointed hazel-eyed gaze at her. This was clearly his stern law enforcement officer face. "One—I'm *not* the Danny Adams you knew. High school was over twenty years ago. Two—don't call me Danny. Ever. Three—I'm a sheriff's deputy, and I take my job seriously. I'd like to keep it. Of *course* I'm not going to drink on duty."

She leveled a gaze right back at him, but her fingernails were tapping rapidly on the counter. She'd known Dan since she was in grade school. Hell, she'd *crushed* on him back when his hair was long and shaggy and his attitude had been pure bad boy. But he'd never stopped being Danny, the kid who'd roughed her hair and thrown popcorn at her during movie nights. Cop face or not, he wasn't going to intimidate her now. She took a long, slow sip of scotch. "Tell you what—I'll try not to call you Danny if you'll promise not to remind me how long ago we met."

He nodded, his mouth sliding into a half grin. Some of the tension left his stance, and she realized her own fingers had stopped their nervous tapping. The adrenaline rush of their violent encounter was fading for both of them. Dan walked toward the counter, his eye on the very expensive scotch. He glanced at his watch, then up at her.

"It really has been a long damn time since we first met, Mack. A lifetime ago. You were just a kid."

"So were you. And you just failed your promise… *Danny*." He rolled his eyes, reminding her again of that high school kid he'd been. He and Ryan met in freshman detention and became fast friends. Mack was in…she paused to think. "Oh, my God, I was in fifth grade when you and Ryan became partners in crime. How is that even possible?"

Dan propped his hip against the counter across from her. Now that they were closer and the lights were on, she could see the deep lines next to his eyes. As if he'd seen a lot of sun. Or a lot of trouble. He was looking at the counter, but she had a feeling he was a million miles away.

"Are you okay?"

His head rose sharply at the question. "Why do you ask?"

"I don't know. You look tired or stressed or something."

Dan grunted in response. "Or something." He looked at his watch, closed his eyes briefly, then reached for the glass of amber liquid. He downed it in one gulp, then gave a loud sigh of satisfaction. "Not my usual end-of-shift choice, but you can never go wrong with Macallan." She held up the bottle to pour a refill, but he shook his head. "I may be off shift, but I'm in uniform."

With a start, she realized she had no idea what kind

of life Dan Adams lived these days. He wasn't wearing a ring, but that might be an in-uniform thing. The guy had to be almost forty, so he probably had a wife and family. She took in his intense composure, his square jaw, broad shoulders and calm—if tired—eyes. Yes, this looked like a man with a Sunday school teacher of a wife, a couple kids and probably a dog, too. She couldn't help thinking that was a damn shame. She splashed more scotch in her own glass and lifted it in a mock toast.

"I don't have that problem, since all I have to do is crawl up the stairs. Did you settle down with anyone I know?"

He lowered his brow. "Settle down? Oh, you mean family? I married Susanne Buckley. You might have known her—she was between our grades, a couple years behind me. Cheerleader. Class president. Homecoming queen."

Mack started to laugh. "*You* landed a homecoming queen? With your reputation? How did her parents let *that* happen?" She had a vague memory of Susanne—cute, perky and popular. No match for Danger Dan.

That odd shadow crossed his face again. He didn't seem to like being reminded of his teen adventures. "We didn't get together until after college, so her parents couldn't do anything about it." His voice dropped so low she barely heard him. "But it didn't stop them from trying."

Silence fell in the store again. Her long day started to catch up with her, and she couldn't stifle the yawn that came out of nowhere. Dan straightened with a smile.

"It's late…or should I say early? Between our little adventure and the booze you've had, I'm guessing you'll get to sleep now." He started to turn away, then stopped. "It wasn't a gun, by the way."

"What?"

"You asked me before if you felt a gun to your head. It

was my baton. Cops don't make a habit of blowing people's heads off for burglary."

She considered that for a moment before nodding solemnly. "Good to know. But that *was* a baseball bat I was swinging."

He huffed out a laugh. "Never thought I'd see the day when sweet little Mackie would try to take me out with her daddy's bat."

"I'm done being sweet little Mackie, Dan. Being sweet got me nowhere."

The truth was, she hadn't ever *been* sweet. She'd acted the part, but only as a means to an end—to make other people think better of her. Being that calculated couldn't really be *sweet*, could it? It certainly hadn't made her a lot of friends. And it didn't help her hold on to a husband.

Dan studied her, and she had a feeling he was trying to put together a profile, cop-style. Trying to figure her out. *Good luck with that.* His slanted smile returned. "It got you back to Gallant Lake, helping your dad. That's exactly what I'd expect from the sweet little Mackie I knew."

She grimaced. It wasn't like she'd had anywhere else to go. Mason had kept both the house and the condo in the divorce. She hadn't had the stomach to fight him. She'd taken the cash and left. She lifted her chin. "I'm turning over a new leaf. One that doesn't include 'little.'" She gestured down to her well-rounded figure. "And especially doesn't include 'sweet.'"

He pursed his lips, tilting his head to the side with a skeptical grin. "Yeah. Okay. Whatever you say. Get some sleep, and don't forget to lock up after I go. In fact…" He picked her phone up from the counter and handed it to her. "Unlock it." She followed his order without question, not realizing she'd done so until he was taking the phone back

from her and started tapping. "Here's my number. Text me
when you're locked in upstairs."

"Yes, sir. Officer, sir." She gave him a mock salute, realizing the scotch might just be kicking in. "Say hi to Susanne for me."

He'd started walking away but hesitated on that last line.
He gave a quick shake of his head, then kept on going. The
back door gave its usual groan as he left. It wasn't until then
that Mack noticed the atmosphere change. Dan seemed low-
key, but his presence had still brought a definite energy to
the place. Energy that evaporated as soon as he left. She
thought about that for a minute, then dismissed it as nothing
more than her adrenaline letdown from being shoved hard
up against the wall by a guy she'd once known as a pimple-
faced kid. She closed up the store and headed back upstairs.

She shoved the still-annoyed cat off her bed pillow and
crawled under the covers after sending a quick text that all
was well. Mack had a hunch her dreams were going to be
filled with golden-green eyes that had more of a story to
tell than just "I'm not that Danny anymore." And damned
if she didn't want to know more about it.

"So let me get this straight." Asher Peyton turned away
from the dresser he'd been building and sat on the bench
next to Dan. His best friend looked puzzled. "You knew
Carl's daughter when she was a kid? And you accosted her
last night in Carl's store?" Asher chuckled, rubbing the dark
beard he was sporting these days. "Good luck getting any
more first-responder discounts from Carl, man."

"I hope to God she doesn't tell him." Dan took a swig
of the cola Asher had given him. He was on duty soon, so
he'd had to turn down the beer he'd been offered. Asher
always had a supply of both on hand for him. "But I didn't

accost her. There was a person with a flashlight in Carl's store in the middle of the night. I *apprehended* her, at best." Sure, he'd been rough with her, but damn. He gave Asher a pointed look. "And let's not forget that baseball bat she swung at my head."

"Yeah, that would have hurt. Makes total sense you'd have a drink with her after."

Dan didn't respond. Mainly because he couldn't explain it. He'd seen Mack a few times since high school, but not up close and personal like last night. Probably the closest they'd been as adults was when he shook her hand at her mom's funeral years ago, but she'd been a shell-shocked college freshman with hollow eyes that day. She probably didn't even remember him being there. Once in a while he'd seen her in the liquor store, visiting with her dad. But Dan had never stopped by. Why would he? He was part of the reason her family—the family that for years had felt like it was *his*—had spiraled into tragedy. He'd supplied the alcohol the night Ryan and Braden crashed, and Braden had died. It was just dumb luck that Dan hadn't been in the car with them.

"Hello? Earth to Dan?" Asher's voice broke into his thoughts, almost making him flinch. But Dan had learned long ago not to show that kind of reaction to anyone around him. Calm and steady was the lawman's mantra. *Never let them see you blink.* He held in a steadying breath, then released it slowly, grinning at Asher.

"Sorry, man. My little run-in with Mack aside, last night was a hell of a shift. Stupid kids drag racing out on Hilton Road. And another damn overdose. It took two doses of Narcan to bring the guy back." The nasal spray superdrug made him feel like some kind of god, bringing the dead back to life. But there was something about the look in the person's eyes when the Narcan kicked in and jolted them back to planet Earth. They'd taken the opioids to escape, and here they were, waking up to flashing lights and yelling voices and all the chaos they'd been trying to get away from. In last night's case, Kyle Alderwood had OD'd in his car, sitting in his parents' driveway in one of the nicest neighborhoods in town. His mom, Barb, was screaming and crying in a panic in the front yard while neighbors tried to comfort her. What a scene. He'd felt everyone's eyes on him. This scourge had come to Gallant Lake under his watch.

"He made it?" Asher asked. Dan nodded, staring into his glass and wishing it was something other than soda.

"How many overdoses does that make in the last month or so?" Asher looked up as a customer walked in.

"Too many." Dan answered. "Too damn many." He needed to figure out who was distributing opioids laced with Fentanyl in Gallant Lake, and why they'd picked his quiet little town, but he hadn't managed it yet. The stuff was everywhere all of a sudden, but the path back to the suppliers was a cleverly knotted mess he hadn't been able to unravel. He just had to hope the new interdepartmental task force would figure it out. Soon.

Asher spoke with the woman who'd come in to check on a sideboard she'd ordered the previous week. He explained that the curly maple she'd requested hadn't even arrived yet. And there were three orders for his custom-built furniture ahead of hers. But he promised her she'd have it in time for her daughter's wedding shower in two months. Reassured, the woman left. Asher stood at the café table he used as a checkout counter, looking out the window at downtown Gallant Lake.

"Does Carl's daughter have lots of blond hair? And a bang-out figure?"

Dan stood, scowling at his friend. "Maybe. Why?"

"I think she just bought out the sports section at Nate's hardware store. She must be into hiking and stuff, huh? Like you?"

Dan ignored the speculative look Asher gave him. Ever since Asher married Nora Lowery, he'd turned into Cupid, trying to help Dan's nonexistent love life. But Dan had two strikes against him with the ladies. He was a cop, with all the stress and weird hours that entailed. And he was a single dad.

He walked toward the window. "Can't be Mack if she's buying hiking equipment. She never did anything that might get her nails dirt—" His voice trailed off. Because hell if that wasn't Mackenzie talking to Nate Thomas on the sidewalk outside Nate's store. She was holding hiking poles under one arm, with a biking helmet dangling from her fingers. Her other hand was holding a… Was that a *kayak paddle*?

"So that isn't your girl?" Asher asked.

Dan pressed his lips together. "You've been watching too many of those mushy movies with Nora on the romance channel." He looked back out the window. "No one is 'my girl.' But yeah, that's Mack."

There was no mistaking her figure, full and curvy. And that thick mane of blond hair, pulled back into a ponytail instead of being carefully styled as usual. She was wearing jeans and a T-shirt. Back in the day, Mack always looked like she was ready for tea with the queen, no matter what she was doing. He couldn't remember the last time he saw her in denim. Not even in high school. Dan stiffened at the sight of Nate's hand on her shoulder as they laughed about something together.

Naturally, Asher picked up on his body language. "Nate's quite a catch, you know. Maybe not the most exciting guy in town, but he's steady and reliable and single…"

"I don't see a hardware store owner as Mack's type."

Asher's shoulder rose. "You didn't see her as an adventurer, either, but it looks like she's ready for hiking, biking and kayaking all in one shopping trip. Either Nate's more of a master salesman than I gave him credit for, or you don't know Mackenzie Wallace as much as you think you do."

Mack turned and walked across the street toward the liquor store, loaded down with shopping bags and supplies. "I knew her as a skinny, stuck-up kid who liked to follow her brother and me around and lecture us like she was our grandmother. But somewhere in the last twenty years, she's clearly blossomed."

Asher scoffed as they walked to the back of the shop again. "Blossomed, huh? Now who's been watching girlie movies? And FYI—you can laugh at that romance channel all you want, but they have some pretty deep stuff, and it puts Nora in the cuddling mood, which suits me just fine." He held his hands up at Dan's expression. "Okay, I'm dropping the subject. How's Chloe doing with school?"

Dan took a sip of soda and smiled. His daughter was a topic he was always happy to discuss. He told Asher how the eight-year-old was acing her grades. Her teacher, Sarah Conway, regularly sent emails saying what a delight Chloe was to have in her class.

Now that he thought about it, Chloe was a little like a young Mack—always eager to please and striving to be the best at everything. The only difference was Chloe was a tomboy through and through and had the scrapes and bruises to show for it. Just this week, she'd tried to slide down the banister in his renovated Victorian house and nearly broke her arm when she tumbled off halfway to the ground floor. His ex-wife, Susanne, had a fit when she saw Chloe's puffy wrist, but the doctor confirmed it was just a minor sprain.

Asher finished his lunch and moved to the unfinished dresser on the work table, and Dan knew it was time to go. He had shift in a few hours. He'd usually spend his extra time with Chloe, but Susanne had taken her into the city to shop this weekend. He could probably use a nap after working overtime last night to help out another deputy. That's what a smart man would do.

But Dan wasn't all that smart, because he headed right down Main Street toward the liquor store.

Chapter 3

Mack sat behind the counter and stared at the hiking poles leaning against the back wall, right between the cognac and the whiskey. She shifted on her dad's weathered old stool, and her hiking boots clunked against the counter. Damn, these things were bulky. Nate had told her they were the highest-rated hiking boots on the market, and that she should wear them a few hours at a time to break them in and get used to them. So here she was, clumping around Dad's liquor store in boots that would horrify the ladies back at Glenfadden Country Club. She grinned. That just made her like these boots all the more.

Her dad's friend Bert Jenkins worked in the store part-time. He'd been covering full-time since Dad's fall five days ago, so she'd given him a couple days off. It was weird being back in Gallant Lake, working the store on a Saturday. Everyone wanted to know about Dad, who had been grumpy as hell when she'd seen him this morning. But everyone also seemed a little hesitant to start up a conversation with her. Most of them had watched her grow up in this place.

To be fair, she hadn't been much of a social butterfly those last few years she'd lived here. It felt like half the town hated them back then because of Ryan's accident and Braden's death. Then Braden's family sued. And lost. Ryan was a mess. Her mom was sick. Dad did nothing but work. And Mack had spent her days tap-dancing like crazy to keep everyone happy at home and get good enough grades to earn a scholarship to a college as far away from Gallant Lake as possible.

She slid off the stool and walked to the back of the store, where the café tables and chairs sat in disarray. The stroll down memory lane wasn't doing a thing to make her feel better about coming home again. She started arranging the tables and chairs.

Dad had told her he'd read an article about having wine tastings to draw in new customers, though he hadn't gotten around to having one yet. But he *had* ordered the furniture. And rearranged the store to shift the wine section toward the back wall, where the tables were. It was an interesting concept, since wine was his biggest seller. Forcing people to walk past the bottles of vodka and gin to get to what they came for probably led to some impulse purchases. Dad had owned this liquor store for thirty years, but he never stopped trying to make it better. She slid two more chairs over to a table. She'd been to her share of fancy wine tastings back in Greenwich and could probably bluff her way through a wine night or two. If she was going to run the place, she should try to contribute something.

Dad had seemed more than happy to give her free rein over the store this morning. It used to be strictly his domain, but he'd shrugged off her news of taking a bottle of scotch last night—she skipped over her run-in with Dan. He told her it was a family business and she was family, so she could make her own decisions. Maybe it was the pain meds making him so amenable. He'd seemed resigned to spending a little more time at the hospital and then going to the rehab center as his ankle healed.

The bell over the front door chimed. She turned with a smile, but the smile faltered when she saw Dan Adams standing there. Her skin warmed at the memory of him pressing her against the wall last night after she'd tried to bash his head in. He was out of uniform now, in jeans and a well-worn henley. But he still sported the slanted smile she was beginning to think was a regular feature. It made him look perpetually amused, but his eyes were watchful. As if the half smile might just be a mask he wore to make him look nonthreatening. For some reason, she wanted to rattle him out of that disguise.

"What can I help you with, Officer? Looking for another Macallan?"

His smile deepened. "In the middle of the afternoon? Seems a little indulgent. I think that's a drink best saved for evening hours." He walked to the back, spotting the chairs and tables she'd set up. "So Carl's going through with his plan for wine tastings?"

Mack shrugged. "I think he's a little intimidated by the idea, since he's not a huge wine drinker himself. But he was all for it when I told him I might give it a try. He has to call the licensing commission to make sure I qualify as a legal agent of the store so it's all on the up-and-up." She stepped back to inspect the tables, trying to determine if they were spaced far enough apart and making sure they weren't blocking access to the wine displays.

Dan gave a low whistle. "Those are some pretty fancy boots you got there, Mackenzie."

She looked down at her sturdy footwear. "I'm breaking them in. Nate Thomas says they'll keep me warm and dry when I hit the trails."

"Hit the trails? You could climb Everest in those things. I watched you grow up, kiddo, and I never once saw you on any trails around here." Dan pulled out a chair and made himself at home.

Mack lifted her chin with a sniff. "I grew up a long time ago. I've changed."

"Yeah? Is this part of that new-leaf thing you talked about last night?"

Her chin rose. "As a matter of fact, yes. It is. I'm tired of the sweater-set-and-pearls crowd."

Dan shook his head. "I don't know what that means, but the Mack I knew wore nothing *but* sweater sets."

She studied him for a moment, tipping her head to the side. "That's the whole point of a new leaf. I think I made it clear last night that I'm not the Mack you knew."

He looked around the store, showing no signs of responding. Was he ignoring her? Dismissing her? Taunting her? Insecurity made her chest go tight. She'd vowed not to give a damn about how anyone judged her, but old habits died hard. Her fingernails dug into her palms. She turned away and straightened some wine bottles, refusing to speak before he did. She could wait him out. Out of the corner of her eye, she saw his slow smile return. Instead of reacting to her comment, he jumped to a new topic.

"You said you weren't married anymore. What happened?"

She huffed out a surprised laugh. "Nice segue, Danger Dan. Just dive right into the deep end, why don't you?"

A flicker of uncertainty passed over his face before he composed himself again. "Sorry. Sometimes I fall into cop mode with the tone of my questions. It's just…" He ran his hand through his hair, leaving finger trails in the short, thick locks. "The last I knew, you were living your dream life over in Connecticut. Big house. Rich investor husband. Queen of the country club crowd. At least, that's the way Carl made it sound." He looked down at her feet again. "And now you're clumping around your dad's liquor store in hiking boots. I'm curious how that happened."

She turned back to the wine display, fussing with the same bottles she'd just straightened, doing her best to keep her voice steady. "Well, you know what they say—be careful what you ask for. Some dreams aren't all they're cracked up to be. So I'm starting a new dream, here in Gallant Lake. And nowhere near my ex-husband and his social circle."

Gallant Lake might not be where she'd planned to be living at this point in her life, but it was where she was needed. It wasn't easy to think about facing everyone and explaining her failed dreams, but she'd just have to suck it up. Hopefully, she hadn't burned *all* her bridges with her *Mean Girls* act in high school. She stared blankly at the bottle of merlot in her hand. It would serve her right if the whole town shunned her.

Dan's voice went hard. "Did he hurt you?"

It made sense that a law enforcement officer would go there first, but the question still made her look up in surprise. The memory of how her marriage collapsed still stung.

"Not the way you're suggesting, no. But it wasn't fun." She'd left everything she'd known behind in Greenwich, including her so-called friends.

Dan sat at one of the tables with a sigh. "Divorce is never fun."

She spun on her heel, which wasn't easy in those boots. "You, too?"

"Three years ago." He nodded, staring at the floor. "Susanne and I were able to keep the focus on what was best for our daughter, but it still feels like a failure, you know? You don't have kids?"

Her heart pinched tight. "No. No kids. And yes. Feels like a failure." She gave him a thin smile. "But I did get custody of our giant grumpy cat."

Dan chuckled. "I can't tell from your tone if that's a win or a loss."

She thought of how Rory had tried to smack Dad's bowling trophies off the shelf one by one that morning while she scrambled to catch them like a juggler, cursing the cat the whole time.

"I'm not sure, either," she laughed. "He's a pain in the ass. But he keeps the bed warm." *Oh, damn.* She waved her hand in dismissal. "Well, crap. Talk about oversharing."

Dan gave her a quizzical look. "Don't take this the wrong way, because it's not a criticism, but... I don't remember you swearing. Like...*ever*."

She gestured to herself. "New leaf, remember? This is new and improved Mackenzie, with no mouth filter. And hiking boots."

And twenty extra pounds since high school. She cringed inside. He must think she'd just let herself go entirely.

"Hey..." Dan's voice was soft as he stood and took a step toward her, forehead furrowed. "New leaves are supposed to make you feel *good*. What's wrong?"

Her breath caught as she tried to steady herself. She could not have a postdivorce meltdown right now. Those were reserved for late evenings, when she was alone and in the dark. She bit her lip hard to bring herself back under control.

"Like you said… Divorce is a failure, and mine's officially only a month old. And look at me. I'm an overweight mess dressed in combat boots." She blinked, willing this pity party to go away. Dan's gentle laughter helped.

"Okay, let's break down that comment. I said divorce *felt like* a failure, not that it *was* one." He ran his eyes up and down her body. "I don't see a mess, or anything wrong with your weight. I see a woman who's just as beautiful as ever, in a very grown-up way." A funny vibration started low in her abdomen. He thought she was beautiful? His hand touched her upper arm gently. "And if you want to call those combat boots, you go right ahead. You'd make a kick-ass soldier, and you're gonna knock the hell out of this new leaf of yours."

Dan sat in his patrol car a few nights later, thinking about that conversation with Mackie. She considered herself a hot mess, but all he could see was her sass and sharp humor. The new fighting spirit she seemed to have. She'd stood her ground that first night, wielding a baseball bat. Every inch of her was an intoxicating, curving temptation. If that was a hot mess…he was into it.

He shifted on the seat, glancing at the radar as a sedan rolled slowly and carefully by. He'd intentionally parked so he'd be easily visible to drivers. Anyone who whipped by him tonight over the speed limit was literally begging for trouble. But he was really hoping no one would. He was worn-out and looking forward to a few days off. The swing shift schedule was a killer, but he didn't have much choice.

When Gallant Lake decided it couldn't afford its own

police force ten years ago, the county sheriff's office had taken over. Dan was a wet-behind-the-ears rookie back then, but the town and county made an agreement. They made a position for him as a deputy sheriff, along with the former police chief, Mike DiNofrio, and gave Dan and Mike the Gallant Lake district to cover. It was the county's way of reassuring the locals that they'd still have coverage by guys they knew.

But they were stretched thin these days, thanks to budget cuts. If there was something going on elsewhere in the county, Gallant Lake was out of luck, with the nearest on-duty sheriff up to twenty miles away. The state troopers helped with coverage, but again, it depended on who was where. There were too many times when there wasn't a law enforcement officer anywhere near Gallant Lake, much less patrolling its streets on a regular basis.

And now that the Gallant Lake Resort was expanding and bringing a lot more tourists and workers to the area, the town needed *more* law enforcement coverage, not less. There'd been some talk about restarting the local police force, and the new mayor was behind the idea. But it wasn't going to happen anytime soon, thanks to politics—one of the few things Dan hated almost as much as he hated the cheap, deadly drugs coming into this area lately.

Several more vehicles meandered past his post. The last one gave him a glare and jumped on the gas shortly after passing him, as if taunting him. He was too tired to play games today. He didn't hit the lights right away, watching to make sure the guy wasn't stupid enough to stay at the high speed. Sure enough, the truck slowed back down again. Good thing. He was in no mood to deal with some hotshot kid in a jacked-up truck.

When Dan picked up his daughter the next morning,

after far too little sleep, Chloe had enough energy for the both of them. As usual, she was the life force that kept him going.

"Dad! Oh my *God*! Did you *hear*? There's a fashion show at the resort and Mom said I could be in it! I'm gonna be a *model*! In a real fashion show!" Chloe grabbed his hand on the sidewalk and tugged him toward Susanne's house. Which used to be *their* house. Back when they were a family. His daughter's words didn't sink in until they were walking inside.

"Wait…did you say you're going to be in a fashion show, Chloe? Is it a contest or something?"

"I don't think it's a contest. But Miss Mel at the shop said she'll order me something special to wear, and she said it could be purple!" Dan couldn't help smiling, despite his confusion. Chloe's entire room was purple, from walls to curtains to carpet. At both houses.

Susanne stuck her head out of the kitchen doorway and waved at Dan. "Hey! Come have a cup of coffee while she gets her stuff ready. I'll fill you in on the big fashion show." She winked. "No reality TV stuff, I promise!"

While Susanne was pregnant, she and Dan had made themselves a few promises, as all new parents do. They'd provide a united front at all times. They wouldn't be over-protective helicopter parents, but they wouldn't be free-range parents, either. And they'd never push their child to do something they didn't want to do. No screaming stage mom. No cursing hockey dad. No unhealthy competition of any kind. They'd let their child *be* a child. No overwrought reality show parenting.

That became their mantra for all of it. *No reality shows!* Susanne had a particular hatred for the cable shows that seemed to glorify horrid parents exploiting their children, who were pushed to win dance contests or kiddie beauty pageants or whatever. After Chloe was born, they realized parenting—not to mention *marriage*—was a lot more complicated than they'd ever anticipated. When one of them thought the other—or Chloe—might be getting a little too carried away, they'd remind each other there were no cameras around. No need for drama.

A fashion show? That one sounded straight out of reality show land.

"I *swear* she's only doing it for fun," Susanne said as she handed him a mug of coffee. "No competition. It's part of the big charity fund-raiser the resort does for that veterans' group every year. You know, with the golf tournament and the fancy gala? Samir is on the board this year, with Amanda Randall. She said they were going to be looking for local fashion models, including children. So he suggested Chloe."

Dr. Samir Badawi was Susanne's fiancé. He'd come to the country as an orphan from Sudan, sponsored by a church in Gallant Lake, and was now a dermatologist in White Plains. He was a good guy as far as Dan could tell— soft-spoken, kind, smart. Chloe seemed to like him. And Susanne was over the moon for the guy.

It made sense—Samir was everything in a mate that Dan wasn't. Wealthy. Didn't have a dangerous job with crazy hours. Susanne probably didn't text Samir all day just to make sure he was okay. She didn't have to worry that he might die on his shift. Her fears over being a cop's wife had been a big factor in their divorce. He'd tried to explain that her fretting distracted him and actually put him at more risk, but that argument just made things worse. So yeah, Samir was probably a better fit for Susanne. Dan wasn't sure how he felt about the guy making decisions about Chloe's activities, though. He also wasn't sure he wanted his eight-year-old daughter parading around in front of strangers.

"I thought you and I were still making decisions about Chloe as a team." He sounded more resentful than he'd intended. Dan usually swallowed pesky things like emotions to keep from showing them. Susanne's eyebrow rose.

"Samir is going to be Chloe's stepfather in six months. I think that makes him part of the so-called team, Dan. And I *did* text you yesterday to call me, which you never did." She had a right to be ticked at him. He drained half his mug of coffee and reined in his annoyance. She knew he didn't answer her texts during shifts unless she said it was urgent. Call me wasn't urgent. But there was no sense in both of them getting mad.

"I get that, Suze. I do." He splayed his hands in surrender. "And I like Samir. But Chloe's still *our* daughter. A heads-up would have been nice, even if you didn't think my opinion was required." He'd tried to sound reasonable, but he could hear the resentment in his voice, and so could Susanne. Instead of challenging him, she bowed her head and sighed.

"I'm sorry if it felt like a blindside, but I did try. I can't help it that you were working. And we just agreed yesterday after we took her to Five and Design to talk to Mel, and Chloe got so excited about it." She gave him a smile. "As you may have noticed. She'll be wearing a modest party dress. No self-respecting reality show would be interested in this. I promise."

Dan chuckled despite himself, tension leaving his shoulders. Melanie Lowery—no, Melanie *Brannigan* as of last month—owned an upscale women's boutique on Main Street. Mel had married sports agent Shane Brannigan on

St. Patrick's Day at the resort, and it had been a blowout of a party. The former fashion model had settled in Gallant Lake to be close to her Lowery cousins, including Asher's wife, Nora. Their other cousin, Amanda Randall, was the wife of the owner of the Gallant Lake Resort, the town's biggest employer and tourist draw. And a fourth cousin, Bree Caldwell from North Carolina, had founded the veteran support charity with her husband. It seemed unlikely that this was some mad plot to corrupt his daughter. He reached out and clinked Susanne's mug with his.

"If the Lowery women are involved, I'm sure Chloe will be fine. And she's definitely excited." He straightened at the sound of his daughter galloping down the stairs. "Sorry if I overreacted. It's been a tough couple of days."

Susanne nodded. "You look beat. I heard there was another overdose. Are you any closer to finding the bastards selling the stuff?"

His shoulders slumped under the weight of what was becoming a familiar question. "Nothing yet. We need more dedicated investigators, but the department is stretched too thin on this new budget. We don't have the manpower to do the job right."

She put her hand on his shoulder, and he could feel her tension. Talking about understaffing was probably making her even more nervous about his job. "Has there been any more talk about reestablishing a Gallant Lake police department?"

Dan turned to wash his mug in the sink. Treating this little house like home was a tough habit to break after sharing years of family life there.

"The politicians are talking, but that doesn't mean anything. They're *always* talking." Dan hated politicians and their verbal gymnastics.

Susanne watched him dry the mug and put it away in the cupboard. "If you're that understaffed, do you think you'll have to work the night of the gala next month? Chloe will want you there. And she has a fitting at the boutique in a couple weeks. I'll text you once we have a time." Susanne knew he had little control over his schedule. It wasn't as if he ever *wanted* to miss family events. She cleared her throat. "Rumor has it Blake Randall is pushing hard for a local police department, and he has some clout as the owner of the resort. And didn't you say Asher was on some committee about it?" She hesitated. "If you were chief…"

If he was the police chief of Gallant Lake, he'd probably be working even more hours than he was now. Chloe dashed into the kitchen, school backpack over one shoulder and a purple duffel bag over the other. He glanced at his watch. She'd be late for school if he didn't get moving.

"Kiss your mom goodbye, baby, and let's go." He looked back at Susanne as he headed out. "Honestly, Suze, I don't get into what the committees and politicians are up to. It's all just noise until a decision is made." He held the door open for his daughter. "I'll have her back here by Sunday night."

Dan dropped Chloe off at school and drove to the small Victorian house that was his home now. It was just a few blocks from Susanne's place in one direction and the elementary school in another. Close enough that Chloe could ride her bike back and forth between her parents' houses. He crawled into bed to catch as much rest as he could before picking his daughter up later. These swing shifts were going to be the death of him yet.

As usual, every worry from every corner of his life rushed through his mind as he lay there, trying to fall asleep. Among them were the usuals—who was selling drugs in his town? What would happen once Susanne and Samir married? The house Dan and Susanne had bought right after they'd married was a little humble for a doctor. Susanne was still in her thirties. Would she and Samir have children? How would Chloe deal with that?

But today, as had happened every day this week, his last thoughts before closing his eyes were of a sassy blonde standing in her father's liquor store wearing those ridiculous hiking boots with a smile that wasn't quite as sugar sweet as it used to be. Mack now had a daring smile that teased of adventure. And the light in her brown eyes teased at even more. Or maybe he was just imagining that. After all, she'd been Perfect Mackenzie back in school—perfect grades, perfect clothes, perfectly angelic behavior. She'd been the sugary counterbalance to all the trouble her brother and Dan managed to find. Determined to leave Gallant Lake in her rearview mirror, she'd gone off to college in California, then married a banker and moved to a mansion in the wealthiest enclave of Greenwich, Connecticut. Dan had been happy for the kid when he'd heard.

But she wasn't a kid anymore. And he had a feeling she might not be all that angelic, either. And that's the thought that kept him awake the most.

Chapter 4

"Welcome to your first Women in Charge meeting, Mackenzie!" Nora Peyton raised her foam-topped mug of cappuccino in Mack's direction. "The only rule for our meetings is that there *are* no rules. We just brainstorm and try to help each other. There are no bad ideas, because even the worst idea might lead to something brilliant."

Nora's Gallant Brew coffee shop was closed for the evening on Thursday, and the front row of lights was off. There were five other women gathered at the table nearest the coffee machines—Nora, petite and smiling, with her brunette bob tucked behind her ears. Nora's two cousins were there—Mel Brannigan, owner of the Five and Design boutique, and Amanda Randall, whose husband owned the Gallant Lake Resort, and an interior designer in her own right. While the Lowery cousins were new faces to Mack, the other two were much more familiar: Cathy Meadows, the former owner of the coffee shop and current part-time employee there, and Thea Winters, who'd owned the Gallant Lake Flower Shop for at least fifty years.

"So glad you could join us, Mackenzie." Amanda leaned forward. She was petite like Nora but had long blond curls that made her look a bit like Little Bo Peep, especially with the pink polka-dot top she was wearing. Amanda was full of restless energy, shifting in her chair and tapping the side of her mug with her spoon. "The female business owners of Gallant Lake need to stick together!"

"My friends call me Mack. And I don't actually own anything. My dad is the boss…"

He'd surprised her a few times this week, though, repeatedly hinting that he wanted Mack to take a more active role in the family business while she was here. She got the feeling he wanted her staying a lot longer than just to regroup from her divorce. But she wasn't ready to consider a permanent move to Gallant Lake just yet.

Mel put her hand on Mack's arm. "How *is* Carl? I meant to get over to see him last week, but I had an awful spring cold and didn't dare risk making him sick."

"He's good, Mel. Rarin' to go, but the doctors are still worried about his ankle." She'd met with the doctors that morning and had been dismayed at what they'd had to say. Before she could explain, Cathy—of all people—spoke up.

"The doctors think they'll have to do more surgery to repair the tendon." Cathy shook her head, pushing her braid of gray hair back over her shoulder. "If they do, Carl won't be able to put an ounce of weight on it for *weeks*. Silly old goat, climbing on ladders at his age…" She looked up and noted Mack's raised eyebrows. How did Dad's former neighbor know all this when Mack had just heard it a few hours ago? Cathy blushed and rushed on. "I just…happened to stop by…before I came here…to say hi to my old friend Carl…because I was in White Plains to…"

The three Lowery cousins exchanged amused glances. Mack wasn't sure what she was missing. Nora coughed and began nodding quickly.

"I sent Cathy to White Plains to pick up an order and told her she should stop and see her…old friend." Dad had told Mack that Cathy had semiretired a few years ago. She'd sold the shop to Nora but stayed on as a part-time employee. Nora shifted in her chair, then straightened and grinned brightly. "So anyway, we started this group last fall, half as a joke, but we're actually starting to get some things done here in Gallant Lake. We have more members, of course, but this was an impromptu gathering to meet you, and some ladies couldn't make it. Including our esteemed mayor, Margie Malone."

Thea harrumphed, her mouth twisting into a scowl. Mack had known the woman all her life, and she wasn't sure if she'd ever seen her smile. Such an odd personality for a florist.

"Esteemed to *you*, maybe," Thea said. "The jury's still out on her. After all these years, she's—"

"She's making great progress." Amanda finished, but probably not the way Thea would have. "She secured a grant to fix up the park, and she's working with Nate at the hardware store to finish the waterfront project and the boardwalk that runs behind the shops over there."

Thea rolled her eyes but didn't respond, pressing her mouth into a tight, thin line.

"As I was saying," Nora continued, "we started meeting monthly, or as needed, to discuss how our businesses are doing and come up with ideas for promotions and stuff. And we encourage each other."

"Why do you call it Women in Charge?" Mack asked.

"That started at my wedding a few years ago," Amanda laughed. "It was a small wedding…"

"In a castle…" Mel muttered. Mack knew Amanda and her husband lived in the historic old castle named Halcyon, just outside town. The place had been vacant for ages. In fact, when Mack was a teen, the rumor was that the place was haunted.

Amanda lifted a shoulder at her cousin's comment. "Anyway… I didn't want a big wedding party, and there's no way I could choose one cousin over the others, so Blake and I dubbed them the Women in Charge for the day. My friend Julie was my attendant, but these ladies, along with my other cousin Bree, organized every little detail for me." Amanda sat back, sipping from her coffee. "I was recovering from an…accident. And I was pregnant, which my cousins didn't know at the time. It was such a relief to hand off the worries to them. We figured if *we* could help each other like that, imagine if the women in town started lifting each other up? And since we're all involved with businesses here, it just kind of grew from there." She grinned at Mel. "That whole pregnant-at-the-wedding thing seemed to have caught on."

Mack looked at Mel in surprise. "You're expecting?"

Mel used to be a famous fashion model. She went by the name Mellie Low back then. It was easy to see how that career came about—the brunette was tall and striking, even without a bit of makeup on. Her dark hair was pulled back into an artfully messy twist, and Mack suspected Mel's casual slacks and sweater sported expensive designer labels.

The woman's face went pink as she patted her flat stomach. "One month married and three months pregnant. Not the way Shane and I planned it, but we're happy. And terrified."

Nora smiled. "You'll be perfect parents." She patted Cathy's hand. "Even though Cathy isn't a business owner *now*, she was one for years, and knows everyone and everything involving Gallant Lake. We're newcomers, so we rely on Cathy and Thea and some of the other women to keep us from rocking the apple cart *too* much."

Mack nodded. Cathy hadn't changed much through the years—she'd always been such a free spirit. Her hair, now pewter instead of the auburn Mack remembered, was still as long as ever, pulled back in that signature heavy braid. Mom used to call Cathy a "hippie girl who never grew up," but they'd been close, if unlikely, friends. Cathy used to live in the loft over the coffee shop, and Mack's parents were just two doors down. Mack used to run over to Cathy's shop for hot cocoa after school, and Cathy always tossed extra marshmallows on top. When Mom got sick, Cathy was there every day, bringing meals or magazines or just sitting and holding Mom's hand. But Cathy seemed to be having a hard time maintaining eye contact across the table. Maybe the memories made her as sad as they did Mack.

"So…is your dad really going to have wine tastings at the store?" Amanda winked at the women around the table. "That would be so much fun! We could promote it from the resort as something guests could attend, and maybe encourage other shops to stay open later that night. With a little wine to loosen the purse strings, people might spend money more freely."

Thea surprised them all when she agreed. "I'm not sure how ethical it is to rely on booze for business, but we need more bodies downtown before we *all* go belly up." She glanced out the windows to a quiet Main Street. "We need more businesses, too."

It seemed the number of boarded-up storefronts increased every time Mack came home. Dad told her it was better now than it had been, but not by much. Most of the businesses they'd lost during the recession and the resort's struggles twenty years ago were gone for good. Main Street had no bakery, no restaurant, no gift shops. There wasn't even a *bar* downtown. Everyone went to the Chalet for drinks and music. The pizza place and townie bar just outside the village center had been there forever. It was where all the cool kids used to hang out after school, but that had never been Mack's crowd.

"If we get more people," Nora said, "the businesses will follow the money. But I think plying people with alcohol may not be the way to go. I think Sheriff Dan will have something to say about that. And if Dan doesn't want it to happen, it won't."

Mack frowned. Dan was a sheriff, but he wasn't going to tell her what to do with her father's business. Along with the bad news about Dad's foot, they'd had good news today, too—she *was* an official legal agent for the store and *could* host wine tastings there.

"I have no intention of letting people get drunk. If I decide to have wine tastings, Danny Adams can't tell me not to." A strange quiet came over the table, and eyes went wide. Okay, maybe she'd sounded overly defiant, but she was tired of people telling her what to do.

Nora spoke first. "Dan is my husband's best friend, and I've never *ever* heard him called Danny." She grinned. "But I'm thinkin' I'll be doing it from now on. Do you *know* him, Mack?"

Not as much as she'd like to. She held in a little shiver.

Where did *that* thought come from? Probably from the same place that wouldn't let her forget how it felt when Dan had her pressed against the wall in the store last week. She gave as casual a shrug as she could manage.

"I've known Danny since I was in fifth grade." There was a delighted intake of breath from the cousins. "He and my brother were best friends in high school. I was four years behind them and pestered them all the time. And by *pestered*, I mean *tattled on*. They got in more trouble…"

Cathy laughed. "Oh, those two boys had more energy than brains, didn't they? Remember when they spray painted all the senior names right down the middle of Main Street before graduation? And they took the principal's car and put it out on the old pier, and everyone was afraid the pier would collapse before the police could get the car off there."

"That wasn't funny," Thea said with a frown. "That little escapade could have cost their parents a bundle. I don't know how those two didn't end up in jail…" Her voice trailed off. She looked at Mack and had the good grace to show regret, remembering one of *those two* was Mack's brother. "I mean, not that they were bad kids…"

Nora's mouth had fallen open. "Are you telling me that straight-arrow Dan—I mean *Danny*—Adams was a wild child? I don't believe it! He's so quiet and honorable and heroic. He helped save my Asher when he was in a bad place a few years ago, before we met. I mean…he's our Sheriff Dan. He's literally run into burning buildings to save people. He climbs trees to rescue kittens. He's a local legend. Our hero."

It had been enough of a shock to see Dan in uniform the other night. But a *hero*? Well, maybe that shouldn't be a shock. At heart, Dan had always been *good*. She thought of the time she'd fallen off her bike when she was twelve. She'd been bruised, bloody and in tears when she got home. Dan—who was *always* at their house—was the one who'd dried her tears, joked around until he got her to laugh and bandaged her cuts. That day was probably when her girlish crush on him really began.

But oh, he'd been wild. Much too wild for wearing a law-enforcement uniform. Yet here he was, twenty years later, the *hero* of Gallant Lake. Her chest warmed. Good for Danny. While she'd been screwing up her life, he'd been rebuilding his. And she shouldn't be doing anything to tarnish that. She reached for one of the ginger cookies Nora had set out.

"No, they *weren't* bad. They were…energetic." She heard Cathy give a soft huff of laughter. "And yes, they were rascals, but they were just kids back then." She bit into the cookie. "Just a couple of active, adventurous boys."

That was a stretch. The two of them had more than one run-in with the old police chief, Mike DiNofrio. Chief DiNofrio had developed a soft spot for Ryan and Dan for some reason. Mack realized she *still* had a soft spot for Dan. And maybe a little bit of that girlish crush, too.

"Daddy, come *on*. We'll never get to the top if we don't hurry!"

Chloe was running ahead on the path up the side of Gallant Mountain, zigzagging around trees and in and out of his view. Oh, to have that child's energy.

"I'm coming, sweetie. Daddy's a little tired today." He tried to pick up his pace, ignoring the protest from his aching body. Nothing like wrestling with some guy who outweighs you by forty pounds *and* is amped up on meth to make it clear you're getting older. Pete Malteer had taken his mom's front door right off its hinges last night. Not the screen door—the solid wood front door. The guy had been out of his mind, furious that his poor mother refused to give him any more money, knowing he'd just spend it all on drugs and booze.

When Dan responded to the call, Karen Malteer had been cowering in the garage, hiding from Pete while she called 911. Shaneka at the 911 call center kept Karen on the line until Dan pulled in. He could hear Pete inside the house, trashing the place. Idiot. No, that wasn't right. It was the drugs making Pete that way. Shaneka told him where to find Karen, and he got her safely over to the neighbor's place before returning to deal with Pete. Dan called for backup, but there'd been an accident up on Route 28 and a shooting in the southern part of the county, so everyone was busy. He was on his own.

Dan was good at talking people down, but Pete wasn't in the mood to talk. He'd taken one look at Dan in the doorway and charged. They'd landed on the sidewalk three steps below, with Dan generously absorbing Pete's impact. Because he was a good guy like that. Pete started swinging, but Dan had the advantage of *not* being higher than a kite. Pete only landed a few blows before Dan had him cuffed and cursing on the ground a few minutes later. He was paying the price today, though. His ribs were covered with bruises. So were his knuckles, because Pete wasn't the only guy who could land a punch.

A few minutes later, Chloe came back down the trail, running straight at him instead of her usual meandering. He automatically went on alert, looking for other hikers or an animal that might have startled her.

"Dad! There's a lady up there dancing in the clearing!

She's barefoot and she's *dancing*! Do you think maybe she's a fairy? Or maybe it's the ghost from Halcyon!"

Halcyon was a local landmark—an actual castle over a hundred years old. Blake and Amanda Randall lived there with their family. And yes, it was rumored to be haunted, but Dan doubted very much that a ghost was tripping the light fantastic on Gallant Mountain. His first guess? Sounded like someone high on something.

Damn it, he couldn't even enjoy a hike with his little girl without those freakin' drug dealers spoiling his day. And here he was with no gun, no radio, no nothing. Just cargo shorts, a T-shirt and sneakers. And his daughter. Dan hesitated, considering whether to go forward or get Chloe back to the car. If it *was* someone high, they could easily tumble over the ledge and fall several hundred feet down the side of the mountain. Or they could put another hiker in danger.

"Okay, Chloe. We'll go check out your dancer. But you have to promise to stay right with me, okay? And don't say a word until I know it's safe."

Chloe rolled her eyes dramatically, hands on her hips. "Dad, it's just a dancing lady. Of course it's safe."

He felt a sharp regret that his little girl would someday have to know that people were seldom "just" anything, and were too often *not* safe. As a cop, it had always been a tough balancing act for him to maintain—seeing the worst of people on the job and trying to shield Chloe from that when he was home.

"You're probably right, but humor me, okay?" She nodded and followed him up the path. He'd explained more than once that sometimes she and her mom just had to let him be who he was—a man determined to keep them safe, even if it meant he worried too much. Chloe had accepted it more readily than Susanne, who didn't like him scaring Chloe with the way he acted.

The clearing just below the famous Kissing Rock near the top of Gallant Mountain was about an acre. Dan suspected someone had cleared it decades ago, but local lore said the grassy plot was a natural little oasis in the middle of the forest. It was anchored on one end by the legendary bus-size boulder and at the other end by a sharp drop-off with a spectacular view of Gallant Lake and the Catskill Mountains. It was privately owned, but the no-trespassing signs meant nothing to locals who'd been coming up here for generations to make out on the famous Kissing Rock.

Not that Dan would ever ignore the signs. He had explicit permission from the owner, Blake Randall, who owned much of the mountain these days. Blake had bought up a ton of property around the lake a few years ago to protect it from development, and he'd held on to the mountain land.

Dan could see the clearing just ahead, and Chloe was tugging his hand to get him to hurry. Knowing he wanted her to be quiet, she whispered, but in a voice that probably carried halfway up the mountain.

"See, Daddy? See the dancing lady?"

He stopped at the edge of the woods, figuring he could tuck Chloe behind a tree if there was trouble. But he hadn't anticipated *this* kind of trouble.

Mackenzie Wallace was twirling in the center of the clearing, blond hair swinging. She was wearing jeans and a dark blue shirt advertising Nora's coffee shop, the Gallant Brew. And her feet were indeed bare. With fire engine–red polish on her toes. She had earphones on—he could see the bright pink cord leading from her ears to her back pocket. Whatever music she was listening to had made her completely uninhibited. Her hands were up in the air, her eyes were closed and she was lost in herself and in the moment. She swung her arms out and spun again, then started jumping to the beat of the silent song. The sight made his chest go tight. She was beautiful, and it had nothing to do with physical appearance. It was her *spirit*—she was beautiful in her freedom.

Dan felt as though he was intruding on something important. Something deeply personal. As much as he wanted to know what she was doing barefoot in a clearing that was just showing the bright greens of spring, he didn't want to intrude on her moment. He should walk away. But his feet were rooted to the ground as securely as the trees around him. Chloe's attention span was substantially shorter than his, though, and she forgot to even try to whisper.

"See, Dad? I *told* you it was a barefoot lady dancing on the mountain! Isn't she pretty? Can we dance, too?" Chloe's high voice must have broken through whatever music was playing in Mack's ears, because she stopped dancing and started looking around. She froze when she saw them, then squinted. Dan realized they were in the tree shadows and might look threatening, so he stepped into the sunlight.

"*Dan?* What are you doing…?" She yanked the ear pods out and stared, her mouth falling open but no more words coming out.

His smile was automatic. That seemed to be how it worked around her. "I think the bigger question is what are *you* doing? Having a little *Sound of Music* moment up here, Mack?"

Her face went bright red, and she quickly ran her hands over her hair, pushing it back over her shoulders. "I… I'm… hiking. It's been a long time since I saw the Kissing Rock, so…"

His right brow shot up. "So you figured you'd celebrate the occasion with an interpretive dance?"

Mack's laughter was quick and full. "Yup. That's it. You caught me honoring the mountain gods." Her head tipped to the side. "Is that not still the tradition?"

"The tradition these days is for people to honor the no-trespassing signs on the trail." He was still smiling, so she didn't even pretend to take him seriously as she walked their way.

"Looks like I'm not the only one breaking the rules, Officer." Chloe giggled at Mack's observation. Mack looked down at her and grinned. "*And* you're corrupting the town's youth. Who is this pretty lady?"

Chloe jumped forward, her hand extended. "I'm Chloe and this is my dad. Why are you barefoot? Why were you dancing? Do you live here? Are you the ghost?"

Mack's eyes went wide at the barrage of questions, then she gave Dan a quick wink before answering.

"I'm Mackenzie Wallace, but you can call me Mack. I grew up here a long…" She glanced up at Dan. "…*long* time ago. I'm definitely not a ghost. I'm dancing because Whitney Houston was telling me she needed to dance with somebody, and I figured I'm somebody, right?" Chloe nodded enthusiastically in agreement.

But there was one question left unanswered. Dan gestured to her feet. "And where are your shoes, dancing queen?"

Mack's face twisted. "Those weren't shoes. They were torture devices." She held up one foot to expose the ugly, open blister just below her ankle. "The other foot is just as bad. I couldn't take one more step in those things once I got up here."

"Let me guess," Dan said with a chuckle. "You decided

to hike up the mountain in those heavy boots you just bought this week."

"Well, I wore them around the shop for a few days to break them in."

"Because you do so much walking in a liquor store. What did you wear for socks, Mack?"

"Um…my gym socks. You know, tighty-whities?"

He closed his eyes tightly. "That is *not* what tighty-whities are. And those socks are no match for a mountain and a brand-new pair of hiking boots. Where are they now?"

Chloe raised her hand to get their attention. "Wait. Do you guys *know* each other? Daddy, do you know Mack? Did you arrest her or something?"

Mack started laughing again. The sound of her laughter, so deep and free, did something weird to Dan's chest cavity. It resonated there and made him relax somehow. Mack leaned over to face Chloe.

"Actually, your daddy *did* try to arrest me, but it was a misunderstanding. We've known each other a long time. Since I was a little girl not much older than you are, I'm guessing. Are you ten? Twelve?"

Chloe straightened, looking very pleased at those guesses. "I'm *eight*, but I'll be nine in November. What was my daddy like as a kid?"

Mack's eyes flickered up to his face, and she must have noted his tension. Chloe was bound to hear stories of Dan's misspent youth eventually. But not today. Mack flashed him another wink.

"Your daddy was my big brother's best friend, and they did a lot of…fun…things when they were boys. How about you? What do *you* like to do for fun?"

As easily distracted as ever, Chloe launched into a list

of all the things she liked to do. Mack seemed to be listening closely, and Dan appreciated that she didn't talk down to Chloe or treat her as less than a person. He'd dated a few women who seemed to see his daughter as an unfortunate intrusion on their time. Dan followed the two females walking hand in hand toward the Kissing Rock at the base of the mountain peak. Didn't really need to be thinking about *dating* and *Mackenzie* in the same breath. That was a nonstarter for a couple of reasons. But most importantly for how their pasts were tragically entwined.

She'd never blamed him for Ryan's accident, probably because she didn't know—or forgot—that he was the one who'd stolen the gin they were drinking that night. Maybe she'd forgotten his involvement. But Dan never would.

Chapter 5

Mack smiled at the sight of Chloe's small hand in hers as they walked. The little girl had short brown hair just a shade darker than Dan's and wide brown eyes full of interest and energy. She reminded her of Dan's and Ryan's restlessness that always seemed to lead them to trouble. But Chloe seemed to have plenty of positive outlets for that energy, from all the things she was listing as her favorite things to do. Maybe if Ryan and Dan had had those kinds of outlets as kids, they wouldn't have been so bored and drawn to mischief.

"…and I take dance class and piano lessons and I play soccer and I like to ride my bike…"

It was mortifying that Dan Adams had caught her dancing all by herself up here. She hadn't been able to resist, though, especially once she'd kicked those god-awful boots off at the base of the Kissing Rock, vowing to never wear them again. The newly grown grass had felt so cool and soft under her feet.

"…and I like to read! I'm reading a book about a girl who builds a submarine…"

Mack hadn't even made it halfway up the mountain path earlier before she knew those boots were a mistake. It started as an irritating burn, but once the blisters broke, every step was painful. She'd been in tears when she reached the clearing, and she'd immediately plopped down in the grass and pulled off the boots and the cheap socks that had wadded themselves around the arches of her feet.

Then she'd stood in her bare feet and took a step toward the vista of Gallant Lake and rows of blue-tinged mountains marching off into the distance. The dirt and the grass and the wildflowers were cool and soft under her feet. Running around without shoes wasn't something she'd done as a child, any more than climbing a mountain was. She'd been a good girl who wore nice clothes and didn't get into trouble. But her good girl days were over, and she was barefoot on a mountainside on an early-May morning. It felt amazing. Freeing. Exciting. When Whitney's song came up on her playlist, there was nothing else to do but dance.

"…and I like to make jewelry with beads and string, but Mom says I just make a mess. I only knocked over the tray of beads one time, but boy, was she mad. I'll make you a bracelet if you want one, but I'll have to do it at Dad's house. What color would you like?"

It took Mack a second to realize Chloe had stopped for a breath and was waiting for an answer.

"I'm sorry, honey…what am I picking a color for?"

Chloe raised her arm straight up, pointing to the beaded and knotted purple bracelet she wore. "A *bracelet*, silly! *My* favorite color is purple, but you can pick a different color as long I have beads in that color. And I have a lot of beads…"

Dan put his hands on his daughter's shoulders. "I knew letting you have those chocolate caramel pancakes at the diner this morning was a mistake. Why don't you go burn off that sugar high by picking some wildflowers for Mack? See how many different kinds you can find. Just stay away from the cliff."

Chloe took off like she was shot from a cannon, making Mack laugh.

"The apple didn't fall far from the tree with that one. She's as restless as a teenage boy I used to know." She met Dan's gaze. "She's adorable."

Dan looked back at his little girl, darting around the mountainside. Mack could hardly believe Dan was really a *dad*.

"Yeah, I think I'll keep her," he said. "Now, where are those boots? You can't go back down the trail in your bare feet."

"Actually, that's exactly what I plan on doing. There is no way I'm shoving my feet back in those torture devices." She walked over to where she'd thrown them, along with the fancy telescoping walking stick, and handed them to Dan. "Ever again."

He studied her for a moment, his face serious. "What are you doing, Mack? What's with the hiking boots and the biking helmet and the kayak paddle? You were never one for the great outdoors, unless maybe you were playing tennis or snow skiing down the bunny hill, and now I find you *dancing* on Gallant Mountain. Barefoot! I didn't think you even knew about the Kissing Rock or the old trail."

"Oh, please." She waved her hand. "Just because I was too much of a Goody Two-shoes to walk up here, didn't mean I hadn't *heard* about it. It was the most infamous make-out place in town, except maybe for Gilford's Ridge and the old ski place on the other side of the lake. Is that still open?" He shook his head in the negative, and she frowned. "That's a shame. I don't know how you heard about the biking or the kayaking—which I haven't done yet—but I *did* tell you I was turning over a new leaf. Anything old Mackenzie wouldn't do, *I'm* doing. And I started with Gallant Mountain." She held up one foot and wiggled her toes. "And dancing barefoot. Which was unplanned, but also un-Mackenzie-like. So that gets bonus points."

Dan glanced toward Chloe, who was staying a safe distance away from the cliff edge, running in and out of the trees on the edge of the opening with a fistful of flowers in her hand. He looked back to Mack, his brows bunched together.

"I don't think you've told me what exactly was wrong with the *old* Mackenzie." He sat on a smaller boulder at the base of the cliff and patted the stone for her to join him there. "I kinda liked her, except when she squealed on my best friend and me."

"Oh please," Mack scoffed as she sat. "You didn't know her… I mean…me. You and Ryan were off doing your thing and barely knew I existed. No one knew I existed back then, except my teachers and the church ladies and Mom. I made them all so proud…" Her voice trailed off. Approval had practically been an obsession back then. Having people see her as the opposite of Ryan. Having people tell her parents they were lucky to have such a good, sweet child as Mackenzie. The more she'd heard it, the more she'd believed it, and the more determined she was to meet those expectations that everyone placed on her. "You might think it was easy being Gallant Lake's sweetheart, but it wasn't, Dan. It was hard, and it messed me up."

"Messed you up how?"

She sighed, leaning back against the rock wall behind her and closing her eyes. The air was sharp and clear up here, and it felt good in her lungs. She inhaled deeply and imagined it cleaning away the past few years. Her thoughts drifted to Greenwich. The way everyone watched her perform her perfect-wife act for years. The cool admiration in their eyes until she flipped the script and told them all what she really thought of their little games.

"Mack? What happened to you after you left Gallant Lake?" Dan's voice was firmer now, and she opened her eyes to find him leaning toward her in worry.

"*Nothing* happened. That's the point. For years and years, not one damn thing happened in my life that meant anything. And I'm ready for something to *mean* something, Dan. Hell, even these blisters *mean* something. They mean I *did* something. I *felt* something. You have no idea what a big deal that is to me right now. How much I need it." Her fervency surprised her as much as it did him. It was the first time she'd really articulated those feelings out loud since her divorce from Mason. Another milestone. She bumped her shoulder against him. "You told me you're not Danger Dan anymore. That's too bad, because I'm going to give Danger Mack a try."

Dan leaned back next to her. She didn't miss the way his eyes quickly found his daughter before he relaxed. "A couple of blisters don't exactly make you dangerous. If they make you happy, fine. But I can't let you walk down the trail in your bare feet. That's just begging for tick bites and open cuts that could get infected. It's bad enough you've got those blisters to worry about. We don't need you *and* your dad laid up right now." He reached into her boots and pulled out her sweaty white socks. "Let me tie these *tighty-whities* over the blisters to protect them, then you can wear the boots as far as your car."

"Wow. You went from Danger Dan to Captain Responsibility. Impressive. And dull."

He glared at the ground in silence. Before Mack could ask what was bothering him, Chloe ran up, breathless and clutching a handful of flowers. "Here, Mack! I found eight different kinds of flowers and two types of grass. Does that count? Aren't they pretty? Have you picked a color for your bracelet yet?"

"If I remember correctly," Dan started, "Mack's favorite color used to be mint green or anything pastel. That's all she used to wear."

Chloe grinned widely enough for Mack to see she'd recently lost a tooth. "I have pastel colors! Grandma Buckley asked for a bracelet like that. I'll just make two!"

Terrific. Mack and Grandma liked the same colors. She narrowed her eyes when she heard Dan's choked laughter. He wouldn't look up, concentrating *very* hard on wrapping her ankles and sliding those infernal boots on her feet. He wasn't wrong. She'd been the queen of buttery-yellow sweater sets and powder-blue skirts. She carried her tendency for soft, safe, ladylike colors to Greenwich, too, with a few touches of classic black for trips to New York. But to get the same color as Chloe's *grandmother*? Nope. She took the flowers from Chloe and pointed to the girl's sparkly bracelet.

"Actually, Chloe, that's not true anymore." Mack glanced at Dan before smiling at his daughter. "My favorite color these days is the same as yours—purple! Can you do that? A bright purple glittery bracelet?"

"Oh, yes! I have new glitter beads that will be perfect! Daddy, can I make Mack's bracelet at your house?"

Dan's eyes were on Mack. "Sure, baby. Make it as big and bright as you want. Because apparently I don't know Mack as well as I thought."

Mack dipped her head in acknowledgment of his confession. She was no longer a woman of pastel good behavior. And Dan was no longer a guy looking for danger. She couldn't help thinking that was a pity. She was going to be in Gallant Lake awhile—forever if Dad had *his* way—and Danger Dan would have been a fun diversion. But Dudley Do-Right Dan? Not as tempting. Or so she kept telling herself.

Mack stared at the doctor in shock. "Six *weeks*?"

The doctor, who seemed barely old enough for medical school, much less practicing medicine, nodded with a bright smile, as if having no idea what his words were doing to her. She'd figured Dad would be home in a week or two. Hobbling around on crutches, maybe, but home, so she'd be free to figure out *her* life. But now he was having *surgery*?

"Yes, Miss Wallace…"

Dad interrupted with a grumble. "It's Mrs. Burns."

"Actually, Dad…" She gave him a warning look. "It's not anymore. You should be *happy* I took your name back." It was frustrating that her own father refused to accept her divorce. He was still in the *Did you try hard enough?* phase. But then again, Dad had no idea what Mason had done. She looked back to the young doctor, determined to focus on the present, not the past. "You're saying he can't put weight on that foot for six weeks? Not even…?"

The young doctor knew how to scowl. "No weight *whatsoever*. Not a single step. That tendon was hanging on by a thread, and if we don't give yesterday's surgery time to take, it won't heal at all. And there are very few options at this point if it doesn't." He brightened. "But we'll give Carl a scooter to use so he'll still be mobile."

"But his apartment is upstairs." She turned to her father. "Did you *know* this, Dad?"

He was sitting up in his hospital bed. Even in his pea-green hospital gown, he looked surprisingly robust and completely unconcerned at the prospect of not being able to access his home of thirty years. He gave a sharp nod.

"It's okay, Doc. We'll figure something out."

"We *will*?" she asked after the doctor left them alone in the room. "You say that like you have a solution in mind, but I'll be damned if I can see one."

Her father gave her a sharp look. "Watch your language, young lady. And yes, I have options, but I need to talk to some folks first. How's the store doing? Is Bert covering enough hours for you? What were your numbers for last week?"

She followed his lead and talked business until it was time for her to go, but the whole time she was wondering where Dad was going to live. She looked at the hulking shape of Gallant Mountain looming over the town as she parked behind the store. Despite her worries, it made her smile.

Hiking had been fun last weekend, but the blisters *still* hadn't healed, and her feet were too tender to wear those damn boots for a while, even with the extrathick wool socks Dan had dropped off for her yesterday. He'd had a good laugh when he walked into the store and saw her soaking-wet hair and foul mood. She'd discovered shortly before his arrival that kayaking was *not* going to be one of her adventures.

Nate Thomas had loaned her a small kayak and tried to show her how to use it shortly before Dan showed up, but she and kayaks just didn't get along. Maybe it was a balance thing, but she'd wobbled and shaken so much that she couldn't manage to stay upright. And when the kayak flipped, she'd panicked every time. It wasn't the water as much as her claustrophobia—being upside down in the lake while strapped into a vessel determined to hold her there. Nate was a patient soul, but even *he* suggested she might want to try another hobby.

So this weekend, she was going to take her brand-new bicycle and she was going to hit the roads. It wasn't a mountain bike, but she figured one step at a time. Besides, it would help her get in shape, and biking was something she hadn't done much as a little girl. Her bike had been for riding back and forth to school or over to her friend Shelly Graber's to do homework when they were twelve. So pedaling through the hills around town would be fun and at least a *little* adventurous.

She had Shelly Graber—now Shelly Markson—on her mind this week. Shelly had actually walked into the liquor store the other day. Mack wanted to hide behind the counter. She'd left Shelly in the dust back then after Ryan's accident. Things had been chaotic at home, and Mack had started down her path of people pleasing. Or parent pleasing. And teacher pleasing. Not so much friend pleasing. Friends couldn't get her into college and out of the little town that was suffocating her.

But she didn't hide. She'd looked her onetime best friend in the eye and asked her how she could help. Shelly hadn't changed much. Tall, athletic and devil-may-care, wearing jeans and a Gallant Lake sweatshirt, with her long brown hair tucked into a ball cap. Shelly laughed at Mack's expression and asked for two bottles of Mack's best cheap wine. Then she'd invited Mack to join her and her friends at the Chalet. Mack stared in stunned silence at the question until Shelly set the bottles down on one of the café tables and gave her a warm embrace. She said of *course* she'd forgiven Mack for ghosting her all those years ago. Shelly reminded Mack that neither of them were in high school anymore. She told Mack about her four children—four!—and invited Mack to country music night at the Chalet.

She said her older brother might join them for a drink. Mack remembered Owen Graber as a handsome boy who always had an easy smile and a mischievous gleam in his eye. Owen had been part of Ryan and Danny's wild bunch, but Shelly said he was settling down after sowing many years' worth of wild oats, including a short stint in jail a few years back. Shelly warned that Friday-night crowds could get a little rowdy, but Mack waved off her concern. Rowdy was definitely *not* Old Mack's style. Neither were ex-cons. Her heart beat a little faster. Maybe Owen was just the bad boy she needed right now. Maybe Owen's company would keep her from wondering what Danny Adams was up to on a Friday night.

Chapter 6

"Why are we doing this again?" Dan asked as Asher parked at the Chalet. "Like I don't see enough drunks when I'm on the job, you're bringing me to a *bar* on my first full weekend off in ages? Besides, it's late. Why can't we just drink at your shop like we used to...?"

"Whah, whah, whah." Asher slammed his car door. "Will you stop whining? You're not having your wisdom teeth extracted, for Chrissakes. You're going out for a drink to celebrate your friend's engagement. I'm pretty sure it won't kill you." They started walking across the lot. Asher looked over at Dan, then shook his head. "And the only reason we're late is because you were dragging your feet trying to beg off. You used to rag on me about becoming a hermit, but look at *you*. When's the last time you had social interaction with someone that didn't involve hand-cuffs, Sheriff Dan?"

Dan thought about Mackenzie dancing on the mountain

last weekend. Mack didn't seem terribly impressed with his status as Sheriff Dan, Hero of Gallant Lake. Maybe she hadn't heard the wondrous—and often exaggerated—tales of his derring-do. The truth was, he'd never been that comfortable with the title, and he resented the pressure it put on him. The folks new to town knew him as the lawman. A benevolent good guy keeping them safe. And the folks who'd lived here awhile looked at him as the bad boy who'd turned his life around. Both versions of the story ended up with him on some sort of pedestal, and that was a very narrow place to build a life.

When Asher opened the door to the Chalet, noise poured out—laughter, shouting, music, glasses clinking together. A typical Friday night at a townie bar, and the partying was in full swing. It was too late to turn back now.

Shane Brannigan and Nate Thomas were drinking at a booth by the windows. Shane, a sports agent, was married to Melanie, the owner of the upscale boutique in town who was helping Chloe pick out a dress for that gala. Dan spotted Blake Randall at the bar. The owner of the Gallant Lake Resort, with two restaurants of its own, didn't spend a lot of time hanging out at the Chalet. But his wife, Amanda, had insisted that he and the guys celebrate Nick West's engagement to Cassie Zetticci somewhere other than the resort where Nick and Blake worked.

The man of the hour, Nick, was standing next to Blake, accepting well wishes from the crowd. Nick had come to town the previous summer as Blake's director of security. He'd been a police detective in LA before making the move, and he and Dan had become good friends.

Nick saw Dan standing there and waved him over as Asher moved on to the booth. "Hey, look, it's Sheriff Dan in the flesh!" Nick announced loudly. "Let me buy you a beer, Dan-o."

Dan hated that name, but Nick had clearly had a few beers already, so he let it slide. He accepted the beer and shook Nick's hand.

"Stop reminding everyone of my profession tonight—it's a buzzkill." He clapped Nick on the back. "Congratulations, man. Have you and Cassie set a date?"

Nick shook his head. "I've promised to show up at the appointed time, but the rest of the details are up to her." He took a long swig of his beer. Nick was lean and tough—a rock climber and white-water kayaker. Blake's build was broader and taller. And he had that air of being in charge, even leaning on the bar at the Chalet. Blake bumped Nick's shoulder.

"How is it that I know more about your nuptials than you do? You're getting married in September. At Halcyon. On the veranda if the weather's nice. Inside if it's not. The women are all over it."

"Nice." Nick raised his glass, which seemed to have magically refilled itself. "Married in a castle. Who'd have thunk it? Come on, let's get back to Shane and Nate." Nick wavered on his feet, making Dan wonder A—how much had he had to drink? And B—who was driving this crew home? As if reading his mind, Nick gave him a lopsided grin. "Relax, Officer. Shane's our designated driver tonight." They approached the table. "See? He's drinking soda. Or something. What the hell *are* you drinking?"

Shane lifted his glass of ruby liquid. "Cranberry juice. You'd think I'd be sick of it by now, with Mel wanting nothing but for the past month or so, but my pregnant wife has me hooked on the stuff. Although I'll admit, I generally add lots of vodka to mine at home. But not tonight."

He drained half the glass and sighed. "Tonight I'm sober. I promise, Sheriff Dan."

"Christ, will everyone stop calling me that?" Dan sat down with a growl. He glared at Asher. "*This* is why I don't go out. Between everyone calling me Sheriff Dan like I'm some kind of cartoon character and then not being able to get respectably drunk in the same town I'm supposed to be protecting." His glass of beer was still distressingly full. He'd be nursing that one all night, or at least until he got home to have a whiskey—or three—in private.

"Yikes." Shane laughed. "I thought my *wife* was hormonal. What's got *you* in such a twist?"

Asher chuckled. "More like *who* has him in a twist. A ghost from his past has him shook."

Nick set his glass down, his smile fading. "What kind of ghost? Someone you arrested?"

"No," Asher replied, more than happy to speak for Dan. "A *lady* ghost. Carl Wallace's daughter is here to help run the liquor store while he's laid up." Asher gave Dan a speculative look. "And it turns out our buddy Dan went to *school* with Mackenzie Wallace."

Nate Thomas's head bobbed up and down. "We *all* went to school together, but she was a few years behind…" He snapped his fingers. "That's right—you and her brother, Ryan, were best buds! It was you two who tore up the football field doing doughnuts with your dirt bikes, right? Hey, did you know she's…"

"Wait…" Blake held up his hand. "*Sheriff Dan* got in trouble in school? Please, tell us more!"

Nate interrupted. "Dan, she's h—"

Asher jumped in. He knew about Dan's past and knew why Dan didn't want to talk about it. "What are we, a bunch of gossiping old women? We *all* had adventures in high school. And I imagine we all had some girl we'd like to see again..." He glanced at Dan. "Or not. So give the guy a break. Nate, how's business been?"

Music swirled around them. Country wasn't Dan's thing, but judging from the crowded dance floor, people were into it. There was a lot of hooting and hollering involved, which meant Nate had to practically yell to be heard.

"Business sucks, as usual lately. But Mackenzie..."

Asher tried again to distract Nate. "And that stupid parrot of yours—how's he doing?" Nate's parrot, Hank, was a minor tourist attraction. He lived in a large cage in the hardware store and liked to swear. A lot.

"Still likes to curse a blue streak." Nate shrugged. "Might be why business is so bad, but what can I do?" He leaned toward Dan. "She's here."

"Who's here? Your *parrot*?" Nick looked around, as if Nate would actually bring Hank to a bar like some pirate.

"No, you idiot." Nate looked straight at Dan. "Mackenzie Wallace. She's over on the other side of the bar, with Shelly Markson and Kiara Kelsoe. Shelly's brother was over there, too."

Dan went very still. Mack was *here*? With Owen Graber? Christ, he knew she wanted to find her adventurous side, but hanging out with Owen Graber wasn't a great idea. His friends moved on to discussing baseball, which was normally a conversation Dan would gladly be a part of. But he couldn't focus on anything other than Mack being in the bar. With Owen.

Back in high school, Owen had been part of their group of troublemakers. Outsiders on the far edge of polite society. Punks thinking they were clever rebels of some kind. They'd never met a rule they didn't want to break, and Dan really couldn't remember why, or what the point was. Attention? Danger? Fun? For him it was probably just an escape from his parents' divorce and all the tension at home. His father was angry and distant, and often drunk. Dan's friends became his family, even if they were often drunk, too.

Dan outgrew his rebel phase in the span of one awful night, when Ryan Wallace wrapped his car around a tree and Braden Michaels died. It could have been him. He was supposed to be with them. More than once he'd thought it *should* have been him. He'd decided after that night, with a little tough love from Chief DiNofrio, that he was done with the whole criminal-in-training routine.

But Owen hadn't learned his lesson nearly as fast. He'd bounced around from job to job, living with his parents, getting high every weekend, playing video games in the basement. Then he was arrested in White Plains for possession, but Owen always insisted it was a setup. The only reason Owen hadn't done serious time was because the detective screwed up the chain of custody and the case got tossed. Because of that arrest, Owen was one of the names on Dan's short list of suspects for being involved with the recent influx of opioids.

Mack said she wanted a walk on the wild side, but Dan didn't think she wanted to get quite *that* wild. He stood, getting the attention of his friends. He flipped his thumb toward the back of the bar, where the restrooms were. But that's not where he went.

He walked around the bar to the group of tables on the other side. It didn't take long to find Mack. Her golden hair was loose and full, catching the lights from the dance floor. She was in jeans, with a snug black knit top cut just low enough to be interesting. She and Shelly were laughing at something Kiara was saying. And sitting there, with his arm over the back of Mack's chair, was Owen.

Dan wasn't sure what this emotion was flaring up inside of him or where it was coming from. He only knew his fingers curled and his pace picked up as he headed to their table. Was it knowing Owen's shady past that bothered him? Or was it the way Owen was leaning toward Mack, his fingers touching the back of her neck? Whatever it was, it had Dan burning inside.

Mack sensed Dan's presence before she saw him. She was laughing with Shelly, and just like that, she knew Dan was there. They'd just sat down from dancing to a bunch of pounding songs about bonfires and girls dancing in pickup trucks, and Mack had drained her frosty glass of beer. So *not* a country club thing to do. They were laughing at some of the lyrics when she lifted her hair away from her neck to cool off. Owen reached over to "help," and she didn't miss the way his fingers lingered on her skin. He'd been flirting lightly all night, but she had a hunch his heart wasn't in it. He was smooth, but it felt like he was on autopilot. Still, it was fun to be on the receiving end of a man's attention.

She looked up and looked straight into Dan's eyes as he rounded the bar. He was wearing well-worn jeans and a plaid shirt with the sleeves rolled up. And a scowl. What was *that* about?

Giddy from alcohol and adrenaline from all the dancing, Mack jumped to her feet and threw her arms around Dan's neck, surprising everyone including herself. "Danny! What are you doing here? Pull up a chair! We've got a big head start on you, so you have a *lot* of catching up to do, mister."

As she heard the heightened pitch of her voice, Mack knew she'd had too much to drink. But the bar was hot and the beer was cold and had gone down much too easily. Dan set his hands lightly on her waist, his scowl deepening. "I think you might be too far gone for me to catch up, Mackenzie. How many have you had?" She just shrugged, because she wasn't really sure anymore. She smacked his shoulder playfully.

"I'm a big girl, Danny. I don't need some guy with a badge watching out for me."

Dan tensed, his eyes growing hard. "I'm more than a guy with a badge, Mackie."

Was he? She'd yet to see it. Even with his daughter on Gallant Mountain, he'd been cautious and protective. The ultimate good guy. The opposite of what she was looking for. His eyes were darting around the room, as if he was casing the place, looking for trouble so he could rush in and prevent it. A pretty young waitress came over to take Dan's order. He looked at the pitcher of beer on the table and ordered a cola. *Ugh.* Even on a Friday night, he was still Mr. Straight Arrow. Dan's expression cooled even more when Owen stood to hold a chair out for Mack. Was he...*jealous?* Dan grabbed a chair from a neighboring table and slid it close to Mack as she sat down between them.

She pretended to fan herself. "Is it just me or is there a lot of testosterone in the air all of a sudden?"

Shelly giggled. "I should get a pic of this. It's like you have a devil on one shoulder and an angel on the other."

Owen laughed. "And which is which?"

He was just as good-looking as ever, with auburn hair falling across his forehead and a wicked, fun-loving glint in his brown eyes. Looking for laughs, just like in high school. He'd been cracking jokes and buying drinks all night. But, like Dan, he was drinking cola. Kiara, whom Mack had never really known that well, had filled her in earlier that evening on Owen's brush with the law. Kiara told it as a cautionary tale, warning Mack that a lot of people thought Owen was trouble. Which was interesting, because Kiara, with her skinny purple braids pulled high on her head and looking like an African queen, hadn't taken her eyes off him all night. Maybe that was why Dan was all bristly and broody at her side. The lawman versus the lawbreaker.

Mack pretended to consider Owen's question. "Well, you were both devils in high school, but now? I guess I'd need to do more research with each of you to know for sure."

Dan was silent, while Owen just laughed harder, resting his hand on her shoulder. Kiara's face fell just enough to confirm Mack's suspicion that the woman had a mad crush on Owen. Owen's shady past didn't bother Kiara one bit. Owen was either completely clueless or was willfully ignoring Kiara's attraction to him. He was treating Kiara the same as his sister—teasing and…brotherly. Kiara hadn't exactly been welcoming to Mack, but she still felt a stab of pity for her.

Shelly asked Dan about his daughter, which seemed to cool some of the edginess he'd brought to the table. The two of them settled into a conversation about something happening at school. Kiara wagged her eyebrows, looking between Dan and Mack, and Mack shook her head. It would be convenient for Kiara if there was something between Mack and Dan, but it wasn't going to happen. Mack had already lost her trophy husband and all her so-called friends in Connecticut. She didn't dare set her sights on Gallant Lake's local hero. Kiara gave up, then put her hand on Owen's arm and laughed loudly at something he said about the pitcher being empty again.

Mack couldn't remember the last time she'd hung out with friends and shared laughs over a pitcher of beer like this. She sighed. There was a good reason for that—she'd *never* hung out at a bar, drinking beer with friends. Good girls didn't do that. Good girls sipped martinis while squeezed into torturous support garments under their cocktail dresses at parties where a sense of competition lay just under the surface. Who was skinnier? Who had the newest fashion? The most expensive jewelry? The most successful husband? The most interesting lover?

How in the world had fun-loving ten-year-old Mackenzie Wallace, with her pigtails and scuffed-up sneakers, turned into a country club diva? It was a long, gradual descent into living a lie, but she hoped the path back to finding herself wouldn't take nearly as long. And she was determined to make it as interesting a journey as possible. And one without making new enemies. She grabbed Kiara's hand when another fast tune started blasting over the sound system. Kiara hesitated, then nodded and stood. Mack leaned forward when they got to the dance floor and winked.

"Don't worry, I'm not interested in Owen."

Kiara's eyes went wide. "Why are you telling *me*? He's not my guy."

"But you'd like him to be."

Kiara stopped moving and almost got knocked off her feet by some guy behind her. She moved closer to Mack and started dancing again. "Is it that obvious?"

"Well, I don't think *he* has a clue, but yeah, I could see it. Have you told him?"

"No way. We've been friends forever, and I don't want to screw that up." Kiara's eyes clouded. "Besides, it's strictly one-sided." Mack couldn't argue, since Owen had been paying more attention to Mack all night. Kiara glanced over at their table. "Why do you care, anyway?"

Mack missed a step. "Ouch. Why wouldn't I?"

The volume rose on the pounding song they were dancing to, and someone in the crowd whooped, making everyone around him laugh. Mack had to lean in to hear Kiara's answer.

"I don't know," Kiara said, glancing away. Then she looked straight at Mack. "You were kind of a bitch in high school. You acted like you were too good for Gallant Lake or anyone who lived here. Everyone called you the ice queen."

Mack's face felt like it was going up in flames. "I know. I had a lot going on at home, and..." She spread her hands and lifted her shoulders. "I was trying to be the perfect kid. Instead of being a happy kid. Or a nice kid. I'm sorry if I ever treated you bad."

Kiara didn't answer. They kept dancing, but the song soon ended. They headed back to the table, but Kiara stopped Mack at the edge of the dance floor.

"Nothing specific happened with us, but everyone said you were a stuck-up snob." Then Kiara smiled and bumped her shoulder. "You seem cool enough now."

It wasn't exactly a ringing endorsement, but at least it left room for hope. And maybe friendship. If she stayed around for any length of time, Mack would definitely be making more apologies like this. She'd left Gallant Lake after high school in a self-important blaze of glory, doing all but writing the words "See ya, suckers!" on the back of her car. People weren't likely to forget stuff like that, even if it was twenty years ago.

Kiara tipped her head toward the table. "What about you and Dan? Did I pick up on some chemistry there?"

"No, thanks. He's too... I don't know... Mr. Lawman these days. Maybe if he was still the Danny Adams we knew in school..."

Mack's gaze met Dan's as they approached the table, and he gave her a quizzical smile. Kiara was trying to say something, but the music was too loud. They moved closer.

"That bad boy might still be in there. You just have to coax him out!"

"And how do you suggest I do that?"

"Dance with the man!"

Dance with him?

Mackenzie hadn't danced with a man in a long time. Mason would never risk looking foolish dancing to a fast song. He'd told her he couldn't afford to have someone video him and embarrass him with his investors, as if his dancing was really memorable. It wasn't. He'd occasionally oblige her with a slow dance, but in the last few years of their marriage, it had never felt like he was *there*. Even with her in his arms, his mind seemed elsewhere.

Kiara was saying something else, and Mack leaned in and turned her head to try to hear her. Her gaze landed on Dan again. He was looking straight at her. Again. They were almost at the table, and Kiara's voice dropped.

"...hasn't taken his eyes off you. I think you should dance with the guy and see what a little body contact does!"

As enticing as *a little body contact* sounded, it was a bad idea. If she really wanted to move forward and start fresh, dancing with her high school crush wasn't the way to do it. Especially since he'd turned into Captain Responsibility. She wanted an adventure with someone who wasn't afraid to break a few rules, and that wasn't Danny Adams.

Dan leaped to his feet to hold Mack's chair, and Owen scrambled to match his chivalry by holding Kiara's. Then Owen refilled Mack's glass of beer from the new pitcher, smirking at Dan as if he'd just won extra points in some competition. Dan glowered in return. If Kiara wasn't so into Owen, Mack might have flirted back more aggressively, just to see where it might lead. And what Dan would have done. She frowned. All her thoughts seemed to circle back to him.

"How many have you had again?" Dan's brow arched as she took a drink. She set the glass down and met his gaze, refusing to be intimidated.

"I don't see where that's any of your concern, Officer." Mack pulled her hair up and pressed her cool, damp napkin on the back of her neck. "I'm not driving, so put your badge away."

He scowled. "I'm not flashing a damn badge. I'm asking as a friend."

"Is that what you are? A friend?"

"What else would I be?"

They stared at each other in silence, although the din of the bar was pounding around them. People talking, shouting, laughing. Music throbbed, acting as the drumbeat beneath the action. With a start, Mack realized she was starting to lean closer to Dan. *Don't mess with the local lawman, remember?*

"Would you excuse me for a minute?" She stood, and Dan leaped to his feet again to hold her chair. Mack needed to do two things—visit the ladies' room and put some space between her and Danger Dan. She'd felt slightly off balance from the moment he walked over to their table, and she didn't think it was all due to the beer.

She was mortified at her appearance in the ladies' room mirror. Her hair was wild, her face was shimmering with sweat and her eyes were bright. Too bright.

She put a cold, wet paper towel on her face and ran wet fingers through her hair to settle it down. When she came back out into the bar, Dan stood again. He sure was Mr.

Manners tonight. But there was a heat there in his eyes that made her wonder if Kiara was right. If Danger Dan might still be in there.

In an unplanned act of bravado, she grabbed Dan by the hand before he could sit back down.

"Come on, Danny boy, let's dance!"

Kiara and Shelly let out catcalls from the table as Mack led a bemused Dan to the dance floor. A fast song was blaring about country boys and back roads.

Dan protested he didn't know much about country music, but Mack ignored him. Then he spun her effortlessly and she realized he was actually a good dancer. His eyes never left hers as she bounced to the song's beat, but she couldn't read his expression. All those years of law enforcement had taught him how to hide his feelings well.

The next tune slowed to more of a two-step. It was one of those stereotypical country songs—the singer was crooning about how jealous he was of the beer his girlfriend put to her lips. Dan twirled Mack around again, leaned close and said, "Did that singer just say he wanted to check his girl for *ticks*?"

Mack threw her head back and laughed. "Sure—but he wants to do it in the moonlight. That makes it romantic, right?"

"I'd never thought about it, but I can see how that might be fun." Dan flashed Mack a smile that almost made her heart stop. Her smile faltered, but she forced herself to respond lightly.

"It's every country girl's dream."

"Okay, hold still then…" Dan grabbed her tightly by the waist and they both started laughing as his hands moved lightly up and down her back, making motions to check her for pests as she swatted at him.

Then the song stopped, and a slow song came on. Dan pulled Mack close and there they were, locked in an embrace in the center of the floor, swaying gently against one another as the singer crooned about blue not being a good color on his girl.

Back when she'd been a teenager, she'd privately dreamed of slow dancing with Danny Adams. It was surreal to actually be doing it so many years later. As the song continued, she found herself relaxing into his arms. Whether it was the alcohol, the song or his embrace, Mack felt a flood of emotions as they swayed together. She'd spent so much time being angry about the failure of her marriage, but some of that anger was beginning to ease. She rested her head on Dan's shoulder and felt tears threatening to spill. She'd been without a man's caring embrace for too long. She hadn't realized until that moment how very lonely she'd been.

Dan seemed as unprepared for the intimacy the song invited as she was. His hands fell to her waist. She could feel him hesitating, debating with himself. But as Mack snuggled closer, his arms tightened reflexively. One hand moved up her back. When she laid her head on his shoulder, he slid his hand to the back of her neck and dropped his cheek to the top of her head. It was intimate and private and lovely.

The music built, and Dan spun across the floor without releasing her. She moved with him as if they were one, hip to hip, head on his shoulder, secure in his arms. For a moment, the rest of the world fell away. When the music stopped, they stayed locked in their embrace in the center of the dance floor. Mack finally blinked and looked up, surprised to see the floor crowded with other couples. It felt as though they'd been dancing completely alone.

Dan took a deep breath, and his arms loosened enough for her to step back and look up into his eyes. They were dark and intense and were locked on her. His guard had dropped, and she was surprised to see sadness there, and longing. And there was also heat. She felt suddenly sober and stepped away abruptly.

"You know, I'm thinking it's time for me to head home." Mack glanced away to break the intense moment. She'd wanted this, but now that she was confronted with the chance to be a little wild, she felt panic bubbling up.

Dan's brows rose. "You haven't finished your beer."

"I think I can do without more beer, don't you?"

But she followed him back to the table. She tried to avoid Kiara and Shelly's speculative expressions. After that slow dance, she and Dan were going to be gossip fodder in Gallant Lake for sure. When Dan leaned over to answer something Kiara said, Shelly grabbed Mack and started whispering.

"That man has the hots for you! And it looks like it's mutual."

"Shh!" Mack hissed. "You're crazy!" Or was she? "He's not what I'm looking for." Or was he? "I've had way too much to drink." Well, that much was true.

She felt something touch her fingers and looked up to see Dan's hand next to hers on the table. Their eyes met, and he smiled softly as he nodded to something Owen was saying about a baseball game on the television behind the bar. Mack felt an unfamiliar flutter in her abdomen. She was definitely feeling reckless tonight, but the past was whispering warnings even the alcohol couldn't silence.

Mason had been a charmer, too, in the beginning. Mason was handsome and so very civilized in his actions, but he seemed driven to make sure he was always the center of attention. Dan was far more comfortable in his own skin, but he was Gallant Lake's version of Superman. And she had a feeling the *ice queen* wasn't the Lois Lane the locals had in mind for their hero.

Dan walked to the bar. Shelly was calling to her over the loud music. "You're looking mighty dreamy-eyed, girlfriend!"

Mack rolled her eyes. "Wasn't it you who told me we're not in high school anymore? The next thing you know, you'll be asking me to carve our initials inside a heart or toss a coin in the old wishing well on Gilford's Ridge."

Shelly laughed. "Wow, I haven't thought about that old wishing well in ages… I wonder if it's still up there? I should take my kids hiking and see if we can find it. Look, you don't have to *marry* the guy, Mack. Just have some fun. Dan's a good guy, and Lord knows he deserves some fun, too. And after watching you two dance… Well, let's just say there was some hotness goin' on!"

Dan returned, thankfully ending the conversation. He handed her a glass, but it wasn't beer.

"I thought you might want some water to hydrate yourself from all your…uh…activity."

"In other words, you agree I've had enough beer tonight? You're right—this is not a typical Friday night for me." Remembering she was here to start a more fun-loving life, she lifted her chin. "At least it wasn't before tonight."

Owen leaned forward to make himself heard over the music. "Hey, Dan, you bike, right? A bunch of us are going to do the loop around the lake Sunday. Wanna join us?"

Mack's eyes went wide. "Dan, you still have your motorcycle? I used to love the way that thing rumbled…"

Kiara's eyebrows rose, and Mack realized she sounded gushy. But she hadn't thought of Dan pulling up behind the liquor store on that dark red Harley of his in a long time. He'd been every teenage girl's bad-boy dream—handsome, reckless and restless. She used to run to the back window when she heard him coming, just to watch him pull that helmet off and run his fingers through his hair, wearing those tight jeans.

Was it hot in here, or was it her memories that were heating her up right now? She gulped down the cold water, nearly emptying the glass in one pull. Dan was saying something. Oh, damn. Dan was talking and she wasn't even listening…

"…think Owen's referring to *bicycles*, not motorcycles." He nodded toward Owen. "I've got Chloe this weekend, so I'll have to pass." His mouth slanted into a half grin as he turned back to Mack. "But yes, I still have the old Harley. It's been in mothballs for a few years, but I can't seem to part with that last vestige of my misspent youth."

That bad boy might still be in there…

"You know, I've never been on a motorcycle. You should give me a ride sometime…"

Dan coughed and the others laughed. That wasn't the kind of *ride* she'd meant, of course. Or was it? Rather than apologize, she just met his gaze and shrugged.

There was a spark of something in his eyes. Interest? He closed them and shook his head, as if chasing away whatever thoughts she'd put there.

"Okay, Miss New Leaf, I think it's time to head home." He looked toward the entrance, where several men were standing. She recognized Nate Thomas and Asher Peyton among them. Asher was smirking in Dan's general direction. "Looks like my friends are ready to head out. I didn't drive, but Asher and I can drop you."

Owen spoke up. "I can drive her home."

Dan glanced at the cola Owen held. The two men had a brief stare down before Mack had enough of it.

"Before you two cavemen start pounding your chests, I'm *walking* home. Alone." She held up her hand when they both started to object. "I'm a big girl, it's not that far, and there are sidewalks and streetlights the whole way." She glanced Dan's way. "And I have it on good authority that this is a very safe town."

Owen sat back in his chair. "Suit yourself. You coming back next Friday? Third Fridays are..." His forehead furrowed in thought. "Oh, yeah. Classic rock. Always a good time."

"I don't know what my plans are for next week. I have to make living arrangements for Dad at some point." Shelly and Kiara both gave her a wave good-night, with promises to stop by the store. Dan didn't move until she headed for the door, then he fell in step with her.

"I'll walk you home and have Asher pick me up there. You shouldn't be walking alone."

Mack came to an abrupt stop. "Oh, please. Stop being such a knight in shining armor. I'm a grown woman." She pointed at Asher, whom she'd met just that week. Nora's husband, he owned the custom furniture shop a few doors down from the liquor store. "Go home with your pals and leave me alone."

He stared at her, then shrugged. "Fine. Go do your independent thing."

She hadn't expected him to give up his protector role so easily. When he didn't say more, she brushed past him.

She was almost by when he spoke softly, "Text me when you get there."

It wasn't an unreasonable request, so she nodded before heading out the door. It didn't take more than fifteen minutes to get back to the apartment, and the walk through a quiet Gallant Lake helped sober her up. Before she unlocked the door, she sent a quick text to Dan, simply saying, I'm home. As soon as the notice popped up that the message was delivered, she saw headlights come on in the parking lot behind the strip of stores and apartments. A Jeep slowly pulled away, and she recognized it as Asher's. Which meant Dan had made sure they followed her home anyway.

Maybe she should have been annoyed, but the way he'd done it was pretty chivalrous and sweet, and he *was* a cop, after all, and probably couldn't help himself. She waved as she went inside, just to let him know she was onto him. She locked the door behind her, and Rory trotted down the hall to wind between her legs, complaining loudly.

"Yeah, yeah. I hear you, cat. Your dish empty? Whose fault is that?"

She tossed a few pieces of kibble in, and they were gone in a flash. If she fed this cat as much as *he* thought she should, he'd weigh fifty pounds instead of twenty. She had another glass of water before going to her room and crawling into bed. She'd just turned the lights out and Rory was settling on the pillow next to her when her phone chirped with a message. It was from Dan.

Drink some water or you'll have a headache.

Why did he have to be so freaking nice? And why did she like it so much? She debated how to respond, then grinned. Maybe she could get him to blush again.

You know, I have a bicycle-type bike, too. If you ever want to take a ride.

The bubbles appeared, then stopped. Then appeared again, but nothing came through. She chuckled, and Rory let out an annoyed mew next to her. Was Dan lying in bed like her? Staring at his phone in the dark, wondering what they were doing? The bubbles started up again.

Chloe and I are taking a bicycle ride Sunday if you want to join us. Pick you up around noon?

She had a sneaking suspicion one of those first unsent responses was more interesting, but the invitation was a pleasant surprise. And a family bike ride was something new and different, if not all that risky. Bert was covering the liquor store this weekend.

Sounds good.

As she rolled over and closed her eyes, she knew she'd be dreaming of a teenage Dan riding that Harley.

Chapter 7

Dan took Mack's bike out of the back of his truck and looked it over as he held it for her to take. Just like her hiking boots, she'd gone for the top-of-the-line.

"You might want to remove the price tag."

She laughed and tugged at the tag attached to the handlebars. "That does look a little tacky, doesn't it? Don't want anyone to think I'm riding a stolen bike with the local sheriff."

He really wished people would stop saying stuff like that. "I'm not the sheriff today, okay?" He reached into his shorts pocket for his folding knife, reaching over to cut through the cord holding the tag in place. "There you go."

Mack's forehead furrowed. "You said something like that Friday night, too. That you weren't the guy with the badge. Does it bother you being Sheriff Dan all the time?"

He watched his daughter pedaling her purple bike in circles behind the truck. "Chloe, ride on the bike path, where there aren't any cars, okay?" He turned to Mack, handing her helmet to her. "The whole *Sheriff Dan* thing started as a term of affection. Respect. I guess it still *is* that, but sometimes it makes me feel like a cartoon character. Like that's all I am—some 24-7 do-gooder crossing guard or something."

"Uh…you just moved your daughter to the nice safe bike path from the equally safe parking lot. And reminded me about my helmet. And you followed me home Friday night to make sure I got there safely. And you were clearly trying to determine everyone's alcohol consumption at the Chalet. And people like my dad give you the keys to their businesses…"

Dan set his own bike on the ground with more force than he intended. "The job is hard to turn off, Mack." She started to speak, but he talked over her. "But that doesn't mean I don't *want* to be treated like I'm just… Dan…once in a while." He jammed his ball cap onto his head. He wasn't even making sense to himself. Since when had he resented the *Sheriff Dan* thing? Maybe since drugs moved into his town and made him feel impotent. Maybe he didn't mind it when he felt like he might really be the hero. Maybe that made him a jerk. It was all too much to digest at the moment. "It just gets to be a lot sometimes, that's all." He turned away before she had a chance to say anything. "Come on, Chloe. Let's get this show on the road. You ride between Mack and me, especially on the main roads. Mack, you take the lead. We're taking the lake trail as far as we can, then up the hill to the resort, which means we'll be on the main road for a little way, but there's a wide shoulder. It's a busy road, so be sure to look both ways…"

Mack was straddling her bike, giving him a smirky grin.
"What?"

Her shoulder rose and fell. "For someone who doesn't want to be School-Crossing Dan, you really *do* tend to fret over things and boss people around."

She wasn't wrong. "The one job I *don't* want to change is being a dad. I'm just keeping her safe." He looked at Chloe, who was waiting impatiently for somebody to do something. Mack considered that, then tipped her head.

"Fair enough. But let's explore this conversation more at a later date." She waved at Chloe, and he noticed the purple bracelet sparkling on Mack's wrist. It matched the one on Chloe's arm. "I haven't ridden a bike in years that wasn't stationary and in a gym, so don't laugh at me."

He *did* laugh. All three of them did as Mack wobbled and zigzagged and had to plant her feet on the ground more than once to keep from falling over. But she eventually got the hang of it, and Dan wasn't laughing anymore. Riding behind her, watching her rounded butt go up and down, back and forth, over and over…it was enough to make *his* bike zigzag a few times. She was in capris and a knit top—just snug enough to show off all of her rounded lines. Mack used to be obsessively thin in high school. Always on some crazy diet some Hollywood star raved about in a magazine. Ryan used to tease that a good wind would blow her over.

That sure as hell wasn't the case anymore, and it was a vast improvement. She was far more interesting with those lush curves everywhere. She was far more interesting, period. He couldn't believe he'd texted her at almost midnight on Friday, telling her to drink more water. He rolled his eyes at himself. Could he get any nerdier? And then she'd responded by carrying on that embarrassing innuendo game that she'd started in the bar, about him giving her a ride. The Mackenzie Wallace he'd known as a girl would have *never* spoken that way, at least not intentionally. But Mack had been *very* intentional.

Just like when she pressed up against him on the dance floor. Intentional.

"Oh, hell!" His bike went off the path and he barely managed to get it through the grass and back onto the path without going head over heels. Mack and Chloe both stopped, looking back at him in surprise. Not his finest moment. He felt his face heat up.

"Sorry. Bad dad language. I owe you a buck, Chloe. Can I put it on credit for now?"

She nodded with a bright grin. "Sure, Dad. What happened back there?"

As if she knew she'd been responsible for his lapse in attention, Mack joined in with a fairly wicked grin. "Yeah, Dan. What happened back there?"

"I got distracted, smart-a…" He cleared his throat. "Smarty-pants. We're almost to the road. Mack, you remember the way to Halcyon, right?"

"I haven't been gone *that* long, Dan. It's the biggest landmark in town, after the resort, of course." She started pedaling again. "Didn't you and Ryan used to go up there and sneak into the place looking for the ghost?"

He and Ryan used to sneak around the overgrown property surrounding the big stone castle, but they sure as hell weren't looking for some ghost. They used to break into the carriage house through a back window and smoke weed and drink with pals like Owen Graber. Once in a while, they'd take a couple adventurous girls with them and have fun trying to get past second base. He and Ryan really had been a couple of punk kids back then.

Chloe called back to him. "Dad! Did you really break into the castle? Did you *see* the ghost?"

"I did *not* break into the castle." Just the carriage house. "And there is no ghost, Chloe. It's just a story. Mr. and Mrs. Randall live there now with their kids. They wouldn't do that if the place was haunted." Of course, they'd named their daughter Madeleine, after the woman rumored to haunt the place, but they must have just liked the name or something. A large truck passed them but was courteous enough to swing out into the far lane. "Pay attention to the road, sweetheart."

The hill to the resort and Halcyon wasn't steep, but it was long, and Dan could see Mack was struggling a little. He called up to her, "You okay up there? Need a break?"

"Nope…" She sounded winded. "I'm fine. It's not much farther…is it?"

There was so much hope in those last two words that he had to laugh. She must have been exhausted, but she didn't quit.

They passed the entrance to the Gallant Lake Golf Club, and a low stone wall stretched ahead along the road all the way to the main entrance of the resort. The Gallant Lake Resort was nearly a hundred years old, built back in the days when people flocked from the city to the Catskills for weeks at a time during the summer. The movie *Dirty Dancing* wasn't *all* fiction. The resort had even had waterfront camp cottages at one time, and the main building had several hundred rooms.

Most of the cottages were gone now, and the resort had almost met the same fate. When Blake Randall bought the three-story fieldstone and timber hotel, his plan was to tear it all down and build a ten-story casino in its place. But then he met his now-wife, Amanda, and she changed everything. She remodeled the historic castle named Halcyon and captured Blake's heart in the process. They adopted Blake's orphaned nephew and had a daughter of their own, and Blake went from being despised in Gallant Lake to being a community leader and benefactor.

The stone wall rose to form two large pillars on either side of the entrance to the resort. A limo pulled out as they rode by. These days, the remodeled resort was bringing in well-heeled guests from Manhattan and all over. Beyond the resort entrance, the fence changed from stone to wrought iron, signaling they were almost to the Halcyon entrance. When they were opposite it, Mack pulled her bike to the edge of the shoulder and looked back to Dan. Her face was red and shining with sweat, but she was smiling.

"What now? Are we going in?" She winked. "Wanna see if there are any windows unlocked in the carriage house?"

So she *knew* what her brother and Dan had been up to all those years ago. He shook his head. "No, thanks. The place is very much occupied these days, not to mention it's monitored by the security team at the resort. Cross over when it's safe, and we'll grab an iced tea down at the resort."

"Yes!" Chloe gave a little fist pump. "Can we walk down to the lakeshore? Can I go to the ballroom where the fashion show's gonna be? Can I go up the big tree stairs?"

He gave his daughter a don't-push-your-luck look. "Yes. Probably not. Maybe."

Her face scrunched up as she tried to apply the answers to the questions and determine if it was good or bad. Traffic was clear, so they crossed the road and went down to the resort, riding between the big stone pillars and putting their bikes in the rack near the front door.

Mack took off her helmet and shook her hair loose, frowning at her brand-new bicycle. "I don't have a bike lock. Will it be safe here?"

Dan directed her attention up to a small camera on the

building, aimed directly at the bike rack. He waved, and grinned when the green light below the camera blinked twice. Either Nick West was in the surveillance room, or his employee Brad was, and they'd seen him. Dan flashed a thumbs-up and took his daughter's hand, smiling over her head at Mack. "No one will touch the bikes. This place has tighter security than Fort Knox, and probably more cameras."

Mack was amazed by the transformation of the old Gallant Lake Resort. She remembered it being a nice, but really tired even then, place. It had always seemed trapped in a time warp of 1950s mountain lodge kitsch and even more questionable 1980s "upgrades," with gleaming brass everywhere. But there was no sign of that now. The lobby was open and inviting, with a very contemporary nod to camp motif. The main staircase used to be a wide, curving oak affair. It wasn't ugly, but it wasn't pretty, either.

It had been replaced with a massive round pillar in the center of the lobby, carved to look like a tree trunk. An open wooden staircase wrapped around the pillar with a metal banister that was designed with leaves and scrollwork. Large copper leaves were scattered across the ceiling three stories above, hanging down in some places. The effect as a whole made her wonder if there was a wondrous tree house hiding up there. No wonder Chloe had wanted to climb the big tree stairs. Mack did, too.

Dan noticed her gaping and gave her a nudge. "A little different than you remember?"

"Uh, yeah. I feel underdressed." She watched an older couple walk by, the woman in head-to-toe designer resort wear. The kind of stuff Mack used to wear every weekend at Glenfadden.

Dan nodded toward the back wall, where a row of french doors opened to a spacious veranda. "We might not get into the main restaurant for Sunday brunch looking like this, but we're fine for the outdoor grill."

Chloe was already headed outside. They sat at a bistro table overlooking the outdoor pool and enjoyed iced tea while sharing a tray of nachos. Chloe told Mack about the fashion show she was going to be part of in June, and how much she hoped for a purple outfit to wear. She even wanted purple hair. That announcement made Dan blanch a bit, but Mack assured him there were plenty of safe *temporary* hair colors Chloe could use.

When the nachos were gone, so was Chloe. She was determined to see the water, and one of the resort's employees, whom Dan introduced as Brad from Security, offered to take her down the expansive lawn to the lake. Dan watched closely as Chloe ran ahead of Brad, making Mack laugh.

"Do you not trust your friend? The guy from *security*?"

He finally dragged his eyes away from his daughter. "She's my child, Mack. With the job I have... You don't know what it's like to have a child..."

She took a sharp intake of breath and he rushed to backtrack.

"I mean... I just meant that a parent doesn't ever stop being a parent..."

"Which I wouldn't know because I'm *not* one?"

His lips pressed together, and he looked everywhere but at her. His eyes flicked to the lakeshore, where Chloe was running back and forth as Brad watched closely.

"Was that on purpose?" he asked, still not meeting her gaze. "That you and your husband didn't have children?"

From anyone else, the question would be way too personal. Offensive, even. But this was Danny, and she'd known him her whole life. He'd be fine if she told him to mind his own business. But she didn't.

"It wasn't on purpose, but it turned out for the best, I guess. We didn't have to worry about screwing up a child when we…" Her eyes closed. Now it was her turn to be embarrassed.

"When you got divorced, like me and Chloe's mom?" There was no accusation in his voice. If anything, he sounded amused. "One thing's for sure—we're not in high school anymore, Mackie. Let's establish a judgment-free zone between us, okay?"

She looked into his warm eyes and smiled. "Fair enough." She watched him check on Chloe again. "What happened with you and Susanne?"

His mouth twisted. "I don't know if any one thing *happened*. It just ended, and we both knew it. Instead of hanging on so long that we'd end up hating each other, we worked out a split that kept things as easy for Chloe as possible." He looked at her. "What about you? Did something happen, or…?"

She huffed a small laugh. "You could say that. Remember how I was always the good girl?" He nodded. "Well, I never gave that up. Good student. Good college. Successful husband. And I spent every bit of my energy being the good wife." They both stood as Chloe ran up the lawn toward them. This conversation was going to end quickly. "Until the day I learned he was cheating on me with a cocktail waitress at our country club. I was so busy being Patty Perfect, but my husband only wanted Patty Perfect as his respectable arm candy. He wanted a naughty girl in bed."

Dan's eyes clouded, but Chloe was there before he could speak.

"Dad! There were great big fish right next to the shore! Brad said they were carp. What are carp, Dad?"

Dan looked straight at Mack.

"They're bottom-feeders, honey. Nothing but scummy, no-good bottom-feeders."

Mack tried and failed to hold back a smile. He wasn't talking about fish.

Chapter 8

Dan walked around his old Harley and whistled. "Damn, Wyatt. It looks brand-new."

He'd gone to school with Wyatt Henderson, and they'd both gotten married the same year. But Wyatt's wife died of breast cancer before she reached thirty. Wyatt had poured his energy into building this classic car dealership and service shop just outside of town. It had always been his dream, and his wife made him promise to do it after she was gone.

Wyatt nodded with a smile. "It basically *is* brand-new. These babies shouldn't be left sitting in a garage without being run once in a while. She needed new tires, new brakes and a new carburetor. But she's all inspected and ready to roll." He handed Dan the keys. "What made you dust her off?"

He mumbled something about it being the right time, but the truth was he couldn't stop thinking about the gleam in the eyes of a sassy blonde who'd never ridden a motorcycle. The way Mack had talked about listening to the engine's rumble made Dan think it was more than the bike she'd liked back then. Which was a complete shock, because he'd never looked at her that way when they were kids. Not that she wasn't attractive to him, but she was his buddy's kid sister. It felt like she was *his* kid sister with all the time he'd spent at the Wallace home. His brain just never went there, and then she was gone.

Mack's desire to take a walk on the wild side made a lot more sense after their chat on Sunday. Her ass-hat husband had cheated on her. With a younger, *wilder* woman—at least in Mack's eyes. She wanted to see what she thought she'd been missing by being a good kid and a faithful wife.

Before Dan's shift started on Monday, he'd rolled the bike out of the garage and called Wyatt to pick it up and do whatever it took to get it roadworthy. When it was done, he had Asher drop him off at Wyatt's. His pal made a few comments about a midlife crisis before he drove off. But this wasn't about Dan. It was about Mack. It was about helping her find the kind of spirit that had her dancing in a mountain meadow a couple weeks ago.

He realized Wyatt was saying something and followed where he was pointing—to the plywood covering a shattered window. He was asking about the investigation into the break-ins. Dan coughed and nodded as if he'd been listening all along.

"Well…um… I don't think there are any new leads, but Sam's still working the case." Sam Edgewood was the state trooper who'd answered the alarm call. He and Dan were friends, and both were on the new antidrug task force in the county. "He won't let it go until he has something. He's one of the best."

Wyatt shook his head. "I'm sure it was some kids looking for easy money. A pro never would have left all these vehicles and parts here. They went to the cash box and that was it." They started walking up to the showroom so Dan could pay for the bike. "It's probably a good thing I did what you suggested and left forty bucks in there every night when I cashed out to make the bank deposit."

Dan nodded. "Always a good idea to leave a little cash available. Sometimes it's enough for them to snatch and run without trashing the place looking for more."

"My heart just about stopped when I got the call from the security service at three in the morning. I'm looking into installing a camera system along with the motion detectors."

Dan pulled out his wallet. "Talk to Blake Randall or his head of security, Nick West. They've got a primo system up there and might be able to recommend something that would work for you." He'd been looking down as he walked, searching for his credit card. He looked up when Wyatt brought up his least favorite subject.

"I've been hearing stories about drugs in town. It's hard to believe." He printed a receipt and handed it to Dan to sign. "I mean, they're everywhere, but why would they suddenly turn into such a big deal in our little town? Did some drug lord just move in or something?"

Dan shoved the receipt in his pocket. It was a question he heard daily, and he was sick of it. But he also understood the frustration. And Wyatt was a trusted friend. Susanne had been his wife's nurse during those awful final days.

"I don't know, man. We've got a whole freakin' task force on it, and we still can't figure it out. We think the town somehow got selected as a waypoint between the city and upstate, but they must have a local connection that's helping them stay out of sight." He looked Wyatt straight in the eye. "We'll find them, Wyatt. I won't let this happen to our town. I won't give up until we have them."

"I believe you, Dan. And you know I wasn't trying to pin it on you." Wyatt walked outside with him. The air held the promise of summer today, warm with a hint of sultry. Wyatt must have thought the same thing. He clapped Dan's shoulder. "I know you're determined, but you still need to make time for yourself to rest and regroup. It's a great day for a nice long bike ride to clear your head. You'll be better for it, I promise."

Dan was off duty, but the task force was never off the clock. He could check in with Sam and Terry and see if there were any new developments. The sunlight glinted off the mirrors on the Harley. Or he could go cruise around town and see if he could find an adventurous blonde looking for her first motorcycle ride.

He pulled out onto the highway with a wave, and it was even more fun than he'd anticipated to accelerate around the curve at the top of the hill and take in the countryside as he drove the bike back toward town. There was a little spot in his chest that woke up for the first time in years. The sense of freedom that the open road instilled was something he hadn't exactly been nurturing in himself.

He took a deep breath and smelled the damp, overturned earth of the farm he was passing. He smelled the freshness of new leaves on the trees. As he got closer to town, he could smell the clean, sharp scent of the lake itself. He might be doing this for Mack, but there was no arguing that he was enjoying this far more than he'd imagined he would.

"I'm sorry, Dad. I'm pretty sure my hearing is going. *What* did you just say?" Mack was surprised she was able to move her jaw enough to form words after the way it dropped at her father's announcement. He leveled a gaze at her that made it clear she could quickly be on thin ice with him, but she didn't care. "You're moving in with Cathy Meadows? Wha…when did this decision get made? When were you going to tell me? Are you two…?"

He sat on the edge of the bed, fully dressed, bags packed. If she hadn't stopped by this morning, would he have even bothered telling her he was leaving the rehab center?

"Lower your voice, Mackenzie." His tone was even but brooked no argument. Her father wasn't a big guy. He wasn't a loud guy. He was the kind of guy who just plugged along, doing his job, being nice and respectful to everyone he met unless they gave him a reason not to be. He was *not* the kind of guy to hang out with an aging hippie like Cathy. He gestured to the chair near the bed. "Sit down and hear me out before you go gettin' excited."

She never considered *not* obeying him. She'd never disobeyed her father, who'd been the one steady constant in her life. So she sat down and did her best to smooth the shock off her face, folding her hands in her lap. If her fingers were clutching at each other, that just couldn't be helped. He gave a brief nod.

"First, you know I'm ready to get out of this dang place. The food stinks and the bed's uncomfortable and the lights are on in the hallway all night long. I haven't had a good night's sleep since the accident, and I really need one. The only reason they haven't released me is that I can't get up the stairs to the apartment." His gaze darted away from hers. "Cathy has a very nice double-wide with a floor plan that'll be easy for me to maneuver that scooter thing around." He gestured toward the tri-wheeled scooter he had to rest his right leg on for the next six weeks. "Cathy and

I have been friends for years. She helped take care of your mother. She's a lovely person, Mackenzie."

Her mouth opened and closed a few times. She had a sneaking suspicion there was more to this than Cathy being a generous friend.

"So are you going to sleep in a guest room there, or…?"

Dad's cheeks went red, and his mouth thinned to a hard line.

"Where I sleep is none of your damned business, young lady."

Mack straightened. Dad never swore—not even "damn"—in mixed company. She'd heard rumors that his language was a lot saltier when he was playing cards with the guys, but *never* if a woman was present. The fact that he'd just dropped a "damn" on her meant she'd ticked him off big-time.

"Dad, you might be right, but…" He started to argue, but she held up her hand. "*But* I don't think it's an unreasonable question. I'm not judging…" She was, kind of, but she was really trying not to. "And if you have a…relationship…that makes you happy, then…good." Fine. Wonderful. Great. "I just want to know what's going on. I'm your daughter. I mean… I don't need details, but are you and Cathy…an item? Because I sure as hell…*heck*…haven't heard anything about it."

"He didn't know how to tell you." The voice came from the doorway behind Mack. "And he made *me* promise not to." Cathy walked over and sat on the bed next to her father. Mack's *father.* When Cathy took his hand, Dad gave the woman a soft, tender smile with a gleam in his eyes that Mack hadn't seen in twenty years. Her breath came out in a whoosh that left her feeling dizzy.

Her father was in *love.* How had she missed this? And how did she feel about it? He gave her a truly repentant look.

"It started about the time you and Mason were…having problems. You were upset, and I started talking to Cathy over coffee, and then we started talking over dinner, and then we started having nightcaps at my place, and…" He shrugged, knowing he didn't have to fill in the rest.

"So you're saying this…" She gestured between them. "Is *my* fault?"

Her father shook his head. "No."

At the same time, Cathy was nodding. "Yes. And thank you."

A startled laugh bubbled up. "I'm glad my divorce made *someone* happy."

There was a beat of silence as the three of them stared at each other, then they all started laughing. Her dad was laughing so hard he had to wipe his eyes with his free hand, because he wouldn't let go of Cathy's hand with the other. Mack sat back in her chair, shaking her head in amazement.

Cathy's laughter faded. "Honey, you know I loved your mama. She was one of my dearest friends, and…"

Mack waved her hand in the air, as much in surrender as anything else. "I'm sure Mom would approve. She's been gone eighteen years now, and she loved you both. I…" She straightened, then stood. "I don't *object*. I just need to wrap my head around it." Her eyes narrowed on her dad, who glanced quickly away. "It would have helped if I'd known more than fifteen *minutes* before you move in together."

"It's only temporary…" Dad started, then stopped when he saw Cathy's face fall. "I mean…we were going to *say* it was temporary. But the truth is…it's probably not…temporary. This way you can have the apartment to yourself. Do whatever you want to it. Cathy's got a great little place, and it's paid for, and if I start collecting Social Security…"

Whoa. Was he *retiring*?

"What about the liquor store?"

He chewed his lip, and Cathy jumped in. "We were thinking maybe *you'd* take the store. It's past time for Carl to retire. He could still come in and help, like I did after I sold the coffee shop to Nora. But the pressure would be off. He and I could…travel."

Since when did her father care about *traveling*? Mack put her hand over her eyes. This must be what it felt like when a person's head was getting ready to explode. A little dizzy, a little fuzzy, losing the ability to speak coherently. Yup. Her head was going to explode any minute now. She held her hand out to stop Cathy from saying any more.

"I need to go. I need…" She swallowed hard. "I need to go…think. Or something. Do you need any help getting to Cathy's place?"

Her father and his…his *girlfriend*…both shook their heads. "It's all set. There's only two steps up to the front door, and the railings are sturdy enough for him to be able to hop up there. Once he's inside, there's plenty of room. I took up the area rugs for now so he won't get hung up on them. You should come. Well…" Cathy cleared her throat, her cheeks going pink. "Of course you *need* to come. Maybe for dinner? Tonight? Tomorrow? This weekend?"

Her dad nodded. "Yes. And you could bring some of my clothes. I mean, I have some there now, but…"

So her dad already had a stay-over drawer at Cathy's. It would be cute if it wasn't so mind-boggling.

"Do you have enough clothes to get you through to the weekend? Tomorrow's our first official wine tasting at the store. It's just a test, with invited guests, but I still have a lot to do. And I should get started on all that work right now." She really needed to get out of here. "Uh…let me know if you need anything, and um…have fun, I guess."

She stopped at the store long enough to finish getting the tables and chairs in place and lined up the four wines and two craft whiskeys they'd be tasting. It would just be Nora and her cousins, plus Shelly and Kiara. Bert seemed to have everything else under control, which left Mack with little to do. So she changed into her sneakers and went for a walk, heading up the hill toward the resort, her head spinning.

Her dad. Cathy. Mack's failed marriage. Danger Dan. All those boxes she'd put people into. None of those boxes seemed to fit anymore. Was it good? Bad? Or just…life?

She was approaching the resort's golf course when a motorcycle came roaring over the crest of the hill ahead of her. She thought nothing of it until the bike slowed dramatically, then pulled into the entrance of the golf club and stopped directly in front of her. Awkward. And a little scary. She didn't know anyone with a motorcycle in town, and this guy was staring straight at her through his black helmet visor.

He pulled the helmet off, and she started to laugh in surprised relief. Danny Adams. On a motorcycle. Talk about people not filling their assigned boxes. Or into tight jeans. Or…she totally lost her train of thought. Dan's denim-clad legs were braced to hold the bike upright, and he was smiling at her. Wait. He was reaching a hand out to her. For *what*?

"Perfect timing, Mackie. Wanna take that first-ever motorcycle ride?"

The bike was idling with a rumble that vibrated in her chest. He looked like sex on a stick right now, with that leather jacket and his usually neat hair standing on end, clutching the gleaming black helmet in his hand. The thought of wrapping her arms around his waist and straddling that machine was extremely tempting.

"Isn't there a helmet law in New York?"

He reached behind him with a grin, pulling a dark purple helmet out of the saddlebag and handing it to her. What a strange, through-the-looking-glass sort of day this was turning into.

"And you carry a purple helmet with you at all times because…?"

"Because you never know when you might see someone who likes purple and really needs a ride."

Her lips trembled a little. He had no idea. "Was it that obvious?"

His smile slipped. "Is everything okay?"

She looked down at the noisy bike and her smile strengthened. "It is now. Let's blow this Popsicle stand, Luke Perry."

She stepped forward, but he stopped her, looking at her feet. "Whoa. Sneaker laces and motorcycle-wheel spokes are not a good combination."

"I can tuck the laces into my sneaks." She bent over and did that, then straightened and took the helmet from his hand. "Is that better, Mr. Safety First?"

"Much." He helped her adjust the strap under her chin. "Watch the muffler. It'll burn your leg if you're not careful." The seat was more slippery and rounded than she'd anticipated. It also sloped forward so that body contact was unavoidable. Dan pointed out a couple handholds next to the seat and behind it, but *he* was the handhold she preferred. He tensed for a second when she slid her arm around his waist. Then he relaxed and patted her hand. "Good girl.

Your body follows my body, okay? If I lean, you lean. If I don't lean, you don't. Got it?"

"Yes, sir, Officer, sir!"

He rolled his eyes and turned forward. His foot jiggled something, his hand moved something on the handlebars and they were off. He went back up the hill toward wherever he'd come from.

It was loud. And different. She felt very exposed, especially when a big truck passed them from the opposite direction. She lowered her head at first, resting it on the back of his shoulder and hiding her face from the wind. But when he turned onto the side road, she raised her head and kept it up. Cars had plenty of windows all around, but the view was nothing like this panorama in every direction. It felt like she was a *part* of the scenery instead of just driving through it. Dan seemed confident and at ease with the bike, and her grip loosened as she relaxed and took it in.

The lake stretched out below them on the left. On the right, Gallant Mountain rose high above, with heavy forests broken only by the occasional home. They went beyond the mountain and Dan made another turn, taking a road between two high ridges and heading into the rural countryside. She pressed up against his back and raised her voice so he could hear. "Come on, you can go faster than this!"

Dan shook his head, but he accelerated. She was tempted to put her arms out to the side, *Titanic*-style, but she wasn't sure if it would bother Dan. So she tried it with one arm, pointing to a herd of dairy cows and leaving her arm out there. He didn't react, so she slowly moved her other arm away from his stomach. She felt him tighten, but he didn't say anything. And then she was doing it. She was flying, arms out, chest pressed tight against Dan's back for security. They rode like that for a minute, then he glanced back and shook his head. She understood the unspoken command and behaved herself again, holding on to him and the bike. But the sense of freedom remained, burning bright.

Chapter 9

Dan couldn't believe his luck at finding Mackie walking just as he was headed into town to seek her out. And the look on her face when he pulled off his helmet in front of her. Priceless. And then she'd put her leg across the seat, pressing her body so tight up against him he wasn't sure he'd be able to concentrate enough to drive.

If he thought he'd felt free before, that was nothing compared to how he felt with Mack's arms wrapped around him as they leaned into the curves along the country roads. Then she'd put her arms out like a bird behind him, and, as crazy as it was, he'd let her do it. At least for a mile or two. Because he knew she was feeling it, too. Freedom. No judgment. No responsibility. No labels to live up to…or run away from. He wasn't Danger Dan. Well…maybe a little. She wasn't prim and proper Mackenzie. He wasn't a guy with a badge right now. They were just two people cruising down the road on a sunny May afternoon. Dan and Mack.

He headed up the next hill and remembered that Paul Cooper's place was out here and the farm stand might be open. Paul had one of the biggest sugar maple groves in the area and made the best maple syrup around. Dan slowed down as they approached and saw the green banner flying that indicated the stand was open for business. Mack straightened and looked around as Dan brought the bike to a stop.

Today was an honor day at the stand. There was a covered bucket nailed to the post to collect payment and a limited amount of product out. A small sign sat on the plywood counter.

There's the price >
< There's the pay bucket
We have faith in you to do the right thing.
And if you don't pay us, we have faith in karma evening the score.

Mack slid off the bike and laughed at the sign, unbuckling her helmet. "Does that really work?"

"Most of the time." Dan nodded, mesmerized at the sight of her thick hair tumbling free. "Paul doesn't leave enough product out to hurt too bad if someone gets carried away. Usually the worst of it is someone walking off with a can of syrup." He pointed up under the eaves of the rustic-looking stand. "And that digital camera will usually catch the license plate, and maybe even a nice portrait." He waved, not expecting a response. Paul's truck wasn't there, but he might have an alert on his phone for the camera.

"What is up with all the cameras around this town? Is there some vast criminal underground you people are dealing with?"

Dan sorted through the maple sugar candy display and pulled out two small white paper packages from the back, where the afternoon sun wouldn't have melted them. He tossed one bag to Mack.

"These days, half the doorbells in this country are mini-cameras. You probably had just as many cameras in Greenwich, but you didn't have me around to point them out."

"Fair enough." She bit into a piece of candy molded into the form of a maple leaf. "Oh wow, this is delicious. But the sweetness makes my teeth tingle."

"Yeah, it's pure maple sugar. When Paul cooks the syrup all the way down, it turns into this."

"Do I know this Paul?"

"No. He bought the old Kraddock place ten years ago. He's done well with it. Has kids here for field trips, and he and his husband have a big party when the sap starts running in March." Dan popped a piece of candy in his mouth and let it melt there. He'd always been a sucker for anything maple flavored, even as a kid. His phone vibrated with a text. He grinned and nodded up toward the camera. "It's from Paul. He must have gotten an alert on his phone."

The texts came in rapid succession.

Scott and I are staying in the city tonight to catch a show.

When did you dig out the BIKE?

Who's the hot chick?

Dan turned his phone so Mack could read the messages. She joined him in laughter when she read the last line.

"I haven't had anyone think of me as a *hot chick* in a long time." She gave a thumbs-up toward the camera, then walked over to the large tree between the stand and the road.

"I can promise you that's not true."

Her laughter came to an abrupt halt.

"What?"

Dan walked over to where she was leaning against the tree. He brushed her hair back from her face, leaving his fingers on the silky-soft skin behind her ear.

"Come on, Mack. Even if *I* wasn't thinking it, every other guy would be."

Was it possible she didn't know? But then, no other man had seen her dancing barefoot in a mountain meadow. Her eyes went wide and unblinking. Her breath stilled, and he realized his had, too. His hand slid to curl around the back of her neck. What was this woman doing to him? His nice, orderly life was suddenly sliding toward disaster as if a cat was walking along and smacking everything over the edge.

Ryan's kid sister. He'd accosted her in her dad's store. He'd had a drink with her. He'd watched her dancing on the mountain. He'd danced *with* her. And now he was taking her for a spin on the Harley he'd had in mothballs for years. And he was thinking about kissing her. *Really* thinking about it. From the heat in her eyes, she was on the same wavelength he was. They stood like that, staring at each other, for what seemed like a very long time.

Time enough for him to realize that the exact color of her eyes was that of honey and hot cocoa layered over each other, with just a little gold glitter added in. Her thick lashes were approximately three-eighths of an inch long and were the same dark gold as her hair. She had exactly seven freckles on her right cheek and eight on her left. And her lips... Her lips were full and softly tinted pink. And they were parted. Waiting for him.

This was nuts. *Nuts.*

He hardly touched her at first, just brushing his lips against hers so softly he could barely feel it himself. His head lowered a fraction, increasing the pressure. That's when she responded, pushing against him and thrusting her hands up and into his hair, pulling him down. The kiss heated up exponentially second by second, until he had her flattened against the tree trunk, his tongue deep in her mouth and his hands cupping her butt.

He was a man who was trained to be constantly aware of his surroundings. That didn't turn off just because he was off duty. It *never* turned off. But he didn't even hear the approaching car until it was racing past them, a bunch of teens hanging out the windows hooting and hollering. Mack flinched, but he tightened his grip on her. Those high school kids would never recognize his Harley. And they'd never guess dear old Sheriff Dan would be necking with some blonde at the maple syrup stand.

The absurdity of it set off a bubble of laughter deep in his chest. He tried to hold it in until he realized Mack was shaking with laughter, too. He lifted his head and immediately missed the warm comfort of her lips. Her eyes shimmered with humor and heat. She moved one hand to his cheek, smacking him playfully.

"People our age usually know better than to have a make-out session in broad daylight on the side of the road." She tipped her head toward the bike. "Is this a side effect of that?"

"Do motorcycles make women horny? Sometimes."

Her playful slap got a little bit sharper on the side of his face. "*Women?* Excuse me, Officer, but *you're* the one who seems to have a thing for throwing me up against walls and trees and stuff."

"Yeah, I do, don't I?" He kissed her again, sliding her around behind the tree as he did. She giggled against his mouth. The sensation was electric. Her laughter. Her body, all soft and warm. Her mouth moving against his, doing her own exploring. Kissing this woman was like handling dynamite.

Another car went by, but they were out of sight now, and neither of them had any intention of stopping. Which was nuts, right? They were in Paul's front yard, for crying out loud. On a Thursday afternoon. He gave a deep groan of frustration. Mack clutched at him, probably guessing he was going to pull away. This wasn't the time or the place. He lifted his head, and now it was Mack's turn to groan. She grabbed at his shirt, but he took a step back. Time for a reality check.

"Mack...it's four o'clock in the afternoon. And we haven't even talked about...anything." The corner of his mouth lifted. "I know you want to be adventurous, but going any further out here is a little *too* far, isn't it?"

She raised her fingers to her lips and nodded. "Right. Of course. Sure."

A commercial truck went by at a rate well above the speed limit. She flinched, then stepped away from the tree. He watched her eyes, which dimmed for a moment before brightening again. Her mouth curved into a sly smile. She patted his chest and walked by him toward the bike.

"I guess there's a little Danger Dan in there after all."

That was exactly what he was afraid of.

Mack's heart was racing. Not only had she ridden a motorcycle for the first time—with *Danny Adams*!—but she'd also *kissed* the man. Under a tree on a quiet farm road in

Gallant Lake. And he'd said she was *hot*. A hot chick. Tears
burned her eyes.

She'd *never* been the hot chick in high school. That
had been Shelly and Kiara's role, in their short skirts and
cropped tops. Not Mack. She'd been the good student. The
good sister. The good daughter. The good wife. The good
chairperson of half a dozen charities through the years.
She hadn't stopped trying to be *good* until she'd opened
the storage room door at the country club and found her
husband humping Charity Williams. *The irony.*

All that trying. In the process, she'd left friends like
Shelly and Kiara in the dust. She'd left *herself* in the dust.
So eager to escape Gallant Lake. So eager to be Miss Prim
and Proper Housewife. So eager for approval from everyone
else. With never a thought about what *she* wanted.

She pulled in a ragged breath but didn't feel any oxy-
gen reaching her lungs. Of all the places to gain clarity on
the falseness of her entire life, it had to happen at a maple
syrup stand in Gallant Lake.

"Hey…" Dan put his hand on her shoulder. "What's
wrong?"

She started to laugh, and then, to her horror, she began
to cry. To ugly cry, with big ugly tears as well as big dramatic sobs for complete humiliation. She leaned over, hands
on her thighs, wheezing in breaths between the cries rack-
ing her chest.

She was vaguely aware of Dan leading her farther away
from the road. "Jesus… Mackie, what is it? Did I do something? I'm sorry…"

There was a picnic table behind the stand, out of sight
and shaded. As soon as they sat, Dan folded her into his
arms. She shook her head sharply before giving in to the

crying jag that had clearly just been waiting for a chance to humiliate her properly.

"It's not…you. It's me…my life…"

The fear left Dan's voice, leaving only warmth and caring.

"Oh, Mackie. Go ahead. Get it out, baby."

She obliged, sobbing into his shirt while he held her, his hand running slowly up and down her back. He was speaking, but it was more a murmur of comforting sounds than actual words. Her tears didn't seem to intimidate him or make him want to run. That was new. Mason hated it when she cried. He told her it was childish. That was rich coming from a guy who cheated on her with a girl who was barely above the age of consent.

A laugh bubbled up, making Dan's hand freeze. Did he think she was having a breakdown? Who was she kidding—she *was* having a breakdown. And for some crazy reason, that made her laugh harder, with tears still covering her face. She lifted her head and gave him a watery smile.

"I'm sorry. This is horrible timing for an emotional collapse. Don't take it personally. I just…"

She wiped her cheek with the back of her hand, and Dan fished in his pocket for a handkerchief. What kind of man still carried a cotton handkerchief? Her dad. And Dan. She laughed again, then the tears returned. She was completely out of control. He pulled her back into his embrace, and she cried some more, but more softly now. The tidal wave had passed, and she was finding her center again. Slowly. Dan didn't rush her. He didn't talk. He didn't ask *her* to talk, either. He was just…there. Like a rock. Like a good guy.

She pulled in a long, slow breath and put Dan's handkerchief to use. She knew she wasn't a pretty crier. Her face had to be red and blotchy and puffy and wet and…

Dan's fingers raised her chin and his mouth brushed hers before he came in for a deep, hypnotic kiss. He lifted his head and grinned, saying exactly what she needed to hear.

"You're still a hot chick."

She huffed out a genuine laugh, no longer feeling on a razor's edge.

"I'm a hot *mess* is what I am."

He stared into her eyes, then shook his head. "Nah. You're human. A divorce is like a death, and it hits you at weird times. And then with your dad getting hurt…"

"My dad. Yeah." She looked up through the bright green leaves, filtering the sun and looking like a kaleidoscope. "Did you know Dad's been shacking up with Cathy Meadows? He moved into her double-wide today. Dad's gettin' luckier than I am. How is that fair?"

Dan's brows shot high up his forehead. "Carl and *Cathy*? Wow, I…well…yeah, I guess I've seen them together a lot lately. But I figured they were friends. How old is your dad?"

"He's sixty-eight, Dan."

He winked at her. "Good for him, the old dog."

She straightened. "Ew. That's my *dad* you're talking about. No one wants to think of their father getting it on."

"My dad's had a girlfriend for ten years now. Her apartment is right next to his at the senior center in Florida. I'm sure they've had a few sleepovers."

Mack grimaced. "My brain isn't ready to embrace that yet. I just found out this morning."

"Ooh." Dan stretched his legs out in front of him, leaning back against the table. He stared at the ground for a moment. "What bothers you more—that your dad's seeing someone, or that he didn't tell you?"

She didn't answer right away. Did it matter? She pressed her lips together.

"Honestly, being blindsided pissed me off. A lot. Then they told me it all started when Dad started talking to Cathy about *my* problems. How weird is that? My failed relationship led to them being together." She sighed, staring out across the freshly plowed fields on the opposite side of the road. "Oh, and he's *retiring*. They want to 'travel' together." She formed the air quotes with her fingers. She knew she sounded resentful. "He wants me to take over the store for good."

Dan was quiet, then he started to chuckle softly. "Man, you really *have* had quite a day, haven't you? Is that why you were out walking when I found you?"

When he found her. There was something about that word...*found*...that made her feel warm and fuzzy inside. Like he'd been looking for her. Like he cared. Like he'd pulled out that motorcycle just for her. Maybe she didn't need him to be Danger Dan after all. Because she was really starting to like Good Guy Dan.

"Mack..." There was gentle warning in his voice, and she realized she was leaning into him. She also hadn't answered the question he'd just repeated a second time. She pulled back.

"I was walking to settle my head, yes. And then you found me."

"And did I help or make it worse?"

She held up his handkerchief, saturated with her tears, and shrugged. "Both?"

He grinned. "Fair enough. You hungry?"

"I don't need any more maple sugar—my metabolism is buzzing enough already. And my face is way too messy for dining in public."

"I was thinking more along the line of burgers on the grill." He stood and held out his hand. "At my place."

She took his hand. Bad idea? Good idea? Who knew the difference anymore? The only thing she knew for sure was that she was sliding on the back of Dan Adams's bike and having dinner with him. At his place.

Chapter 10

Dan put the perfectly charred burgers on the platter and set the buns on the grill to toast. Mack was just coming out of the house with a tray of condiments in one hand and two bottles of beer in the other. They'd stopped at the store on the way home and she'd juggled a container of macaroni salad and a box of cupcakes on the back of the bike, laughing all the way. He already had some baked beans in the cupboard. It wasn't fancy, but then again, it was Thursday night, which meant it didn't need to be fancy. This was just a midweek dinner between friends. Friends who'd kissed each other's lights out an hour ago.

Right before she'd burst into tears. But if there was one thing Dan was used to, it was dealing with people in emotional situations. He'd learned the worst thing you could do was try to tell someone to *stop* once a hysterical crying jag came on. Best to just support them without judgment while they worked through it.

Knowing what to do and *liking* it were two different things, though. It had broken his heart to see Mack, always so pulled together and in control, just…lose it like that. He wondered how long she'd been holding all that in. How painful that must have been.

"I didn't realize how hungry I was until I stepped out here." She smiled at him. "Those burgers smell amazing. I think I found everything we'll need." She held up the beer. "Even adult beverages."

She hadn't said much about the white Victorian he lived in, or all the signs of Chloe everywhere, from drawings on the fridge to trays of beads on the dining table. Mack knew he was a single dad, of course, but he wondered how she felt about being confronted by it. They sat at the glass patio table.

"You okay?" he asked. "You were quiet after we got here."

She took a sip of her beer. "Always the detective." He tensed, and she set her beer down with a frown. "Sorry. I forgot you don't like being reminded of your job."

"It's not that…it's just…" Dan wasn't sure *what* it was. He didn't want Mack to see him as his job. He wanted her to see him as a man. Maybe even as *her* man.

"I know. Cartoon character and all that. I get it." She looked up at the house. "It's a bit surreal to be here at your house. It's so…domestic."

He chuckled. "That's me. Domestic Dan."

She laughed. "Who knew?" She took a bite of her burger. "Oh my God, you really *are* Domestic Dan. This is delicious."

They ate in comfortable silence, interspersed with an occasional comment about the food or the nice weather or something else with no meaning. They were opening the package of cupcakes when things took a more serious turn again. Mack gave him a level gaze over the top of her bright pink frosted cupcake.

"So you know why I got divorced. What's *your* real story?"

He didn't answer right away. Partly because his mouth was full and partly because he wasn't sure how to answer. He swallowed hard and shrugged as casually as possible.

"I usually say we grew apart, but that sounds like such a cliché. Our jobs didn't help. She's a nurse, and her shifts at the urgent care center tended to be the opposite of mine, until we were just passing each other in the hallway most days. We planned it that way at first, so one of us could be with Chloe. In hindsight, it wasn't the best idea for the marriage." He took a bite of his cappuccino cupcake. "Oh, man, this is good."

He told Mack how he and Susanne became more like roommates than husband and wife after a while. How neither of them seemed to mind that it happened. And how sad that realization made them both.

"She tried. She took a job at the clinic here in town, with more regular hours. But after the local police department dissolved and got absorbed by the sheriff's department, I didn't have much control over my hours. And being a cop is…" He blew out a breath. "It's not a nine-to-five job. We're on call all the time if something big goes down. And we're spread thin, so I might be thirty miles away dealing with an accident at the end of my shift, meaning I'd be way late getting home. And often not in the best of moods. Add in the fact that she was always worrying about me…"

Mack nodded. "It must be hard. What you do. What you see."

She had no idea. No one did, except other first responders.

"Susanne would try to get me to talk about it, but that's not anything a cop wants to bring home with them, you know? She'd freak out if I *did* tell her anything, and it would just make her worry that much more. It reached the point where she was texting me twenty times a shift to make sure I was okay. So I stopped talking about it." He took a swig of beer. Quite a combination—beer and cupcakes. "Eventually she stopped asking, and that's when we knew it was over. We decided to split while we were still friends instead of hanging in there so long we hated each other."

"Much better for Chloe that way."

"Exactly."

"Susanne's still here in town, then?"

"About a ten-minute walk."

Mack set what was left of her cupcake down.

"You live in the same neighborhood as your ex?"

"I live in the same neighborhood as my *daughter*. And technically, they're different neighborhoods, just close. This place is a hundred years old, while their house is in a more recent development." He looked up at the house. It had taken him a couple years of hard work to bring it back from the brink of disrepair, but it was turning into a home he was proud of. "Chloe can ride her bike back and forth easily, she can catch the same school bus from either house, and she's close to her friends no matter where she's staying."

"Wow." Mack finished her beer. "That's very…civilized." He started to roll his eyes at the sarcasm, but she quickly corrected him. "No, I mean it! Not many people would be willing to do that, even for their children's sake, but you and Susanne figured it out. Good for you."

Yeah, good for him. Their marriage had failed. Because of who he was. But at least they *had* managed to do the right thing by Chloe. He nodded, staring at the table for a minute before meeting her eyes.

"There was no single trauma that tore us apart. No affairs. No big fights. No games. Our marriage faded more than died. Not like yours, I'm assuming."

She huffed out a laugh. "My marriage blew sky-high, Dan. Nothing left but ashes. If I'd been paying attention, maybe I'd have seen it coming. All the signs were there. Staying in the city overnight. All those work trips. Late nights 'with the boys' at the club. The way our social group—I can't really think of them as friends—couldn't maintain eye contact with me after a while. They all knew, of course. Not one of them told me I was being made into a laughingstock."

She told him how Mason loved having her on his arm at business functions and formal parties. How well she'd played the part, charming his clients, chatting with their wives, golfing with the ladies at the club every Thursday, running fund-raisers for the trendiest of Greenwich charities, sitting in the same church pew every Sunday at her husband's side. It was all about appearances.

"It wasn't even a so-called friend who told me. It was Carly Fitzgibbons, the backstabbing president of the ladies' charity society at the club. She and I had tangled over which charities the society funded. I didn't think the ritzy private school in town needed help as much as the homeless shelter might, and she never forgave me for calling her out on it at a meeting."

Mack went quiet, and Dan had a feeling she was done talking. That was okay with him. He already knew her husband had cheated on her. He didn't need the sordid details. He started to stand, figuring they should move inside before the bugs came out. Springtime in the mountains meant blackflies, or what some called "no-see-ums." They were nasty, tiny bugs with bigger appetites than the summer mosquitoes, and that was saying something.

He was just starting to stack the plates when Mack spoke again.

"Carly sent me to the storage room in the middle of the annual fund-raiser for the society. She said they were short a centerpiece and asked me to go get one because the staff was busy serving appetizers. Made a big deal out of it and said the florist must have left one in there when they were setting up." Mack ran her finger around the top of her empty beer glass. "I thought it silly, but I was on the committee and she was chair, so away I went. I walked in on Mason and one of the cocktail waitresses." Her gaze met his. "She was up on a stack of boxes. His tuxedo pants were down around his ankles, and her legs were wrapped around his waist like a nutcracker. The three of us just looked at each other, then I walked out. I left the door wide-open behind me and told everyone I passed that there was free champagne being served in there. Quite a few guests got an eyeful before Mason could hobble over and lock the door."

"Good for you, Mackie."

"You'd think so, but people were more scandalized over *my* actions than his. I ruined their very classy event, you see. Mason's behavior was bad, but boys will be boys, right? Wives aren't supposed to be tacky about it."

"Screw that."

"Indeed."

They both laughed, and the tension that had been growing around her eyes disappeared. They moved everything inside and loaded the dishwasher. She asked if he wanted another beer, but he declined. He wasn't on shift until tomorrow, but with the task force investigating the opioid crisis, he was always on call.

"A crisis? In Gallant Lake?"

"The theory is we've somehow become a substation for a supplier who's funneling the stuff into the city, but they're very happy to sell it locally, too. It's getting bad fast. We're losing too many good people. All incomes. Any neighborhood. The task force is working with the DEA and the state police to figure out who the local connection is and where they're stashing the stuff. Hopefully we'll get the head of the snake, but right now I'd be happy to just get this crap out of my town."

She hung the dish towel on the oven handle. "I'm sorry. That must be tough."

She didn't pry any more than that. Didn't ask for details. Didn't shrug it off. Didn't get dramatic. Just empathized. It resonated inside of Dan. Maybe it was his nonstop focus on finding who was responsible and dreading that it might be someone he knew, like Owen Graber. Or maybe it was the way Mack made him feel. Like she *got* it. Like she accepted that he'd said all he could and all he wanted to. It was nice. *She* was nice.

His kitchen wasn't that big, so it was easy to reach over and pull her close. Was that first kiss just a motorcycle and maple sugar sort of thing? Or had it really been as good as he'd thought? Judging from the way Mack melted against him, she was more than willing to explore that question with him. In fact, it was Mack who went up on tiptoe to press her lips to his. It was Mack who went exploring—first with her tongue, then with her hands, which wandered down his back and squeezed his butt the same way he'd done to hers out on the farm.

The kiss heated up as if doused with gasoline. Their hands were moving, their heads were turning and they both grabbed quick gasps of air before connecting again. Faster. Harder. And he knew where this was heading. Right up that center staircase and straight into his room. He started backing up in that direction, pulling her with him. She laughed against his mouth as she followed. They got to the staircase, and he stumbled, too focused on what she was doing to him to be bothered with what his feet were up to. Their momentum carried them down until he was sitting on the steps with her straddling him. *Yes, please.*

He slid his hands under her top, fumbling with her bra while she did the same with his belt buckle. Dan normally craved control, but right now he was very okay with shedding their clothes on the wooden stairs and making love right here, right now. Green light all the way. They were both chuckling under their hurried breaths as they worked with all the frustrating fasteners keeping their clothing in place. His fingers finally moved the bra in the right direction and the hooks came free. Oh yeah. This was happening. He was vibrating with need. Vibrating…

Damn it. That vibration wasn't from need. It was the phone in his pocket. The pulsing vibrating pattern meant the worst possible thing. The task force.

No no no no no!

He considered ignoring it, but that wasn't a serious option. He dropped his head back and it thunked against the step. Then he reached around and pulled the phone from his pocket with a groan.

"Mack…babe…gotta get this…work…"

She froze above him, raising her head and staring, wide-eyed. Her mouth opened, then snapped shut when she saw he was swiping to answer the call.

"Adams." He barked his name into the phone.

"Easy, Dan." It was Sam Edgewood from the state police. "It's not like I'm calling at three in the morning."

He didn't bother apologizing. He was too distracted by Mack lowering her head and running her lips...and her tongue...up the side of his neck. He bit back a moan, sliding his hand up to fondle her breast.

"What is it, Sam?"

Mack giggled against his neck, but thankfully Sam didn't seem to hear.

"A car was stopped on the Thruway for speeding this afternoon. The trunk was loaded with little baggies full of little white pills." Sam paused for dramatic effect, which was almost Dan's downfall as Mack continued to unbutton his shirt, tracing kisses across his shoulder. He bit the inside of his mouth to keep from groaning out loud. He was grateful when Sam continued, giving him something concrete to focus on. "The driver clammed up, but the car's GPS shows it came from Gallant Lake. A parking lot at some abandoned ski slope, then out to the Thruway. Oh, and he had a sawed-off shotgun under the front seat, as well as a handgun stuck in his belt. These guys ain't playin'. The trooper saw the guy reaching and drew his weapon before he could do anything."

Dan sat up and Mack moved off him, sitting on the step below and watching in concern. Fun and games were over. "A ski slope? Gallant Lake Ski Resort? That place has been closed for ten years." Dan did the occasional drive-by to check for vandalism, but he'd had no idea anyone was using it for drug trade. "You wanna meet me up there?"

"I'm on my way now. We won't have a lot of daylight, but we should see if there's anything obvious before this guy has a chance to warn off his bosses. Who knows where his one phone call will go?"

With a look of apology to Mack, Dan stood, extending his hand to help her up. She'd already fastened her pants again and was reaching back to hook her bra. It was one of those mysteries of women that men would never figure out—he'd practically needed an engineering degree to unhook it, and she had it refastened behind her back in seconds. He told Sam he'd see him in ten and ended the call. Mack gave him a slanted smile.

"Duty calls?"

"Damn, Mack. You have no idea how sorry I am. Of all the lousy timing. I…"

"Hey, it's okay. You told me you were on call. Task force?"

Dan hesitated. This is where he always got in trouble with Susanne. Holding back. Or telling so much that she worried.

Mack stared hard, then shook her head. "And if you told me, then you'd have to kill me, right?" She tugged the hem of her shirt, covering the last tempting stretch of flesh above her waist. "Can you drop me at home?"

"Uh…yes. To both." Her brows lowered in confusion. "Yes, I'd have to kill you. And yes, I can drop you."

The corner of her mouth tipped up. "Right."

She started toward the door, but Dan stopped her. "Mack…this interruption might be a good thing. That was a little…crazy and…"

"Frantic? Dangerous? Fun?"

He pulled her in for a quick kiss. "All of that. It's been one hell of a day."

"I don't have any regrets. Do you?"

He looked her straight in the eye.

"Only that my phone rang when it did."

She patted his arm.

"Yeah, that was a mood killer." She opened the door, looking back over her shoulder with a bright smile. "But there's no reason we can't try again some other time."

"Wait, this is sauvignon blanc?" Nora raised her glass. "I don't like sauv blanc. But I like this."

Mack's role was more hostess than expert tonight, on the trial run of ladies' night at Wallace Liquors. She turned to Marie DuCoq, the sales rep from one of the wine distribution companies Dad worked with. Marie held up the bottle she'd been pouring from.

"Oh, yes, this is a lovely wine. The citrus notes are pronounced, but not as harsh as some lesser sauv blancs can be." She looked at the puzzled expressions on the women's faces around the tables and cleared her throat. "It's dry without being bitter." Heads nodded at the simplified explanation.

Mack felt a small pulse of panic. There was no shame in her friends not being wine experts. But *she* was going to have to learn a whole lot more than she knew now if she was really going to take over the family business. Marie was pouring a "buttery chardonnay with a soft mouthfeel and a hint of melon and baking spices."

Shelly caught Mack's eye and mouthed, "What?"

She gave a thin smile in response. She'd asked Shelly and Kiara to join them for a layperson's opinion, since the Lowery cousins were business owners and looking at this as a new event to promote the town. Her two friends admitted they didn't know much about wine, which made them perfect guinea pigs. Mack tried to pay attention to Marie's descriptions, but she could tell Kiara was doing her best not to giggle at the over-the-top phrasing. This was supposed to be fun, not feel like a college lecture. She wanted people to *buy* wine, not be intimidated by it.

Amanda Randall leaned over from the next table, her voice low. "I'll introduce you to our sommelier at the resort. He's a laid-back California surfer dude who grew up on a vineyard. He has a degree, of course, but Gavin can help make this a lot less…" Amanda glanced toward Marie and lowered her voice. "…stuffy."

Mack's shoulders relaxed. It wasn't just her, then. She nodded in thanks as Marie moved on to the reds, pouring a pinot noir. Mack jumped up to replace the cheese platters on the tables with plates of fruit and chocolate. Mel Brannigan was the only one not drinking. Even if she hadn't been pregnant, she'd explained to Mack last week that she'd had a problem with substance abuse when she was a young fashion model and had been in a twelve-step program for years. Mack told her she didn't have to attend, but Mel said it wouldn't be an issue. She was sipping a "very fine vintage" of peach-pear sparkling water from a champagne glass.

It was nice to have these women here to support her, laughing with her behind Marie's pompous back. She thought she'd had friends in Greenwich, but they'd dropped her like a hot rock after the night she exposed her husband's bad behavior. The divorce made her the odd one out at events. She was no longer part of a couple, *and* she'd been tainted by scandal, so invitations dried up overnight. Mason's father and grandfather had been members of the Glenfadden Country Club, so the members naturally gravitated to him, at the expense of all contact with her. It hurt. A lot.

Who'd have guessed that she'd come back to Gallant Lake and...*like* it? That she'd go for a motorcycle ride with Danger Dan Adams? That he'd *kiss* her? That they'd come so very close to having sex on his Victorian staircase?

Marie took the ladies through three more wines, finishing with a white port. Mack thanked her and rang up the purchases she'd told everyone they didn't need to make.

Nora was the last to leave. Asher's Jeep was parked out front, and he was leaning against it, scrolling through his phone as he waited. He was tall and rugged, with a dark beard that was just touched by gray. Amanda's husband, Blake, had picked her and Mel up a few minutes earlier. The men didn't want their women to drive after the wine tasting. It was something she'd have to consider once she opened these events to the public. Limiting the number of wines and the amounts being poured. Maybe offering a discount to designated drivers if they agreed to drink sparkling water the way Mel had.

"Tonight was great," Nora was saying. "Something like this could really help increase evening foot traffic downtown. Maybe some of the other businesses would be tempted to stay open if they knew the sidewalks wouldn't roll up at six o'clock." Nora tipped her head. "Are you really taking over the store? Cathy said..."

Mack tensed. She still hadn't worked out her feelings about Dad and Cathy yet. "Did you know they were together? Dad and Cathy? Why didn't anyone tell me?"

Nora's cheeks went pink. "I honestly didn't know it was a secret. I figured you knew until Cathy warned me that your dad never told you. For what it's worth, they seem good for each other. Your dad anchors Cathy's flightiness, and she's made him a little less...reserved."

Mack sighed. That made sense, actually. "It was a shock,

that's all. Not that I have anything against Cathy—I've known her my whole life. But that Dad wouldn't tell me... I don't know, maybe I can't blame him. There was a time when I'd have been horrified at the thought of my father shacking up with a woman as out there as Cathy can be. I still remember when she was growing pot in her loft. She's lucky Dan never caught her."

Nora laughed. "There's not much that goes on in this town that Dan doesn't know about. He told Cathy back then that if she started selling the stuff, he'd arrest her in a heartbeat. If not, he'd pretend they were tomato plants as long as she didn't get carried away."

"Good Guy Sheriff Dan ignored a marijuana operation in the center of town?"

"Dan knew Cathy only started growing that stuff after a friend of hers got cancer. That was before medical marijuana became legal. I'm not saying she didn't enjoy a little recreationally, but from what I heard, most of it went to people who needed it and didn't have the money or the nerve to get it on their own. Dan's always been a compassionate guy. He could have arrested Asher years ago for being reckless, but he knew Asher was in a bad place. Dan drove him home and checked up on him every night for over a year. That's how they became friends."

As if he'd heard his name, Asher walked inside. "You about ready, babe? Or are you two gonna have a sleepover and do girl talk all night?"

Nora smiled and stepped into his embrace. "I was just telling Mack about how you and Dan became friends. How he isn't *always* Dudley Do-Right."

Asher nodded. "I kinda miss those nights when he'd stop by my place and have a drink after his shift. We had some good talks." He kissed the top of Nora's head. "Not that I'd trade it for what I have now, but I think it was as good for Dan as it was for me. It was a pressure valve for him, where he could shed whatever he'd seen on shift before he went home." Asher gave Mack a pointed look. "I heard he put his bike back on the road this week. He hasn't ridden that thing in years. Wonder what brought that on?"

She didn't answer. Judging from the speculation in Asher's eyes, she didn't have to.

After Nora and Asher left, she finished cleaning up and locked the doors. She'd just gotten upstairs and was giving Rory a late-night snack when her phone chirped with a text from Dan.

How'd it go?

She knew he was still on shift, but it made her heart jump to know he was thinking of her.

The wine lady was a snob.

She hit Send, then followed it up.

I thought you might stop by.

The bubbles floated on her screen.

In uniform? That would put a damper on the party.

She thought about what Asher had said about Dan needing to decompress after his job.

Stop by for a drink after shift? Still got that Macallan open.

There was a long pause before she saw he was typing again.

I'm sitting surveillance after shift on that other thing. Tomorrow?

She smiled.

Sure. Be safe.

Always.

Chapter 11

Dan was only five minutes late to Five and Design Saturday afternoon. Considering he was on shift, that wasn't bad. He could have been on the other side of the county, but he'd lucked out. He parked the patrol car in front of the boutique and called in that he was grabbing lunch in Gallant Lake. Only a slight fabrication, since he'd picked up a sandwich to go at the Chalet before dashing over to watch Chloe try on party dresses for her big modeling gig at the upcoming charity event.

"Daddy! Look at all these dresses!" His daughter ran to give him a quick hug, then pointed to the rack full of purple glitter and lace. Dan looked at Susanne and tried not to sound too much like an old grump.

"Those are a little grown-up for an eight-year-old, don't you think?"

He must have failed at the not-an-old-grump thing, because his ex-wife narrowed her eyes at him as Chloe ran back to the dress rack.

"They're *party* dresses, Dan. Little girls like to dress up. Just because it has sequins doesn't mean it's risqué."

Mel Brannigan walked into the shop from a back room. "*Risqué?* Relax, Dad. You know I'd never do that." She smiled at Chloe and pulled two sparkly, princessy dresses off the rack. "Let's try these first, okay?"

Chloe clapped her hands. Maybe Dan *was* being a fuddy-duddy. After all, Chloe was happy, and the whole thing was for charity. He was able to stay long enough to see Chloe twirl around in three purple dresses before he had to get back to work. Susanne gave him another dose of stink eye, as if she didn't know what he did for a living or what his hours were. He'd told Mack his marriage ended because of crossed hours and growing apart, but really his job had killed it. And Susanne's fears over it.

He was tempted to stop by the liquor store to see if Mack was there, but he'd been out of his vehicle long enough. Time to get back to work. Besides, he'd said yes to sharing a Macallan with her later tonight, so he had that to look forward to.

But by the end of the shift, he wasn't sure that was such a great idea. It had been a miserable Saturday night. An overdose on a country road, which he'd luckily been able to reverse with Narcan. But the screams of the woman's three young children in the back seat, thinking their mommy had died, would haunt him for a long time. Then there was a break-in at the hair salon. No one was there by the time he arrived, but they'd clearly been looking for cash. When they didn't find any, they'd crowbarred the cash register right off the counter and took off with it. That's when someone spotted them running out the shattered front door and called it in.

Martie Williams had owned the salon for thirty years. She'd been adamant that she didn't need an alarm system. And she'd told Dan he was crazy if he thought she was going to leave any of her hard-earned money around "as bait." She'd refused to listen when he'd explained that if thieves found easy cash they were less likely to destroy property. Now the old-fashioned cash register her late husband had bought for the shop decades ago was gone. And Dan had gotten an earful from Martie about it—if he hadn't let these drugs into town it wouldn't have happened, blah, blah, blah. Sometimes this job made him tired.

That call had been followed up with a domestic disturbance in the upscale Walnut Point neighborhood along the lake. The complaint was for noise. Mr. and Mrs. Quenton had enjoyed a few too many martinis and started a screaming match that escalated to bottle throwing. In their living room. It was the first time he'd ever been called there, so Dan got them both calmed down and made them a pot of coffee. By the time he left, they were sheepishly picking up their mess and apologizing to him and each other.

He was glad it had ended well, but every domestic call took a toll. They were fraught with the unexpected and were among the most dangerous calls an officer could respond to. He'd seen more than his share that had ended in injuries, jail time, restraining orders and, twice in his eighteen-year career…death.

And the night *still* wasn't done with him. He ended the shift with a vehicular call that put him on the scene of a fatal accident in the next town over. He suspected drag racing was involved, judging from the twin burn marks on the remote country road. But there was only one vehicle when first responders arrived. And it was wrapped around a tree, with a dead teenager in the front seat. A family would be forever changed because of a moment's decision to race a one-ton vehicle with nearly bald tires. It looked so easy in the movies, right?

It was after midnight by the time Dan got back to Gallant Lake. He stopped home long enough to shower and change, then drove his truck to the parking lot behind the liquor store. And that's when his momentum slowed and the shift caught up with him. He was both exhausted and wired. Not a good combination for socializing. He texted Mack.

Rough night. Rain check?

Her response was swift.

Get out of the truck and come upstairs.

He looked up and there she was, standing on the metal fire escape behind the apartment. She was leaning on the railing, looking straight at his car, bathed in the light from the open door behind her. Her hair was loose around her shoulders, nearly white against the darkness of the night. She looked like…

Dan gave his head a shake, but that didn't change the illogical truth. She looked like exactly what he needed right now.

She waited for him, studying his face silently as he walked up to her. Then she opened her arms, and he didn't hesitate to walk into the embrace. Her arms were firm and tight around him, like she wanted to hold him up. And she almost was. He dropped his head on hers with a deep sigh, and they stood there for a beat. No words. No need for them.

He could feel her trying to infuse him with comfort, and damn if it wasn't working. He felt better already. But the night's darkness wouldn't be chased off that easily.

"Come inside," she whispered.

He nodded against her. "Yes."

Mack could see the tension pulsing under Dan's skin. She didn't know why or what happened, but she had a hunch that "rough night" was probably an understatement. They sat at the kitchen table, where two glasses of scotch waited. Dan drained his before Mack could even start hers. Her eyebrows rose, but she didn't say a word as she refilled his glass.

Dan drank this one more slowly, holding the amber liquid in his mouth and closing his eyes before swallowing. He let out a long sigh, then opened his eyes and started to cough and sputter.

"What the hell is *that*?" He pointed to where Rory was stretched out on the back of the sofa, easily occupying three feet of space with his legs extended the way they were.

"That is Rory. He's a Maine coon cat. Remember I told you I won him in the divorce?"

The cat lifted his head and gave Dan a bored look before dropping back to the sofa.

"I was about to call animal control and tell them a mountain lion had invaded Gallant Lake."

Mack chuckled. "I named him Rory because he looks like a big old lion. He's harmless as long as you don't scratch his belly. Do that and you'll see more bloodshed than you can imagine…" She looked at Dan. "Well, probably not more than *you* can imagine. Sorry."

He went still. She reached out and covered his hand with hers.

"It really was a rough night, huh?"

"I don't want to talk about it. And trust me, you don't want to hear about it."

"You're not injured or anything?"

He gave a sharp shake of his head and took another sip of whiskey.

"Just a long night, Mack. Let it go."

That was hard to do, when it was lurking in the room like a heavy shadow. She had a dozen questions. But she stayed quiet.

Dan's tension eased a bit as the minutes ticked by and the whiskey did its trick. Mack shifted in her chair, and the corner of Dan's mouth lifted.

"It's killin' you, isn't it? Waiting me out."

"A little bit, yeah." She nodded.

"I'm trained in interrogation." He turned his hand to twine his fingers with hers. "You won't be able to outwait me. I will never feel the urge to fill the silence with the answers to your unspoken questions. But honestly?" She looked at him in curiosity, and his smile deepened. "It's nice to sit here with you. I feel better already."

"I'm glad." She squeezed his hand. "Anything else I can do to help?"

"Yeah. You can kiss me."

She was more than happy to oblige. She leaned toward him, and he met her halfway, just as eager for it as she was. And no wonder. Their kisses were like wildfire fueled with kerosene and sprinkled with gunpowder. *Hot.* The chairs scraped loudly across the tile floor as they both stood, eager to be closer as the kiss grew deeper. *Hotter.* His hands were under her shirt, sliding across her skin. Her fingers were in his hair, pulling him closer, even though their teeth were already clicking together as the kiss went out of control and their heads turned for better access. *Even hotter*. He pulled his mouth away long enough to say one word.

"Bedroom?"

"Yes. Upstairs."

Hottest.

She wasn't sure how they got there. There was a vague recollection of hands and kisses and clothing coming off, and then they were in her room and on her bed. Not quite naked, but not exactly dressed, either. And thoroughly out of breath. Dan was kneeling over her, and she saw a flash of concern in his eyes.

"Mack…are you sure…?"

She arched one brow. "Seriously? You think we need the consent conversation after the way we just came up those stairs?" He started to answer, but she put her fingers on his mouth. "Kidding. It's a good thing. And yes, I'm sure." A thread of doubt went through her. "Are *you* sure? After your day…"

He lowered his head and kissed her without a word. The kiss confirmed her suspicion—Dan was, at least to some extent, using sex to forget his terrible shift. After she'd asked how she could help. So they both knew what was what. She returned the kiss with enthusiasm. They both wanted this.

What difference did the motives make? She was providing an escape. He was providing…hope. A glimpse at a new beginning for her that included a night of passionate sex with her high school crush. What could possibly go wrong?

Dan's hands slid up to cup her breasts over her bra. He squeezed, and she let out a groan, arching against him. He murmured something that sounded like "so beautiful" before his hand slid lower, slipping his fingers under the elastic of her panties. He sat up and slid the lacy hipsters down her legs. He removed his boxers and started looking around.

"Son of a…where are my pants?"

She huffed a laugh. "Leaving so soon?"

He gave her a crooked grin. "Not likely. But the consent conversation goes hand in hand with the safe-sex conversation. My condom is in my wallet, which is in my pants. Which are somewhere between the dining table and your bed." He started to move off the mattress, but Mack stopped him. "Nightstand. Top drawer."

"So you were prepared for tonight, eh? Naughty girl." He crawled over her and pulled the drawer open.

"Let's be clear—if it's okay for you to walk around with a condom in your pocket, then it's okay for me to have some by my bed."

He pulled a strip of packets from the box. "Absolutely. Didn't mean to sound judgy." He winked at her. "We good?"

"Nope."

His eyes went wide. "What? Why? Mack…"

She started to giggle. "I just meant that you're too far away."

"That's easy to fix." In the blink of an eye, he was settling between her thighs as he tore open a foil wrap. She pulled down her bra straps and shifted to reach behind her back, but he stopped her. "I can fix that, too." His body pressed on hers, and his hands moved behind her back and made quick work of her bra, which was soon flying across the room to land by the dresser.

They were both still laughing, and she loved that. The laughter was an expression of joy more than humor. As if neither of them could hold it in. Dan kissed her, his fingers twisting in her hair. She let out a low moan as he sank into her and began to move. He traced kisses from her mouth to her shoulder, where she felt his teeth pressing on her skin. Nipping her lightly, then moving to her breast, all the while moving inside her. She traced her fingers across the dragon tattoo on his shoulder—she hadn't seen it since they were kids. It was…hot. Her moans were no longer low. She cried out and rose to meet his hips. Her fingers dug into his back.

"Mackie…oh, Mack…" His face was against her neck now, his words growing more tangled as the pace increased. She curled her hand around the back of his head, whispering…something. They were her words, but she had no idea what they were anymore. All she knew was emotion and sound and sensation. So much sensation. She burned with it, and when it reached the point where she couldn't take anymore, she begged him.

"*Please*, Dan…please…"

"Just go, Mackie. I'm right there with you, baby. I'm right there…"

There was a burst of light behind her eyes, and she was pretty sure she screamed, but it was drowned out by Dan's bellow as he joined her. There was a beat of silence, or at least silence other than their heavy breathing as they lay there. And then they were laughing again, softly, both shaking from it. Like a pair of shell-shocked teens who'd had no idea what was going to happen just then.

"Mack…holy…" Dan spoke against her skin, as if unable to raise his head. She knew the feeling. Her heart felt like it was trying to beat its way out of her chest.

"I know. That was…really something."

It had been *more*. More than sex. More than…anything.

Dan shifted his weight from her and grabbed a tissue for the condom. Then he settled back at her side and threw his arm over her, burying his face in her hair. "I won't spend the night. But God, I need to sleep. Just for a little while."

She didn't bother answering, because she could tell from his breathing that he was already asleep. She listened to the steady rhythm, feeling her own pulse slowing to match it.

There had been chemistry between them from that night when she'd swung a bat at his head in the store. As much as Dan had insisted he wasn't that bad boy anymore, she'd tapped in to the thrill seeker somehow. She suppressed a laugh. She'd just had crazy wild sex with the local hero. She wondered how that would fly with all the folks in Gallant Lake who adored their Sheriff Dan and put all those expectations on him. His arm tightened around her waist, and he muttered something in his sleep.

Too late to worry about that now.

For tonight, Sheriff Dan was all hers.

Chapter 12

Dan was warm. Too warm. He went to toss off his covers, but there was only a light sheet over him. And a soft, warm body next to him. His eyes snapped open. It was dark, and he lifted his head to check the clock. Almost four. He should go. Mack shifted and murmured something, then settled back against him.

There was just enough glow through the curtains from the lights in the parking lot to cast soft shadows on Mack's face. He studied her, wondering what it was that made her completely irresistible to him. She was pretty, but he knew plenty of good-looking women. She was fun, and that was different, but then again... Gallant Lake was full of fun-loving people. But no woman made him laugh as easily as Mackenzie Wallace did. And for sure, no woman made him lose his head the way she did when they kissed.

And the sex. The sex was incredible. The stuff of wet dreams, not reality. He frowned. He'd been in a bad spot when he got here last night. He probably shouldn't have come up. But she'd ordered him to. He ran his finger down her arm. She twitched but didn't wake. Big bad police officer taking orders from a woman he couldn't shake. Not from his dreams. Not from his life. Not yet, anyway.

He kissed the soft skin behind her ear, and she stirred again. She made a low sound, and her eyes swept open. She turned and smiled at him over her shoulder.

"Hey, you." Her voice was still thick with sleep.

"Hey, yourself."

Tonight was great, but it wasn't serious. He had to leave. He couldn't sleep over. So many smart things he should say. He rolled her onto her back.

"I want you."

Funny how the truth always came out when he was with her. Her eyes went dark, and her smile deepened.

"You had to wake me to tell me that?"

"Yup." He kissed her, grinning against her mouth as her arms wrapped around him.

"Good choice."

Mack whispered his name, and any scraps of doubt left his head completely.

Their first time had been intense. Hard. Fast. Passionate. Fun. But this time was slower. Smoother. Softer. Quieter. And even better.

Afterward, they stayed locked in an embrace. Mack quickly fell asleep, but Dan was wide-awake. He stared up into the dark. He hadn't exactly been celibate since his divorce, but it wasn't easy doing the casual dating thing when you were the local law. He had to be careful about whom he socialized with in public. He didn't need people seeing him partying or having a one-night stand with some woman or catching him sneaking out in a walk of shame afterward. His reputation wasn't just important to him per-sonally—it reflected on his job, his daughter, his ex, his whole *Sheriff Dan* shtick. He drew in a long breath. It was a lot to live up to.

Right now, wrapped up in Mackenzie Wallace, all he could think was how much he wanted to *stay.* How much he wanted to make love to her again tonight, and tomorrow night, and the night after that. How much he didn't think he'd ever have enough of her. How she made him laugh. How she made him relax. How she'd taken the blackness of a bad shift and erased it with her kisses, her smile, her body.

But in the real world...his truck was parked out back, and everyone in town knew whose truck it was. Nora's cof-fee shop opened at six for early birds. It was almost five now. A groan of disappointment escaped him, and Mack pulled her head back to look at him.

"Are you in pain?"

He kissed her pillow-soft lips. "Yes. I'm in pain at the thought of leaving this bed. But I have to."

"Why? The sun isn't even up yet." She burrowed closer. "And you must be exhausted after all that sexing."

He huffed a soft laugh, lowering his head to press his face against her neck. "That was some pretty amazing sex-ing, that's for sure. But people will recognize my truck. The café opens at six. I don't want people thinking...you know."

"That two grown-ups spent the night together? Has Gal-lant Lake grown so provincial since I left that consenting adults can't have sex?"

He lifted his head, serious now. "Mack, it's a small town. Small towns talk. And I'm Sheriff Dan, remember? That name carries a ton of baggage and expectations. Not to mention I have a daughter and an ex-wife living here."

Now it was her turn to groan. She threw her arm over

her face. "Okay, okay. I get it. I wouldn't want Chloe hearing about us from anyone but you. If there is an us." She sat up, not bothering to cover herself with the twisted sheet. "I couldn't care less what anyone else thinks or knows. I spent twelve years worrying about what people thought of me, and I'm over it." She stood, her body bathed in the soft gray light. "But you do you, Danny. I'll just remind you that it's Sunday, and Nora doesn't open until eight on Sundays, so you have time for a very early breakfast before you sneak out of here and make me feel like a scarlet woman." She yanked on a long robe and tied the belt snugly. "Omelets okay?"

Once again, he was stuck between what he *should* say—*no, thanks*—and what he was *going* to say. The internal debate wasn't even worth the time it would take.

"Sounds great."

They gathered up their discarded clothing on their way downstairs without saying a word. Dan made the coffee while Mack chopped up mushrooms and spinach and whipped the eggs. The sun was just turning the sky a peachy pink when they sat at the table where this had all started a few hours ago. When a kiss turned into a race up the stairs and into her bed. Mack must have been thinking about that, too. She reached over and put her hand on his arm.

"I know you didn't want to talk about it last night, but if you ever do want to get a bad shift off your chest, I'm here to listen. I know you used to unwind with Asher some nights, and…"

Dan couldn't stop his grin. "Asher and I never unwound like *that*, believe me."

She barked out a bright, sharp laugh. "I'm sure you didn't, but you know what I'm saying."

He frowned at his plate. "I appreciate it, Mack, but it's hard to talk to civilians. Susanne used to get mad that I didn't share stuff, and then she'd get upset if I *did* share. And frankly, her anger was easier to handle than her tears and the way she'd worry. So me not talking is really just me protecting you. No one needs the gory details." He took her hand. "But having you waiting up for me helped. Having someone to just sit with. To help me reenter the regular world again. And I gotta say, all that sex was the icing on the cake."

Mack smiled. "Glad to be of service, Sheriff Dan." He winced, and she rushed on. "I'm sorry. I know you don't like that, although I'm not sure I understand why. The more I talk to people here, the more I can see how much they love you. There's even talk about a push to start the police department up again, and your name is on everyone's lips as the future police chief."

Dan had spoken with Mayor Malone a few times about that possibility, but the plan was supposed to be hush-hush while the mayor lined up both support and funding. "At the moment, there *is* no Gallant Lake Police Department, so the talk is just talk." He leaned toward her. "And the only lips I want my name on are yours." He gave her a soft kiss, but the embers were right under the surface, ready to flare out of control all over again. It wasn't easy to pull away. "I gotta go. I need to grab some shut-eye before I'm back out with the task force and then my regular shift."

She followed him to the back door, still in her robe, which was falling open just enough to tease. She followed his gaze, then leaned back against the hallway wall in a movie-perfect pose, one arm over her head, the other hand tugging at her bottom lip. Marilyn had nothing on Mack.

She gave him a sultry smile, half in jest, but there was a very real heat in her chocolate-colored eyes.

"Will I see you tonight, Officer?"

She squeaked in surprise when he moved against her, holding both hands over her head and pressing her against the wall with his body. Turned out two could play this movie-scene game, and she knew all the shades of what happened in that infamous elevator kiss. Her mouth fell open, and he took her chin in his hand, holding there as he kissed her. Hard. Deep. Hot. Then he stepped back, trying his damnedest to look cool and detached—and knowing he'd probably failed.

"My shift won't be over until after midnight."

She straightened with a sassy wink.

"I'll wait up."

He didn't bother answering before he walked out the door. They both knew he'd be there.

Nora couldn't take her eyes off Mack as they sat in the coffee shop later that morning. Finally, Mack couldn't take it anymore.

"Do I have spinach in my teeth or something? What are you staring at?" Naturally, her outburst brought the other women's attention to her, so now all three cousins were staring.

"I don't know," Nora said. "There's something…" She gestured in Mack's general direction. "…different this morning. Your hair's a little messy. Your eyes look sleepy, but your face is freakin' glowing for some reason. And your mouth…"

Mel raised a manicured eyebrow as she sipped her herbal tea. "Oh, yeah…those lips look like you've either used a good volumizer or you've been kissing somebody. A lot. And recently."

Nora nodded in agreement with her cousin. "That's what I was thinking. She did not have this sexy, satisfied look Friday night when we left the wine tasting. Which makes me wonder what happened on *Saturday* night?"

"And with whom?" Mel asked.

Amanda snorted. "Please, we all know *that* answer. Paul Cooper told Blake that Dan got caught on camera making out with some blonde up at his maple stand this week. Paul was teasing that he might put it on Facebook, but Blake talked him out of it."

Nora reached for a croissant. "That must have been Thursday. My daughter Becky lives over by Dan's place, and her husband…" She glanced at Mack. "Who happens to be Asher's son…long story. Anyway, Michael saw Dan and a woman leave the house together Thursday night and get in Dan's truck."

Mack's cheeks were burning. First from embarrassment, but then anger took over. "Wow. Dan wasn't kidding about how bad the small-town gossip is around here."

All three women sat back a bit. Nora spoke first.

"Mack, just because we share with each other doesn't mean we share it with the world. I'm sorry…"

Mack waved her hand, freshly embarrassed. The whole gossip thing reminded her too much of Greenwich, but that wasn't fair. "No, it's okay. I know you all can be trusted. I just didn't believe Dan when he said how careful we'd have to be. How much people would care." He was well-known and much loved. There was nothing some people enjoyed more than bringing down a hero. And wouldn't they love it if the ice queen Mackenzie Wallace was the one to ruin their precious Sheriff Dan? She shuddered at the thought.

Amanda's blue eyes went round. "Excuse me, but did you just say you and Dan are a 'we'? It's not gossip if it comes straight from the source, so *spill*, girl."

She'd come home to Gallant Lake to find some peace and quiet. Help her dad for a while. Lick her wounds in solitude while figuring out her next move. And here she was, thinking about taking over the liquor store for *good*, falling for the local lawman and making friends who wanted to know all about it.

Mack was exhausted from very little sleep and very much activity last night. Her feelings were all over the place, and she was having a hard time putting them in any order that made sense. She glanced around the café, but it was quiet at the moment, in the lull between the before-church crowd and the after-church crowd. Cathy was behind the counter, keeping her distance from the younger women today. Probably because of Mack. And because Mack's father was now *living* with Cathy and they hadn't had a real discussion about it since he left the rehab center Thursday.

"Dan spent the night," she blurted out. "Or…most of it, anyway. He stopped for a drink after work, and we were at the kitchen table and…"

"And one thing led to another until you were in bed together?" Mel smiled. Her smile was warm. Even a little dreamy. "I love when that happens. Shane and I started in the kitchen the first time."

Amanda nodded. "Our first time started in the living room before we headed upstairs." She winked at Mack. "But our first *kiss* was in the kitchen."

Nora chuckled. "We were in a half-built house on the side of the mountain when…" She winked. "One thing led to another." Her smile faded a bit. "Mack, Dan's one of the best guys I know. You couldn't find a better one, other than the three we've already taken." The others nodded in agreement.

Mack ran her finger around the top of her coffee cup. "I know he's a good guy. I just don't know if that's what I need right now. I'm a newly divorced woman who never took the chance to be footloose and fancy-free. I don't even know what we're doing. But when we're together, it's…wonderful. We laugh all the time, at the silliest stuff."

Nora's forehead furrowed in thought. She pulled apart the last bit of croissant and popped it into her mouth, staring off into space somewhere over Mack's shoulder. "You know, as well as I know Dan, I don't know if I've heard him laugh a lot." She tipped her head. "That's so weird. I mean, he's funny and kind and always smiling. But he's had dinner with us tons of times, and I'm sure he's laughed, or at least made *us* laugh, but…huh." She frowned. "I honestly don't think of Dan and immediately think of laughter."

Mack didn't know what to say. His easy laugh was one of her favorite things about Dan. They'd laughed all the way into bed last night, giddy and breathless with the joy and adventure of the moment. Was he different when he was with her? The thought made her pulse quicken. She looked up at Nora.

"He laughs with *me*. We took a motorcycle ride…" She gave Amanda a pointed look. "Where we stopped at the maple syrup stand." Where Dan said she was hot. "Then he grilled some burgers at his place and things got crazy and funny and pretty amazing. And then last night, he'd had a rough shift, and was looking for a way to unwind…"

Mel grinned. "Oh, is that what they're calling it these days?"

Mack joined the laughter. "Well, it seemed to work. For both of us. But now I don't know where we're going with it.

He's got an ex-wife and a little girl and a job that seems all consuming. I've got an ex, too, but he's nowhere near here, and we don't have any kids tying us together for the rest of our lives." She drained her mug of coffee. "I'm looking to kick my heels up, but Dan's so serious about his responsibilities. I'm not sure there's a long-term there."

"You say Dan is serious, but you also say you two laugh and have fun together. So maybe you're just what he needs." Amanda stood, gesturing for Mel to join her. "I'll drop you off on the way back. Zach has a Spanish-class project due tomorrow that he just told me about last night at dinner. He wants to teach the class how to cook paella. Which means *he* has to learn to cook it. And have me video him doing it. After I teach him the recipe. God save me from teenage boys."

Mack helped Nora clear the table, carrying the empty mugs and dishes to the small kitchen behind the coffee counter where Cathy was working. The older woman's hair was usually in a braid, but today it was wound into a knot low on her neck. She used to be a lot more bohemian, with a wardrobe full of floor-length broomstick skirts and peasant-style tops. But Cathy seemed to be changing up her wardrobe. Today she was in slightly rumpled chinos and a dark green Gallant Brew polo shirt. She'd been avoiding Mack's eyes, and that wasn't what Mack wanted. She may not have fully embraced what her dad was up to, but she didn't blame Cathy for that. She waited until Cathy was done filling a customer order before she spoke.

"How's Dad settling in at your place?"

"Uh…fine." Cathy sorted out the customer's change, then broke a fresh roll of quarters open, dumping it in the drawer. "He says it's nice and quiet there—a lot easier to sleep there than the hospital." Cathy finally stopped moving and met Mack's gaze. "You should come over for dinner tonight. I'm making lasagna. Well, I'm reheating lasagna from the grocery store—you know I was never much of a cook—but there's plenty."

Mack nodded. Dan had said his shift wouldn't end until after midnight. "I'd like that, Cathy. And…thanks for being there for Dad. He put us both on the spot by not wanting to tell me, but I'm okay with it. Really. If he's happy, then I'm happy."

Cathy's smile brightened. "Thank you, Mack. I told him keeping it secret was a bonehead move, but your dad can be stubborn. What about the store? Are you going to take over?"

"I don't have a choice at this point. It's the family business, and Ryan doesn't seem interested. If Dad really wants to retire, I'm the last one left."

She'd texted her brother after Dad's bombshell announcement on Thursday but hadn't heard from him yet. That wasn't all that uncommon. He was working as a firefighter out west, and he'd texted a week ago that his team was headed to a fire in Arizona and might be off the grid for a while. Ryan had his hands full just surviving, and she was sure he'd be happy with whatever decision she made. Gallant Lake didn't hold warm, fuzzy memories for her brother.

He'd called Dad right after the accident, and again after the surgery. But he hadn't called his sister. Just because he was sober these days didn't mean he couldn't still be a jerk. He'd told Dad this was a bad time of year for him to get away, when the wildfires were just getting started out there. Dad told him not to worry. He was proud of Ryan for pulling his life back together.

Cathy's hand rested on Mack's arm. "That's going to

make your dad really happy, Mack. He was having a hard time imagining that store leaving the family, but he really wants to retire."

Mack nodded absently. One more thing her father hadn't mentioned in their regular calls. What was he afraid she'd do? Cry? Get mad? Refuse to come home?

She walked back to her place, unable to avoid the truth. All of those things were possible. If Dad had asked her to come home while she and Mason were married, she'd have been horrified. It wasn't until she'd lost everything that she'd come back into Dad's world. He knew that as well as she did.

The sting was no less painful that night, when her dad confirmed it over dinner.

"I've been ready to cut back for a few years, Mackie." He scooped an enormous mound of lasagna onto her plate and handed it over. "I didn't want to pressure you or Ryan to take over the business," he said, "but I didn't want to *sell* it, either. It was great timing when you ended up getting…well…"

"Great timing for me to get *divorced*, Dad?" Mack smirked. "Yeah, I thought so, too." Dad's face went red. He didn't like talking about the failure of her marriage. He and her mother had had a forever kind of love, and it was tough for him to understand that not every marriage was like that. He cleared his throat awkwardly but didn't argue, so she pressed ahead. "I get it. If my marriage had lasted, I wouldn't be here helping you. Just like Ryan finding the firefighter team and finally figuring out who he was meant to be. Your kids are late bloomers, Dad. But we're figuring it out."

He mulled her words for a moment.

"So you're saying you'll take it on?"

She huffed out a laugh. She hadn't known what she was going to do until that moment.

"Sure, Dad. I've got nothing else to do."

He stared at his plate, frowning. "Not exactly the enthusiasm I was looking for."

"Give me a break, Dad. I'm here, aren't I? Isn't that what you want?"

Cathy cut in. "Your dad is very proud of both of you, Mack. You and Ryan. He says it all the time."

Mack's fork rattled against her plate. He *did*? Her father wasn't one to talk about feelings or affection, although she'd always felt he supported her and Ryan. And loved them in his quiet way. To hear that he talked about his feelings with *other* people—with his *girlfriend*—stirred some mixed emotions. On one hand, it was nice to think he was so proud of her that he'd say it out loud to someone. On the other hand, it hurt more than a little that he couldn't say it to *her*. She looked across the table at him and realized she needed to hear the words.

"*Are* you, Dad? Proud of us?"

The only other time she'd seen his face this red was when he told her he was moving in with Cathy. His jaw worked back and forth a few times, and he gave Cathy an annoyed look for starting this. Cathy cupped her chin in her hand and stared right back at him in mock innocence. The corner of her father's mouth lifted in a smile that had warmth and—uh-oh, was that *heat*?—in it. If she'd had any doubt about whether or not her father and Cathy were more than just friends, that silent exchange between them confirmed it. And Mack was surprisingly okay with it. Her dad shook his head and turned to Mack.

"Of course I'm proud of you. Both of you. You were always a good girl, of course. And Ryan? Well, Ryan worked hard to get himself right."

The words were the ones she'd wanted to hear. But then he'd ruined it.

"Was it just because I didn't cause problems that you were proud, Dad? Compared to Ryan?"

He gave Cathy a quick glance, looking for help. But Cathy sat back in silence, her face carefully blank. He was on his own with this one. He harrumphed a few times, but eventually he leaned forward and looked straight into Mack's eyes.

"Mackenzie Elizabeth Wallace, your mother and I were *always* proud of you. Not because you behaved. That's a pretty low bar, don't you think? We were proud because of *why* you were such a sweet girl. At twelve, you decided to do that for us because Ryan was getting in so much trouble. We tried to get you to ease up on yourself, but you just became such a driven kid. And when Mary got sick, you stepped up again. We worried, but there was no stopping you." He took a long drink of water, as if this much personal conversation was exhausting him. "When you and Mason got married, I was relieved. I figured you'd finally relax and live your own life." He gave her a sheepish look. "I guess I was wrong, huh?"

She started to answer, but he waved her off.

"And now you're back. And I have a feeling you're *finally* starting to live for yourself. So don't take on the store only to please me. I'll be proud of you no matter what, Mackie."

A thick silence fell on the table. Mack's throat was so full of emotion that she wouldn't have been able to speak if she wanted to. Dad looked like he'd just run a marathon and was ready to collapse of exhaustion. His glance darted around the room for a safe place to land. Cathy was biting her lip, her eyes shining with tears. She started to nod and kept nodding as she stood.

"I almost forgot dessert!" Cathy spoke rapidly. "I bought strawberries and angel food cake today. Let me just clear this..."

Mack got up to help, and as she passed behind her father, she patted his shoulder, still not trusting herself to say anything. He nodded, and she almost laughed. The three of them looked like a bunch of bobblehead dolls right now.

Wait until she told Dan about this later... His was the very first name that came to mind. Not her brother. Not her new friends. Dan Adams.

She checked her watch. Still a few more hours until he'd be at her place. Her heart jumped in anticipation. Good thing she'd grabbed a nap that afternoon.

Chapter 13

Sundays tended to be quieter on-duty days. Not always, but usually. Dan's biggest challenge that day had been exhaustion and impatience to get back to Mackenzie. He'd texted her to let her know he was headed her way, just in case she'd fallen asleep. Or changed her mind. But her response came back almost instantly.

I'll pour the scotch.

When she opened the door and saw the box in his hand, she started to laugh. He'd missed that sound all day. He'd missed *her*.

"You brought a *pizza*?" She looked at her watch. "At twelve thirty in the morning?" She stepped aside to let him in. He gave her a quick kiss as he passed.

"Don't be too impressed. It's cold and half of it's been eaten. A pizzeria dropped half a dozen of them off at the station tonight. One of those thanks-for-your-service things. I haven't had dinner, and it smelled too good to leave it there." He took his jacket off and went to toss it on the chair, then stopped cold when an orange pillow started to move. "Damn, I forgot you had that mutant cat."

The cat was curled up on the chair seat, but a cat that large couldn't curl up enough to hide his gargantuan size. He studied Dan with tawny eyes the same color as his thick coat. Dan reached down, and those eyes narrowed dangerously. Then he stretched just enough to brush his head against Dan's fingers.

"Ooh, you should feel honored." Mack put a slice of pizza on a plate. "That's *almost* a sign of approval."

"What's his name again?"

"Rory."

"Right." He moved his fingers against the cat's head. Rory tolerated it for a minute, then reached up and put his teeth on Dan's finger. He didn't bite, just held him there. Dan waited until Rory released him, then slowly pulled his hand back. There was no malice in the cat's expression, and he finally lost interest and started cleaning his paws. Dan wasn't much of a cat guy, so he'd accept this truce as a win.

He took his glass of scotch and sat. "There's enough pizza for two in there if you want to join me."

"I had lasagna with Dad and Cathy." She sat next to him and propped her chin in her hand. "You had an okay day?"

"Blissfully boring. How did your dinner go?"

"Um...not boring, but not bad." It was nice, sitting there discussing their day. She told him about her conversation with her dad while he ate. When she said she was ready to take over the liquor store, he set his pizza slice down and stared. Something weird fluttered inside him at the thought of spending more evenings unwinding with Mack.

"So you're really staying in Gallant Lake?"

Her mouth twitched. "Would that be a problem, Officer?"

"Not for me." He leaned over and kissed her lips, pulling back quickly to avoid being pulled into the kiss vortex that tended to spin the two of them out of control.

They chatted more as he devoured the rest of the pizza. As always, Mack was easy to be with. As he drained the last of his scotch, he said so. She tipped her head, and her honey-colored hair tumbled over her shoulders.

"You're pretty nice to be around, too."

They continued chatting as they cleaned up. She told him about her father's unexpected declaration that he was proud of her. To Dan, that seemed obvious. But when he saw how much the words meant to Mack, he wondered if maybe it was a guy thing to assume people knew your thoughts. It was a damned shame Mack had gone all these years not knowing for sure how much her father cared. The next time Dan saw his daughter, he'd be sure to tell Chloe how proud of her he was.

Dan put the empty pizza box into her recycle bin. They were being so very domestic at one o'clock in the morning. After this weekend, he should be exhausted, but being with Mack energized him.

"So you're going to run the liquor store. I'd have never guessed *that* one twenty years ago. Is that part of Mackie's adventurous new leaf?" Another question rose up before he had time to think it through. "For that matter, am I?"

They stared at each other for a long moment. He wanted to kick himself for taking the conversation in such a serious direction. He had no right to press her for a declaration of her feelings about them when he hadn't examined his own yet.

She blew out a quick breath. "I guess it is. And you could be. We haven't really talked about what it is you and I…" She gestured between them. "…whatever this is we're doing…"

He took the towel from her hands and set it aside, tugging her close. "I didn't mean to be such a wet blanket. Sorry, babe."

She considered his words, frowning. "It wasn't a bad question, though. What *are* we doing? Is this a relationship now? Is it serious or just for fun?"

He had no idea how to answer.

"Can't we figure that out as we go? Take it a day at a time? No strings…"

"No strings?" She pulled back and looked up at him, her brows furrowed. "You don't think we've already created strings?"

Yeah, they had. Strings slicing right through the center of his heart. He released her and scrubbed his hands down his face.

"I don't know, Mack. I haven't had a serious relationship since my divorce, and I'm guessing you haven't, either."

She laughed. "Turns out I didn't have a serious one *before* my divorce, either. This is new territory for both of us." She shrugged. "Maybe we should stick to that one-day-at-a-time plan for a while."

"If nothing else, I need to make sure Chloe's okay with it before anything gets serious." He gave her a wink and ran her fingers down her arm. He loved the way her skin trembled at his touch. "But we don't have to worry about any of that tonight."

Mack started walking backward, taking his fingers in her hand and pulling him along. "Agreed. And just because

I didn't want any pizza doesn't mean I'm not hungry for something else."

That was all the invitation Dan needed. They were upstairs, undressed and in bed in less than a minute, but then he took his time exploring her. He hadn't seen her naked body in almost twenty-four hours, and he wanted to memorize every inch of it. He didn't just explore with his hands, either. He kissed her from her toes to her thighs and beyond. Just as dangerous to handle as ever, she came fast and loud when his mouth found her. And again when he sank into her.

They moved together in perfect time, whispering and pleading and saying very naughty words. But it was her name he cried out when he came, right after she'd shuddered in his arms with another orgasm. She had a hair trigger, and he'd never realized how exciting that could be. How exciting *she* could be. He pulled her in close, their hearts and their breathing falling into sync. She was asleep in seconds, but Dan lay there wide-awake, trying to make sense of it all.

He'd never wanted a woman the way he wanted Mack. With every fiber of his being. With a love so strong…

Wait. *What?*

She shifted in his arms, as if sensing his tension. He kissed her temple and whispered for her to go back to sleep. She did, but he couldn't. Was he falling in *love* with her? Was it possible for that to happen so quickly? Mack let out a little sigh in her sleep, and his heart swelled.

It felt very possible right now.

Mack barely woke when Dan whispered an apology and slipped out of bed, saying something about meeting someone named Sam. She brushed her hair up off her face and tried to remember what day it was. Wednesday? Thursday? He'd spent every night, or at least part of every night, at her place this week. They hadn't had a chance to discuss what they'd do when Chloe was staying with him. Well, they'd *had* the chance, but they'd decided to use those chances for *other* things, like making love all night. Every night.

She was so tired when Dan left that she'd just muttered something and rolled over. When her phone rang ten minutes later, she figured it was him, calling with something naughty to say. He did that a lot, but not usually this early.

Her voice was still husky from sleep when she answered. "Hey, lover boy, did you decide you'd rather come back and have *me* for breakfast?"

Her brother coughed on the other end of the call, choking on laughter. "Well, hot damn. I was going to ask how you were coping after the divorce, but it sounds like you're handling it just fine, sis. Way to get back in the saddle again!"

Mack groaned, sitting up and rubbing her eyes. "Jackass." She glanced at the time. "Aren't you three time zones away? Why are you calling so early?" She was suddenly fully alert. "Did something happen? Are you okay?"

"Relax, Mother Hubbard, I'm fine. We're working wacky shifts on this fire, and I don't get a lot of downtime for family calls." Ryan hesitated. "I talked to Dad yesterday, and he dumped a few surprises on me. Is he *really* shacking up with Cathy Meadows? And are you *really* taking over the store? Is that what you want?"

"Why?" She pulled on her robe, wondering if she'd misread her brother's plans. She worked her way past the hungry cat, who seemed more determined than usual to trip her up. "Do *you* want the store? You know I'd never do anything official without talking to you first. If you…"

"Seriously, Mackie?" Ryan sounded as tired as she felt. "Gallant Lake and me is not happening. Been there. Done that. Know I'm not welcome. At least not by some people. And I get it. Mrs. Michaels doesn't need to be bumping into me on the sidewalk."

Mack stopped so fast that Rory ended up two feet in front of her instead of between her feet. He looked back in annoyance, clearly frustrated that he couldn't trip her from that far away. Ryan rarely talked about the accident that took the life of his friend and nearly his own. When she didn't respond, Ryan filled in the silence.

"I talked to her a couple months ago, you know."

"Mrs. Michaels? *Why?*" Both boys had been drunk that night, but the police report determined it was Braden Michaels who was behind the wheel, just as Ryan had said. Braden's family refused to believe it at the time and took Ryan to court for wrongful death. Mom and Dad used up most of their savings defending him, but the case was eventually dismissed.

"There are twelve steps, Mack. And I'd reached the atonement step. I was too chicken to face her, but I did call and tell her how sorry I was."

She drew in a sharp breath. "Was that wise? *Apologizing?* Doesn't it make you sound responsible?" She pushed the button on the coffee maker and brushed her hair back again. She really needed to find a hairdresser.

"It's part of the program, sis. Had to do it. I wasn't driving, and I told her that. But Braden and I stole that booze from Dad. And I hopped in the car with him, knowing how trashed he was. I was, too. Anyway..." He sighed. "I called. She listened. She couldn't give me more than an 'okay' when I was done, but that's probably more than I deserved." There was a pause. Mack had no idea what to say. Ryan sighed again. "And that was a really long-winded way of saying I have no intention of returning to Gallant Lake. It wouldn't be fair to them. And as far as the store is concerned, probably not the best idea for an alcoholic to be selling booze. The store's all yours."

"Thanks, Ryan." She grabbed the box of day-old doughnuts Dan had brought with him last night and opened it. *Breakfast of champions.* "I'll be buying it from Dad, so I'm sure you'll get a share, either now or later." There was a rustling in the background on his end, and it sounded like he was settling onto a cot or sleeping bag. He'd been working on this fire for weeks, and he had to be exhausted. "To answer your *other* question—yes, Dad *is* shacking up with Cathy. And no, I couldn't believe it, either. But they're actually pretty cute together, which is weird. He seems… happy."

"Well, good for them, I guess. Mom's been gone a long time, and he deserves to be happy again. And speaking of getting some…who the hell is 'lover boy'?"

Mack hesitated, not sure if Ryan would want to know she was sleeping with his onetime best friend. But she'd been mad at her father for keeping secrets, and she didn't want to turn around and do the same thing.

"It's just casual. And very new."

"Considering you just got free of the other jerk a month ago, I would *hope* this is new. Anyone I know?"

"Um…yeah, actually." She took a steadying breath. "Dan Adams."

The silence stretched on for what seemed like hours. And then her brother started to laugh.

"Are you kiddin' me? Dan Adams?" He laughed some more, and someone there must have said something about the noise, because Ryan wasn't speaking to her when he said, "Sorry, man, but my kid sister is screwing my best friend. Or former best friend. Like, she's got a whole town to choose from, and she chooses *that* guy." His voice got more clear as he started talking to her again. "So how *is* Danny? And I don't mean how is he in the sack, 'cause I don't need to know."

They talked for a few minutes about Dan, and Ryan seemed genuinely cool with it. He said he regretted the way their friendship had faded after the accident, but he understood it. After Braden's death, Dan had found the righteous path of law and order, while Ryan had continued drowning his sorrows in a bottle for a decade or more.

"I suppose I owe him some apologies, too. I gave him a lot of crap when he turned his life around. The truth was, I was jealous." Ryan paused. "He made it look so easy. Just woke up one day as one of the good guys. And I never figured out how to do that."

"Yes, you did. You're a good guy, Ryan. A hero firefighter."

"Don't call me a hero, sis." His voice hardened. "I never know what to say when people use that word. I've got a job and I do it. That's it."

Dan had said something similar more than once. He was uncomfortable with the whole Sheriff Dan, Hero of Gallant Lake legend. Ryan ended the call after explaining that he had to get some sleep before his next shift. The good news was the fire was 70 percent contained. The bad news was it was still 30 percent *un*contained. He promised to call again the next week.

Mack finished her doughnut and gulped down some coffee before starting a load of laundry. Once in motion, she stayed there, vacuuming and picking up around the apartment. Dad had told her it would be hers. Did she *want* to live here, where she'd grown up? Or would she be better off buying a house and renting this out? Her divorce settlement had been generous enough that she could probably afford it. The settlement was *too* generous, according to Mason, but he'd wanted the marriage to be over with as badly as she had. She'd taken a lump sum instead of alimony, but she didn't want to spend it all on buying the store. Her conversation with Ryan had made her realize she'd have to find a bank and get a loan.

Bert was manning the store until five, so she headed down a little before that to see how things were going. He was a funny guy—quiet and introverted, but knowledgeable about their inventory and happy to share his knowledge with customers. As Dad told her, Bert wouldn't come close to hard selling anyone, but he managed to do well just because people liked and trusted the former schoolteacher in his cardigan sweaters and comb-over hair. If he recommended something, they didn't hesitate to buy it. Dad called him an accidental salesperson. Bert didn't seem to sell anything on purpose.

She and Bert went over their stock orders for the next few weeks. There was a big charity event coming up at the resort that apparently brought a lot of high spenders to Gallant Lake, so they were planning for that with more upscale product than usual. After Bert headed home, Mack went through the wine section, dusting shelves and bottles while taking inventory. The bell over the door tinkled, and she turned to see one very familiar young face and an adult one she didn't recognize right away. But she had a hunch who it was.

"Mackie!" Chloe released the hand of the woman and ran over to Mack. "We were just looking at websites with

Mel to pick out a dress for me. I'm gonna be a model, re-member?"

Mack smiled and walked toward the front of the store with her. "I remember. Did you find something pretty?" Mack looked up. "You must be Chloe's mom. Susanne, right? I think I remember you from school. I'm Macken-zie Wallace."

Susanne Adams gave her an appraising look. It didn't feel adversarial. Yet. She was petite and trim, with shoul-der-length brown hair and a very put-together look. An *expensive* look. Dan had mentioned his ex was dating a doctor now.

"Yes, I think I remember you, too. And of course, I know your dad. How is Carl?"

"He's recuperating well, but not quickly enough to suit him."

They were being oh so polite. This was brand-new ter-ritory for Mack, and probably for Susanne, too. Dan said he hadn't been in any relationships to speak of since the divorce. Dan had also said he hadn't told her yet, but Mack definitely got the vibe that she knew. Chloe was checking out the mini bottles on the counter, straightening them on the little display shelves.

"Be careful with those, honey," Susanne said. "Don't drop any."

Mack waved her hand. "Most of those are plastic these days. She's fine. Are you looking for anything in particu-lar?"

Susanne didn't answer right away, studying Mack. Fi-nally, she tilted her head toward the back of the store, where the wines were. Oh yeah—she knew. Mack followed. When they were far enough from Chloe, Susanne turned and got right to business.

"I hear you're dating my ex."

Great.

"Yes, I guess I am." Although this week they'd spent more time in her bedroom than out on any dates. But his ex probably didn't want to hear that detail any more than her brother did. She wondered who'd been talking.

"I wasn't sure how I felt about it, but we had a teacher's conference yesterday, and Dan was more…relaxed…than usual. Happier. It was nice." She pursed her lips, lost in thought, before looking up with a soft smile. "It's a small town, Mack. People talk. And *everyone* knows Dan, so they're even quicker to talk. And everyone knows Carl, so *you're* on their radar, too. And not always in a good way—you were a bit of a brat in school."

Susanne shrugged as she continued. "I just wanted you to know the word's out there. Chloe told me Daddy had a new friend. She told me you three went bike riding together. And I'm totally fine with it. I mean, obviously." She held up her left hand and flashed an enormous diamond. "I'm remarrying, so there's no jealousy between Dan and me." She glanced toward Chloe. "But the simple truth is, he and I will be connected for the rest of our lives because of our daughter. And anyone coming into our lives needs to know that." She leveled her gaze at Mack. "I guess you could say we're a package deal."

Was this a warning or a welcome? Mack couldn't tell. Susanne was being nice enough but still guarded. Mack gave her a bright smile. "I totally get that. But just so you know, Dan and I are…new. Casual. That being said, I adore Chloe and I'd never want to upset her. If people are talking, Dan should probably…"

"Exactly. I'd rather Chloe heard it from her father than

some kid at school joking about Sheriff Dan's new girl-friend." Mack cringed. She appreciated how cool Susanne was being about all of this, but that didn't make it any less awkward. Susanne picked up a bottle of Finger Lakes char-donnay. "Do you want to talk to Dan about it or should I? I'm assuming *you'll* see him before I will."

Without thinking, Mack glanced at her watch, and Su-sanne laughed.

"I'll take that as a yes." Chloe was just finishing up the last shelf of tiny bottles. Susanne pulled a folded piece of paper from her pocket. "Here's my contact information. Cell phone. Work phone. Chloe likes spending time with you, and you should probably know how to reach me if Dan has to leave and Chloe needs anything. He's basically on call all the time, you know."

Mack took the card, then shook her head with a grin. She remembered the call he got when they were making out on his stairs a week ago. "Yeah, I know. You're mak-ing this feel very…normal."

"Dan's a good guy and a great father. We were lucky enough to part as friends, which will make the rest of Chloe's life a lot easier." She smiled at her daughter, who'd just walked over to join them. "We're a team, and that includes the people we…well…" She rolled her eyes in Chloe's direction. "The team includes our new friends. That's why I thought we should meet."

"I'm glad we did." Mack slid the bottle of chardonnay into a paper bag. "Take this home with you. On the house."

Susanne's eyes brightened. "Really? I used to tell Dan he had good taste in women. I guess I was right. Thanks."

Mack watched Chloe and her mom head out the door. She'd worried a little about the whole family dynamics issue of getting involved with a single dad, but it seemed that was one thing she didn't have to worry about. Now she just had to figure out what she and Dan were really doing, and how far it was going to go. The one thing she *did* know for sure was that she couldn't wait to see him again tonight.

Chapter 14

"Just hold my hand and step in, Mack. It's a lot more stable than a kayak, I promise."

Dan tried not to laugh at the doubt and fear in Mack's eyes. She'd told him about her experience trying the kayak with Nate and how she'd freaked out when she couldn't get out of the thing. That wasn't going to be a problem in his aluminum fishing boat. Sixteen feet long, with three bench seats and a reliable outboard motor on back, it was his getaway from the real world. At least, it *had* been. For the past week or so, Mack was his getaway. When he was with her, some of the pressure always simmering under his skin seemed to ease. He could laugh with her. Or laugh *at* her, which he was about to do if she didn't get in the boat.

"Mackie, trust me."

At that, she reached out from the dock at the public boat launch and took his hand. She was shaking, but she managed to get into the boat and quickly plunk down on one of the bench seats. When she realized the sturdy old boat was barely swaying from her entry, she grinned up at him.

"That wasn't so bad."

"Told you so. Now hang on—I'll get us over to Muskrat Bay and drop anchor, and we'll see if we can find any fish."

Gallant Lake was a little choppy that afternoon, but the rainstorms had let up and the afternoon sun was warming things up in a hurry. Summer was definitely on its way, and there was already a touch of humidity in the air. The bay was protected from the breeze, so the water was quieter there. Dan got the anchor set and handed a fishing pole to Mack. She looked at the pole with the same amount of suspicion she'd had for the boat.

"I know I grew up here," she said, "but Dad was never big on fishing, and I certainly wouldn't be caught dead touching a worm back then. So I have no idea what to do here."

Dan opened the container of worms he'd picked up from the bait shop near the park and put one on Mack's hook. She didn't squeal in fear or anything when he handed the pole back to her, just inspected what he'd done in fascination, then watched as he put a jointed lure on his fishing rod.

"Why aren't you using a worm?"

"I probably will later, but as long as you're using worms, I'll use the lure and we'll see what works."

An hour later, they were both using worms. And they had a basket hanging off the side of the boat that was quickly filling with lake perch. It was fun when you found a school of perch like that, and Mack was having a blast. She'd start laughing the minute she got a nibble, and Dan couldn't help joining her. She was putting her own worms on the hook now, even if she made a lot of faces while doing it. But Dan took the fish off the hook for her. She had no interest in touching the fish while they were still wiggling, and he didn't want her stabbing herself.

Eventually, the perch moved on and things slowed down.

"This is perfect fishing," he told her with a smile. "We had our fun. The basket's full. And now we can just relax."

Mack frowned. "You don't want to move the boat to find more fish or something?"

"Sometimes the best thing about fishing is the peace and quiet. No one around. No demands. No complaints." He nodded toward the village in the distance. "It's nice to see the town from this perspective. Close enough to enjoy it, far enough away to not have to…react…to anything."

She nodded. "It's like that thirty-thousand-foot view they talk about—far enough removed to see the big picture, but not the details."

"Something like that."

She dropped her hook back in the water, letting the line out a few more feet. She was up in the bow of the boat, and she leaned back and stared up at the sky, which was beginning to darken again.

"Do you take Chloe fishing?"

"I've tried, but containing all that energy to a boat this size is…challenging." Frankly, the girl freaked him out on the water. She had zero fear, and sitting still was next to impossible for her.

Mack laughed, sitting up again. "I can imagine. And with you being Mr. Safety and all, I bet you're a nervous wreck. That girl is always on the go." Her smile faded. "Have you talked to her about us seeing each other? Is she okay with it?"

Dan jiggled the fishing rod to move the bait around before setting it back down again. "She was excited about it. She likes you, Mack. We made sure she got counseling after the divorce, and she still goes once a month." Dan hadn't want to think his little girl needed professional help at such a young age, but Susanne had insisted. And she'd been right. Having someone to talk to had helped Chloe process all the changes in her life without taking things personally. "She's already seen her mom dating and getting ready for a wedding, so I think she gets it. Don't be surprised if she starts talking weddings, though. I think she figures that's how it works after Susanne and Samir got engaged. Boy meets girl. Boy dates girl. Boy and girl get married. Little girl gets a pretty dress and a part in the wedding." The tip of his fishing rod dipped and he reached for it, but it was just a nibble.

Mack's forehead furrowed. "I hope you told her not to expect any wedding bells with us."

He absorbed the sting of her words and tried to smile. "Is it such a revolting idea? Wedding bells?"

"Slow down, Danger Dan." Mack moved her fishing pole, mimicking his actions. "We've been together less than a month. I'm looking for fun, remember? Not a shotgun wedding." She laughed. "I don't mean *that* kind of shotgun wedding, but you know what I'm saying. We haven't even said the *L* word yet, and I think the proper order of things is for that to come before wedding bells."

Dan swallowed hard. There were some big things in those few sentences. The first was the reference to a shotgun wedding. Meaning she'd be pregnant. He hadn't even considered more children, but the idea of Mack carrying his baby filled him with anticipation. Pride. Desire. And then she'd mentioned love. Not directly—she'd used "the *L* word" as if saying it would be some sort of jinx. But he'd already been dealing with feelings for her that felt a hell of a lot like love. She was right, though. It was probably too soon for that.

"Do you want kids?" The words tumbled out before he could stop them. Mack's eyes went wide.

"Where did that...? Oh, the shotgun-wedding thing." She looked off into space for a moment before continuing. "It never happened for Mason and me, but the doctors said they couldn't see any reason why it shouldn't have. So I guess it's possible it could happen, even at this late date."

"Mack, you're thirty-six. That's not a late date." He hesitated, not sure if this conversation was a good idea. "If that's what you want. And that's all I was asking."

A smile played at the corners of her mouth. "I've *wanted* a lot of things, Dan. And I got a lot of them. And most turned into dust. I don't mean to sound melodramatic, but I kinda stopped wishing and wanting. If it happens, it happens. And if a baby happens someday, I'd be thrilled. I think." She gave her head a quick shake, nearly losing her brimmed hat in the process. "I have a hard time picturing that, but it would definitely qualify as an adventure, wouldn't it?"

Dan thought of his boisterous daughter and grinned. "I can tell you that every day is an adventure with the one I have."

"As long as we're on the subject, how do you think Chloe will feel if there's a new family member? Are Susanne and Samir planning a child together? Would Chloe welcome that?"

"*Would* she?" Dan laughed. "She's already asking for a brother or sister or both or several of each. Chloe's always been a the-more-the-merrier kind of kid. I know she's only eight, but she's never been selfish about people or things."

He paused, emotion filling his throat. "She has the biggest heart of any kid I've ever met."

There was a gentle rumble in the distance, and Dan pulled out his phone to check the weather. "Looks like more rain might move in. Let's get back while we're still dry." They both started reeling in their lines. He hadn't had a chance to address the whole *L*-word thing. But Mack was staying in Gallant Lake, and they had plenty of time.

Even with a storm on the distant horizon, Mack was relaxed as Dan steered the boat toward the public docks at the park. Getting him away from town had done a world of good for all that tension he'd been carrying. No one was around to bug him about solving crime, and he'd gradually shed that hero cape that usually weighed him down. His joy when the fish started biting was infectious, and they'd both been laughing and teasing as they brought the fish into the boat. He said it was plenty for a meal and promised to fry them up that night. Mack had never eaten a meal she'd caught herself—unless you counted shopping at the fish market—so it was another adventure to add to her list.

Dan helped her out of the boat, then had her hold the lines while he backed his trailer down the ramp and into the water. A few minutes later, he drove the truck forward, with the boat safely on board and secure. She hopped into the passenger seat, and he started to drive, then stopped abruptly.

"Look at that!" Dan pointed past her, out the window toward the lake. Although it wasn't raining where they sat, it clearly *was* raining on the other side of the water. A soft gray curtain of rain blurred the rounded mountains in the distance. As the rain approached, the surface of the lake changed from smooth blue gray to rain-dappled pewter.

They watched as the little downpour came all the way to the shore, then swept over the truck and over Gallant Lake. It pounded on the roof of the truck cab.

"Wasn't that cool?" he asked. His eyes were bright and… happy. Mack thought about what Susanne had said. That Dan seemed happier since meeting her. The thought filled her with warmth. She nodded in agreement.

"Very cool. At one point it was raining on the end of the dock but not over us. We got back just in time."

His smile dimmed. "We weren't in any danger, Mack. That thunder we heard was off to the north. I'd never—"

She rolled her eyes at him. "Oh my God, Dan. Do you become Captain Responsibility the minute your feet touch land? I never once thought we were in danger. I just meant we didn't get *wet*." She looked back out at the rain, still coming down straight and heavy. "But then again, what's the big deal about getting wet?"

When she grabbed the door handle, Dan reached for her, but it was too late. She was out and jogging backward away from the truck, gesturing for him to join her. "Come on, Danny boy. You won't melt!" She twirled, arms outstretched. The rain was cold, but it felt great. Refreshing. Daring. She turned away from the truck, away from Dan's shocked and disapproving face, and looked out over the now-silver lake. If only that carefree guy she'd seen in the boat could find a way to exist on shore.

The clouds looked so low she could almost touch them. The top of Gallant Mountain was completely hidden. She lifted her head, closed her eyes and let the rain hit her face. This felt better than the best facial she'd ever had. Her eyes snapped open when she felt two strong arms wrap around her waist. She was tugged back against a solid chest. A familiar voice spoke right next to her ear.

"You're crazy. You make *me* crazy, Mackenzie Wallace." His voice lowered so she barely heard the next. "And I think I'm falling in love with you."

"What?" She spun in his arms, laughing at the sight of his hair plastered on his forehead, raindrops rolling down his face. She could only imagine what she looked like, but... she honestly didn't care. "What did you say?"

He shook his head with that half grin she'd thought was his mask to hide his emotion. The one that said the world amused him, but that he wasn't part of the world. But the deep, dark flame in his gaze told her he was very present in this moment.

"I'm not going to repeat what I know you heard." He lifted a shoulder. "Probably shouldn't have said it so soon, but the sight of you out here, dancing in the rain... Thinking I'd join you..." He kissed her, hard and fast. The rain made the kiss taste fresh. "And here I am. You do something to me, Mackie. I don't know if it's good or bad, but I'm pretty sure that *L* word is behind it. And I'm falling. I'm free-falling. You pushed me—or maybe pulled me— right over the edge." He cupped her face in his hands and kissed her again. The rain was coming down so hard she could hardly keep her eyes open, but she couldn't not look into his emotion-filled gaze. "So tell me, baby. Are we falling together?"

She felt a quick shiver of fear, followed by another shiver...of desire. She wrapped her arms around his neck.

"The question isn't if we're falling, Danny. It's where are we going to land? And what's going to happen then?"

"Well, girl. You said you were looking for an adventure. Tumbling through the unknown is about as adventurous as it gets. Let's see where it takes us." He tugged her arm and took her hand, entwining his fingers with hers. "At least we'll have good company. But you didn't really answer my question. *Are* you falling, too?"

"I'm falling, Dan. Believe me, I'm falling."

The truth was, she'd fallen already. She was in love with Danny Adams. Before she could say so, he looked up at the still-pouring heavens and tugged her toward the truck.

"We'll both have pneumonia if we don't get out of this rain."

They went to Dan's house. Susanne had Chloe that day, and Dan didn't expect her to bike over for a surprise visit in the rain. They parked the boat next to his garage. Dan tossed the fish into the spare refrigerator in the garage. Then they ran inside to take a steaming hot shower—together. And then, well…then they made love, of course. In the shower. Then again in his bed. They probably would have continued the activity straight into the night, but Dan reminded her they had fish to clean.

"Uh-uh. *You* have fish to clean. I'm not going there." They'd tossed their clothes into the dryer, so she was fully dressed again, standing in the kitchen.

He shook his head. "Haven't you ever heard of the rule— you catch 'em, you clean 'em?"

She lifted one brow. "Haven't you ever heard of the rule—you could have thrown them back?" She pulled a head of lettuce from his fridge. "I'll put a salad together and mix up a box of brownies. While *you* take care of the fishies."

An hour later, they were sitting down to a delicious meal of pan-fried perch. The small fillets were mild but still flavorful. She thought of their conversation and realized that if they landed like this, sharing meals they caught in Gallant Lake and laughing about who did the most work, she'd be a very happy woman.

They were talking about her dad and Cathy while they were washing dishes later, and Dan asked how Ryan took the news.

"He's fine with it." Mack set her towel down and turned to face him. "What happened between you and Ryan, Dan? You were best friends, and now you have no contact at all. He said he understood, but I'm not sure *I* do."

Dan's smile was gone in an instant, and his face went gray. "You know what happened. The accident…"

"Uh, yeah. I remember. But you weren't even in the car. Ryan was in the hospital for weeks, and you barely showed up. You stopped coming to our house. You avoided my parents…"

He put the last of the dishes in the strainer and stood staring at it as if he wished it could remove him from this room. But they'd handled some big topics that day, and she wasn't going to let this one slide. She really wanted to know. She put her hand on his shoulder, shocked at how tight and tense he was. He kept staring at the clean plates when he spoke, his voice devoid of emotion.

"I couldn't face your parents, Mack. I never knew when they'd show up in Ryan's room, and I couldn't face them. Or the Michaels family, for that matter. I didn't know what to do."

"Why couldn't you face them? I don't understand…"

He closed his eyes, his fingers curling into the towel he held. "I got them the booze that day, Mack. I wasn't in the car, but only because my dad had grounded me for mouthing back at him. He was drinking a lot back then—hell, so was I—and we had a stupid argument. One of those rite-of-passage arguments where teenage boys take their first swing at their dad. It was a mess. Anyway, he grounded me for the first time ever. I had to go straight home after baseball practice at school. But I didn't go to practice. I met Ryan and Braden up on Hill Road, and I gave them two bottles of gin I'd lifted from my grandparents' liquor cabinet." He shook his head, his eyes still tightly shut. "I got them drunk. It was *my* fault. My fault Ryan was in the hospital." He finally turned and looked at her. "My fault Braden was dead. I'm sorry—I didn't know how to tell you. If this changes anything…"

Mack started to laugh, low and soft. Dan recoiled from the unexpected reaction. She took his hands in hers and held tight.

"Dan, have you really been thinking that all these years? That night wasn't your fault." He started to object but she talked right over him. "Okay, fine, you contributed some booze. But that was in the afternoon, and they didn't hit that tree until three in the morning. I remember the night as if it was yesterday. Ryan and Braden took something like half a case of bourbon from Dad's store. And by took I mean stole. Mom and Dad were visiting my grandparents in Syracuse. The boys were supposed to be watching me, but they were playing video games and doing shots for *hours* that night." Her parents kept trying to give Ryan responsibility in hopes that he'd grow up, but it didn't work. "I put myself to bed. Ryan told me afterward that they got into an argument about whether Braden's car was fast enough to catch air on that little rise out on Marshfield Road. They got the bright idea to go try it." Dan was scowling at the counter, and she squeezed his hands again to make sure he was hearing her. God, had he been carrying this around all these years? "I don't know how they even made it to the car, much less drove it up there, but they did. Those two bottles of gin eight hours earlier didn't cause it. It wasn't your fault."

"Maybe I could have stopped it if I'd been there."

"I just let you off the hook for one guilt trip, and you're grasping at another one? Stop, Dan. You didn't do this. And honestly, I'm *glad* you weren't there. I'm glad you were safe at home that night. The thought that you could have been killed, too…my God." She leaned forward and kissed him softly on the mouth. He didn't respond at first, but then his hand came up to cup the back of her neck, tugging her closer.

The kiss deepened, and Mack felt something shift between them. As intense as their lovemaking had been before, she hadn't realized until this moment that there'd been something between them. Something he'd been holding in. But that something was gone now. His head tipped for better access, and he murmured her name against her lips. His arms went around her, sliding up under her top, hot against her skin. *Yes, please.*

"I need you, Mack. Spend the night." She hadn't done that yet—stayed at his place. He'd been worried about Chloe stopping by on the way to school or something.

"Dan…"

"It's okay. It'll be okay. We'll make it all work. Stay the night. Stay with me…" His hand slid beneath the waist of her jeans, his fingers curling around her backside and pulling her in tight. She let out a low moan. Who was she kidding? She was putty in his hands when he let down his guard like this.

"I'll stay, Dan. I'll stay."

Chapter 15

"Wow, what a view!" Mack was staring out the windshield as Dan parked the truck in front of Asher and Nora's log house on Gallant Mountain.

Dan stared at her for a moment. Her hair was pulled back in a low ponytail. She was wearing crisp white jeans and a fluttery blue top that just brushed across her curves. It was low cut, and as she leaned forward, he couldn't help but smile and agree.

"Yeah. The view's *very* nice."

She looked over, then followed where his eyes were focused, promptly sitting up.

"What are you, sixteen?" She frowned at her outfit. "Is it too low? Too fancy? Not fancy enough?"

"Whoa, calm down, girl. You look perfect. Just do me a favor and don't bend over like that in front of Asher." Dan opened the truck door and winked over at her. "I'd hate to have to punch my best friend in the nose because he couldn't keep his eyes where they belong. And relax. It's just dinner with friends."

They walked up the steps hand in hand. Asher was an architect as well as a furniture maker, and he'd designed the big house to look like it had just grown there at the edge of the trees. The dark green metal roof blended with the pines, and a wide porch wrapped around three sides.

"I know I've said this already," Mack said, "but…wow." She stopped and looked at the lake far below. "When Nora said she lived in a log house, I pictured *Little House on the Prairie*, not *Architectural Digest*."

"It was actually featured in the magazine last year. Asher designed it and basically built it all himself, too. Wait until you see the…" The door flew open, and Nora stood there with a dish towel in one hand and a bottle of wine in the other.

"You're here! Come in! I just pulled my famous shrimp toast out of the oven, and Asher and the guys are out front at the grill." Nora waved them in. "Mack, why don't you join Mel, Amanda and me in the kitchen, and Dan, you can go watch the fire with the other cavemen."

"Actually," Dan started, not ready to lose Mack's company just yet, "I was going to give Mack the grand tour, if that's okay."

Nora froze, her eyebrows slowly raising. Mel and Amanda had stopped talking and were staring at Dan. They all seemed to be biting back laughter. Nora regained her composure, but he couldn't help noticing her southern accent deepened.

"Why, sure, Dan! Y'all go on ahead and tour the place. With your girl." She leaned toward Mack and spoke in a stage whisper that could be heard on the second floor. "Dan's never brought a girl here before." Nora looked back to Dan, holding the dish towel over her heart. "And he doesn't want to leave your side. Which might just be the cutest thing ever."

Dan had taken his share of razzing from Nora since she came to town and bought the coffee shop next door to Asher's business. She and Asher fought like hellcats right up to the moment they'd fallen in love. Dan had been happy for the two of them. But right now he was wondering if he really needed Nora Peyton teasing about how cute he was.

Mack was looking at him funny. "You've never brought a date here to meet your friends?"

"What friends?" He glowered at Nora, but that just made her laugh harder.

"You don't scare me with that lawman glare, Dan Adams. And to answer your question, Mack, no—he hasn't ever brought a date here. I don't know if I've ever *seen* him with a date, now that I think about it. He's a bit of a hermit when he's not working." She stepped back and gestured toward the curving staircase. "Feel free to explore the place. Dan helped Asher build a lot of it. And despite the way he's pouting at the moment, he loves me."

He sighed. "Yeah, yeah. You're pretty irresistible." He flipped the bottom of her hair as he walked by, making her squeal and smack at his hand. "Like an annoying big sister."

The men and women separated again after dinner, and this time Dan joined the guys on the screened porch. Mack had gone to the kitchen with the women. He'd heard another bottle of wine being uncorked in there. Good thing Mack didn't have to work the next morning.

Blake settled into a large wicker rocker and pulled a slender cigar from his pocket. He leaned forward and peeked into the house to make sure he couldn't be seen before lighting it. "I was at our Barbados resort last week, and a guy hooked me up with some hand-rolled cigars." He looked around. "Anyone want one?"

Shane took one, but Asher and Dan were satisfied with their brandy. Shane sat and looked over to Dan. "So things are getting serious with the woman you body slammed against the wall a month ago?"

Dan shook his head. He'd probably never live down that night. But *last* night, he'd had Mack against the wall in a whole new way, so that was his new favorite memory when it came to walls.

Shane chuckled. "From that grin on your face, I'm guessing the answer is 'why yes, Shane, things *are* going well.' Not that it matters, but I like her. She's got sass."

Dan tried to think if he'd seen Shane and Mack together. "Is this your first time meeting her?"

Shane took a puff of his cigar. "Other than a quick wave in passing, yes. I've been on the road nonstop, man. The basketball draft is in a few weeks and I've got two kids who might make the first round, and I've got a baseball player looking to make a big move this summer."

He glanced at Dan. "I hear there's been some drug drama in our little town. Mel said there's actually a task force now. Are you any closer to figuring it out?"

Dan didn't answer right away. He was tired of the question, but he understood why people asked. They were concerned. So was he. And these guys were friends with an interest in the safety and reputation of the town they did business in as well as called their home. But still, he couldn't divulge too much.

"We think it's a New York gang looking to expand north. We're not their target market, but they seem to be stashing the stuff in our area. Treating this like a warehouse between the city and upstate. The volume is more than we've ever had in our area, and they're tossing it around like freakin' candy. We just can't keep up with where they're hiding it. Every time we think we have a line, it dries up. We thought they were using an old grain mill on the north shore, but we searched the place and found nothing." Nothing other than a suspicious amount of tire tracks and fresh scrape marks across the old plank floors.

"I heard the old mill was in foreclosure," Blake said. "You might want to check with real-estate brokers."

The other guys nodded, and Dan drained his glass in one gulp. They were trying to be helpful, but did they really think he hadn't thought of that already?

"Good thought. We're looking into all angles. We'll find them."

Asher patted his shoulder. "We know you will, Dan. I'm glad you've got Mackenzie as a distraction."

Dan went still. "Nothing distracts me from my job. You know that."

"Easy, big guy." Asher leaned against the railing. "I didn't mean she was taking you *away* from your work. Just that she gives you an escape from it when you're off duty. A chance to relax, like tonight. You know what they say about all work and no play." He hesitated. "She's good for you. She makes you laugh. She makes you more... I don't know...happy?"

Blake nodded in agreement. "Amanda said the same thing. You're different since Mack came to town. In a good way."

Dan wasn't sure he wanted to be different, but he knew they were right. Mack was changing him. Love was changing him.

"She wants me to go to the llama farm."

Asher choked on his drink. "There's a sentence I never thought I'd hear you say."

"You and me both." Dan shook his head. "I don't know what's happening."

The three men looked at Dan, then at each other, and started to laugh.

"Oh, I think you know exactly what's happening," Blake said. "Only love could get *me* to a llama farm. Don't bother fighting it. And whatever you do…" He snuffed out the cigar. "*Whatever* you do, don't screw it up. And if you *do* screw it up, which is likely…" The other guys nodded. "Make sure you fix it fast. Seriously. If you're in love with her, don't let her go."

Dan glanced into the house just as Mack threw her head back and laughed at something. She was sitting up on the counter, wineglass in hand, smiling at his friends. Her friends. In his world. Right where he wanted her to stay.

One of the weirdest things about moving back to your hometown was the way you kept running into familiar faces, but not *completely* familiar, because you've been gone twenty years. Mack looked around the bank and blinked, trying to put names with faces. Kiara was the easiest—she was a teller behind the counter and waved as soon as Mack walked in. Her braids were down and swinging around her face today. One of the other tellers looked familiar… Joy something? The big-haired lady who owned the hair salon… Martie Kennedy? Between the teased and sprayed-solid hair and the scowl on her face, Mack was pretty sure she'd be going outside Gallant Lake to find a decent haircut.

And now here was Wes Compton, former class president

and all-around Mr. Popularity in school, walking up to her with a wide, toothy smile and his hand extended. His dark hair was trimmed short and neat.

"Mackenzie Wallace! Wow, it's great to see you!" He gripped her hand and shook it hard enough to make her neck snap a little. "Come on back to my office. Your dad called yesterday and said you might be stopping by. You're really taking over the store, huh?"

She didn't have much of a chance to answer, as Wes just kept talking. He'd always been a charmer in school, too, but now his charm almost felt aggressive. He was dressed in the new-slash-old *Wall Street* style, with his blue shirt with the white collar, pleated trousers and…suspenders. It was a trend Mack didn't think needed to return. Especially in Gallant Lake. But she returned his smile and shook his hand without grimacing. She needed this loan, and he was the loan manager at the only bank in town.

He barely looked at the store's tax records and profit reports she'd brought with her once they sat down. Wes was too busy talking. About himself. Thirty minutes later, Wes had filled her in on his success as a banker and investor. He had a big house on the lake with a wife and three kids. He'd married Mandi Sue Moore, who was probably the one girl in school disliked more than Mack had been. Mack had just been laser focused on grades and *accidentally* ignored everyone else. Mandi sincerely thought she *was* better than everyone else. Made sense that she'd go after Wes and his family's money. Mack looked at her watch.

Dan had agreed to go to the llama farm out beyond the maple syrup stand today. Mack had read about it online and saw that they had baby llamas now. Dan had been so tense and tired this past week, working long hours and getting frustrated with the drug case he was on. Doing something silly like watching baby llamas would be a great stress reliever. But the place closed in three hours. She tried to catch up with what Wes was saying.

"…let me tell you, the difference between a Mercedes and a Bentley is night and day. I mean, Mandi doesn't mind the Mercedes, but I'm just not impressed."

"Well, they both sound expensive, that's for sure." She wondered how much the little bank in Gallant Lake paid him. He must have read her expression, because he rushed to clarify.

"Oh…uh… I've had some recent property investments do very well."

"Really? Around here?"

"Yes. There's money to be made in foreclosed properties, if you know what I mean."

She didn't, but she really needed to speed this along.

"So about that loan…"

He waved his hand at her. "It's a no-brainer, Mackenzie. It's a local business with a local family. Your credit's stellar. Just the sort of thing the bank wants to promote. Fill out these forms and let me bump it up the ladder, but I'm sure there won't be any problem."

She blew out a sigh of relief. As she filled in the paperwork, Wes kept talking. He was an adviser for the business chamber in town. Chair of a committee exploring growth opportunities. President of the parent-teacher organization. He was even thinking of running for mayor. Mack was looking forward to the *quiet* of a llama farm almost as much as she was looking forward to seeing Dan. Her ears were practically ringing from the constant sound of Wes Compton's voice.

He was ushering her out of the bank when a man walked in whom Mack didn't know but Wes clearly did. He went completely still—and silent—at her side as the broad-shouldered man approached. The stranger was dressed in dark jeans and a black T-shirt two sizes too small. His hair was slicked back with so much hair product it was almost shining. Wes's smile abruptly changed to an angry straight line.

"What the fu—" He glanced around, then at Mack, and that smile returned like magic. "What a *fun* surprise, Carter. I didn't ever expect to see you here at the *bank*. Where I *work*. In *town*."

Carter shrugged, clearly unconcerned. "The boss needs us to move on something. Now."

Wes was a completely different man. His face fell, and instead of anger, Mack saw a hint of fear in his eyes. What the hell was going on? It was like the most puffed-up man in town had been deflated right in front of her. He hustled her down the sidewalk and toward the parking lot with a hurried goodbye and a promise that he'd take care of the loan.

An hour later, she was telling Dan about it at Larry's Llama Farm. He didn't seem concerned. But he'd had a bad overnight shift and was sleep deprived as well as frustrated over their lack of progress on the drug ring.

"Wes likes to be involved with everything in town. He's an overachiever."

"But who do you think that slimy guy was that showed up and freaked him out so much? He called him Carter."

"I don't know, Mack. Maybe a disgruntled customer. Wes can be annoying, but…"

She nodded and took his hand as they walked along the path toward the paddocks. He was probably right. "He told me he's making a bundle from foreclosed properties, which seems like a conflict of interest, but he's getting me a loan, so I guess it's none of my business. Oh, Dan! Look!"

The path curved to the right, and there in front of them was a large pasture with a dozen llamas wandering about grazing, or just lying in the grass, their jaws moving back and forth rhythmically as they watched Dan and her walk by. Some were solid colored—white, brown or gray. Others were spotted black and white.

"They're so big!"

Dan's shoulders began to ease, and he smiled. "They look like they were made from leftover parts, don't they? Chloe came here a few weeks ago on a field trip, and she said they can be three hundred pounds or more. I didn't know how *tall* they could be." A steel-gray llama walked toward the fence, his tail curled tight over his back and his eyes fixed on Mack. Dan took her hand and tugged her away from the fence. "Don't forget they can spit."

"Yeah, he wouldn't be so cute if he spit regurgitated food at me." Dan laughed at that, and she knew he was beginning to relax at last. His pace slowed, and he slid his arm around her shoulder.

"It's pretty up here." The lake was hidden by the mountain, but the farmland rolled over the smaller hills. Crops were showing bright green shoots in the plowed fields across the road, and the pastures looked lush and green.

She leaned into his embrace. "It is pretty. Summer's almost here—you can feel it in the air."

Dan kissed her temple. "All the better for dancing in the rain."

Oh yes. That *was* a good day. She grinned up at him.

They didn't see any babies until they walked a little farther. There was a smaller paddock near the barns, and a cinnamon-colored llama mama stood in the corner. A tiny baby of the same color was toddling around.

"Oh my God, look at that fluff of hair on his head! He looks like you, Dan!" He grimaced at her, which just made her laugh more. "He has gorgeous big eyes like you. And he's frisky!" The baby started jumping around, then ran a mad dash in circles around his mother.

They sat at a nearby picnic table to watch him. Dan checked his phone and frowned.

"Damn it. No signal out here. I was afraid of that. We should probably go…"

"Are you on shift today?"

"No, but…"

"Are you on call today?"

"Technically, but…"

She took the phone from his hand.

"Just put this away and let someone else save the world today."

"Mack…"

She darted in quickly to kiss him and stop him from thinking. Judging from the way he reacted, she was successful. His arm tightened around her, and she let him take over. He was hungry, demanding. And neither of them cared if the llamas watched.

But it was the middle of the afternoon, so they eventually cooled it and settled back against the table, watching the baby llama prance around. They didn't talk much, just sat there in the sun, pressed close together, and breathed. It was nice. It was perfect until Dan couldn't sit still any longer. The real world was out there, and he didn't like being cut off from it.

He checked his phone three times on the way back to

the truck, muttering every time. As they crested the first hill on the way back toward town, he pulled the truck over.

"Seriously, Dan? You can't wait? This is supposed to be a break."

"It *was* a break, babe. And I appreciated it. But I can't hide from the job."

She was beginning to realize the absolute truth of that statement.

Chapter 16

Dan's phone lit up with a string of missed calls and texts. All from Sam Edgewood. He muttered a curse and called Sam.

"Where were you, Dan? We've been calling for two hours."

"What happened?"

He'd known there was no reception on the far side of Gallant Mountain. He'd *told* Mack that. But she was so determined to go see that damn llama farm. To give him some much-needed fun. And Lord knew he couldn't say no to her.

"What *happened* was that we had the bastards, Dan." Sam's voice was angry and clipped. "We missed the actual exchange, but Terry's DEA guys told us a car matching this one was seen going in and out of the auto shop in Brooklyn where they think the ring is being run from. We know he's part of it. But we lost them just outside Gallant Lake. You know, that place where *you* live? That town where *you* want to be police chief?" Sam took in a long, heavy breath, then blew it out again. His voice lowered in resignation. "Sorry, man, that wasn't fair. It was a souped-up Dodge, bright blue. Stolen tags. I swear that thing had jet engines. We were too far behind him and never had a chance." He paused. "And we don't know the area as well as…you."

Mack watched in silence from the passenger's seat, reading his expression plainly enough and knowing to stay quiet. If he'd been near town and gotten the call, he could have intercepted the car. Maybe.

"I'm sorry, Sam. I was in a freakin' dead zone. No signal." Mack reached over and put her hand on his, but he jerked away. He wasn't sure why, and he regretted it as soon as it happened. Especially when he saw the hurt in her eyes. He cleared his throat and spoke into the phone. "Where did you lose him?"

"He came down by the Chalet…"

Dan stiffened. "You ran a high-speed chase through *my* town?"

"Of course not, you idiot. We were a couple cars back, tailing him. Everything was fine. Then he turned onto Hill Road on the other side of town. There's no traffic out there, so he made us right away and took off. Those roads have so many twists and turns and dirt roads that aren't on the damn GPS. He was just…gone."

Dan pinched his nose, closing his eyes tight. He thought of that poor woman who'd OD'd in her car with her kids in the back seat. In *Gallant Lake*. She wasn't a local, but that didn't matter. It had happened in his town. These drugs were coming into *his* town. He cleared his throat.

"Okay, Sam. We'll recap with Terry and his DEA team in the morning. This gives a lot more weight to his theory that Gallant Lake has become a waypoint between New York and their expansion into Albany."

He ended the call and stared out the windshield. He almost forgot Mack was there until she spoke.

"Something bad happened." She didn't state it as a question.

"Yes."

"Have there been casualties?"

He huffed out a humorless laugh. "Have there been *casualties*? Christ, Mack, do you have any idea how many OD calls I get these days? It feels more common than traffic stops. In Gallant Lake! And I just missed a chance to stop it." His teeth ground together as he turned the key and pulled back onto the road. "For llamas."

"Dan, you're off duty until tonight. It's a Wednesday afternoon. Even cops get to have lives once in a while."

"I was on *call*. I should have made sure I could actually receive a call, don't you think? I told you it was a dead zone, but no, you had to see the baby llama." He was being an ass. He knew it. But that mother and her kids…

Mack recoiled, but her voice stayed calm. Steely calm.

"I know you're upset. But this is not my fault. It's not *yours*, either. It's not feasible to be on call every hour of every day. You'll have another chance to get them…"

"Yeah? You're an expert on how often law enforcement gets a chance to shut down a drug highway, huh? That's great. What would you suggest we do next, *boss*?" He turned onto the main road, driving past Halcyon and the resort. He was baiting her, looking for a fight. And she wasn't going to give him the satisfaction, sitting there in silence.

He parked behind her place, his fingers tight on the wheel. She didn't leave the truck. He didn't say anything.

Knowing he was acting like a jerk didn't make it any easier to stop. He scrubbed his hands down his face.

"I think I'd better just go home tonight, Mack. I clearly won't be good company."

"Dan...no. Come upstairs. Tell me what happened. Let's—"

"No. That's not what I need." He had a feeling it was *exactly* what he needed, but it wouldn't help him figure out how to break this drug case. And that had to be his focus now. He glanced at Mack. He couldn't afford to be side-tracked. The town was depending on him.

Mack shook her head, but she reached for the door handle. "You're wrong. But you're too stubborn to listen, so...fine. When you're ready to talk, I'm here." The door opened, and she looked back over her shoulder. "For what it's worth, today was great until you got that call."

His chest went hollow. "Don't you get it, Mack? That's my life. There will *always* be a call that ruins a fun day. I am *always* going to have half my mind on my job at any given moment. And I won't be able to talk to you about most of it. I won't want you to know. I won't want to answer the questions. I won't want to bring the crap I see into your world. But that's what you get with me. The people of this town rely on me, and you have no idea what that..." His words caught in his throat. He was so damn tired. Her hand touched his, and he froze, closing his eyes. "Don't."

He wanted to follow her up to her bed and bury himself in her. Let go of everything weighing on him. But he couldn't do that. He had a responsibility, and today, he'd dropped the ball. That couldn't happen again.

Mack waited for a moment, then muttered something and pulled her hand away.

"You know, you complain about feeling like a cartoon

character with the whole Sheriff Dan thing, but here you are, acting like you really *are* some kind of superhero. But you're not. And the sooner you realize that, the happier you'll be." And she was gone.

He couldn't fault what she'd said. But his priority in life wasn't being *happy*. It was…

His tires spun on the way out of the parking lot. Damned if he knew *what* it was anymore.

People hadn't been kidding when they told Mack the Travis Foundation charity weekend was a really big deal. Not only did it raise tons of money for the foundation to help veterans, but it was also a boon to Gallant Lake. Mack couldn't believe the swanky crowd strolling the sidewalks on Friday afternoon. Athletes—many of them clients of Mel Brannigan's agent husband, Shane. Hollywood faces recruited by the cousin who ran the event, Bree Caldwell— a former reality-TV star turned North Carolina farm wife. Dad had warned Mack to be stocked and ready for crowds, and she was glad she'd listened. He also told her to make sure she had lots of top-shelf stuff, and she'd been selling it.

She should be happy. Hell, she should be *ecstatic*. Her dad was wheeling his scooter around the store and smiling ear to ear as he made recommendations to customers. He loved being in the store, and she suspected he was loving it so much because he didn't *have* to be there. She hadn't realized how much pressure he'd been feeling the past few years trying to keep the store going while she and Ryan figured out what the heck they wanted to do with their lives. So now Dad was having a great time and the store was doing hot business. Why wasn't she happy?

Dan hadn't been back to her place since their argument on Wednesday. She wasn't sure if she could really call it an argument, since Dan seemed to be carrying on the whole thing on his own. He'd wanted to fight, but she wasn't going to be a part of him beating himself up. And she sure wasn't going to take the blame for whatever it was that went wrong while she and Dan had—horrors!—been having fun on his day off.

He'd said he liked coming to her to forget what he dealt with on his job. But what if he couldn't ever *really* forget? If he'd never be able to share more with her than his *need* to forget? What was there for *her* in a relationship that revolved around Dan basically using her as a release valve?

To be fair, it wasn't like he ghosted her completely. He'd texted, explaining he was on surveillance with the task force when he wasn't on shift. She knew he was trying to make up for what happened Wednesday by working nonstop. He couldn't keep going like this. But she didn't bother pointing that out. He'd rewired himself from Danger Dan to Sheriff Dan, and he seemed determined that there was no middle ground between the two.

Because she loved him, she was willing to give him a little more time to figure things out. She'd been through it herself after her divorce, finding the sweet spot between People-Pleaser Mackenzie and Free-Spirited Mackie. Dan had helped her with that. So she'd return the favor. If he'd let her.

"Mack! Oh, good, you're here!" Mel rushed into the store, waving at Dad. "Hi, Carl!" She turned back to Mack. "I have a double-malt scotch emergency."

"Well, *there's* something I never thought I'd hear from my pregnant, alcoholic friend."

Mel barked out a quick laugh. "One of the resort guests is being fitted by Luis for a gown for tomorrow's gala. Her husband is running out of patience, and she's afraid he'll tell her to just wear the dress she already has. She doesn't want that to happen, and considering the cost of the dress she's looking at, Luis and I don't want it to happen, either." She paused for a breath. "She says hubby *loves* top-shelf double malt. Got any that might impress him enough to soothe his grumbling?"

Mack turned for the counter, but her dad beat her to it, handing Mel a bottle.

"This'll keep him happy," he said.

"You're a lifesaver, Carl!" Mel clutched the bottle to her chest. "How much…?"

"A lot." Mack's dad winked. "But you can catch up with us later. That's what neighbors are for."

Mel turned to go but paused as she passed Mack. "Your dad's the best. You and Dan are coming to the gala tomorrow, right?"

"I… I'm not sure." She and Dan were supposed to be going together, but she wasn't sure where they stood after this week.

Mel came to a full stop. "What happened?"

Mack glanced back at her father, but he'd moved to the back of the store, out of earshot. "Dan's really busy this week…"

Mel waved her hand. "He'll be there—his daughter's a model. And even if he's on call, you should be there for Chloe. All she talks about is how you and she both love purple. In fact…" Mel looked Mack up and down. "Stop by the shop later. Luis has a dress that would be perfect for you with a little nip and tuck here and there."

"That's sweet, but I can't afford a Luis Alvarez gown, Mel." Luis Alvarez was Mel's best friend and business partner. He was also a well-known fashion designer. He maintained a fashion studio above her boutique that was usually appointment only, but he and his husband, Tim, were in town all week for the big event.

Mel reached for the door, distracted and on the fly again. "Don't be silly. It's a loaner. You can be one of our models. My cousins are all modeling dresses, too. They do it every year." She winked over her shoulder as she left. "And it's got purple in it. You'll be Chloe's hero!"

Mack was pretty sure she'd never worn a purple couture dress in Connecticut. She couldn't help smiling. If it was something the old Mack wouldn't have done, then it was something the new Mack should embrace. And what better way to knock Dan's socks off than showing up in an Alvarez Designs creation?

Chapter 17

Mack paced nervously as she waited for Dan to pick her up Saturday night. She had no idea where they stood. The weight of the heavily sequined gown gave her some comfort. Between the shapewear she wore under it and the way the gown hugged her body, it was like wearing her very own ThunderShirt, like the snug ones dogs wore to comfort them during storms. The bold colors gave her a jolt of confidence, too—swirls of deep purple, turquoise and white. The off-the-shoulder design was simple and form-fitting, with a thigh-high side slit and a plunging neckline.

Luis Alvarez had made a few adjustments to accommodate her ample cleavage, and Mel had shown her how to tape those babies up and secure and then how to tape the dress to her skin to avoid any nip slips. She felt strapped in and ready for battle.

She opened the door almost as soon as Dan knocked, and they stared at each other in silence. Dan was in a tux. A *tux*. And the man, who wore a uniform like it was his second skin, was doing the same with this tuxedo. He looked as cool and comfortable as he did in his cargo shorts and T-shirt out in the fishing boat. And just as delicious. But after the past week, she didn't feel she could jump into his arms and tell him so. So she waited, chin held high, tummy pulled in, hand on her hip as if she was just waiting for him to fall to his knees before her. It was all an act, of course, as she tried to suppress her fear that things were worse between them than she'd thought.

He let out a low whistle as his gaze traveled up her body. When his eyes met hers, there was a welcome and familiar heat there, and his mouth slid into a slanted grin. Danger Dan was back.

"Damn, Mack. You look…" He gestured at the dress. "… amazing. I mean, you're always amazing, but…hot damn. That dress looks like it was poured onto you. And this…" His gesture moved to her chest. "How are you keeping those things in there?"

The blurted-out question made her laugh, and just like that, the tension eased between them. "Don't worry, there's enough tape in here to keep everything in place."

He stepped inside, and he smelled as good as he looked, all spice and pine and mountain air. The minute his fingers brushed hers, she started wondering if they really *had* to go to the gala. Would they be missed? Could she convince him to follow her upstairs, where she'd relocated her things to the large master bedroom this week? The master bedroom with a king-size bed?

Clearly reading her mind, Dan shook his head slowly. "As much as I want to untape you piece by piece, Chloe's waiting for us." His smile faded. "I know we have a lot to talk about, Mackie, but for tonight…"

"For tonight," she finished for him, "I'm Cinderella and you're my Prince Charming. And you have another little princess who needs you, too. The clock won't strike midnight for hours yet, so let's enjoy it."

His arm slid around her waist, and he kissed her lightly. "I don't want to mess up your makeup." He winked. "At least not yet. But God, Mackie, it feels good to be with you right now. We both know I've been avoiding you, and I'm sorry. I'm just trying—"

"Hey, Prince Charming." She cupped her hand on his cheek. "No talking until later. It's been a hard week for both of us." His eyes glowed with warmth and regret, and she almost bolted the door behind him so they couldn't leave until they'd solved this problem. But Chloe was waiting. "I love you, so I'm giving you time to figure your nonsense out. For tonight, let's just go live the fairy tale, okay?"

He tugged her in close, kissing her again, a little more passionately this time. "I'm always living a fairy tale with you, Mackie. You make me feel...well, you make me feel *everything*. It's a blessing and a curse, to be honest. Maybe we can find a fairy godmother to lift the curse part, because my heart and my head are so damned tangled up right now." He looked down at her chest pressed tight against his, so close to overflowing the confines of her dress. "This dress isn't helping. I'm going to be watching all night to make sure that tape is really going to hold. And I'm damn sure looking forward to peeling it off later."

"Be careful, Caveman Dan. This is a borrowed dress, and if it's damaged, it might turn into a very expensive pumpkin."

He rubbed the back of his neck. "I'm wondering how I'm going to get you up into my truck. Maybe I should have hired a limo."

She managed to get into the truck just fine, thanks to that very long slit in the side of the dress and a little boost from Dan. She wasn't sure if he did it to help, or if he just wanted a chance to put his hands on her butt. Either way worked for her.

Hell, everything worked when they were together. Maybe this week was just a speed bump for them. A blip on the story of their love. Because she *did* love him.

When they walked into the ballroom, it took Mack a moment to realize this was the same Gallant Lake Resort ballroom she'd been in as a girl. When she was growing up, she'd been to a few weddings and parties in this room, but it never looked *anything* like this. The walls and chandeliers shimmered. Thousands of tiny fairy lights strung across the ceiling made it feel like she really *was* in a fairy tale. Multiple French doors opened onto the wide stone veranda overlooking the lake, which was smooth as glass as the sun sank low in the sky. The round tables had floral centerpieces that cascaded down from the tops of tall glass pillars, creating the sensation when you sat down that you were sitting under an arbor of roses and lilies.

The crowd was just as spectacular as the setting. Television celebrities. Broadway stars. Athletes. CEOs. The men were in tuxes, and the women were in the most beautiful dresses Mack had ever seen. She breathed a silent thanks to Mel for providing a dress that held its own in this room.

"Dad! Mackie! You're here!" Chloe came running at them, hugging Dan before turning to Mack. "Your dress has purple in it! We match, Mackie!"

Chloe twirled, the grape-colored organza skirt flaring out around her she did. The skirt had glittery three-dimensional flowers scattered on it, and the top was a lighter shade of purple, with puffy sleeves of organza and lace. Mack laughed.

"We *do* match, but your dress is better for twirling than mine! And look at your shoes!" The flats were covered in purple crystals. "They look like something you could click together and get any wish you wanted!"

Chloe extended one leg, admiring her shoes. "Mel said I could *keep* the shoes. I'm going to wear them every day."

Dan frowned. "I don't know how practical—"

Mack cut him off. "You get to keep the magic wish shoes? That's awesome. Isn't it awesome, Dan?"

She gave him a pointed look. He didn't have to be such a Be Honest at All Times buzzkill. He apparently got the message, shaking his head with a smile.

"It *is* awesome. Make sure you thank Mel later. You look really pretty, sweetheart."

Chloe beamed. "Thanks, Dad!" She turned back to Mack. "Wouldn't it be cool if they really were magic shoes and granted wishes?"

"That *would* be cool." Mack started to lean forward, then thought better of it. No sense testing the strength of that tape. She grabbed Chloe's hand and bent her knees instead. "You know, when I was a little older than you, my friend and I found a magic wishing well just outside Gallant Lake. Have you ever heard of the wishing well up on Gilford's Ridge?" She had no idea if it was still a legend or not. For all she knew, the old Gilford homestead on the ridge had been bulldozed and built over years ago. But Chloe jumped on the story.

"Really? A wishing well in Gallant Lake? Dad, did you know about that? Is it still there? Can we go to it?"

Dan rolled his eyes at Mack, but a mischievous grin played at the corners of his mouth. "It's been a long time since I was up on Gilford's Ridge, honey. And I wasn't there for any wishing well."

Mack blushed. She'd forgotten the abandoned farm had been a popular lovers' lane for horny high school kids back then. Of course, *she'd* never been taken up there for that. She'd been a serious student. But she and Shelly *had* walked through the woods one summer afternoon in junior high and found the wishing well.

After a five-course dinner and a fashion show put on by *real* models as well as a quick walk about by volunteers like Chloe and Mack, the dancing commenced. Dan and Mack were seated with Nick West and Cassie Zetticci. The newly engaged coworkers were clearly head over heels for each other. No one could miss their affection. The furtive, heated glances. Hands held under the table. The occasional quick kiss. His hand brushing the back of her head, fingers twisting in her dark hair briefly before he sat up straighter and pretended it was accidental.

Mack leaned over to Dan when Nick and Cassie were out on the dance floor, cheek to cheek. "Are they the cutest couple or what?"

He gave her a bemused smile. "Yeah, I love to look at my friends and think how cute they are. Adorable, even."

"Stop being such a Joe Cool, Dan. You keep forgetting I know there's a heart in there." She tapped her fingers on his chest, right over the top of one of the round buttons on his shirt. Before she could pull back, he grabbed her fingers and held her hand there.

"I'm sorry things got weird with us this week. I'm tryin', Mack. It's just these drugs are coming into town out of nowhere, and I can't let myself be distracted. It's my town…"

Mack stood, still gripping his hand, thinking of their first dance at the Chalet. "Come dance with me, babe."

He stood but didn't move toward the dance floor. "That won't solve anything, Mack."

She gave him a soft smile.

"It'll make you forget, if only for five minutes." She patted his chest again, this time over where his phone was tucked inside the jacket. "And you're not in a dead zone here, so relax. You're still on call, locked and loaded." He hesitated, then nodded.

They'd barely taken a step when Sally Vincent from the post office stopped them. Mack always thought she was a sanctimonious old busybody. "Oh, Dan, you look so fancy in that tux! And Mack…" Her eyes took in the neckline on the gown. "You look…very daring tonight." Sally turned back to Dan, clearly her target in this conversation. "I heard about Kyle Alderwood overdosing last week. How awful! Where are these drugs coming from? Are you close to solving it? Why haven't you arrested anyone yet?"

Well, this wasn't helping at all. Mack tried to intervene.

"Thanks for admiring my dress, Sally. It's by Luis—"

Dan squeezed her fingers, talking over her. "Mrs. Vincent, we're chasing down every single lead, and believe me, we'll get the people responsible."

Mack nodded briskly, trying to move Dan toward the dance floor. "Yes, he *is* working hard, but right now he's—"

Sally held up her hand. "Look, Mackenzie, we all know you're only here to help your dad. Lord knows your brother can't. Not after he killed that Michaels boy."

Mack couldn't answer. Not without air in her lungs. Sally rounded on Dan again.

"I hope you solve this problem soon, Dan. The Alderwoods are neighbors of mine. Kyle is a friend of my grandson. Thank goodness he survived, but everyone's very upset…"

"Yeah, well… I'm upset, too, Mrs. Vincent." Dan's voice sharpened, catching both Mack and Sally by surprise. "I'm really goddamned upset." He jammed his fingers through his hair. "I said I'll *catch* the bastards, okay? I won't quit until I do."

Sally looked at Mack, her lips pressed thin, then back at Dan.

"And you think the drug dealers are out on the dance floor?"

Dan released Mack's hand like it was on fire.

"You're right. I was here tonight for my daughter, but I need to get back to work."

Sally just sniffed and walked away. Dan headed for the exit, and Mack had to move fast in her stilettos to keep up with him.

"Dan, it's just one obnoxious old woman. Don't…"

He yanked his arm away from her when they got to the hallway. He kept his voice low, but his anger made it heavy and thick. "Just one? Mack, that's the *third* person to ask me about the drugs *tonight*. And who can blame them? People are dying and I'm here in this penguin suit sipping champagne. They're right. I *shouldn't* be here. I shouldn't be with you. I'm dropping the ball and it's…"

"And it's *my* fault?" Mack glared at him. Enough was enough. She wasn't going to be his scapegoat.

"No." The edge dropped from his voice. "No, it's not. Look, my job destroyed my first marriage, and it'll do the same with us." He dropped his forehead to hers. "I was right to back off this week. It's hard for me to think straight around you, and now more than ever, I *need* to think straight."

"You're saying you can't do your job and love me at the same time?"

He stepped back. "I don't think I *can*, babe. I want to, but I really don't think I can." His devastated expression told her those words hurt him as much as they did her. He gestured toward the ballroom. "Those people are relying on me. They all remember what a screwup I was, and now they'll think I'm one all over again. I have to—"

"Those people are *killing* you, Dan, and you're letting them do it. Your *job* is law enforcement, but you're a man who deserves to have love in your life. And you *can* do both. You made mistakes when you were a kid. So did Ryan. You have to stop taking responsibility for every bad thing that happens in Gallant Lake." She put her hands on both sides of his face. She could feel him slipping away from her. "You're a good man. A good cop. You'll solve this. But you can't carry the whole town on your shoulders. You need a safe place to rest."

The hallway was silent and empty, with only the muted sound of music in the background. He stood there, eyes closed, as if absorbing her words and trying to hold on to them. She willed him to be successful. She needed him to believe.

"Dan, I love you. And you love me. That's a good thing. The *best* thing. Let me be where you come to rest and laugh and love. To let go of the expectations and all the darkness with me. Let me be your safe place, Dan. Go do your job and know that I'll be waiting with open arms and a glass of scotch. You deserve that. We both do." She took a deep breath. "And if I'm not the one you can talk to, find someone you *can* talk to. A professional."

She held her breath until his eyes slowly opened. There he was. The man she'd fallen in love with. The tender glow in those green-gold eyes of his. She saw a flicker of hope there. He was trying so hard to believe. She stared at him, silently pleading for him to accept her help. To accept her love.

"Mackie…" His voice broke. "I don't know…"

"Yes, you do. You *know*. Let me in, Dan."

He moved closer, his hand gripping her waist. Before he could speak, there was a commotion at the end of the hall. Nick West came rushing at them. Dan stepped back from Mack, leaving her feeling suddenly cold and lost. Blake Randall was right behind Nick. Both men looked grim.

"What is it?" Dan's voice was all business now.

"We've got trouble." Nick was talking fast. "Some guests got their hands on the tainted Oxy."

Blake's face was like thunder. "There are ambulances and state police out front, Dan. It was an overdose. At *my* hotel!"

Mack bristled. "That's not Dan's fault!"

Blake looked at her in shock. "I *know* that. Christ, I wasn't *blaming* him, Mack. But this is a big damn problem, and he's…" Blake looked at Dan. "You know this isn't your fault, right?"

Nick, a former cop himself, shook his head. "We don't have time to hold hands and sing 'Kumbaya' right now. We need to contain this. We don't need the gala interrupted by flashing lights in the parking lot."

Dan moved farther away from Mack. "Fatalities?"

Nick shook his head. "The guy was touch and go, but they should both pull through."

Dan started walking away with Nick. Mack called his name. He stopped and turned back as if he'd forgotten she was there. Nick and Blake walked on.

"Mack, I gotta go."

"I know you're going. Just tell me you're not *leaving*."

Dan stared at Mackenzie, his heart heavy. She was everything. Everything he didn't deserve and couldn't hang on to.

"These drugs may not be my fault, Mack, but they *are* my responsibility. My community—my friends—are relying on me. If you can't get that…"

She shook her head, refusing to listen. "I understand your responsibilities. But you're letting everyone else define your success or lack of it. No one's working harder on this problem than you." She took his hand and squeezed, like a mother would to a child. "Trust me, I know from experience that you can't make everyone happy. It's impossible. You'll lose yourself—"

He stopped her with a kiss. It was a dangerous move, because their kisses so often spun out of control. But this one was necessary. And sweet. And…final. He lifted his head and looked her straight in the eyes to leave no doubt to his words. He steeled himself against the tears he saw shimmering there.

"This job saved me, Mack. It's who I am, so how can I be losing myself?"

Truth be told, he felt like he was losing himself right now. Losing himself in her eyes, which were quickly filling with tears. Why couldn't she understand? His shoulders fell. How could he expect *anyone* to understand what he couldn't fully understand himself?

He brushed a loose strand of hair behind her ear. "Maybe I am stretched too thin. I don't think I can be what *you* need and what everyone else needs. I need my focus, and you're bad for it." Nick barked Dan's name from the end of the hall, and Mack flinched.

"Are you saying *I'm* what needs to be out of your life?"

Dan looked at her with regret pressing him down like an anvil resting on his shoulders. There was a voice in his head whispering this was the wrong choice, but he dismissed it. He had to be able to control one effing thing in his life, and he could control *this*.

"I'm no good for you, Mack. Look at us. You told me once that it felt like I was using you. You were right. I am. And I love you too much to do that to you. You deserve better."

"Dan…" His name came out on a breath. Her tears were ready to spill over, and he wasn't strong enough to watch that happen.

"I'm no good for you, Mackie. I'll ruin us one way or the other. If not now, then eventually."

Her eyes went hard behind the tears, and she jerked away from him.

"You've been hiding behind your Good Guy Dan disguise for so long that you actually think it's *true*." She poked him in the chest with a brightly polished fingernail. "You're a coward, Dan Adams. You're afraid that wild, reckless kid you used to be is going to bust out, take over and destroy you. But you don't have to worry about it." She poked him again. "You're doing a great job of destroying yourself, twisting yourself in knots, determined you deserve the worst. Which is a damn shame." She backed away, putting her hand on her own chest as if it ached. He knew the feeling. But she wasn't done with him yet. "That wild, happy kid is who you really are. But you're killing him, and you're killing us." She pulled her shoulders back. "I can't be the only one fighting here, Dan. That's not the kind of adventure I came home for. If you're too scared to believe in a future for us, then what's the point?"

Her mile-high shoes clicked like gunshots on the marble tiles as she walked away and left him standing there alone.

Chapter 18

Mack thought she'd braced herself sufficiently before knocking at Dan's front door the following Saturday, but… no. She wasn't at all prepared for the sweet stab of loss when he opened it. He stared at her in steely silence. He was in uniform, physically and mentally. One hundred percent pure cop. Annoyed cop.

"Mack, I don't know what you want, but I don't have time." Even his tone was on duty—authoritarian and cold. He'd clearly made his decision on who he wanted to be. "I'm on duty in just…"

"Mackie!" Chloe came pounding down the stairs behind her father. "You remembered!"

Mack ignored Dan's confusion and smiled at Chloe. "Of course I did. A deal's a deal, right?"

"Right!" Chloe plunked down on the bottom stair and pulled on her sneakers. "Girl code." She gave her father a disdainful look. "You wouldn't get it, Dad. But when girlfriends make promises, we keep them. We're going to find the old wishing well today, and then we'll each make a wish and it'll have to come true! Did you bring an old penny?"

Mack reached into her shorts pocket and pulled out the 1936 coin. "That was a great idea you had. It took some digging, but I found a treasure trove of them. Do you need one?" After searching the apartment for old pennies, she'd called her father. Turned out Cathy still had her old penny jar from when she owned the coffee shop, and it was loaded. So loaded that when Mack left, Dad was sorting them all out on Cathy's dining table to see if maybe they were rich.

Chloe shook her head. "Nope. Mom's boyfriend, Samir, had some. But now you can make more than one wish!"

Mack shook her head. "You can't get greedy with wishes. The wishing well might get mad and not give us *any.*"

Chloe's mouth dropped open in horror, but Dan spoke before she could say anything.

"What the he…heck are you two going on about?"

Chloe finished tying her sneakers and ran to Mack's side, grabbing her hand. Mack gave Dan a cheery smile, hoping it wasn't trembling as much as her heart was.

"You remember the story, Dan. About the old well up on the ridge, where the Gilford farm used to be? Stories say their well has the power to grant wishes. I was up there once as a little girl with Shelly, and we tossed in quarters and made wishes, but it turns out we were doing it all wrong." She gave him a quick wink to let him know her speech was for Chloe's sake. "Your daughter figured it out. She thinks maybe the well only grants wishes for *pennies*, and the pennies have to be from the years when the Gilford place was an active farm. The house burned down in 1945, so…" She held up her old penny. "We had to find pennies that were older than that, because that's when the well was magical."

Dan's gaze went from the penny to Mack and quickly back again. He seemed distracted by her presence, and she had a feeling he hadn't listened to a word she'd just said. This friend zone was new territory for both of them, and he was wearing it as uncomfortably as she was.

"Bye, Dad!" Chloe waved, tugging on Mack's hand. "Let's go!"

Dan shook himself out of whatever thoughts he'd been lost in and gestured to his daughter. "Hey—you're not going anywhere without a kiss, kiddo. Come here." Chloe obliged, but only long enough for her father to barely brush his lips on her hair before she was out the door. He straightened with a resigned half laugh. "Pretty soon I won't get her to hold still for even that little bit." He looked into Mack's eyes. She wanted to ask for a goodbye kiss too, but she could see he was slipping into his protective cop-mode armor again. "It's…nice of you to do this with Chloe…" He swallowed hard. "After…you know…you and I…"

For some strange reason, she felt compelled to come to his rescue. "There's no reason you and I can't be civil to each other, right? Or why Chloe and I can't be friends."

Dan's shoulders dropped a bit, and there was a quick flash of sorrow in his expression before it hardened once again. "Right. Friends. Uh…" He straightened, reaching for his gun belt and avoiding her eyes. "Do you mind dropping her at Susanne's when you're done? She's staying there this week."

"Sure. No problem. I'll text Susanne when we're on our way. Should only be a few hours. I'd like to find the old well, but I have no desire to spend the entire day traipsing around the hills looking for it." Dan nodded, busy buckling his gun to his hip. Mack couldn't resist a little jab. "Look at us, all grown-up and mature, carrying on a casual conversation as if we…"

He met her eyes then, his angry gaze slamming into her as he barked a one-word command.

"Don't."

And there it was, all the emotion she'd been trying to convince herself she didn't have anymore. "Don't *what*, Dan? Don't stop pretending that we're suddenly just *pals*? Don't act like I still love you? Don't push you to admit you still love me too? What is it you *don't* want me to do, exactly?" Her words were low and sharp, just between them. "'Cause I've got a news flash for you—whether I'm your so-called *friend* or your lover, I *still* don't take orders from you."

He scrubbed his hands down his face, eyes squeezed tightly shut, lips pressed tight.

"God*damn* it, Mack. I don't have time for this right now. I… I can't do this, okay?" His eyes opened, his golden gaze level and cool. "It won't change anything. We made our decision." He looked out toward the street. "Chloe's waiting. I gotta go."

He ushered her out to the porch, then locked the door behind him. She wanted to argue. To rant and rave right there on the porch. But he was right about one thing—this wasn't the time. So she followed him down the sidewalk to where her car was parked. Where his daughter was waiting. He rubbed his knuckles in Chloe's hair, chuckling when she hollered in protest. Then he walked away.

"Do you think the wishing well will grant us anything we want?" Chloe jumped out of the car as soon as Mack pulled off the side of Marshall Creek Road, behind Gilford's Ridge. Shelly had agreed with Mack's memory that they'd found the well ages ago by coming up the hill from this direction, rather than from Ridge Road. There were some worn and faded no-trespassing signs on random fence posts and trees, but this was Gallant Lake. She knew pretty much everybody, or had at one time. It wasn't like she and Chloe were looking to do any cattle rustling. They were just hiking. After covering each other in bug spray, they headed into the woods.

Mack finally answered Chloe's question. "I don't think the wishing well can grant *anything* we ask for like a genie in a bottle, honey. But sometimes the act of wishing and hoping for something specific can create the right energy in our lives to make it happen. Does that make sense?"

Chloe dashed toward the trees. "Not really, but kinda. I know what I'm gonna ask for. Do you?"

Mack didn't reply, instead directing the girl to the left, where she thought the old homestead might be. What *would* she ask for? Dan back in her life? In her bed? What point was there in that if he didn't stop being so tough on himself? If he didn't see himself as a man outside Sheriff Dan? That's what Mack had to wish for. Dan's job might have shaped him, but it didn't have to be who he *was* at heart. She'd wish for him to see that. But she wasn't very hopeful as she hurried after Chloe. He was a stubborn one.

Two hours later, they'd zigzagged their way to the top of the ridge. The view of Gallant Lake stretching out in the distance was beautiful. But Chloe was unimpressed. The eight-year-old wasn't here for sightseeing.

"Are you sure this is the right hill? I haven't seen anything that looked like an old house *or* barn *or* well." Chloe's brows bunched together as she gave Mack a skeptical look. "You are getting old, you know. Maybe you forgot which hill you climbed."

"Thanks a lot, kid." Mack handed her a water bottle from

the small pack she'd carried. "Enjoy the view for a minute while I try to get my bearings." Mack looked around the ridge. It would have been easier if she could use the map app on her phone, but the area was yet another dead zone, with no signal at all. They seemed to be hugging the western end of the ridge. The homestead must be to the east. "This is the right hill, just the wrong end of it. We need to go east. Do you know how to tell which way is east?"

Chloe rolled her eyes. "Duh. The sun rises in the east, so it's that way." She gestured widely, basically covering every direction but due west. "How much farther is it?"

"Do you want to quit? Are you tired?" She wouldn't have objected if Chloe was ready to pack it in. It was getting warm, and they only had two bottles of water left.

But kids were resilient, and Chloe shook her head emphatically. "No way! I want to make my wish!"

They walked east for half an hour, and the trees started to thin. Mack could see an overgrown field, and the roof of an old barn straight ahead. The old Jessup farm was on this end of the ridge, but as far as Mack knew, no one had lived there in a long while. That's why she was surprised to see the glint of windshields and chrome from several vehicles parked there. She and Chloe stopped at the edge of the woods. Those were all late-model cars, and there were four of them by the old barn—two sports cars, a luxury car of some sort, and a pickup truck. One of the sports cars was low, sleek and electric blue.

Something sent a trickle of warning up the back of her neck. She remembered the call Dan had gotten from his task force friend about the guy they'd missed. The guy driving a souped-up bright blue Charger. Just like the one she was looking at right now. She took Chloe's hand and stopped her.

"We've gone too far, honey. This isn't the place we're looking for. Let's go back toward the car. We'll have to come back another time to look for the wishing well."

"But maybe those people know where it is!" Chloe pointed as four men came out of the barn. Three were wearing ball caps pulled low on their foreheads, with loose-fitting dark clothing, carrying large duffel bags. But one was in chinos and a bright white business shirt and tie. And suspenders. His gait was familiar. So was his dark hair, short and neatly styled. He carried a leather satchel. All four of the men's heads were on swivels, looking around as if they sensed they were being watched. Just about the time Mack realized who the businessman was, he looked up the hill and straight at her and Chloe. Wes Compton from the bank. She *knew* he was up to something fishy that day in the parking lot.

Chloe started to wave, but Mack squeezed her hand in a signal to freeze. The girl seemed to pick up on her sense of danger, staying quiet and alert at her side. Dan seemed to dismiss her suspicions about Wes, but she was more certain than ever that she'd been right. Wes said something and the other men separated, two heading toward the vehicles and one—the largest—jogging to the south side of the ridge. The guy loading the back of the blue car was Carter, the man she'd seen at the bank. Wes waved at Mack and Chloe.

Mack tugged Chloe under the shadow of the trees. Something was very wrong here. She and Chloe should not have seen this. Her heart started racing. Maybe he hadn't recognized them. But where had that other guy gone? Wes shouted something up at them. She couldn't make out all the words, but she clearly heard her name. She waved, giving him a wide smile.

"Hey, Wes! We got turned around hiking up here, but I

know where we are now." Somewhere they shouldn't be. "Gotta go! Bye!"

She backed up, ignoring whatever he shouted in response, and started jogging into the woods with Chloe running at her side.

"What's wrong, Mackie? Why are we running from Mr. Compton?"

"I think Mr. Compton is doing something…secret…on that farm, honey. And he might be mad that you and I saw him. Let's get back to the car." They headed down the hill, but she could hear footsteps keeping up with them. *Damn it.* Wes's voice called out again, closer this time.

"Mackenzie! Stop! I just need to talk. You're not going to outrun us."

Us.

The other man was chasing them, too. That couldn't be good. She and Chloe ran past a huge downed tree, roots sticking up in the air at the base. She tugged Chloe behind the roots and up against the thick trunk, holding her finger to her lips to silence her. It wasn't a perfect plan, but she needed to do *something* to protect Chloe.

"Don't question me," Mack said in a rushed whisper. "I need you to hide here. I'll cover you up. Don't make a *sound* until your dad or I come for you, okay?" Chloe's eyes were wide as silver dollars, but she immediately knelt near the trunk of the tree. Thank goodness she was wearing dark clothing. It would be hard to see her through the leafy branches Mack was tossing over her. "I'm going to pretend you ran down the hill, so don't say anything if you hear me calling for you. Don't make a sound, okay?"

"Okay, Mackie. But…what about you?"

"I'll be fine. I'm gonna text your dad to come." Hopefully a text would get out, even if a call wouldn't. They heard heavy footsteps getting closer. "You'll be safe here. Wait for your dad or me—no one else." Their eyes met through the leafy shelter. Mack's chest went tight. "I love you, Chloe. I won't let anything happen to you."

Mack turned and started running straight west, as far away from the tree as she could get. When the footsteps got close enough that Wes didn't have to shout when he told her to stop, she kept her back to him, putting her hands up to cup her mouth. She started shouting off to the west at the top of her lungs as if Chloe had run in that direction.

"Run, Chloe! Run to the car and call your dad! Run!"

She pulled out her phone, but Wes grabbed her arm and knocked the phone to the ground. He spun her around, glaring at her as he tried to catch his breath.

"Damn it, Mackenzie! Why did you have to run like that?"

The second guy, looking angry and rough, ran up behind Wes, who nodded off in the direction Mack had been shouting. "Go find the kid. She's trying to get to the car, which must be over on Marshall Creek. Don't hurt her— just get her back here."

As the man took off, Mack pretended to be upset, but she was secretly relieved. The ruse had worked. They were moving away from Chloe's hiding place. Wes released her, shaking his head as if he was deeply disappointed.

"Mackenzie Wallace, what are you doing? I just wanted to talk to you both so there weren't any misunderstandings about what you saw. There was no need to panic."

"Really? Then why did you just send that guy running to catch a *child*? You could have cleared up any misunderstanding with a phone call. You didn't have to chase us through the woods. In fact, you know what?" She stepped back, testing him. "I think you *should* call me later and explain it all. Or not. Whatever. I need to go..."

He took her arm, less gently than before. "I don't have time for this, Mack. Your boyfriend and his posse have been getting on my last nerve these past few weeks, so I need to get this barn cleared out today." He started walking, pushing her ahead of him. "It's too bad. We had a good thing going in Gallant Lake."

"Look, I don't know what you're doing up here, and I don't *want* to know. Seriously, I don't want to be involved. I don't care. And Dan isn't my boyfriend anymore, so don't worry about that."

His eyes narrowed. "You expect me to believe you and Dan broke up, and you just happen to be out here with his *kid*? That's quite a coincidence, don't you think? I'm not an idiot, Mackenzie."

Before she could answer, the big guy came thumping through the trees and back to them. He shook his head at Wes.

"No sign of the kid. The car's still there. No one else around, so she hasn't raised any alarms yet. Maybe she got lost. Maybe she's hunkered down in the woods somewhere, hiding."

Wes gave Mack a long, calculating look, then gave her another shove as he answered Big Guy. "Forget the kid. Let's get the rest of the stuff loaded and get the hell out of here." He looked at Mack. "You're staying with us, at least for now."

Resisting made no sense. Running would be futile. And if she cooperated, they might forget about Chloe all together. She yanked her arm away from him but started walking back to the farm.

"Fine."

* * *

The radio in Dan's car crackled before Terrance Lewis's voice came over it, low and steady. "Everyone's in place. Hold tight for now. Let's see if any bigger fish show up." Terry was with the DEA and the leader of the task force operations.

"Roger that. They're loading the vehicles now. Canvas duffels. Looks like Carter, Martinez, Compton and some big guy I haven't seen before," Sam Edgewood replied. Damned if Mack hadn't been right about good old Wes Compton being up to no good. Mr. Clean Cut was the local freaking drug lord, right under Dan's nose. He shifted in the seat of the unmarked sedan, parked under the shade of a maple tree just fifty yards from the dirt driveway leading up to the "abandoned" farm currently in foreclosure. That's why they could never catch up with the product. Wes kept moving it from one vacant, foreclosed property to another.

They'd caught a break when the woman who'd almost died at the resort last weekend told investigators that "some guy at the bank" had sent her and her brother to meet the man who sold them the drugs. Dan remembered what Mack told him about Wes, and they'd started checking all the foreclosed properties. There was a suspicious amount of activity at this place, with the buildings up a long curving driveway, out of sight from the road. They'd had someone sitting on it for days now.

"Hold on. Something's happening." Sam's voice was quiet on the radio. He was hiding behind the barn. "Compton and the big guy just went up to the woods in a hurry. Maybe there's another stash up there?"

Dan didn't want this bust going sideways after all this work. "Have they made us? We have anyone up there?"

"Negative," Terry responded. "Too many of these gangs

use wildlife cameras with motion detectors, and we didn't want to risk triggering one. We've got one agent at an up-stairs window in the old house." The agent acknowledged with a click on the mic. "One of your fellow deputies down by the road. One with Sam." Two more mic clicks. "Two cars of federal agents waiting on side roads for once it all goes down. Hopefully without a fight." There was a pause. "If it goes sideways, just remember Yosemite Sam up there is the best shot of us all. Those guys won't sit for a week."

Sam would never be able to live down the day he'd shot a carjacker in his left butt cheek. Dan chuckled, then pressed the button again. "Jesus, don't say that out loud. His ego's bad enough."

One of the SUVs full of DEA agents clicked their mic so the raucous laughter could be heard. Sam was also laugh-ing softly. "I keep telling you guys I hit him right where I was aiming." There was a quick pause. "Hold on." Sam's tone was suddenly all business. Something was wrong, and everyone went silent.

"Jesus. Okay, be advised Compton and his buddy have emerged from the woods and are returning to the farm-yard. They have a woman with them. I repeat, they have a civilian woman with them, and I don't think she's there voluntarily."

"A hostage?" Terry asked. "That's not their style."

More static, then Sam's whisper. "Style or not, her body language screams 'unhappy.' Disgruntled customer?"

"We've been camped out at this farm for two days," Terry replied. "They haven't had any clients here. Descrip-tion?"

"Long blond hair. Average height. Jeans. Blue sweater. Small backpack."

Dan's vision blurred, making him blink almost as rapidly

as his heart was pounding. It took all his concentration to draw in a breath and hold it, trying to slow his adrenaline to a more functional level. Mack had been wearing jeans and a blue sweater this morning. He remembered noting the bright pink stripe around each cuff and the hem. It matched the thick socks she'd been wearing. The socks *he'd* bought her after she got those blisters weeks ago.

He squeezed the mic button so hard it was a wonder it didn't snap. "What color are her socks?"

Silence. Then Terry spoke. "Did you just ask about her *socks*?"

Before he could reply, Sam answered with the one word Dan had been dreading.

"Pink."

"Is she alone? Is there a little girl there? An eight-year-old?" Dan was almost shouting, which he knew was a no-no when guys were using earbuds.

"Dan…" Sam started, still in a near whisper. "Are you asking about Chloe? Do you think your daughter might be out here? I haven't seen anyone but the woman… Oh, crap. Are you saying this woman is Mackenzie Wallace? Your girlfriend?"

A new low voice came on the radio. "Smith here, from the upstairs window. I can confirm it's Mackenzie Wallace. My sister went to school with her."

"She's arguing with Compton." Sam's voice was level, as if he didn't know Dan's entire world was falling away from his feet. "He's pointing to the barn. She's pointing to the ridge."

"Gilford's Ridge." Dan didn't bother stating it as a question. That stupid wishing well was on the burned-out Gilford farm. Mack had taken Chloe to Gilford's Ridge. Which, by some ridiculous chance of fate, was where Wes

Compton's current storage place was. Dan had been too distracted that morning to make the connection, but then again, this operation hadn't been on his radar when Mack picked up Chloe. Sam had been on surveillance today and noticed the jump in activity. Suspecting Wes and his men were clearing out, Terry made the call to grab them.

"What are we doing, guys?" It was one of the federal agents from the waiting cars. "These roads are remote, but they're not abandoned. We've had two local cars pass us already. All it takes is someone getting nosy, or sending a text to one of Compton's guys, and we're blown."

Terry said something about waiting for *bigger fish* again. Smith was talking about the men loading more duffels into their trucks. The feds were offering to grab the trucks as they left the farm. But the only thing Dan cared about was where his daughter was.

The radio buzzed with static, and another unfamiliar voice came on. "Okay, we're on Marshall Creek Road behind the ridge, and there's a blue Ford compact here. Parked and locked tight. No one around."

"That's Mack's car." Dan's mouth was dry as cotton. "My daughter was with her. She's *eight*." He swallowed hard. "If Compton's done anything… I'm going up there now."

"Negative! Sit tight, damn it." Terry's command was quiet but firm.

Sam joined in. "Agreed. Don't make things worse, Dan. Chloe's not here, and the woman isn't sobbing or distraught. She's just pissed." There was a pause. It couldn't be easy for Sam to be operating so close to Wes and his well-armed men. He was hiding in the old pump house, but the thing wasn't soundproof. Or bulletproof. Terry's mic clicked again.

"Dennis, take your team up the hill from the car. Use stealth, but find that kid."

"Roger. On our way."

It was the logical course of action. Dan would have made the same call in Terry's position. But Terry wasn't in *his* position, with his daughter and the woman he loved in danger. The *L* word settled his pulse more than any breathing exercise ever could. He *loved* Mackenzie, and his job didn't have a damn thing to do with that. His job sure as hell wasn't more *important* than that. Than Mack. Than Chloe. They were his *family*. He opened his car door slowly and slid out, moving along the tree line near the road as he inserted the earbud and tapped the mic.

"Be advised, I'm out of my vehicle, moving closer to the driveway."

Sam let out a string of hissed obscenities in his ear.

Terry's voice came on again, sounding more resigned than angry.

"Roger that. Do *not* come up the drive until we know what's happening. A shoot-out doesn't help anyone."

"Affirmative." Charging in, guns blazing, only worked in the movies and would put Mack and Chloe in more danger.

The next few minutes of silence felt like an eternity as Dan hunched under a large eucalyptus bush. He was so tense that his whole body twitched when the earbud finally clicked.

"Be advised," Sam said. "Two of the vehicles are preparing to leave. Carter's in the blue one. Martinez is in the other." A pause. "The woman is sitting on the back of a farm wagon in the yard. She keeps glancing up the hill when Todd's not looking. Dan, I have to think your girl is still up there."

He closed his eyes, praying to whoever might be listening that Chloe was okay. Going forward without that little girl in his life just wasn't an option.

Another click. "Dan, we found her. She had a good hiding spot." Dennis's words were the sweetest Dan had heard. "She said she was ordered not to move until she heard from the woman or you. Say something so she knows we're the good guys."

Dan's eyes burned, and his throat was thick with emotion. "Baby girl, it's Daddy." The word broke as it came out. His whole body shook with relief. "Dennis is a friend of mine. I need you to go with him, okay?"

Silence. Then Dennis responded. "Got her. She's fine, just scared about the woman. On our way to the vehicle now."

Sam said the words Dan couldn't form. "Thank God. Now let's get this son of a bitch."

"Team Two will grab the vehicles heading out now," Terry whispered. "Everyone else stay outta sight."

"Roger that."

Dan flattened under the shrubs as the two vehicles raced down the drive, throwing up dust and stones. They both headed east, toward the interstate, but he knew they'd never get that far. Using the dust cloud as cover, Dan moved farther up the drive. He could see the remaining two vehicles, but they were blocking his view of Mack and the two men.

Sam came on the radio. "Be advised. Compton said something that pissed off Dan's girlfriend. She's up and arguing, dropping f-bombs all over the place."

Dan grinned through his worry. *Thatta girl, Mackie. Give him hell.*

"Compton wants her inside the barn, and she is not having it." A pause. "Be advised, the big guy is heading down the drive in his truck, which is loaded with product. Don't let him get far."

Terry chuckled. "I'll take care of him. Go get your girl, Dan."

Dan moved up the hill, only stopping long enough to duck when Elliot went by. His eyes narrowed when he saw Wes grab at Mack's arm.

"Roger the hell outta that. Everyone else stand down. Compton's *mine*."

Chapter 19

Everyone knew that you never let a bad guy take you into a vehicle or an abandoned barn. Mack had read it a dozen times. *Don't let them take you anywhere alone.* Wes grabbed her arm again, fingers digging in hard enough to make her cry out. But not so hard that she couldn't call him every name she could think of while digging her heels into the dirt driveway. His face reddened with anger.

"Damn it, Mack, I'm not going to violate you or anything. I'll just tie you up in there and let my bosses decide what to do with you after I'm long gone." He yanked sharply. "You're not that hot that I'd risk my escape taking the time to do you."

She tried to pull away, but he wasn't letting go this time. Fear and fury were fueling her in equal measure now.

"A—I'm *totally* hot enough, you ignorant ass hat. And B—I am *not* letting you tie me up in some barn in the middle of nowhere. I'll die out here!" And who'd save Chloe?

His grip tightened again, and he pulled hard enough to send her stumbling forward. "Okay, okay. I'll tell you what—forget what I said about my bosses. We don't need to get them involved." His voice was so smooth and smarmy that she knew he was lying. "I'll call your boyfriend and tell Dan where you are once I'm at the airport and ready to book outta here. You'll be fine. Now be a good girl and get moving. I wasn't kidding when I said I don't have time for this."

He pushed again, and she didn't even try to stay on her feet. Let him drag her if he wanted. She hit the dirt and glared up at him, slapping at his hands when he reached down to grab her.

"I am so sick and tired of men saying they don't have time for me, Wes. And I am damn sure *not* anyone's good girl. Oh, and I'm not going in that barn either, so you can just—"

A glint of rage in his eyes silenced her. Maybe lying on the ground under him wasn't the best idea she'd ever had. His hand curled into a fist, and he pulled his arm back.

"No wonder Adams dumped your obnoxious ass," he snarled. "You never know when to shut the hell up."

Before he could take the swing, there was a roar from her right and a blur of dark motion. Wes vanished under whoever had just tackled him. Mack rolled away from the scuffle, only to have someone's hand wrap around her arm as she stood. *Oh, hell no.* She came around swinging, connecting with the stranger's face right about the time she noticed he was wearing a bulletproof vest and a cap with the letters "DEA" printed on it.

The tall black man shook his head and grimaced, but he was laughing. "That's a hell of a right hook, Mackenzie. I'm one of the good guys. It's over." He let go of her arm and stepped back. Law enforcement officers were coming at them from all over, with the same dark hats and black vests. On the ground, one was wrestling with Wes. She saw a familiar shock of sandy hair. *Dan.* He was on top now, throwing a flurry of punches at Wes and cursing him in a voice filled with rage. She heard him say something about his daughter.

Chloe...

She must have spoken out loud, and the agent she'd just punched tipped his head at her. "Chloe's safe. She's with my team." He looked over at one of the men watching Dan beating on Wes and raised one brow in question. "Sam, you think you might want to get your friend?"

Sam jumped forward and grabbed Dan's arm before he could land another punch.

"Enough, man. I think you made your point."

Dan struggled against his grip for a moment, then stopped, glaring at Wes. "It'll never be enough for me, but yeah. I'm done. Facedown, asshole." He spun Wes over in a flash, cuffing his hands behind his back, then standing. His eyes went right to her. And...wow.

Her knees nearly buckled from the emotion swirling in his gaze. Rage. Desperation. Relief. Love. He swept his gaze up and down her body, checking for damage, then pulled her into his arms. He nearly crushed her, but she didn't object. She knew he needed it as much as she did. She soaked it up, then started trying to explain.

"I'm so sorry. I had no idea. I never would have put Chloe in this—"

His hand cupped the back of her head, holding her against his shoulder. "I know. I'm just glad you're both okay." A shudder went through him as he drew in a deep breath. "You're all that matters to me. You and Chloe. That's it."

"Did I mess up your bust or sting or whatever this is? I punched your boss. Will you be in trouble? I'm sorry…"

"Baby, hush." Another shudder. No, wait. That was a shake. He was shaking. He was…laughing. And so were the agents around them. Mack pushed away, but Dan kept her in the circle of his arms. One of the two female agents spoke up.

"It's true. She clocked Terry right in the nose. It was pretty sweet." The woman winked at Mack. "Couldn't have happened to a nicer guy."

The man she'd hit—Terry, apparently—rolled his eyes. "Ha ha, very funny." He smiled at Mack. "No harm done, I promise. And I was in charge today, but I'm not Dan's boss. In fact, I'm thinking he won't have *any* boss before long. After today, I think he's a shoo-in for that chief of police opening I hear is coming."

Dan started introducing her around as two agents roughly lifted Wes to his feet and walked him to the waiting black SUV with dark-tinted windows. Just like in the movies. A matching SUV pulled up behind it. As soon as the door closed on Wes, the back door on the second vehicle flew open.

"Daddy! Mackie!" Chloe bolted out of the car and ran to them. Moving as one, Dan and Mack bent and opened their arms to pull her into their embrace. She ended up sitting on Dan's hip but had a death grip on Mack's hand. She realized with a wave of sadness that she didn't belong in this family embrace. But when she went to move away, Dan's hold tightened around her waist. He shook his head at her, even as he talked to Chloe.

"Baby girl, I am *so* happy to see you. And I am so proud

of you for listening to Mack and doing what she told you."
He kissed her cheek, then let her slide to the ground. "Why
don't you let me thank Mack for a minute, then we'll go
home, okay?"

"But Dad, I have to tell Mack—"

"Just give me a minute, okay, baby?"

Chloe opened her mouth to argue, then shrugged and
walked over to climb on the old farm wagon. Mack smiled.
Dan had been right about her—perpetual motion.

"Dan, I really am sorry…" He wasn't listening, intent
on examining her arm where Wes had grabbed her. Rings
of bruises were already visible.

"Do you need to have this looked at?" His hands slid up
to her shoulders, resting at the base of her neck. "Are you
hurt anywhere else?"

"What? No. I'm fine. I'll just catch a ride back to my car
with someone and be out of your hair. I should never have
brought Chloe up here. I wasn't thinking…"

"Mack, you had no idea this was going to happen. Hell,
I had no idea this was happening until a few hours ago.
And I never connected in my mind that this place was on
the edge of Gilford's Ridge or that that's where you were
going to be. It's not your fault. And the way you protected
Chloe, at your own expense… Mack, I don't know how I'll
ever thank you enough for that." He put his thumbs under
her chin and raised it until she was looking right at him.
"But I'll spend the rest of my life trying."

Her heart jumped. He didn't mean it the way she hoped,
of course. He only meant they'd be living in the same town,
as *friends*, and he'd be grateful. How nice. But there was
something shining in his eyes that made her go very still.
Something warm and deep and true.

"Mack, I was an idiot. You were right about me hiding in

the job, using it as an excuse, being a coward. All of it. You were right. I love you so much, and when I thought I might lose you…" He swallowed hard. "Everything just fell into place in my head. Like tumblers in a lock. Boom. It was clear as a bell. This job might be my calling. But it's not my life. *You're* my life. You and Chloe." He cupped her face in his hands. "I *love* you. And if it's not too late, I'd really like you to love me back. It still won't be easy. I might end up being the local police chief, which is a big job. I don't know how we'll make it all work, but Mackie… I need a safe place. I want that safe place to be you."

He kissed her, and she kissed him back with everything she had. Neither of them cared about the catcalls coming from the agents milling around the farmyard. It was Chloe's voice that finally pulled them apart.

"Yes!" She shouted from the farm wagon. "It worked!" She gave a little fist pump, and everyone laughed.

"What worked, sweetie?" Dan asked.

"The wishing well! We found it, Mackie, on the way back to the car. Mr. Dennis didn't want to stop, but I told him it was *very* important. He carried me over and let me throw my penny in real fast. I made my wish, and it worked!"

Mack had a feeling she knew the answer before she even asked. "What did you wish for, Chloe?"

The girl gave them a wide, gap-toothed grin. "I wished that you two would get married!"

There were more catcalls while Dan coughed and Mack's face went burgundy.

"Well, I don't know if I'd say it really worked then…"

But Dan stopped her, sliding his arm around her waist and reaching up to the wagon to hold Chloe, too.

"Actually, baby, I think your wish did come true. Or

at least, it's *going* to." He looked into Mack's eyes with a heated gaze that made her toes curl. "What do you say, Mack? Do you think Chloe's wish will be granted?"

She settled in the crook of his arm, trying to hold her smile back, but failing badly.

"I do."

Those two words made Dan straighten with a smile. "Perfect answer."

* * * * *

We hope you enjoyed reading

Fever Pitch

by *New York Times* bestselling author

SHERRYL WOODS

and

Her Homecoming Wish

by JO McNALLY.

Both were originally Harlequin® series stories!

From passionate, suspenseful and dramatic
love stories to inspirational or historical,
Harlequin offers different lines to
satisfy every romance reader.

New books in each line are available every month.

HARLEQUIN
SPECIAL EDITION

**Believe in love. Overcome obstacles.
Find happiness.**

*The Sweet Magnolias legacy continues
for a new generation of women!*

Keep reading for a sneak peek at
Home in Carolina
by #1 New York Times *bestselling author Sherryl Woods.*

Chapter One

Settled at her usual table near the kitchen of her mom's restaurant,
Annie Sullivan ate the last of her omelet and opened the local paper
to the sports section. Even though she and major league pitcher
Tyler Townsend, a hometown boy, had been apart for a long time
now, it was a habit she hadn't been able to break. She kept hoping
that one day she'd see his name in print and it wouldn't hurt. So far,
though, that hadn't happened.

Today, with the baseball season barely started in mid-April,
she was expecting nothing more than a small jolt to her system
from the local weekly. Instead, her jaw dropped at the headline at
the top of the page: Star Pitcher Ty Townsend on Injured Reserve.
The article went on to report that after pitching just three games,
the baseball sensation from Serenity would be out indefinitely
following surgery two weeks ago for a potentially career-ending
injury to his shoulder. He'd be doing rehab, possibly for months,
and he'd be doing it right here in town. He was, in fact, already
here.

Clutching the paper in a white-knuckled grip, Annie had to draw
in several deep breaths before she could stand. Shouting for her
mother, she headed straight for the restaurant kitchen, only to be
intercepted by sous-chef Erik Whitney.

Regarding her with concern, Erik steadied her when she would have dashed right past him. "Hey, sweetheart, where's the fire?" he asked.

"I need to see my mother," she said, trying to wrench free of his grasp.

"She's in her office. What's wrong, Annie? You look as if you've seen a ghost."

Though she'd poured out her heart to Erik as a teenager, right this second she was incapable of speech. Instead, Annie simply handed him the paper.

Erik took one look at the headline and muttered a curse. "I knew this was going to happen," he said.

Annie stared at him, her sense of betrayal deepening. "You knew about this? You knew Ty was back in town?"

Erik nodded. "Since the day before yesterday."

"Mom, too?"

He nodded again.

Now it was Annie who uttered a curse, made a U-turn and headed back to the table to grab her purse. What had everyone been thinking, conspiring to keep something this huge from her? Especially her mom, who knew better than anyone the damage secrets, lies and betrayal could do.

Erik stuck with her. "Come on, Annie, don't blame your mother for this. Go to her office. Talk to her," he urged as she stormed past him through the kitchen. "She was just trying to protect you."

At the door, she turned and asked angrily, "So I could be blindsided, instead? Ty had surgery two weeks ago, Erik! He's been in town how long—a couple of days? A week? It's not as if this happened yesterday."

Don't miss Home in Carolina *a Sweet Magnolias novel available wherever MIRA books are sold!*

MIRABooks.com

♦ HARLEQUIN
SPECIAL EDITION

**Believe in love. Overcome obstacles.
Find happiness.**

Save **$1.00**

on the purchase of ANY
Harlequin Special Edition book.

Available wherever books are sold, including
most bookstores, supermarkets, drugstores
and discount stores.

Save **$1.00**

on the purchase of ANY Harlequin Special Edition book.

Coupon valid until July 31, 2021. Redeemable at participating outlets in the U.S. and Canada only.
Not redeemable at Barnes & Noble stores. Limit one coupon per customer.

52617078

Canadian Retailers: Harlequin Enterprises ULC will pay the face value of this coupon plus 10.25¢ if submitted by customer for this product only. Any other use constitutes fraud. Coupon is nonassignable. Void if taxed, prohibited or restricted by law. Consumer must pay any government taxes. Void if copied. Inmar Promotional Services ("IPS") customers submit coupons and proof of sales to Harlequin Enterprises ULC, P.O. Box 31000, Scarborough, ON M1R 0E7, Canada. Non-IPS retailer—for reimbursement submit coupons and proof of sales directly to Harlequin Enterprises ULC, Retail Marketing Department, Bay Adelaide Centre, East Tower, 22 Adelaide Street West, 40th Floor, Toronto, Ontario M5H 4E3, Canada.

5 65373 00076 2 (8100)0 12499

U.S. Retailers: Harlequin Enterprises ULC will pay the face value of this coupon plus 8¢ if submitted by customer for this product only. Any other use constitutes fraud. Coupon is nonassignable. Void if taxed, prohibited or restricted by law. Consumer must pay any government taxes. Void if copied. For reimbursement submit coupons and proof of sales directly to Harlequin Enterprises ULC 482, NCH Marketing Services, P.O. Box 880001, El Paso, TX 88588-0001, U.S.A. Cash value 1/100 cents.

BACCOUP20993MAX

Love Harlequin romance?

DISCOVER.

Be the first to find out about promotions, news and exclusive content!

Facebook.com/HarlequinBooks

Twitter.com/HarlequinBooks

Instagram.com/HarlequinBooks

Pinterest.com/HarlequinBooks

ReaderService.com

EXPLORE.

Sign up for the Harlequin e-newsletter and download a free book from any series at **TryHarlequin.com**

CONNECT.

Join our Harlequin community to share your thoughts and connect with other romance readers! **Facebook.com/groups/HarlequinConnection**